35'
8M 01-18

THE FLYING CIRCUS

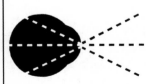 This Large Print Book carries the
Seal of Approval of N.A.V.H.

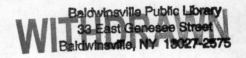

THE FLYING CIRCUS

SUSAN CRANDALL

WHEELER PUBLISHING
A part of Gale, Cengage Learning

GALE
CENGAGE Learning·

Farmington Hills, Mich • San Francisco • New York • Waterville, Maine
Meriden, Conn • Mason, Ohio • Chicago

GALE
CENGAGE Learning·

JAN 2 7 2016

Copyright © 2015 by Susan Crandall.
Wheeler Publishing, a part of Gale, Cengage Learning.

Wheeler Publishing Large Print Hardcover.
The text of this Large Print edition is unabridged.
Other aspects of the book may vary from the original edition.
Set in 16 pt. Plantin.

LIBRARY OF CONGRESS CATALOGING-IN-PUBLICATION DATA

Crandall, Susan.
 The flying circus / by Susan Crandall. — Large print edition.
  pages cm. — (Wheeler Publishing large print hardcover)
  ISBN 978-1-4104-8304-1 (hardcover) — ISBN 1-4104-8304-5 (hardcover)
  1. Stunt flying—Fiction. 2. Nineteen twenties—Fiction. 3. United States—Social life and customs—20th century—Fiction. 4. Large type books.
 I. Title.
 PS3603.R375F59 2015b
 813'.6—dc23   2015025572

Published in 2015 by arrangement with Gallery, an imprint of Simon & Schuster, Inc.

Printed in Mexico
1 2 3 4 5 6 7 19 18 17 16 15

In loving memory of my father,
Vic Zinn,
a man who loved machines and the sky

I know that I shall meet my fate
Somewhere among the clouds above;
Those that I fight I do not hate,
Those that I guard I do not love;
. . . .
A lonely impulse of delight
Drove to this tumult in the clouds;
I balanced all, brought all to mind,
The years to come seemed waste of
breath,
A waste of breath the years behind
In balance with this life, this death.

— William Butler Yeats

1

May 1923

Disaster lived by its own rules. Most times it crept up from behind, wiping out everything with a single blow, a bully and a coward. Lightning strikes. Train wrecks. Someone shoots an archduke and starts a bloody war. But disaster had veered from its sneaky, obliterating path with the Schuler family. It had taken them down one finger flick at a time. First baby Marie. Then Ma. Then Peter. Finally, Pa. For the past five years, Henry had been the last Schuler standing.

And now disaster had come for him. For the second time its ugly hands had shoved Henry out of his own life. At least it hadn't taken him down. Not yet. At least this time he wasn't a powerless boy. He was an eighteen-year-old man. He could choose. Running was wrong, a coward's way. And maybe he was — as much of a coward as that bully disaster. But it was either run or die.

Since he'd been orphaned, Henry had been living on a farm with Anders Dahlgren, his wife, and seven daughters. During those years the second eldest, Emmaline, had convinced many folks he was a deceitful, untrustworthy boy. If he had stayed, all anyone would see was his aggressive, hateful *German-ness.* All anyone would hear were the echoes of Emmaline's claims. Justice might be blind, but it heard plenty.

The fresh scratches and bruises were even more damning than his heritage or his reputation.

Even Mr. Dahlgren couldn't save him now. Wouldn't even try. Not when Henry had betrayed him in the worst way imaginable. That thought just about tore out Henry's heart.

He walked along the river in step with a heavy-booted chant in his mind: *Kill 'im. Kill 'im. Kill Heinrich the Hun* — words his schoolmates had hurled like stones at his back during the Great War. Unlike the taunting of grade school, this time the threat was as real as the dirt under his feet. The only thing behind him was a noose.

After a day and a half on deer trails and farm paths, he'd probably traveled far enough no one would recognize him. He crawled out of the bramble beside a covered bridge, crouching like the animal he felt himself becoming — dirty, hungry, desperate — and looked to make sure no one was in sight before he stepped onto the road. The second his feet hit the packed, rutted dirt, he felt naked and defenseless. *All animals have to come out sooner or later or they'll starve to death.* Every hunter knew that. Probably every lawman, too.

By midmorning, Henry hadn't seen a single solitary soul on that road. Maybe his luck was changing. He breathed some easier. The past was done. Finished. Gone. From here on, he'd only look toward the future. Toward Chicago. The Cubs. Yeah, he'd think about the Cubs. Peter, his older brother, had been crazy about the Cubs. He and Henry used to huddle over the weekly paper Pa splurged on, memorizing players and statistics. At first Henry had only done it to be with Peter. Before long, he, too, was standing on the front porch waiting for Pa to arrive with the paper.

He spent some time thinking about what Cubs Park — it had been called Weeghman Park when he and Peter had started following the Cubs — would look like. It could seat fifteen thousand people. He'd never been in a *town* with fifteen thousand souls all totaled. He was trying to imagine that many people all in one place at one time — the jostle of bodies packed shoulder to shoulder, the swirl of smells coming off that many different sorts of folks, the noise — when he heard the clatter of tack and the roll of a wagon behind him.

As the plodding hooves and rumbling wheels got closer, Henry's skin drew up prickly and his privates tried to crawl up into his belly. His feet wanted to light out. A new chant filled his head. *Steady. Steady. They don't know me . . . don't know me . . . don't know me . . . don't know me.*

The road was barely wide enough for a pair of mules to walk side by side, so he moved to the weeds for the wagon to pass. Three steps in, he flushed out a rabbit, sending it skittering across the road and his heart nearly shooting out of his mouth.

As the mule team pulled past, he moved his lips into a strawboard smile. A little boy with red hair under a beat-up straw hat looked down, smiled, and waved. He was missing his two front teeth. Something in that kid's earnest smile made Henry feel as if he'd lost something he'd never get back. What, exactly, he couldn't say since he'd lost most everything that meant anything by the time he was twelve.

He raised a hand and kept that mock smile on his face, thinking innocent thoughts, hoping they'd shine through his eyes.

He braced for recognition; waited for the man to look at him, stand, and glare down, pointing a damning finger of accusation. But the boy's pa stayed put on that creaky wagon bench, slump-shouldered with his hat pulled low. He didn't even glance Henry's way. Every line of the man's posture reminded Henry of his pa, completely used up by life. Henry felt a stab of pity for the kid and hoped to high heaven his life took an easier road than Henry's had. He continued to put one shaky foot in front of the other until the wagon and the dust it kicked up rolled out of sight. Then the dry heaves grabbed him. He bent over and braced his hands on his knees until they passed.

How was he going to live a life on the run if he threw up every time a stranger approached? He had to convince himself of his innocence before he could convince anyone else.

After a while he came to a little town that either didn't matter enough to name, or nobody had bothered to post a sign to let

13

folks know what it was. It sat on a straight shot of road and had about a dozen houses, most of them peeling and tired. T's of utility poles ran down the right side of the unpaved street, draping lines to the buildings like Chautauqua banners. The brick sidewalk started at a two-room school that reminded him of the one he and Peter had gone to, with tall windows and a bell tower over the double front door (damn few happy memories there). After that was a feedstore, a white-painted church (services at nine o'clock and six thirty on Sunday, seven o'clock on Wednesday evenings), Castetter's Grocery and Variety, a brick-and-limestone bank, and a grain elevator.

Best to just walk right through, not too fast. Meet people's eyes. The visible bruise at his temple would probably draw attention. His fingers went there, prodded the soreness. If asked, he'd just pile on another lie.

Back when disaster ended his first life, Henry had picked a fake name to dodge those mealymouthed, do-gooder welfare folks who would have sent him to the County Home — a hulking brick place filled with orphans, kids whose families couldn't afford to feed them, and thrown-away old people. A nice patriotic-sounding *American* name that wouldn't draw the suspicious looks his German name did: Henry Jefferson. But Anders Dahlgren had come to take him in, fully aware that Henry was a Schuler. Now that the law was after him, Henry Jefferson was who he would be.

There weren't many people around this nameless town. A couple of kids played marbles in the dirt. A horse-drawn delivery wagon sat in front of Castetter's. A woman rocked on a front porch, shelling early peas into the apron on her lap. Two babies crawled around her feet. She looked as tired as Henry felt and didn't give him a second glance. When he passed the feedstore, an old guy wearing overalls was leaning in the doorway. He eyed Henry long enough that the urge to run washed over him, but he put one foot steadily in front of the other. He even managed an I've-got-nothing-to-hide wave. At first the man only stared. Then he gave a slow nod. Henry kept going, counting his steps until the sidewalk stopped as abruptly as it began.

The scenery rolled back into farmland and the town disappeared. The hours came and went, step after step, thirst, hunger. He welcomed the exhaustion and numbness, it made it easier to forget the horror of what he'd left behind. He kept himself going by

15

listening to the regular rhythm of his pants legs rubbing against each other.

The sun had slipped into late afternoon when his feet decided to stop. He blinked, somewhat surprised to find himself in the middle of a crossroad. A crow cawed overhead, a harsh, unwelcoming sound. A single dove sat on the wire strung from pole to pole alongside the road, its mournful *hoo-ah hoo-hoo-hoo* making him feel more alone than he ever had in his life.

He wished he knew how far he'd gone. But this Indiana road was the same as all of the others he'd crossed, marked by more horse hooves and wagon wheels than automobile tires, passing through a rotating kaleidoscope of woods tangled with grapevine, fields sprouting green shoots of corn, and grassy pastures dotted with spring clover and livestock. This was the only landscape he'd ever known. From the newspapers he knew Chicago was crowded and noisy, full of mobsters and speakeasies. He reckoned he'd just have to get used to the idea of a world filled with brick and stone, noise and people. He was really going to miss green meeting blue on every horizon.

As he stood there sluggishly debating whether to continue west or turn north, a muted buzz vibrated the air. A *mechanical* buzz. And it was approaching. Too deep for an automobile. Closing in too fast to be a tractor. His curiosity kept him from diving for the weeds and hiding.

It got louder, stealing deep into Henry's bones. When he set eyes on the airplane overhead, something fluttered to life in his chest. It was a beauty for sure; stacked wings and throaty roar against the blue sky. He'd only seen airplanes in pictures, and those pictures hadn't been able to fill his heart with the raw power of that thrumming motor.

His mechanic's hands itched to tinker with those valves and pistons.

Suddenly, the plane rolled to its right and made a U-turn, heading back the way it had come. He stood there wishing it would turn around again.

And then it did.

Well, if I'd known there was a wish to be granted, I'd have made better use.

The plane skimmed low over the far side of the broad cow pasture on Henry's right.

Then he noticed something else. Below the plane. Matching its speed.

He shaded his eyes and squinted.

A motorcycle tore along at breakneck speed, bouncing on the rough ground, looking as if it were bucking to throw off the

17

rider, who was leaning forward over the handlebars.

A tree row stood about two hundred yards ahead of the motorcycle and the plane. Who would blink first?

The plane stayed lower than the treetops, edging just ahead of the motorcycle.

The motorcycle did not let up.

Even if the plane pulled up now, it looked to be too late.

"No, no, no, no, no!" Henry jumped over the water-filled ditch, vaulted over the wire fence. He felt caught in a dream, his body moving unnaturally slowly, the pasture growing wider as he ran.

Just when he thought the plane was going to hit the trees, it pulled up with a mighty roar, nose nearly straight up in the air.

The motorcycle disappeared into the tree line. The crashing sound rolled across the field. The engine whined high, as if the wheels had left the ground.

The plane's drone moved away.

Henry ran faster. He ducked and swatted through trees and scrub where the motorcycle had left a trail of broken branches and flattened weeds. It was on its side, front wheel bent, handlebar plowed deep in the mud beside a large pond.

The rider?

There! Facedown in the water.

Henry splashed into the pond, praying it wasn't deep; he could keep himself from drowning, but that was about it. The water dragged on his clothes. Each step in the muddy bottom was harder to pull free than the last. Once chest deep, he stretched his reach, but fell short.

The rider's head jerked up. Sputtering, he flailed.

Henry lunged forward to grab the collar of the leather jacket, but missed.

"Hold still!" He took another step and slipped under as the bottom fell away under his feet. When he bobbed back up, an elbow caught him in the eye. A foot landed a kick on his right thigh.

"Stop moving! I'll *ggg*—" Water splashed into Henry's open mouth and shot down his gullet. He coughed and grabbed blindly for the rider.

He dodged an arm and managed to get one of his own wrapped around the man's waist and half swam, half drowned, back to where he could set his feet on the bottom. The body beneath the leather jacket felt more like a fourteen-year-old than a man.

Now that he was towing a thrashing body, Henry's feet sank deeper into the bottom.

The choking, gasping kid kept fighting

and Henry almost lost his grip.

"I have you!" Henry pulled one foot from the mud and nearly went under again.

He shifted his grip to the collar of the leather jacket. His chances of staying on his feet were better dragging a floating body, even if it was flopping like a banked bass. He leaned away and pulled the boy behind him, one sucking step at a time.

By the time they reached the edge of the pond, the floundering stopped. The boy gasped for air. Henry's legs were lead. He let go of the jacket and fell to the ground himself, muscles burning, heart ready to explode. He lay on his back sucking air into his starved lungs, listening to the kid cough and wheeze.

A couple of minutes later, Henry was still getting his breath when a curious cow stepped close and looked down at him. A long string of drool hung from her lips. Henry put up a hand and swatted her away, realizing too late that if he startled her, her next step could be in the center of his chest.

The cow didn't move, but the drool let go and landed in a slimy *plop* on Henry's forehead. He swiped at it, but the snotty stuff just smeared.

The cow blinked her huge brown eyes and mooed. Henry was pretty sure she was laughing at him.

"Oh, shut up, Tilda." The rider's voice was gaspy and graveled from coughing.

Henry took the kid's ability to speak — and his sense of humor — as good news. "You know this cow?"

"She's a" — he coughed and spat — "a troublemaker." The boy pushed himself to sitting.

"Careful! Something might be broken."

"Nah." The boy was still breathing hard as he rotated wrists and bent elbows and knees to make sure. "Just got the wind knocked out." He pulled off his gloves and swiped some of the mud from his cheek before reaching for the buckle on his leather helmet.

"Sure you're okay?" Henry's own eye throbbed. He figured it for a shiner.

The cow walked between them and stepped into the pond. Henry dodged, but her flitting tail caught his cheek. "You've got a real sassy attitude there, Tilda."

The kid laughed, then started coughing again.

There was a whir as the plane, now on the ground, bumped along the rough pasture coming toward them. The propeller and engine sounded different from when it was airborne. Henry looked through the trees, eyes and heart drawn to the machine. The plane swung sideways before the engine shut off. It took a second for the propeller to come to a jerky stop.

Henry got up and went to get a better look. He might never see an airplane again. A clump of green leaves stuck in the tail skid. That pilot couldn't have cut it any closer.

"Dear God, is he okay?" the pilot shouted. He was out of the plane by the time Henry reached the wingtip. The man's leather helmet was in one hand and his goggles hung around his neck. His face was sooty. He looked like a reverse raccoon.

"Says he is." Henry heard the pilot thrash through the trees behind him, but kept his eyes on the plane, listening to the pops and clicks as it began to cool. The upper wing had a wider span than the lower; the two were tied together with wood poles and a whole lot of wires and turnbuckles. The entire plane looked as if it were held together by wires running in all sorts of angles, above the wing, between the wings, between the body and the tail. The purpose of the half-circle hoops under the tips of the bottom wings was a mystery.

He reached out slowly, laying his fingertips reverently on the gray fabric of the wing.

"Damned idiot!" the pilot shouted. "You could have gotten yourself killed!"

"Pretty smart talk from a fella who'd rather crash his plane than lose a race!"

That voice sounded even younger than Henry had thought.

"*You're the one* who crashed —" The pilot's words cut off. "Ho-ly hell."

Henry turned. The kid had pulled off the leather helmet and was standing with hands on hips. Not a kid. A *girl* . . . with a long, brown braid . . . wearing *trousers* and lace-up knee boots . . . racing like the devil on a motorcycle.

"What?" she asked, raising her chin. "Embarrassed to be beaten by a woman?"

"The one whose machine ends up mangled after a tie is the loser," the pilot said. "And a fool to boot."

"You both look like idiots to me," Henry said as he walked toward them, wringing the water out of the hem of his shirt, his shoes squishing. "If I had either one of those machines, I sure wouldn't treat them like that."

They both turned to Henry and said, "Well, you *don't.*"

Henry stopped short.

"Sure you're not hurt?" The pilot sounded more disrespectful than worried, which rubbed Henry the wrong way.

"Yes, I'm sure! Too bad the motorcycle didn't fare as well." Her voice slid down a steep hill from defensive to sad. "My brother wouldn't like it."

"You have a brother who lets you get out on that thing and do dangerous stunts like this?" The pilot had a point.

"I said he *wouldn't* like it. He's dead."

"If his judgment was anything like yours, he was probably killed on that motorbike."

Henry cringed. *Who talks to a girl like that?*

"His was worse actually." A whole lot of I-dare-you was in her voice. "Signed up and got killed by German mustard gas."

German. Familiar guilty dread crept over Henry. Would the stink from that word ever leave him?

The pilot sucked in a breath as if he'd been gut-punched. After a few seconds he said, "Sorry. I'm an ass."

"Obviously."

It got quiet again.

While those two stood and stared at one another, Henry went to check the motorcycle.

HENDERSON was written in gold letters across the rectangular gas tank. He wasn't familiar enough with motorcycles to tell if it was an expensive model. The front fork

24

looked okay, hard as that was to believe. The front wheel was tweaked too far to rotate, its fender twisted. The chain drive remained in place, even though the guard had been ripped half off and would flap like a broken wing once the motorcycle got moving.

He reached down and grabbed the handlebars. When he pulled to right the cycle, his feet slipped in the mud and he landed on his backside.

Tilda mooed loudly, making sure the pilot and the girl looked Henry's way. That cow was really itching to turn into a side of beef.

"Now who looks like an idiot?" the girl said.

The pilot walked toward Henry and gave him a hand up. "Charles Gilchrist. Call me Gil."

"Henry S — Jefferson."

"What's the *S* stand for?"

Stupid. "Sam-uel." All the way with the red, white, and blue.

Gil turned toward the girl, his voice sounding the slightest bit apologetic. "And you?"

"Cora Haviland — of the New York Havilands." The way she said her name made Henry think he should have heard of her family — as if she were a Carnegie, Ford, or Rockefeller. Henry didn't know anything about society, so he glanced at Gil. He didn't look as if her name meant anything to him either.

She nodded toward the cow. "You've met Tilda."

Henry swiped his forehead again and felt the slime. "Unfortunately."

He and Gil got the motorcycle up on its wheels. It was like wrestling a boar hog. No wonder he'd fallen on his ass.

Cora took it out of gear. Gil lifted the bent wheel and they rolled the cycle on its rear tire to the tree line and leaned it up against a trunk. That's when Henry realized the flat-bottomed, U-shaped piece of metal on the ground near the tree row must have been a stand that could be rolled under the rear wheel to hold the cycle upright. He went over and picked it up. He didn't see how it could be repaired, but hooked it under the seat anyway, so it stayed with the motorcycle.

"Not sure how you're going to get it home," Gil said.

"Is it far?" Henry asked.

"A mile or so. But we can't just go dragging it up the lane." She shot a challenging look at them, as if she was daring them to argue about the *we* part. "Mother thinks it's long gone."

If her mother didn't know about the motorcycle, how did Cora explain dressing like that?

Gil didn't look confused at all. He just raised a brow. "Quite the rebel, are you?"

"Flyboy, you have no idea."

Cora insisted that taking the motorcycle home by way of the road was out of the question. Only an approach from the back of the barn wouldn't risk being seen. Whatever way they went, Henry figured it was going to be a whole lot easier to move the cycle if that front wheel turned. He tugged on the fender and straightened it enough to allow the wheel to pass through. Then he picked up a thick, downed tree limb and tried to lever the rim until it was true enough to spin. Gil stood off to the side with his arms crossed, telling Henry it was a waste of time. Which turned out to be right.

"Do you have any ideas?" he asked Gil.

"Too heavy for the three of us to carry any distance." He glanced at the sky, impatience on his face. Then he looked at Cora. "If you keep this thing in the barn, your father must know you have it. Maybe he could bring a wagon and the three of us men could lift it in."

"He's dead, too."

Henry couldn't believe how matter-of-fact she was when she talked about her war-killed brother and her dead father. Maybe the crash had knocked her head and she didn't know what she was saying. She was a girl, after all. The Dahlgren girls cried over everything: baby birds fallen from the nest, moths trapped in spiderwebs, mud on their dresses. They even got weepy when anyone mentioned the name of a barn cat that had been trampled by a mule years before. From his first day on that farm, Mrs. Dahlgren had preached to Henry that girls had delicate sensibilities and it was every male's duty to protect them. One of Henry's jobs had been to scout the chicken yard and henhouse before the girls went to fetch the eggs in the morning, just to make sure no foxes had raided and left a bloody trail of chicken guts.

He was starting to think chicken guts wouldn't even make Cora blink.

"Well, then," Gil said, "I say we park it in this tree row for tonight, out of sight. Miss Daredevil here can get some help and haul it home tomorrow."

"Hey!" Henry said. "She's just a girl. We have to help. Besides *you're* the reason she wrecked."

"Just a girl!" Both Cora and Gil said. Henry wondered how two people who'd barely met could chime in with the exact same words twice in less than fifteen minutes.

Cora's mouth snapped closed, as if she realized she was starting to argue against what she wanted to happen.

Gil looked to be gritting his teeth. "Look." He jabbed a finger in her direction. "She wrecked because she used poor judgment. Women and machines don't mix. Who would have thought a *girl* would be out here tearing around a farm field on a motorcycle? This" — he shifted his finger to the motorcycle — "is *not* my fault. And in about forty minutes, I'm going to lose the light and be stuck in this pasture until sunrise tomorrow. Which will be *her* fault."

"Ducky, then." Cora sounded as if she were agreeing with good news. "You'll have all night to help us get this back to the barn."

Henry looked at the sinking sun. "Where were you heading? You from around here?"

"I'm not *from* anywhere, but I need to get to the next sizable town sooner rather than later."

"Why?" Cora asked. "The day's almost

over anyway."

"I need people in a number greater than the two of you and gasoline for what I do. County seats are the best bet."

Cora looked puzzled. "A business that requires people and hooch; now there I can see lots of possibilities. But people and *gasoline*? What exactly *do* you do?"

"Barnstorming."

Henry didn't want to show his ignorance, so he kept quiet.

"What in the Sam Hill is that?" Cora asked. "Got anything to do with bootleg?"

Even out in the country, enough people ignored the Volstead Act that it barely seemed like a crime.

"No." Gil gave her a scowl — Henry was beginning to think that was the man's normal face. A weary, angry tension steadily vibrated under his skin.

"So what is it?" Cora asked.

"I buzz over a town, do a few stunts to get people's attention, then find a field to land in. The curious always come."

"For what?" Henry felt bolder now that Cora had admitted she didn't know what barnstorming was, but one look at her face said she'd already figured it out.

"Rides," Gil said. "Five dollars for ten minutes. If they want a loop or a barrel roll, it's extra."

Five dollars! No wonder he needed a town full of people — bankers and lawyers and the like. Henry'd give his right arm to fly in that thing, but five dollars was something he couldn't imagine ever having to spare.

Cora tilted her head. "You make enough kale to live on just by selling a few rides?"

Gil made a face that wasn't quite a smile. "I make enough to keep my plane in the air. That's all I need."

"So where do you plan to sleep tonight?" she asked.

"Camp, like always."

"Well, Aunt Gladys's arthritis says it's going to rain. If you help me get this motorbike back to the barn, you can sleep there." Cora raised a brow. "*And* you can come in for dinner. I'm sure I can talk my uncle into letting you use the field for your barnstorming, too."

The thought of a hot meal nearly made Henry cry like the Dahlgren girls.

Gil looked at the sky.

"Sounds like a good deal, Gil." Henry tried to keep the needy hope out of his voice. "You won't get far before dark anyway."

Gil stood there looking stubborn. "Not enough people around here to make this pasture worthwhile," he finally said.

"But you're already here," Cora said. "Why not cash in before you move on? I know *I'd* like a ride, so you have your first customer already."

"What about you?" Gil asked Henry. "Don't you have somewhere to be?"

"I'm on my way to Chicago. Got a job waiting. I could use a place to sleep tonight." *Inside. Where no one will find me.* "Your uncle's name is Haviland?" Not one Henry was familiar with, but what if it wasn't Haviland and Cora's uncle knew Anders Dahlgren?

"No. It's Fessler. Aunt Gladys is Father's older sister."

Henry nodded. Fessler was just as unfamiliar as Haviland.

Gil looked at Cora. "You're sure your uncle will go along?"

"Ab-so-lute-ly."

"All right. Deal."

Henry's mouth started to water. But his hopes for a quick meal were squashed when Gil said they had to tie down the plane before they could leave it. He retrieved a cross-peen hammer, three lengths of rope, and a couple of stakes from the plane.

Cora watched them with her hands on her hips. "Afraid it'll take off without you?"

The thing was designed to ride on the wind. *She* said weather was coming in. Gil was right, women and machines didn't mix.

Gil gave a head shake and went on about his business. Henry didn't feel it was his place to explain.

Gil finished tying the tail rope to the trunk of a nearby tree. Then he wiped his hands on his thighs. "That should do it."

Cora nudged Henry's shoulder. "Let's go, Kid."

Kid? She looked eighteen, nineteen at most. But he kept his mouth shut. Right now, the less said, the less likely questions would be asked.

He focused on supper. During his time on the Dahlgren farm he'd forgotten how to live hungry.

Gil carried the front of the motorcycle by the bent wheel while Henry pushed from the rear, feeling as if he were herding a reluctant donkey. Cora walked alongside, steadying the balance. Tilda followed them all the way across the pasture to a back gate that led to a cornfield. When Cora closed the gate behind them, the cow bellowed like an abandoned kid.

Before they started moving again, Cora took off her jacket and threw it over the handlebars, where Gil's already hung. Henry's mouth went dry at the sight of her. Her white blouse was stuck to her skin and wet enough to show more than a hint of what was underneath. No matter how many times Henry forced his eyes elsewhere, his curious gaze slid right back to Cora. Gil proved a gentleman, which was a surprise after the way he'd talked to her, turning his back the second she'd slipped the jacket off her shoulders.

Henry was torn between relief and regret when they started moving again and all he could see was her back.

It was almost dark when they went through another gate. Henry's nose told him they were in the pig lot. The barn was a hulking, dark shadow on the far side.

Cora scouted the open stretch between the row of hedge apple trees and the barn. When she was satisfied the coast was clear, they rolled the motorcycle across the final, sour-smelling stretch. By then Henry's eye was throbbing and his back felt as if he'd been lifting hay bales every day for a week.

Directing them to a lean-to on the back side of the barn, she said, "Here."

She opened a door barely wide enough for the handlebars to pass through. It was pitch-black inside. Stepping around Gil, she disappeared in the darkness. After a second, a light flared and she reappeared in the glow of a small oil lantern. Shameful as it was, Henry was disappointed to see her blouse had dried.

The inside of the lean-to wasn't packed with stuff the way Henry expected it to be. Against the back wall was a stack of wooden crates covered with about a hundred years of dust, a chair with a missing leg, and a rusty scythe. Nearer the door was a tarp-covered pile about two feet by three feet and a red, two-gallon gas can.

"Nobody ever comes in here. Uncle Clyde thinks the door is still stuck."

Henry noticed the ground beneath the door swing had been dug down. He wondered if Cora had shoveled it herself. He'd never seen a girl lift a tool of any kind, so he doubted it.

"*Nobody* knows you've got this thing?" Gil asked.

"After Jonathan was killed, it sat in our garage at the country house under a tarp. Everyone forgot about it . . . except me. When we packed up and moved here, a couple of sawbucks got the men to crate it up without a word to Mother. And here it is."

"Where'd you live before?" Henry asked.

"I told you, New York City. But Mother preferred that dreadfully boring Hudson Valley house most of the time. We wintered on Jekyll Island. It was all very . . . you know" — she gave a flip of her head and lifted her nose in the air — "high-hat."

Gil whistled through his teeth.

Henry had no idea where Hudson Valley or Jekyll Island were. Anybody with more than one house was rich, that much he *did* know.

"If you gentlemen will wait outside, I need to change my clothes."

Henry hurried out, the image of her body under that wet blouse burning in his brain. Gil followed more slowly, then leaned against the barn, putting one foot on the wall behind him, and pulled out a pack of Chesterfields from his shirt pocket. He held the pack out to Henry, who waved off the offer. Gil shook one out, struck a match, and lit it.

"Been flying long?" Henry asked.

Gil pulled a long drag on the cigarette, then blew out the smoke. "A while." He kept his eyes on the sky. It was dark enough that a few stars had peeked out.

All of the questions that came ready to Henry's mind could easily lead to questions asked back. Keep to the machine. That was safe. And he was curious about it. He'd always liked figuring out ways to make something useful out of scraps and discards. Early on he discovered his knack for patching the irreparable back together — necessity had been a good teacher. During the past five years he'd earned his keep by coaxing Mr. Dahlgren's finicky Fordson tractor into good behavior, finally silencing the man's threats to return to mule power. Henry's ability to decipher the code that smoothed out an engine's running had been a bitter pill; he blamed tractors for stealing his pa's job and the last of his will to live. But once his love for the hum of pumping pistons, the clatter of a crankshaft, became useful to Mr. Dahlgren, it felt a little less like betrayal.

"How fast will it go?" Henry asked.

"She ain't fast and she ain't agile. She ain't reliable, either. Tops out at around seventy-five. Lucky to get sixty."

"Seventy-five!"

"That's *not* fast. And speed burns too much fuel."

"Eight cylinder?"

"Yeah. Water-cooled Curtiss OX-5."

"I read about Glenn Curtiss in *Scientific American.*"

Gil finally looked at him. "Most folks only

37

know about the Wright brothers, Eddie Rickenbacker, and the Red Baron when it comes to planes."

"Yeah, well, I know about them, too. Love machines. What's the horsepower?"

"When she's working good, ninety. She's usually not working good."

"Maybe I could take a look at it. I'm pretty good with engines."

Gil picked a piece of tobacco off his tongue and flipped it onto the ground. "Nobody touches her but me." He said it as if the plane were his woman.

Cora came back out of the lean-to. Her hair was pinned up proper and she had on a dress with a low sash and short, sheer-ruffled sleeves — far too short for decency according to Mrs. Dahlgren; the loud arguments between her and her older daughters came up like clockwork, right after the arrival of *Harper's Bazaar* magazine or the new Sears, Roebuck catalog. Other than that, she looked like the well-dressed Dahlgren girls. Her wide-brimmed straw hat had a ribbon band that matched the green stripe in her dress, and she wore tan stockings and strap shoes. Over one arm she held a basket holding a book and some pencils. You'd never guess she'd just crashed a speeding motorcycle.

"Oooh." She reached her palm out and flicked her fingers at Gil. "Give me a puff of that ciggy."

He passed it to her as if women smoked all of the time. The tip glowed orange as she drew on it. She handed it back and waved a hand to shoo the smoke away when she exhaled.

As they walked toward the house, she said, "I must warn you, everyone here is quite serious and old-fashioned. I'm losing my mind stuck out here with nobody but the three Victorians. But" — she changed to a high voice that Henry took to be mimicking her mother's — *"we must do our best until our circumstances improve."* She sighed. "Mother's spent the past four months eating humble pie — and looking for a way to change her daily diet. Which means looking for a rich husband for me." The last words were said with a detached flatness that said Cora wasn't all that happy with that solution.

They reached the back door of a regular farmhouse, a nice place, but not a rich man's house. Cora stopped. "You two are welcome to concoct any story you like to explain why you're both stranded here at nightfall. *I* came upon you both in the pasture as I was returning from my nature walk — all civilized young ladies of breeding take nature walks. I'm quite enthralled with them. Sometimes I completely lose track of time." She turned and stepped through the door.

Gil raised a brow to Henry and shrugged.

As they followed her into the house, Henry thought Tilda probably wasn't the only troublemaker on this farm.

2

Cora's aunt and uncle didn't seem old-fashioned, or even all that serious. They were just like most farm folk Henry had ever met. Mr. Fessler had work-rough hands, a stooped back, steel-gray beard, and bald head. Mrs. Fessler had pure white hair and wore an apron over a plain housedress. What Henry couldn't figure was how a girl whose family was New York "high-hat" and had more than one house ended up living on an Indiana farm.

Cora had brought them into the house through the back porch. A couple of trunks were sitting there. She'd stopped so quickly Henry had almost run into the back of her. She'd given a low, throaty growl and kicked one of the trunks hard enough that it scooted a couple of inches, even though the *thunk* said it was full. Then she'd gone on as if she hadn't stopped at all.

Once in the kitchen, she'd made quick

41

work of introducing him and Gil to her aunt and uncle, then disappeared to find dry clothes for Henry.

Mr. Fessler asked them to sit.

Mrs. Fessler went back to rolling out biscuits, but kept casting cool and curious looks toward Henry's muddy clothes, scratched face, and throbbing eye while she worked. Mr. Fessler was more direct in his inspection, sitting at a scarred drop-leaf table with a newspaper and a cut-glass toothpick holder in front of him. Like most farm folks, they did not pry. But they were probably churning out all sorts of supposings about Henry in their heads. He felt obliged to satisfy their curiosity, if only to keep Cora out of trouble. Once he gave his fictional explanation for his pitiful state, Mrs. Fessler warmed right up. She invited Henry and Gil to dinner. They accepted as if Cora hadn't already made the offer . . . Mrs. Fessler was the one cooking, after all.

As Mr. Fessler picked up the newspaper, he muttered a few polite words about the weather, the predictions of the *Farmers' Almanac,* and the sad state of farm-commodity prices. It didn't take long for things to fall quiet. Gil picked up a section of newspaper and opened it, just as if he sat at that table every day.

Henry watched their faces as they read, nervously searching for a glimmer of curiosity cast his way, a hint of recognition, a breath of shock. What had happened to Emmaline — that was the only way he'd allow himself to think of it, as if he'd had nothing to do with it — was surely in the newspapers. Maybe he was far enough away that it wasn't front-page news.

He tried to sit still, but his hands didn't seem to know where to settle. Too dirty to touch the table, they did a flighty rotation: knees, thighs, tucked under his arms, knees, thighs . . . the hands of a man with something to hide.

Mr. Fessler's eyes stayed on the paper and Missus was busy adding two more potatoes to the pot. Still, Henry couldn't shake the feeling that he was on display, like the Incredible Fish Boy in the traveling freak shows, those that came to town one day and were gone the next. Something decent folk couldn't help but part with a nickel to see, but would only look at from the corners of their eyes and always made up for it by muttering sympathy when they came out.

Cora finally came back. "You gentlemen are all set to use the lavatory."

Henry was quick to volunteer for the first turn. He followed her through the house, up the stairs, and down a long, narrow hallway.

"Everything you need should be in there," she said as she stopped at a door at the end of the hall. "If not, just give a shout."

He thanked her and stepped into a black-and-white-tiled bathroom. He tried not to stare like a yokel at the fancy indoor plumbing, the claw-foot tub, and the big mirrors, at least until he got the door closed.

Just before it latched, Cora's fingers wrapped around the edge and stopped it. He pulled it open far enough to see her face.

"Just so we have our stories straight, what did you tell Uncle Clyde?"

He looked down into her green eyes and was for an insane moment tempted to unburden himself of his whole story. "Family's all dead and I'm headed to Chicago for work."

"And?" She raised her brows, looking at his clothes.

"I tripped into the ditch while I was watching Gil's plane. You passed us on your way home."

"And Flyboy?"

"He told your uncle that he got caught short of his destination when the light started to go and he needed a place to land for the night. The pasture looked safe and he hoped Mr. Fessler didn't mind him using it." Henry paused. "Only he didn't use that many words."

She gave a quick nod and left.

Henry closed the door, then pressed his forehead against it. He tried to keep his lies as close to the truth as possible, but they still clung to his tongue, reluctant to leave his mouth. He hated lies. They always grew legs after they were uttered and ran out into the world all on their own. That's when the real trouble started.

After a moment, he took a deep breath and went to the sink. He checked his eye in the mirror. It was going to be a shiner all right. With all of Cora's thrashing around, he figured he was lucky he didn't have a matching pair. There were cuts, too; not from Cora, but from his last horrible minutes on the farm.

He washed his face, neck, and hands, amazed at all that hot water with just the turn of a handle. A box of tooth powder was on the glass shelf under the mirror. He put some on his finger and ran it around his teeth. He needed a shave. No help for that. Luckily his beard was as fair as his hair and kept him from looking too much like a tramp. He combed his hair with his wet fingers and decided that was as good as it was going to get for now.

It had taken a couple of seconds to figure out how the flushing toilet worked. Once he did, he flushed it three more times, just to watch it. He stopped when Gil knocked and asked if Henry was all right.

After that, he got on with changing his clothes. The motorcycle wasn't the only thing of Cora's brother Jonathan's that she hadn't been able to part with. The shirt he put on had a monogram on the cuffs, JHW, and was much finer than any he'd ever touched. She'd given him a collar and collar pin, too, but Henry had never worn a collar before and felt foolish with the stiff, white band cinched around his neck. He took it right back off. The trousers were fine, too, although they were too big around the waist and he felt a little like a circus clown the way they hung from his suspenders. There were socks, dark with a pattern running up the side, and a pair of . . . slippers? They sure weren't shoes. He changed into the socks, but put his own damp shoes back on.

He opened the door with his folded clothes in hand. Gil leaned against the wall with his arms crossed and his chin on his chest. He didn't move. Henry paused and leaned close. The man was dead asleep.

Henry snapped his fingers under Gil's nose.

Before Henry could blink, he was up against the opposite wall, with Gil's forearm pressed against his throat hard enough to cut off his air. It took a second before Gil's eyes changed, as if he were just now seeing, then he jumped away from Henry, looking at him as if *he'd* been the one to attack.

"Sorry." Gil sucked in a deep breath and blew it back out quickly. "Sorry."

Henry stayed against the wall. He was good at keeping himself in check, at least he had been until two days ago. Finally, he felt safe in moving. His hand went to his throat, as if his fingers could read the damage.

Gil ran his hands through his hair, then stepped closer, his bewilderment replaced by anger. "Do not *ever* do that to me again." He disappeared into the bathroom and closed the door.

Henry stood there for a minute. He understood the kind of confusion he'd seen in Gil's eyes, the kind that follows blind rage and unthinking action.

What dwelt in the darkness of Gil's cellar? He was probably Peter's age — the age Peter would be had he not gotten killed in the war. Henry wondered if Gil had gone to war, too. Some men came home different

47

from when they'd left. A man in Delaware County, a teacher before the war, now walked around constantly dodging and ducking things only he could see and hear. Henry had no idea if Gil's reaction was from the war or if he was just crazy on his own.

Once Henry's breathing evened out, he picked up his dropped clothes and headed downstairs.

When he entered the kitchen, the smell of hot food grabbed all of his senses, driving away his ability to do more than breathe and salivate. Cora was alone in the room. She held out her hands, palms up. He stood there looking at her for a minute, trying to figure out what she wanted. She flipped her fingers. "Your clothes."

"Oh." Henry hesitated. It didn't seem proper to have a strange woman handling your clothes, and his were particularly dirty and worn. "Um, just let me know whe—"

"Come on, now. I promise to give them back." She snatched the clothes from his hands. He stood there like an idiot while she shook out the pants and shirt, then pulled two chairs close to the stove. She hung his pants on the back of one. As she was draping his shirt on the other, she asked, "Where are your drawers?"

"Beg pardon?"

She straightened and rolled her eyes. "Your underwear. You do wear underwear, don't you?"

He crossed his hands over himself and took a step backward.

"Give the kid a break," Gil said as he walked into the kitchen. "His union suit is no concern of yours."

"But it has to be damp."

"It's fine," Henry said quietly, avoiding looking at her. The underwear she'd given him upstairs was made of something fine and flimsy — almost girlish. There was only so much humiliation he was willing to take for the sake of a little comfort.

"Suit yourself." She started toward the swinging door to the dining room. "Come on, then."

Henry's stomach tensed. "What?"

She stopped with her hand on the door, looked over her shoulder, and crooked her finger.

"Are we . . . I mean . . . aren't Gil and I eating in the kitchen?" He'd never eaten in a real dining room; and he couldn't say he wanted to start with a bunch of strangers he was lying to while wearing a dead man's clothes.

"Don't be silly." She pushed the door open.

Gil followed her without visible reluctance. Henry trailed behind, wishing he had the nerve to just stay put in the kitchen where he belonged.

Mr. Fessler was seated at the head of the table. Cora's aunt sat on his left, bib apron still in place. A stiff-looking woman wearing a dress with a lot of lace and beads and more jewelry than Henry thought any one woman owned, let alone wore all at once, sat at the other end. And she had on *gloves.* A fluffy, little feather was stuck in her hair. Her green eyes matched Cora's.

"Mother, I'd like to introduce our guests. Charles Gilchrist, an aviator." Cora had changed her voice, using the one she'd used when she'd said she was "of the New York Havilands."

Gil moved to Mrs. Haviland, took her offered hand, and bowed over it. Cora's mother got close to a smile, but it was too thin and held no warmth.

"And Henry Jefferson." Cora motioned toward Henry. "Who is traveling through to Chicago."

He stayed planted just inside the door and nodded. "Ma'am."

Cora's mother looked at him a lot like

Mrs. Dahlgren used to.

He'd never minded living alone in a barn, but right now he felt like a hog let into the house and invited to the table. Sure, he knew to hold a door open for a lady and not to scratch himself in public, but he was, as he'd so often been reminded, "unfit for polite society."

He wished he could hop up on his hog hooves and snort his way back into the kitchen — or better yet, right out the back door and on down the road. Only his hunger kept him where he was.

"Mr. Jefferson," Cora said, "you may sit next to Aunt Gladys."

Henry stood there for a second before he remembered *he* was Jefferson.

As he took the seat, he noticed Mr. Fessler looked about half-perturbed. "Apologize for the late hour, boys. Mrs. Haviland prefers to eat supper closer to breakfast. Since she's our guest . . ."

Cora cast a grateful look Mr. Fessler's way. "Uncle's been so kind to make us feel at home and indulge us in our city ways."

Henry sent a quick, uneasy glance toward Mrs. Haviland. He imagined changing her ways would be a lot like trying to change Mrs. Dahlgren's. *That woman thinks it was etched in stone and handed down from*

Moses. How many times had he heard those words uttered in Mr. Dahlgren's thick Swedish accent? Henry wouldn't ever again hear that man's voice. Another cobweb gathered in his soul.

"Yes." Mrs. Haviland offered a smile that reminded Henry of something reptilian, cold and scaly. Other than the eyes, nothing about the woman hinted that she and Cora were related. "I'm sure Clyde and Gladys will be happy to return to their usual ways."

The way she said "usual ways" made Henry think that their usual ways might include dancing around a bonfire naked and eating their meat raw.

Cora and Gil went to the other side of the white-lace-covered table. He pulled out Cora's chair for her.

Mr. Fessler said grace. Henry grasped on to the familiarity of it. After most of his mother's teachings had fallen to neglect, grace had been one he'd tended.

After the "Amen," he picked up his napkin and tucked it into his collar.

Mrs. Haviland cleared her throat loudly and looked at him with disgust.

Cora made a big show of taking her napkin, shaking it out, and putting it on her lap. Henry's cheeks got hot as he grabbed the tail in his lap and inched the napkin from his collar.

Cora smiled at him, lifted her chin slightly, and turned her head to the side and her nose up in the air. *High-hat.* Then she winked and he felt only a little less stupid.

From then on he focused on not wolfing down his food and avoiding being drawn into conversation. Maybe everyone would forget he was there.

Cora spoke like a shy girl when she told her family how surprised and frightened she'd been when she'd seen Gil's airplane land in the pasture.

"Oh, Uncle, you *must* go look at it," she said. "I've never seen anything so dangerous and fast."

Gil choked a little and reached for his glass of water.

Her mother's face soured. "And you felt it proper to stop and engage with strange men while you were alone? Really, Cora. You must exercise better judgment."

"Yes, Mother."

Henry's eyes snapped up to meet Gil's. Cora had obviously changed more than her clothes in that shed.

"Mr. Gilchrist, did you learn to fly in the service?" Mr. Fessler asked in a way that made Henry think he was speaking more to rescue his niece than out of curiosity.

"I did. The Jenny . . . my plane . . . was a surplus trainer left over from the war."

"A horrible thing," Mr. Fessler said. "We lost Cora's brother Jonathan in France. My great-niece's son came back in one piece, but the shell shock ruined him. Tragic, just a tragic, tragic waste."

Mrs. Haviland suddenly stood and dropped her napkin on the table. "If you'll excuse me . . ."

Mr. Fessler and Gil stood also. Cora and Mrs. Fessler stayed seated. After a second, Henry got the idea and stood until Mrs. Haviland had left the room.

As the men sat back down, Cora said, "Please don't take offense, this happens all of the time. Mother simply detests *any* unpleasant topic of conversation at the table. She's trying to teach us all a lesson."

Mr. and Mrs. Fessler stayed quiet, but both of them looked more relaxed — more as they had in the kitchen when Henry had first arrived.

Henry wondered how it could be much of a lesson when the entire room felt better without Mrs. Haviland in it.

Cora looked at Gil. "You named your plane *Jenny*?"

"That's not her name. That's what she is,

a Curtiss JN-4 . . . everyone calls them Jennies."

A devilish twinkle came to Cora's eye. "Ah, but she is a female."

Gil looked perturbed. "All ships are *she*s."

"That's right," Mr. Fessler said. "Because they're the only females a man can control."

"Clyde." Mrs. Fessler sounded scandalized, but her eyes sparkled and a smile played on her lips.

"Sorry, dear." He reached out and wrapped his blunt fingers around her blue-veined hand. It struck Henry as the most loving gesture he'd ever seen. "I don't get the pleasure of masculine company very often. I lost my head."

"You're entitled, Uncle. After all, you're always so outnumbered," Cora said as if she were forgiving a transgression — and maybe she was. In the world of good manners, how would Henry know? "That's one of the reasons I asked Mr. Gilchrist and Mr. Jefferson to dinner. And I know how you support our veterans. I told Mr. Gilchrist you might be willing to let him use your pasture for his . . ." She batted her eyes and looked at a loss. "What did you call it, Mr. Gilchrist?"

A prick of unease nibbled the back of Henry's neck. She was so convincing in her feigned innocence, so skilled at her duplicity.

Gil slid a look her way. "Barnstorming." He explained to Mr. Fessler as he had to Henry and Cora.

"People pay money to risk their lives like that?" Mr. Fessler asked.

"There's nothing that compares to how it is up there." The tension slid from Gil's face like melted wax; his eyes glowed as if he'd just seen the face of God. "The wind. The power. The isolation. The view. It's like you don't even belong to the earth anymore." He sat there staring into space for a moment, then seemed to snap back to himself. "I'll be happy to take you for a ride. No charge. Aviation is going to change the world."

"Can't see much use for it outside of the military. Read about them planes being used for the mail. Been more mail lost in crashes than made it to its destination. Trains are trustworthy. Airplanes . . ." Mr. Fessler sat back and shook his head. "I'll pass on the ride, but if you want to use my pasture, it's all yours, son. I doubt you'll get many customers around here, though."

"Oh, Mr. Gilchrist says they always come, Uncle!" Cora then lowered her eyes to her lap, as if she were embarrassed by her lack of restraint.

She'd turned completely into that "young lady of breeding" who was "enthralled" with nature walks.

He'd only ever known one girl who could change herself this convincingly.

Ever since he'd laid eyes on that plane, an idea had been playing in Henry's head. He needed to put more distance between himself and Delaware County. And planes travel faster than feet.

He and Gil went to the barn for the night, Henry back in his own clothes, dry and brushed free of crusted mud. They climbed to the hayloft. Once they were settled in the silver moonlight coming through the open hayloft doors — so much for Aunt Gladys's weather prediction — breathing the comfortingly familiar smells of alfalfa, motor oil, and animal, Henry decided to inch his way toward his new objective.

"Does the Jenny use a battery or a magneto?" he asked.

"Magneto. Battery adds too much weight."

"But there's no crank."

"Sure there is. The propeller."

"But you're by yourself. You set the brake first, then?"

"There are no brakes."

"But" — Henry leaned up on one elbow — "it'll run right —"

"Oh, yeah. You spin it and get your ass out of the way."

"Do you use wheel chocks to keep it from moving forward?"

"Some do. I'm fast."

Henry wondered how fast a man had to be to start the engine, run around the wing, and clamber up into the cockpit. "Be easier with two people I imagine."

"It is. But you can't let just anybody prop it; severed body parts are bad for business."

Henry barked out a laugh. "I would imagine." Here goes. "There must be a lot of upkeep on a machine like that one."

"Endless."

"You know, a good mechanic could get that OX-5 singing like a bird."

"I don't make enough to pay a mechanic. I can barely feed myself."

"What if one would do the work for a ride to the next town?" A break in the trail. Did they have dogs after him? There'd be no way to know until he heard them barking at his heels. He'd made one scent break by walking in the river for a long, slow, ankle-turning, mud-sucking mile. But thirty miles in the air, no dog could pick up that scent again.

I'm thinking like a guilty man.

And he was acting like one. Guilty men always run.

"I'll give you a ride if you want one."

"I can't take something for nothing and I don't have any money."

"I told you, I'm the only one who touches her. You can help me haul gasoline out to the field when we get to Noblesville. It'll be a fair trade. Now shut up and go to sleep. I want an early start."

Even before Henry could spit out his gratitude, Gil's breathing changed. He was asleep.

Sleep should have been easy for a man as tired as Henry. But he watched through the open doors of the hayloft as the moon tracked across the night, unable to still his mind. In a bit, Gil's breathing grew rough. Henry heard small movements, twitching against the straw.

Did the green-eyed monster-men of the Kaiser's fill Gil's dreams? Was he dodging and ducking bullets? Was he rolling his plane through skies filled with artillery fire?

Henry had been nine years old when the war started in Europe — a place so far away that Peter, then sixteen, said it wouldn't mean anything to the folks of Delaware County. But that's when things in Delaware County had begun to change. Subtly at first. So subtly that Henry initially thought he'd done something, broken some rule, misbehaved in some way, to draw the nasty looks and turned backs. An invisible cold hand touched the back of his neck every time his teacher walked past his desk, it brushed his cheek when he passed someone on the sidewalk, and it gripped his heart when he sat with his head bowed in prayer in Sunday school. So he tried to be more respectful, more cheerful, more helpful.

Things only grew worse.

The first time some kids mocked him with fake German accents, calling him Heinrich the Hun, he finally got it. It wasn't his fault. It was worse. And damn it, his name wasn't even Heinrich. It was plain old American Henry.

German hate became a national pastime after that German sub sank the *Lusitania.* When the United States joined in the fight, the frosty attitudes turned into flaming rage. German hate even got its own poster and slogan campaign. The one in Henry's classroom said *Beat Back the Hun with Liberty Bonds.* The Hun was a gruesome green-eyed monster of a man with a bloody bayonet and crimson-soaked fingers. *Once a German, always a German.* And Germans ravaged all civilization — usually starting with the women and children.

Then someone had set fire to Wuesthoff's Bakery — after the police had hauled Mr. Wuesthoff to jail for "disloyal utterances against the United States."

Henry had thought nothing like that could happen to his family. Mr. Wuesthoff *acted* German. He wore that stupid hat. Even after the first weeks of the war, he continued to stick little German flags in his strudels. Maybe he *was* a spy.

Peter had been the one to point out the error of that thinking. "Good God, Henry, do you think he'd do any of those things if he *was*? He's not stupid."

Spy fever caught on. The *Schulers* might be spies! Watch them carefully.

It didn't matter that the only thing to spy on where they'd lived were cornfields and cows. Wells could be poisoned. Stores of gasoline and grain burned.

No one cared that Peter and Henry were raised as American boys. Henry didn't even speak German. When he'd been really little, occasionally he'd heard his parents late at night talking softly to one another in a language with hard corners that didn't lend itself to quiet whispers. It had made him feel he was being kept from a secret. But after the war started, he was glad he'd never learned the language. It made it easier to believe the Kaiser and his killer-filled country had nothing to do with him.

What would Gil do if he discovered Henry was a German-bred Schuler and not a star-spangled Jefferson?

He bet he'd never sit inside the man's plane, that's for sure.

At some point Henry must have fallen asleep, because Gil was kicking his shoe. "It's time."

As they walked toward the pasture, the sun inched over the horizon, silvering the mist that clung to the low spots and snaked in the ditch beside the road.

"How many people do you think'll show up today?" Henry asked.

"None."

"But you said they always —"

"There aren't going to be any people because we're flying out of here right now."

"What about Cora?"

"I can't afford to waste a day hoping a couple of farmers show up. I need to harvest a *town.*"

Henry had already decided not to trust

her. And the way he'd caught her looking at Gil when she thought no one was watching, as if he were the most interesting man she'd ever set eyes on, told him there could be trouble. What if she got Gil to hang around here another day that could lead to still another? A willful woman could change the course of history — the path of a man's life was easy pickings. Henry had learned that firsthand. The sooner he and Gil and that airplane were away from here, the better. Yet, sneaking off seemed the wrong way to go about it. "She did feed us."

They were getting near the pasture. Traveling the distance had taken a tenth of the time it had taken last night, wrangling that motorcycle across country.

"I'll send her a nice thank-you note."

"But you said you'd give her a ride."

"I did not. I offered her uncle a ride. He declined. And her *aunt and uncle* fed us."

Henry couldn't ignore his relief. "She's gonna be mad as a wet hornet."

"No doubt — Oh, shit!" Gil broke into a run. "Hey!" he shouted as he leaped the wire fence. "Get away from there!"

Henry looked across the pasture. Tilda stood eating the wing of Gil's plane. Henry took off on Gil's heels.

"Shoo! Shoo!" Henry waved his arms over

his head as he ran.

"Get!" Gil swatted the air.

Tilda finally turned their way. As Henry got closer, he'd swear he saw bored defiance in her big brown cow eyes.

Gil thumped her hindquarters.

She took a reluctant step away from the wing.

Gil growled and ran his hand over the fabric.

Henry took a step closer. The cow hadn't been eating it exactly. More like licking it like a lollipop.

"Why would she do that?" Henry asked.

Gil poked at the wet spot with a finger. "Not too bad," he muttered. "Some cows like to lick the dope on the fabric."

"Dope?"

"The stuff that stretches it tight." He flicked a finger against the dry area of the wing. It sounded like a drum. Then he did the same to the wet spot. It sounded a little duller, but still sounded solid. "The vapors will knock you on your ass when you're putting it on. Worse than a bad drunk. Maybe it gives 'em a cow buzz. I should have stayed with her last night."

"Tilda?"

"You're a real vaudevillian."

Henry shrugged.

Gil untied the ropes that kept the Jenny anchored to the earth, and Henry pulled up the stakes.

"We're really going without seeing her?"

Gil didn't pause coiling the ropes. "You're more than welcome to stay behind, Romeo."

"I'm not the one she —" Henry decided to quit while he was ahead. "Where do you want these stakes?"

Gil took them and stowed everything behind the rear cockpit. Then he climbed back to the ground with an oil can in his hands and stepped up on one of the wheels. Henry figured he was lubricating the rocker arms. Gil did the same on the other side of the engine. After that he walked around the plane, ran his hands over the propeller, checked tautness on some wires, looked at and moved the flappers on the tail and upper wings. Then he went back to the front and rotated the propeller a few times.

Henry braced for the roar of the engine before he realized Gil hadn't turned on the magneto switch yet. Wouldn't that give a lot of credence to his claim of being a good mechanic if Gil had noticed?

"If you're coming with me, climb up into the front cockpit. Careful. Just step right there close to the fuselage or you'll go through the wing."

Henry hopped to, figuring the fuselage must be what a pilot called the body of the plane. "Fasten that belt around your lap," Gil called as he put his hand on the propeller.

At first Henry couldn't find a belt; then he located the two halves on the floor on each side of his seat. His stomach got a little queasy as he fastened it. Never in his wildest dreams had he imagined he'd be sitting where he was right now.

Gil gave the propeller a hard pull. The engine caught in a deafening roar. The wind from the blades sucked Henry's breath away and tried to rip the hair from his scalp.

The plane inched forward. He located the magneto switch in his cockpit, in case he had to cut the engine before the plane ran over Gil.

But Gil was as fast as he claimed. By the time Henry spun around to look for him, he was already stepping into the rear cockpit. He sat down, pulled on his goggles, and gave Henry a salute.

That tiny gesture made him realize how much he missed being a part of something outside himself. It was almost as great a gift as his first flight.

Gil throttled the engine and swung the nose toward the expanse of pasture. Before

Henry could blink, they were bouncing along, gaining speed. The nose of the plane was so high that Henry couldn't see where they were going. Gil was even lower behind him.

"How can you see?" Henry shouted, but his words were torn away and tossed into the air.

The plane crabbed a little sideways, giving him a glimpse of what was in front of them, and then straightened out.

The vibration set Henry's teeth to clattering against one another. His eyeballs shook. He slid lower in the seat and braced his arms and legs against the inside of the cockpit.

The noise! The wind! The jouncing!

Suddenly the bumping stopped. The noise of the wheels on the ground silenced. The vibrations changed, and Henry's stomach slid to the tail of the airplane. For a moment he was so dizzy, he thought he was getting ready to have a fit of some sort.

He inched his eyes up over the leather-wrapped edge of the cockpit, careful not to lean too far to the side, just in case it might throw the plane off-balance.

Oh my God in heaven! The ground was falling away. Trees had shrunk to the size of bushes. Cows were team oxen for toy soldiers.

He was flying. *Flying!*

He sat up straighter. Now that he was looking at something outside the plane, the dizziness left him. The wires between the wings began to sing in the wind, adding to the magic of the music of the machine.

Impossible!

The wind buffeted him, making it hard to breath and his eyes water, but if he kept low, it wasn't so bad.

The road was an endless arrow shooting to the horizon, the creek a winding ribbon tucked in rounded mounds of trees. Fields were patchwork squares and rectangles in shades of green and brown.

Gil tilted the plane to the side and Henry grabbed hold, fearing he'd tip out. What must it be like to go upside down? The plane circled and lost a little altitude. They cleared the lightning rods on the Fesslers' barn by only thirty feet, the rooftop of the farmhouse by slightly more.

Amazing! He was a hawk. An eagle.

In leaving the ground, he left all of the craziness behind. Nothing could touch him, no hatred, no rumors, no law. If only it were possible to just keep flying, on and on until the land turned into ocean and back to land again. If only he could go far enough to be certain what was left behind him never caught up.

But they didn't fly on. Gil circled the farmhouse again. Saying thank-you and good-bye? Or taunting Cora?

Just then she shot out the back door, her hair flowing and the hem of her robe flapping behind her. She waved her hands in the air.

Gil waggled the wings and veered away from the Fesslers' farm.

Henry's last look down at Cora made him a little sick.

She was jumping up and down, shouting, shaking her fists. Henry didn't need to hear her to know what she was saying.

3

Henry had never had the audacity to imagine he would someday fly in an airplane. Such things were for heroes and adventurers, not orphans of poor immigrants. But last night in the hayloft, his heart had lifted and soared above the earth on slippery currents of air.

Reality turned out to be nothing like his imaginings.

In his mind, flying was smooth and graceful, like sliding on ice or bobbing gently on a river current. Birds sure made it look that way. But the air turned out to be unpredictable, as bumpy as the roads below in places, just trembling roughness in others. He quickly got used to the isolating noise of wind and machine and the steady vibration of the engine, which numbed his butt in short order. The jostling and jerking soon ceased to spur fear that the plane was disintegrating around him — it was nothing but stitched fabric and wood strapped behind a ninety-horsepower engine, after all.

Even after he settled and began to understand the normal ways of the plane, his stomach still lurched when the plane fell straight out from under him. Henry knew engines well enough to know one irrefutable fact: they were unreliable. The first time his seat dropped from beneath his butt, he figured he was good as dead. The spike of desire to live had surprised him, especially after the number of times over the past two days self-pity had made him half wish he could disappear from this earth.

After a handful of intermittent sudden drops, he realized the engine had nothing at all to do with it. It was air, all air. Once that became clear, he immersed himself in appreciating this incredible gift Gil had given him. He would never again take his first flight . . . or likely any flight at all.

From up here with this larger-than-life view he felt detached from the earth and all of its creatures. Henry began to understand the change he'd noticed come over Gil when he'd looked over his shoulder at the man. The tightly wound tension that was ever present when he was earthbound had vanished; without the tightness around his mouth and the furrowed forehead, he could have passed for an entirely different person — a younger person. Henry wondered if the man Gil had been before the war was the one in the air, or the one on the ground.

Henry counted every mile west as a mile banked toward safety. If only they would cross a mountain range or vast canyon, some substantial landmark to stand between him and his past. But he had to satisfy himself with counting land parcels and dots of towns as evidence he was indeed putting distance between himself and those who hunted him.

Everything looked the same in all directions: planted fields in corrugated stripes of green and brown; woods like rough, rumpled green blankets; rivers and creeks green-brown yarn batted around by a cat. Even the grids of towns all looked pretty much alike — and they all looked too small from up here to actually hold people and stores and automobiles. It made him feel insignificant, a nearly invisible speck in the vast world that spread beneath him. It made him believe Henry Schuler *could* disappear forever, replaced by Henry Jefferson, a man untainted by a past. His irrelevance would be his protection.

He would start a new life. His third in

eighteen years. It hadn't been of his choosing, but he now had the opportunity to reinvent himself. And he would. He would leave the Schuler name and its shadow of disaster behind him once and for all.

He reached his fist out of the cockpit and into the buffeting air. He opened his fingers one by one, releasing his disaster-shadowed name on the wind. When he brought his unclenched hand back in, he was, and would always be, Henry Jefferson.

A smoking curl of shame rose inside his chest.

Oh, Pa, I am not the man you and Peter were. I am weak. I am afraid. I am lost.

Please forgive me.

Henry's pa had died one month to the day after Armistice — and not of the influenza like everybody else in 1918. Poverty and grief had slowly rolled him into his grave. With the rest of his family already collected by disaster, Henry alone sat vigil beside his pa's pine box. He turned the oil lamp low, to conserve the last of the fuel. In the long, cold night hours, frost bloomed on the inside of the window glass as Henry thought about what he'd do next.

The Schulers didn't have friends, not after the war broke out, and few before. People

73

had never understood Pa's quiet, stern ways. Ma had been sociable enough. Lucky for her she was dead before the war started; it'd have broken her heart to suffer the scorn of the ladies she'd sewed quilts with and helped tend their sick children. Henry's parents' people were still in Germany, if they were still alive. Ma had had a brother, an aunt, and two cousins that Henry knew of. Pa never talked about the life he'd left behind. There hadn't been any letters from overseas — even before the war.

Pa had been convinced that once Peter went to war, everyone would finally understand that the Schulers were as American as any other family in Indiana. If only Pa hadn't put so much faith into that sacrifice, Henry would still have someone.

He would not go to the County Home. He would be spurned for his German-ness even among the outcasts and throwaways that lived there. He decided he would run away.

He only had the little bit of money left in the coffee can. Most likely he'd have starved on the road. But Anders Dahlgren came with his offer of a new home, a new family. He arrived as Henry stood in the cemetery next to the four crooked crosses that were all that was left of his family. Peter wasn't even buried beneath his. Henry had just planted the one he'd made from fence pickets on his pa's grave; a cross he'd carved with carefully chosen words: GEORG SCHULER, DEAD AMERICAN.

It had been snowing when Anders Dahlgren turned his wagon into the lane of his large farm. When Henry set sight on the big, two-story house with smoke curling from its chimneys, he'd been stunned by his good fortune. Hunger, cold, and loneliness — in truth, he'd felt alone since the day Peter had left for the Marines — would soon be distant memories. A man with a passel of daughters, Mr. Dahlgren had told Henry he wanted a boy to help him with the farm — a *son* he'd said. Henry hadn't been sure how he felt about becoming another man's son.

To meet the family, Henry put on a face that made people like him, that of a nice, fun-loving boy. He knew what that face felt like because he'd worn it before the war.

The daughters stood behind their mother, blond stair steps, with big bows in their hair and polished shoes. Mrs. Dahlgren was dressed fancier than Henry had ever seen a farmer's wife — even for church. The instant she set eyes on Henry, her welcoming smile disappeared.

"Girls! Get back!" Her lack of accent told Henry she hadn't come from Sweden alongside her husband. "To your rooms!"

The eldest girl picked up the youngest and they all disappeared like yellow leaves on the wind.

Mrs. Dahlgren snatched up a nearby broom. "Anders! Get that urchin out of here!" She took a couple of pokes in Henry's direction, making him step back into the doorway. "No one is allowed inside this house that doesn't live here. The epidemic! How can you risk our daughters?" She jabbed the broom Henry's way, backing him down the first step.

She had reason to worry, he reckoned. Two kids at his school had died from the influenza before the health board had closed all the schools and churches. Maybe more had died since.

Mr. Dahlgren put a hand on the broom handle. "He is well. No fever. And *he* lives here now."

"What are you talking about?" She pulled the broom free from his grasp and raised it again, her squinty eyes hard on Henry.

"I told you I was looking for a boy."

"You said that *months ago* —"

"*Ja.* And here he is. He is orphaned." Mr. Dahlgren reached back and put a hand on the top of Henry's head. "And smart. He will stay."

"You don't know what filthy diseases that boy is carrying! Get rid of him, then wash up and change your clothes in the barn." The broom jabbed again. "I will not have my daughters living under the same roof with some ragamuffin orphan." She had them backed up far enough to slam the door.

For a moment, they stood on the steps staring at the closed door with the snow falling quietly around them. Then Mr. Dahlgren turned and put his arm around Henry's shoulders. "Do not worry about her," he said as they headed toward the barn. "The disease will pass. She will come around."

"I don't think so, sir." The disease might pass, but Mrs. Dahlgren's opinion of him would not. He'd seen it before. Only he'd never thought being poor and an orphan could provoke as much hate as being German — Mrs. Dahlgren hadn't even learned that part about him yet.

Mr. Dahlgren set Henry up in a small bunk room tucked into the back corner of the barn. He lit the coal stove before he returned to the house and brought out supper, both his and Henry's.

"Aren't you eating with your family?" Henry asked.

"Too many high voices." Mr. Dahlgren tucked a napkin in his collar. "And you are now family." He'd nodded. "Eat."

That meal was the best Henry had eaten since his ma passed, with a big serving of meat — good meat, not the kind that was tough like leather or so stringy it gagged you when you tried to swallow it. He was warm and his belly was full for the first time in a long time. But after Mrs. Dahlgren's reaction to his arrival, he knew he couldn't stay.

Mr. Dahlgren left Henry with a good night. As soon as the man had gone, Henry looked around for something to write a note, but didn't find anything. *Thank you for trying,* that's what his note would have said. Instead, he took his harmonica out of his canvas bag and left it on the pillow, a fair trade for a good meal he figured. He didn't reckon it was enough to cover the trouble with Mr. Dahlgren's wife, but it was the best he could do.

He waited a bit to get good and warm and let everyone in the house go to bed, then he put on his jacket with the too-short sleeves, snuffed the oil lamp, and left the barn.

When he stepped outside, the cold slapped

his face like an angry hand. The sky had cleared and hardened like flint, making the snow look blue under the white sliver of moon. He'd always liked the quiet of a country night wrapped in snow and wondered if it would soften the sounds of the city, too. He had to get to Chicago, where he wouldn't stand out, where he could live on the streets and make up a story about where he lived and no one would know any different. City children worked in factories, just as they worked on farms in the country. But Henry could probably get a man's job with a man's pay, he was big for thirteen.

The frigid snow squeaked under his shoes. As he passed the house, he stopped and sniffed. Matches and tobacco.

"You made me a promise, young Henry." Mr. Dahlgren's quiet voice came from the porch, deep in the shadowy corner of the ell of the house.

The man stepped to the edge where Henry could see him. Smoke curled pale gray from the bowl of his pipe in the thin moonlight.

"Yes, sir. I did. But that was before . . . Well, I just figured it'd be easier for both of us if I moved on."

"I did not ask for easier. I asked for you

to give me time."

"But Mrs. Dahlgren —"

"Bah!" He waved a hand to swat Henry's words away. "She is an excitable woman. She will get used to you." Mr. Dahlgren shrugged, and Henry realized the man was coatless in the cold. "She got used to me."

That seemed an odd thing to say about your wife, but Henry didn't understand much about married folks, so he didn't question. "I don't want to make trouble for you."

"I am not a young man, Henry. And I have waited a long time for you. I do not mind a little trouble, as long as it stays inside the house. I know the barn is not what I promised, but if you can stand it for a while —"

"Oh, no, sir! It isn't the barn. That room's better'n our house."

"Then you will stay." Mr. Dahlgren turned around and disappeared back into the house and closed the door quietly behind him.

The smell of his pipe hung in the air as Henry stood thinking. His pa had always said a man's work was his worth and his word his most valuable possession. Mr. Dahlgren seemed like a man who thought the same. And on that wagon ride, Henry *had* given his word to try.

He'd turned around and traced his steps back through the snow, to the little room in the barn.

It hadn't taken long to understand he would never have the family Mr. Dahlgren had promised. But it hadn't mattered. In fact, it eased his mind some, not having to figure out if accepting a new family made him disloyal to his dead one. He'd been happy to live in his little room in the barn. He'd been warm and dry and had committed himself to being as invisible as possible to the females and useful to Mr. Dahlgren.

All in all, Henry had figured mistreatment from the womenfolk was little enough to pay for his new hunger-free life. He'd modeled himself after his pa. He hadn't argued with rumor and opinion. He'd never retaliated for slights and slurs. He'd not disrespected Mr. Dahlgren by complaining or discrediting his family in public. As his pa used to say, "Words are only words. A man's deeds show what he is."

As it turned out, Henry's deeds had been confined to the farm, hidden from the sight of those whose opinion of him had been formed by the belittling tongues of the Dahlgren women.

He'd been mistaken to accept the opinion others had cultivated of him. Words might

only be words, but they could be as powerful as bullets.

As things were now, Henry bet Mr. Dahlgren wished with all of his heart that he'd
never stopped Henry from leaving that
night.

Even if it had meant he'd have starved to
death, Henry wished it, too.

Henry's worry that he'd leave a brown
streak in his pants when Gil stunted over
Noblesville to draw a crowd proved unnecessary. When the courthouse clock tower
came into view, Gil started losing altitude.
The sun reflected off the rails of the train
track that led into town.

How could Gil tell where he could land
from up here? Everything looked the same.
But Gil must have seen something Henry
didn't because he circled around and lost
more altitude.

There wasn't any place that looked big
enough to land. And Jenny didn't have
brakes.

It sounded as if one cylinder wasn't firing
— when had that started?

Henry sat as tall as he could, leaning right
and left, trying to see where they were
headed. The sound of the engine changed
as Gil throttled back a bit.

The left wing dipped and they swung sideways. Henry's stomach jumped up and slid across the wings.

Gil brought the wings back to level.

All Henry could see were trees ahead. He slid low and braced himself.

The nose of the plane lifted slightly. His seat dropped as if he'd gone over a hill.

There was an impact, a rough jolt. Then the plane bounced along on its wheels. With a little jerk the tail skid hit the ground.

Henry's head popped up. They were in a pasture, the trees behind them . . . no cows in sight . . . unless they were directly in front of the plane where neither Henry nor Gil could see over the high nose.

Henry slithered a little lower and kept his eyes squinted, just in case a propeller-ground cow splattered them.

They stopped rolling. The engine cut off.

No cow guts.

A minute later he stood beside Gil on the ground, wiping the oil spatter off his face and wiggling his pinkie fingers in his ears trying to get them to clear. It seemed the roar of the engine and the rush of the wind continued inside his head after the propeller had stopped.

"What'd you think?" Gil asked, looking like the owner of the blue-ribbon boar at the county fair.

"Amazing! Just incredible!"

"You're shouting. It's the ears." Gil tossed his leather helmet and goggles up into the cockpit. "Time to earn your ride." He started walking toward the dirt road on the far side of the pasture.

Henry wiped the oil from his face and hurried to catch up. "You've got a cylinder not firing."

"I'll clean the spark plugs before I take off again."

"You shouldn't do it with people watching. You'll scare them out of riding."

"Bullshit. They'll be more confident knowing I take care of my ship."

Henry shook his head. "No, sir. Once they get the idea that a machine isn't one hundred percent reliable, you won't get them in the plane."

"How would you know?"

"It's the reason most farmers won't get off mules and horses. Worry over a tractor breaking down. Only *you* want people to trust their lives to a machine racing along hundreds of feet off the ground. You can't let them get even a hint that the thing could fall out of the sky. They need to see it as infallible."

"Never bothered anybody before."

"I'll bet you scared plenty of them off. You just didn't notice." *If not by working on the plane in front of them, then just by your general contrariness.* "Of course, you might be a whole lot more persuasive and likable when you're working an exhibition."

Gil shot him a narrow-eyed look that made Henry wish he'd just kept his mouth shut. He'd wanted to travel on with Gil before, just to get farther down the road, but after flying in that mechanical miracle, he didn't ever want to leave it. And what better way to get lost in this world than to never stay put in one place, never let anyone really get to know you?

They reached the road. A truck was coming toward them, kicking up a rolling plume of dust. It skidded to a stop and an angry man hopped out. "Hold on there, young fella! What gives you the right? Get on" — he waved his hand at Gil as if he were scaring off geese — "and get that contraption outta my field."

Gil kept walking. "Can't. Needs gas."

"Well, that's poor plannin' on your part. You got no right just droppin' down on my land like you own it. Scare the milk right outta my cows."

"Airplanes don't bother cows." Gil sounded so condescending that Henry

85

cringed.

"So you're a dairy farmer," the man said. "Know all about it." Not questions.

Gil huffed, "There aren't even any cows *in* that pasture."

"Neither was I." The man pointed to the sides of his red-faced head. "They got ears! I want you off my land."

Henry stepped between Gil and the farmer. "Sorry, mister. We came on your land without your say-so, and that's not right, for sure. But, you see, there's no way for us to ask from up there, so we gotta land first, then ask. Which is what we were just heading to do." The man continued to frown. "Hope you'll give us pardon." Henry looked things over. The truck was old. The man's barn needed paint. Farm prices were in the shitter. "And we'll . . . we'll pay for the privilege." Gil groaned behind him. "And as soon as we get fueled up, we'll be off to find another pasture nearby to hire out for our barnstorming act. So don't worry about the crowds."

"Hire out?" The farmer stopped straining forward in rage.

"Yes, sir. Captain Gilchrist here is a *bona fide* war hero. A flying ace." The regard Henry saw bloom in the farmer's eyes prompted him to take it another step.

"Fought the Red Baron himself! Why, people line up just for a chance to pay for a ride with him." Peter had been the best at convincing people to do things, clever about it, too. Henry had watched and learned. It'd been a long time since he'd put those skills to much use; the war had made everyone so mistrustful, the use of persuasion only made them more suspicious. He *had* coaxed the two littlest Dahlgren girls with some success — he hadn't wasted his breath with the older ones or their mother.

"I can see you wouldn't want all those folks milling around in your pasture," Henry went on. "The crowd sometimes stays all day just to watch — sometimes runs over into two. We usually try to find a place where a wife wants to make some pocket money selling food and drink. We'll be gone as soon as we can. Promise. But we need to gas up first."

"Well, now, maybe you should tell me more about this barnstorming act."

Gil opened his mouth, but Henry cut him off before he ruined everything. "Captain Gilchrist here . . . once his plane is all fueled up . . . takes off and does a death-defying exhibition of flight, just like he's dogfightin' those dirty Huns over France again. People fall all over themselves getting

87

to where they see his plane land. He charges a reasonable fee for a ride." According to Gil, some folks thought five dollars was reasonable. "Then maybe he'll do some more stunts in between, just to keep people entertained while they wait their turn. There's nothing like flying over your own town and seeing it from the air. Nothing!"

"I don't think folks round here'd be interested."

"I used to think like that, too. Turns out people *everywhere* are *crazy* about airplanes. But not to worry. Captain Gilchrist always respects a landowner's wishes, so we'll be gone as soon as we get some gasoline."

The man rubbed his chin. "We might could work something out. Pasture's empty right now anyhow." Then he gave Gil a harsh glare. "Gotta be compensated for the milk scared outta my cows, of course."

Gil rolled his eyes. "Cows —"

"We can work something out," Henry cut him off.

Fifteen minutes later, not only had they settled on a deal to use the pasture, but the farmer was driving them into town with several old milk cans to get gasoline. Henry insisted he and Gil ride in the truck bed, just to make sure Gil didn't open his mouth and say something that'd put the man off.

Henry sat with his back against one side of the truck bed, Gil the other. "We could have found another pasture — probably for free." He sounded mad.

"And burned up time and gas doing it."

After sitting with his lips pressed together for a while, he said, "I wasn't an ace. You can't tell people that."

Henry shrugged.

"And I *didn't* fight the Red Baron. I didn't fight anyone."

"Come on. You're selling a show, an image for people to get excited about. You did fly in the war, right?"

Gil sat stone-faced and crossed his arms over his chest, but didn't disagree.

Henry thought about the medicine shows and carnivals that traveled around, drawing crowds and relieving folks of their hard-earned money. Plenty of their barkers stretched the truth to get people's blood up. "You know the Lizard Boy in the circus really wasn't born from an alligator egg, don't you?"

Gil stared at him.

"All I'm saying is that you *could have* been up there when the Red Baron was. All show folk do a little truth-stretching."

Gil's breath was rough, the way it had

been when he'd been having his nightmares the night before. He looked as if he wanted to take a swing. "*Not* about the war. Honors were hard earned — and not by me." He scrubbed his hand across his mouth. "As far as war goes, the truth is horrible enough, no need to stretch it."

Peter's face flashed in Henry's mind, a face forever frozen at seventeen. It made his chest hurt, even after all of these years.

"Okay. Okay," Henry said. "Sorry. I was just trying to whip up some excitement. You said yourself the biggest danger a barnstormer faces is starvation."

Gil was silent a minute. "I make *my own* deals with landowners."

"With your sensitivity and understanding of farm folk," Henry said, his own irritation rising, "it's a blue wonder you haven't been shot yet."

"I do fine."

"You could do better."

"Not your concern." Gil shifted his gaze to the passing fields.

"You're right. Makes no difference to me if you starve to death and your plane falls to pieces when a little showmanship could prevent both." And it shouldn't matter to Henry. But he felt invested. Today was the first day since Peter had left that the world showed all of its colors. It was as if a gray fog had lifted from Henry's heart. It got his nanny just thinking how Gil was ruining the opportunity to live the life he wanted just because he couldn't stop being a sullen ass.

What Henry wouldn't give to be in Charles Gilchrist's footloose shoes.

It took a long time to repeatedly fill the large glass reservoir at the top of the gas pump and empty it into milk can after milk can. Gil said it was a rare thing to have this many containers. Normally he had to make multiple trips for gasoline, often between giving rides, making people wait. *Or wander off with their five dollars still in their pockets,* Henry thought. For a man who continually griped about burning daylight, Gil sure wasted a lot of time searching and borrowing to transport fuel. The system begged for improvement.

Henry waited on the tailgate for Gil to go inside the station building and pick up a case of oil and pay. The courthouse clock chimed the hour. Henry glanced at it over the top of buildings across the street. He was damn lucky not to be sitting in one of those right now. The fact was, he was only two counties away from the Dahlgren farm. Not near far enough to be out of danger.

Would he ever be far enough?

Nothing but forward. Nothing.

So he sat tight and swung his feet, trying to look as if he didn't have a care in the world.

Being in a town full of people was different. Someone could be watching him that he couldn't see. To keep the nervousness from giving him away, he busied his mind with ways to improve Gil's efficiency. How much gas Gil's plane must burn per hour; dividing that by the number of rides he could probably give in that much time and how many miles he probably averaged between towns. How far could that engine go between overhauls?

The farmer returned from Craycraft's Dry Goods with a brown-paper-wrapped parcel under his arm, whistling an off-key version of "Put On Your Old Gray Bonnet."

A shout sounded from across the street and down about a half block. A tall, skinny man wearing a blood-smeared white apron ran out of a small storefront, a meat cleaver in his hand. "That's the last time you steal from me, you little bastard!"

Henry got up and looked to see whom the man was chasing.

A silver-gray streak ran past Henry's knees. A single dark sausage link landed near his feet.

The skinny butcher held the cleaver over his head, barreling straight for Henry. The man stepped on the sausage and his foot logrolled forward, throwing him off-balance. The meat cleaver sliced so near the side of Henry's head that he felt the air move.

Oblivious of Henry's near de-earing, the butcher regained his footing and followed the thief's path around the truck.

The streak passed Henry's knees again. A dog. With a rope of cured sausages hanging from his mouth.

The butcher screamed in frustration and passed Henry a second time.

On the dog's third orbit of the truck, he jumped up into the bed and hid behind the milk cans. A single sausage link remained visible.

The butcher caught himself on his fourth lap around the truck, realizing he was chasing only himself. He looked right, left, up and down the street, toward the open station door.

Henry stepped between the butcher and the telltale sausage. "He took off down the alley. That way."

The butcher took off, shouting and shaking the cleaver.

"You'd probably do better if you sneaked

up on him!" Henry called behind the man.

Gil came out of the brick building, looking around. "What's all the shouting?"

The station man followed him out, laughing. "Third time this week the little booger's made off with some of Chet's goods. That stray is so good at it I've started rooting for the pooch. He deserves to win."

Henry knew something about being a hungry stray. He climbed in the truck bed, sitting between Gil and the dog's hiding place. The mutt could use a few miles between himself and that meat cleaver.

Gil cranked the truck, then came around and hopped on the open tailgate.

When the truck started, Henry worried the dog would bolt. He looked up to see the butcher coming back their way, taking time to look behind every trash barrel and stacked crate in the alley.

The dog stayed put. Henry supposed the stray hadn't survived this long by being stupid.

At the edge of town, they stopped for a train to pass. Gil sniffed. "I smell . . . sausage."

Henry lifted his nose and made a show of smelling the air. "Really? I don't smell anything."

Gil looked puzzled and shrugged.

A loud belch came from behind the milk cans.

Gil shot a look over his shoulder at Henry.

Henry patted his chest and covered his mouth. "I do beg your pardon."

Gil shook his head.

The train passed.

They traveled on, back toward the Jenny.

Henry steadied the cans as they bounced across the pasture. They stopped at a place where the gasoline could be stored in the shade. Gil hopped off and Henry started to move the heavy cans to the tailgate. The dog stayed hunkered down, looking up at Henry with unsure brown eyes, holding half of a chewed sausage between its paws.

"It's okay," Henry whispered. "I'm on your side." He reached down and picked up the scruffy terrier. The matted fur and prominent ribs confirmed the filling-station attendant's claim that this was a stray; a dog this size should weigh eighteen or twenty pounds. He didn't feel as if he was anywhere in that neighborhood. "Can't blame a starving animal for fighting to survive."

Gil came back and looked up. "Oh, hell no."

"He needed help." Henry set the dog back down on his paws. "Now he's going on his way." Henry took the half-eaten sausage and tossed it out of the truck, expecting the dog to follow. Instead the pooch just sat there and stared up at Henry with hope in his eyes.

"Maybe Mr. Sowers" — Henry had read the farmer's name written in the shingles of his barn roof — "will keep him?"

The farmer shook his head. "Dog's no hunter. Why would I keep him?"

At that the dog jumped out of the truck bed, picked up the half sausage, and headed toward the road.

The sight of that skinny mutt walking slowly away with his head low made Henry sad. But a man who wasn't sure how he was going to feed himself had no business taking on a dog. No matter how much he sympathized with the hungry stray.

4

The crowd did come, just as Gil had predicted. It came smelling of the anticipation of discovery. People came on foot and in cars, in wagons and on bicycles, in groups and alone. They gathered around the field in little knots made colorful by women's spring hats and dresses. The bolder of the men and boys ventured close and asked Gil questions about the plane. Two different times, Gil swatted a boy away when he tried to climb up onto the wing. Must have been a bold little devil; the scowl on Gil's face was enough to scare most folks off.

The whole atmosphere reminded Henry of a medicine show he and Peter had seen years ago. Henry had watched the performances. Peter had watched the crowd.

Even with the good turnout and the excitement, when Gil stood in the seat of his cockpit and invited anyone with five dollars to come and take a ride, people fell silent, their eyes shifting to the ground beneath their feet, to the person next to them. Anywhere but Gil and his Jenny.

"This is a once-in-a-lifetime chance, folks," Gil said, his hands on his hips. "How many airplanes have you even seen in this town?"

Plenty of folks looked as if they had money in their pockets. Many faces held a spark of longing and curiosity. Henry spied a man in a nice suit and starched collar standing with an equally starched and knickers-clad boy of about twelve. Alongside them was a girl a year or so younger than the boy. Her dress, shoes, and bows would have made the Dahlgren girls jealous. The boy was pointing toward the plane, a pleading look on his face as he chattered to his father. The girl had her hands clasped over her heart, bouncing up and down on the balls of her feet so vigorously her ringlets looked like springs.

For one instant Henry was ten years old again and watching his big brother at the Harvest Festival. Henry had stood in grass so heavy with early-morning dew that it seeped through his shoes, at a time of day when most folks held on to their pennies, carefully deciding where to spend them. Peter opened the Lutheran church's booth, whose purpose was to raise money for Christmas gifts for the children at County Home. (Ironic, when Henry now thought about how close he'd come to becoming a resident there.) Peter started talking, a smile on his face, his arms open and hands gently gesturing for people to come to him. People stopped. Inched closer. Moments later they began to hand over their pennies. Peter's skill at gathering the crowd and separating them from their money had been so good that the medicine-show man came up and tried to convince Peter to come and travel with his show. Ma chased the man off in short order. Later, when Henry asked Peter how he'd known what to say to get people to spend their money, he'd said, "Just stay friendly and keep talking. Don't push too hard. Watch their eyes. Everybody wants to feel like they're doing something special. Make them think they are and you'll get that first penny, that's the hardest one. People follow people, money follows money; it's a fact of life."

From that moment on, Henry had made a game of studying people, trying to read what they were thinking, figuring how they'd react if he said or did certain things. By looking at their eyes and the way they held their bodies, he could tell if he had a chance of softening them up, or if he should just keep his head down. This became a handy tool of survival when the rules of civility were devoured by German hate . . . and then later with the Dahlgren women.

He slipped through the crowd around the Jenny, keeping the man with the two children in sight.

Less than a minute later, Henry was escorting the trio toward the plane. "Here!" Henry shouted. "Captain Gilchrist! We have our first adventurers. These children refuse to miss the chance to tell *their* children that they flew in an airplane with a war hero!"

Gil glowered. Henry hoped no one else noticed.

At least Gil managed a smile as he reached down and pulled the boy up onto the wing. Gil instructed where it was safe to step and not put a foot through the fabric, then helped the boy with the deep step-over into the front cockpit. Once the kid was seated, Gil hopped down, turned his back to the crowd, and whispered to Henry, "How'd you do it?"

"The boy flies free. The dad and daughter go together for five dollars."

"That's fifteen dollars' worth of rides!" Gil hissed.

"We need to break the ice. Show folks it's

safe. What better way than seeing a parent let his kids fly? Besides, the father's sworn to secrecy about his special deal."

Gil's glower returned.

"Maybe you'd rather get back up there on the wing and try to intimidate these folks into handing over their money."

"I don't intimidate —"

"You intimidate just by the way you stand up there with your hands on your hips. People need to be courted, not scolded."

"I can't buy gas if I fly people for free."

"Oh, you'll make money. Leave it to me." Under his breath Henry said a prayer hoping he could deliver. "Climb in. I'll prop the plane."

Gil didn't move.

"They came because they're curious." Henry looked over his shoulder. "Check out their eyes, the way they're standing. We have 'em. Let's not lose 'em."

"There'd better be a line when I get back down here," Gil groused as he hoisted himself up onto the wing.

Henry gave a confident grin.

After the spectacle of the Jenny lumbering airborne and people oohing and aahing as the boy waved his cap as he flew overhead, Henry went to work. When Gil landed ten minutes later, four people stood behind the man and his daughter, their five dollars each already safely in Henry's pocket — insurance against second thoughts.

Once the boy bounced excitedly around the crowd, describing the miracle of flight and the amazing sights to be seen, ten more got in line.

Henry took the money, assisted people in and out of the Jenny, and propped the plane, cutting Gil's time on the ground by at least half. While Gil was in the air, Henry entertained the folks with stories of dogfights and heroism (based on newspaper accounts and his own imagination). He left Gil's name out of the stories, just in case he got wind of Henry's exaggerations. Henry even drummed up a little business for farmer Sowers's wife, who, in addition to refreshments, had a nice assortment of jellies, early peas, cheese, cream, milk, and fresh eggs for sale.

The line for the Jenny was still growing, as was the crowd, when Gil and Henry had to fuel the plane — another process that went much more quickly than usual with Henry helping filter the gasoline through a chamois to reduce the amount of crud that ended up in the plane's tank. Gil was back on the ground with the empty milk can and Henry was just screwing on the plane's gas cap when he heard the sound of a high-winding motor. Voices in the crowd started to rise.

From his perch on the wing, he saw Cora and her motorcycle cutting pell-mell across the pasture. She seemed oblivious of the flapping of the broken chain guard that downed the occasional wildflower like a scythe. Once she got in front of the crowd, she perched one knee on the seat and held her other foot out behind her, much the way Henry had seen on a poster for the circus, only those girls were wearing feathers and sparkles and were on horseback.

Cheers and whistles went up.

Gil muttered a string of curses.

Henry's heart seized up. She was going to ruin everything.

When Cora maneuvered back onto the seat, she was close enough that Henry saw the gray fluff he'd taken for a neck scarf tucked into her jacket was actually a familiar scruffy gray face nestled just under her chin. She aimed her bike at the side of the Jenny and hunkered down, the Red Baron zeroing in on a dogfight.

Gil shouted for her to stop, spread his arms, and braced his feet, as if his body could shield the Jenny from the momentum of nearly four hundred speeding pounds of mammals and machine.

Henry shook off his stunned amazement, jumped off the wing, and rolled away from the plane.

Was she that crazy?

She sped up.

Flat out on the ground, Henry waited in stunned horror for the destruction of two machines, their owners, and one innocent mutt.

Just a few feet shy of Gil, Cora cut the handlebars and spun the motorcycle 180 degrees. The bike leaned over so far she put her foot on the ground — as if she had a chance in hell of stopping the downward momentum. Instead of slowing, she added power — an act totally against instinct and the only hope she had of keeping the machine from landing on its side and sliding out from under her. The turn complete, the bike righted, its rear tire spinning. Soil and grass clumps peppered the Jenny like hail. Henry, on his belly, received a mouthful of dirt. A rock caught his forehead, stinging like fire.

The crowd roared.

When Henry opened his eyes, Gil was on his ass, legs splayed, having stumbled backward.

Thirty feet away, Cora slid the motorcycle

in a quarter turn and stopped dead, revving the engine twice before she cut the power, pulled off her leather helmet, shook out her hair, and held her fists over her head.

"A woman!"

"Have you ever . . . ?"

"Good heavens!"

"Bravo!"

"Well, I'll be!"

"Did you see that?"

Before Henry could spit the dirt out of his mouth, Gil was up and stalking toward Cora, clumps of dirt and grass falling from him as if he'd sprung from the depths of the earth itself.

Henry scrabbled to his feet, stumbling to catch up. Gil was about to make a horrible mistake.

Gil hooked Cora by the waist and yanked her off the bike, which fell to the ground with a thud. He had her by the shoulders, nose to nose, looking ready to give her a swift shake when Henry threw his arms around both of them in what he hoped appeared to be a celebratory three-way hug (four if you counted the wriggling dog inside Cora's jacket). He tightened his grip when Gil tried to shrug him off.

Gil growled, "You spoiled little bit —"

"Spoiled! *I* wasn't the one who sneaked off —"

"Listen!" Henry shouted in Gil's ear, shaking both him and Cora. "Listen! They love her!"

Murder raging in his eyes, Gil kept struggling to be shed of Henry.

"No harm done." Henry squeezed again.

"Only to Flyboy's overblown pride." Cora's body was as stiff as Gil's.

"This is money in your pockets!" Henry said, giving them both a shake.

The dog whimpered.

Henry eased his grip — for the pup's sake. "People love a spectacle. The more unexpected and daring the better." Harry Houdini came to mind. "Cora's definitely unexpected."

"Know who she is?"

"Pretty little thing, ain't she?"

"Is that a dog inside her coat?"

". . . not from around here . . ."

"A woman! How . . . how . . ." This last from a female, definitely not in the same enamored tone as the man who'd uttered the same words earlier.

Henry released them and grabbed a hand from each, spinning them around to face the crowd, keeping himself in the middle. He raised their hands over their heads and grinned victoriously. *A stunt well planned and executed.*

A cheer went up.

He bent at the waist, forcing Gil and Cora to share a bow — not that Gil did much more than lower the shoulder Henry dragged down.

Then, just when Henry thought he'd saved them all, Cora chirped, "See what an asset I am to the team!"

Henry had to tighten his hold on Gil to prevent him from strangling her right there in before a hundred adoring people.

Gil spent the rest of the day in simmering silence. Dark moods made Henry edgy, always had, even when they were no particular threat to him. His natural inclination was to cajole — teachers' frowns were appeased by generous good deeds, Ma's anger cooled with a sweet smile and a corny little soft-shoe, Peter's rare spates of irritation were diluted with a joke, the littlest Dahlgren girls' foul humor nearly always succumbed to funny faces. But today Gil's face had been so thunderous, his body so tense, Henry hadn't even attempted to nudge him out of his mood.

As the sun set, Gil climbed into the passenger seat of the dusty Model T owned by the last customer and drove off toward town without so much as a wink or a wave — or pausing to tie down the Jenny.

Henry secured the plane, driving the stakes with heavy blows that did little to release his own frustration. Gil hadn't welcomed Henry's involvement in his business, but the man's irritation had been salved by the steady flow of five-dollar bills. Cora on the other hand, well, she was nothing but pure aggravation. She had to go.

He went over to where the motorcycle leaned against a tree to remove the last remaining piece of the chain guard so no one would get cut on it. Then it hit him. He didn't know why it hadn't before then. That front wheel shouldn't have been rolling at all. His pride took a lick when he saw it was straight and true as new.

"Hey, how'd you fix this wheel?"

Cora stopped unloading the knapsack she'd retrieved from the edge of the field where she'd left it before her grand entrance. "I didn't."

"Looks fixed to me."

"It's a different wheel. That tarp in the shed covered a bunch of spare parts that Jonathan kept."

"You had a spare wheel all the time!"

She smiled sweetly and shrugged.

"We could have changed it yesterday and not broken our backs."

Tilting her head, she said, "And Gil would have flown out of there before dark. Probably without either one of us."

A manipulator, just as he'd thought. He shoved his hands on his hips and briefly wondered if Cora and Tilda had been in cahoots.

He knelt and checked the installation of the wheel; did she even know how to do it right? "This axle nut is loose! The whole wheel could have come off and you'd have broken your neck."

"But I didn't," she said matter-of-factly. "I only had one wrench, so I did the best I could."

"How'd you get the bent one off without some leverage?"

"It wasn't all that tight either."

"It's a miracle you're alive."

"Jonathan used to tell me that a lot — mostly when he was trying to scare me out of running across or doing handstands on the rafters of the stable at the Hudson Valley house."

How was he going to discourage a girl with an attitude like that?

Henry needed to ease his way in with Gil, one town at a time. He was counting on the growing stream of cash to make his company less objectionable; God knew he'd had plenty of experience in minimizing his presence when need be. Encroaching on Gil's solitary life needed to be handled subtly and gradually, by quiet inches, not by loudly declared miles.

Cora was a declaration with shouts and fireworks.

Henry arranged the sticks and deadwood he'd gathered to start a campfire. Cora sat down on the ground opposite him, drawing the dog onto her lap, looking as if she was settling in for the duration.

"Shouldn't you be getting home?" Unlike Henry, she *had* a home. With people who seemed to care about her, even if they didn't understand her. "It'll be dark soon and your people will be worried."

She stopped picking at the tangles in the dog's coat and looked at him. "I'm not going home, Kid. I'm joining the show."

"There isn't a show."

"What was that we just did this afternoon, then?"

"Well, it was a show all right." He couldn't deny that. My God, the sight of her tearing along on that motorcycle on her knee . . . He ducked his head so she couldn't see his smile. He put a match to the fire.

"They loved it, didn't they!" She grinned like a kid with her first chocolate bar.

"Gil's not interested in a *show* or an *exhibition.* And he's the one with the airplane. I managed to get a lift closer to Chicago in exchange for helping with the gasoline today. Tomorrow he'll be gone on his own and I'll be back on foot. There. Is. No. Show."

"I disagree. We just have to make Gil see the benefit." She held the dog close to her face, oblivious of the animal's smell. "We can perform during fuel stops, keep the crowd entertained while they wait."

True. They loved her. And that the dog acted as if he'd been waiting his whole life to ride on that motorcycle made it even more outstanding. But Gil wouldn't see beyond his anger. If there had been enough daylight left, Henry was pretty sure Gil would have flown out of here and not hopped a ride to town.

She looked more serious than he'd ever seen her when she said, "I *will not* go back. I can go with you. Or I'll do it on my own. I'm committed to the road."

Henry stopped poking the growing flames and sat back on his haunches. "I can't imagine your mother sending you off with her blessing to run all over the country with two men she didn't even want you to talk to in the first place."

"Well, here's the thing, Kid. I'm a grown woman. She might not like it, but she can't do anything about it."

"You just up and left? Do they know where you went?"

"My family isn't your concern."

"I beg to differ. If your mother sends the law after you, it's going to be both my and Gil's concern." *Especially* mine.

She scoffed, but he thought he saw a flicker of uncertainty in her eye. "As I said, I'm a grown woman. Mother will have to marry a rich husband herself if she wants to return to our old life so badly. I'm taking charge of *my* life. If I were a man, everyone would think I was ambitious. Strong. Daring. Bold. Courageous. Admirable." Her hand flitted in the air to indicate the list would go on and on.

"But you're *a woman.*" *Man's sacred duty is to protect women and children.* It was the code of his life, taught by his pa, his church, Mr. Dahlgren.

"In case you missed it, women got the vote. I won't be like my mother, tiptoeing along a path lined with fences erected by parents, only to walk through a gate to tiptoe on another enforced by a husband."

She was so worked up she was stabbing a finger toward him. "Those days are gone, Henry. And good riddance."

She knew nothing about living without those protections, about being alone and vulnerable. If she did, she wouldn't be so quick to toss it all to the wind for the sake of doing whatever she pleased. There was always a cost. Always.

The crickets had begun to chirp and the mosquitoes to take daring attempts at his neck. Henry fanned the fire to get it burning better.

"What about you? You can't really want some drudge job in Chicago when you could do something special with Gil and his plane."

He shrugged. "Drudge it may be, but a man's gotta eat. And Gil doesn't make enough to feed himself, let alone three of us. You should rethink your plan. A rich girl like you doesn't want to live like a starving gypsy."

"You don't know anything about me, Henry Jefferson. Just like I don't know anything about you. So don't suppose you know what I do or do not want. I wasn't born to live behind velvet curtains, wedding rings, and tea sets. Father promised me a life of my choosing, and that's what I'm going to get."

"That sounds pretty selfish."

"Oh, yes, easy for a man to say. Men aren't brokered and sold like their father's sailboat or their mother's fur coat."

Exaggeration; spoiled girls were so good at it. "There's a reason men have more freedom; it's dangerous for a woman with no one to protect her." He ignored her scoff. "You're lucky to have a family who cares about you enough to worry about your future. You have a home, even if it's not what you're used to. Let me ask you this. Would you want to run off and do this — go hungry, sleep outdoors, perform like a circus act — if you still had money?" Henry's entire life had been hunger and uncertainty. Nobody would live penniless if they had a choice.

"*I* never had money. I had promises."

"You had security . . . you still do. You don't know what it's like to be hungry, or cold with no hope of getting warm, alone, powerless."

"Did you hear yourself? Powerless. That's *exactly* what I've been!"

"Okay, I take that one back. But the rest stand. And believe me, if you have a choice, you don't want to experience any of the others. Go home."

She looked at him across the growing fire, the light catching in her green eyes. "I'm sorry that your life has forced you to experience those things. But I'm *choosing.*"

"You're choosing. Choosing with no idea what your choice means."

"I do know what the alternative means. That's enough."

"What? Get married to a rich man who'll spoil you like your daddy did? Poor you."

"And bury my true self for the rest of my life. Do you know what that's like, Henry, to go through every day forced to live behind a mask?"

He did. But it wasn't the same. "We all do things we don't want to. That's life."

She sighed. "When I was a girl, Father took me to an exclusive gambling room — oh, don't look so shocked, he took me lots of places Mother never knew about. Anyway, it was filled with the whiskered sons of oil and coal and railroad fortunes. They smoked cigars and threw around incredible sums of money, as if they were betting peanuts or pea gravel. And the way they talked! Those men disregarded *every-thing* but money. It justified the most callous and inhumane acts. But I knew Father was different. He came from a farm and knew what it was like to dream and work hard; he knew what it was like to reach for something people told you that you could never have. He respected a person's ambitions. He respected *mine*."

Her voice broke and Henry worried she was going to cry. Then what would he do?

But she didn't cry. She sat up straighter and cleared her throat and started finger-combing the dog's matted fur. "But when Father had to choose between his dreams and mine . . ." She pressed her lips together and shook her head, but it wasn't with sadness, it looked more like anger.

"If only Jonathan had lived, I'd have remained a spare tire; you know, inconsequential. But when you lose one tire on the road, everything depends on that spare." She shifted and crossed her legs, cuddling that filthy dog closer. When she spoke again, her tone slid low and settled somewhere between sadness and desperation. "But he was killed. I became the sole vessel for the Haviland for-tune" — she slipped briefly into her high-hat voice — "and its descendants throughout eternity, *amen.* Father suddenly decided my aspirations were childish, foolish, ridiculous ideas and I needed to get them out of my head immediately. Women did as they were told, and I was no exception." The way she said it told Henry those were her father's words exactly.

She sat there looking into the flames for a bit. Henry stirred the fire, and firefly sparks rose into the darkness. The tree frogs had joined the night ruckus around them, making her next, soft-spoken words hard to hear.

"It was like he died with Jonathan and one of those whiskered men from that gambling room took his place. He stopped taking me places. Stopped joining me in inappropriate behavior behind Mother's back. He stopped being Father."

Henry had been well acquainted with death and the changes it brought. Baby Marie and he had caught (ironically enough) German measles at the same time. He remembered Ma's broken heart when Marie died. Ma eventually learned to smile again, but something was missing in her eyes. Try as he might, nothing Henry did brought it back. Eventually Peter had told him to stop trying so hard to cheer her, that it just made Ma sadder. Henry hadn't understood that until Ma passed two years later. Peter had forgotten his words to Henry, and everything he did to make Henry feel better only broke his heart more. By the time Peter died, no one was left who cared enough to even make the effort.

He heard Cora draw a deep breath. "Here I am. So it all worked out." Her voice had regained some of its buoyancy. "By the grace of God — and some shifty shenanigans on my father's part — I was spared being married off to a husband chosen for his wealth and business acumen. I avoided my single life-duty of birthing a brood of little tycoons and debutantes and serving a man I didn't even care to know, let alone live with.

"The money's gone. The promises were ash in my father's mouth all along. My mother only knows one way to live, and I'm the only bargaining chip she has left to get it back. I'm not the commodity I once was; a penniless daughter of a scalawag is a hard sell to all but the most desperate of wealthy men. So don't talk to me about being selfish, Henry Jefferson. I won't be sold twice in one lifetime. This is my chance. I'm taking it."

Her voice changed. "I don't know if Father killed himself because the money was gone, or because he knew he was going to jail for how he got it." She drew a deep breath. "Doesn't matter I suppose. The end result is the same either way."

"I'm sorry." A little seed of hate for that man started in Henry's belly. No matter how awful things got, his pa had stuck it out. What kind of man sets up such foolish expectations in his daughter, takes them away, then deserts her? Suddenly he didn't feel like picking on her anymore. "So your dream and ambition was to ride a motorcycle with a traveling air exhibition?"

"Why, yes." She smiled. "Isn't it every girl's dream?"

He added a log to the fire. "Really, what did you want to do?"

"Have you ever heard of Nellie Bly?"

Henry shook his head.

"Of course not, she was a troublemaking woman. She was a daredevil journalist, got herself into all sorts of places using secret identities. Told stories nobody wanted the public to see, treatment of female inmates in jail, inhumane treatment of workers in factories. She angered all of those whiskered tycoons when she wrote about the Pullman strike from the strikers' perspective. Best of all, in '89 she circumnavigated the globe — *alone*. A *woman* unchaperoned on ship, train, and burro! The scandal! She did it in seventy-two days." The excitement in Cora's voice rose. "And she didn't have the benefit of Jules Verne dictating her story."

"Oh."

"That's all you can say?" Cora shook her

head. "Harriet Chalmers Adams, then? She explored and photographed South American jungles, Mayan ruins, and the like — lectured extensively on it."

Henry shrugged. Despite all of his reading, he suddenly felt his lack of education.

"You *did* hear about Howard Carter finding King Tutankhamen's tomb in Egypt last fall? He was a *man,* after all."

"Everybody heard about that."

"*That's* what I want!" She raised her hand in the air, startling the dog into raising his head. "To make my mark on the world. I want adventure. Discovery. I want to be known and remembered."

Henry wanted just the opposite.

"And I'll still do it. Carter proved you don't need *your own* money — his was provided by a woman, by the way." Cora relaxed a bit. "I *will* do it. Just you wait and see."

Henry thought riding a motorcycle like a madwoman with a dog in her jacket was probably a good start to getting folks to take notice.

Cora pulled a wax-paper-wrapped sandwich from her rucksack. She handed half to Henry. "When do you think Gil'll be back?" she asked, as if her arrival had nothing to do with driving him off.

Henry shrugged. *Hopefully not before I get you on your way.*

They ate in silence. Cora shared every other bite with the dog. If Henry's sense of charity hadn't been overpowered by his hunger, he might have done the same.

He stole an occasional look across the campfire, trying not to be conspicuous as he considered the best way to make her leave. At last, the dog got the final bit of bread crust and lay down at Cora's side. She pulled her long hair over her shoulder and began to slowly braid it. The light brown strands sparked gold in the firelight as her fingers wove with unthinking habit. The dog's eyes closed. His matted fur was not in the least enhanced by the fire's glow. Henry was pretty sure he and the dog shared yet another commonality in that.

Henry chuckled as he thought of the dog trailing sausages and being chased by the butcher.

Cora looked up. "What's funny?"

He shared a dramatized version of the thievery and how the terrier had hitched a ride out of town. Tears ran down Cora's cheeks by the end of the tale. The dog didn't seem to have anything to add — or refute. He did occasionally open his eyes, shooting Henry a curious look.

"What made you stop and pick him up?" Henry asked.

"Never can resist a stray." She scratched behind the dog's ears. "Give them the tiniest bit of attention and you get complete adoration in return." She cupped the dog's face in her hands and looked into his eyes. "I'm going to call you Mercury."

"Because of his color?"

"After the Roman god Jupiter's son. He was a bit of a thief, too, but was such a cutie that everyone forgave him . . . plus, he could fly."

She's gotta go.

"I think you may have overestimated the mutt's charm. That butcher wasn't swayed by those puppy eyes in the least."

She pulled the dog into her lap. "I'm sure darling little Mercury would never have taken those sausages if he hadn't been starving."

The dog looked over at Henry so smugly that Henry wasn't so sure. Maybe the pooch did it for the thrill — he did like riding the motorcycle.

"He's probably got a family somewhere," Henry said. "It wouldn't be fair to take him away. You know families grieve when one of their own disappears."

She shot him a look. "Don't even waste

your breath on that kind of crap with me." Then she shifted her attention back to the dog. "Just look at him! If he has family, they don't deserve him."

They sat quietly for a bit. Her eyelids begin to close as she watched the flames.

He took one last stab at changing her mind. "You do know you aren't going to be remembered for being a barnstormer. Money will stay scarce because that airplane is constantly hungry and ready to fall apart, and it gets first dibs on the cash. Maybe another avenue would be better for you to reach your admirable goals of fame and discovery."

"Everybody's got to start somewhere." She yawned as she lay down. "You know, the journey of a thousand miles begins with a single step."

"Well, now, aren't you a sage."

She laughed. "Not me. Lao-tzu. He was a Chinese philosopher. Good night, Henry."

Eventually Henry fell into a fitful sleep with little hope of leaving Noblesville in the cockpit of Gil's Jenny.

Gil returned early the next morning, red-eyed and grouchy. He nudged Henry with the toe of his shoe and dropped a brown paper bag in front of him. "Breakfast," he

123

said flatly, then sat down, lit a cigarette, and unfolded a newspaper.

Henry rubbed his eyes and looked across the fire. Cora was gone. His words must finally have sunk in. He felt bad for her and her circumstance, but she was better off with her family no matter what she thought.

How had he not heard the motorcycle start up?

He opened the bag. It held half a loaf of brown bread and an apple. "Thanks." As he pulled out the bread and tore off a chunk, he saw the motorcycle was still where it had been last night. His heart sank.

"Where —"

"Don't. Talk." Gil winced as if Henry had yelled.

He finished the bread and ate the apple. Still no sign of Cora.

He got up and walked around. He looked in the little copse of trees. No Cora. No Mercury.

Standing by the Jenny, he heard something. A soft, piglike snuffle.

He climbed up on the wing. Cora was asleep in the cockpit, Mercury curled on her lap. Cora was doing the snoring. The dog looked up and cocked his head.

"Bet you need to visit the doggie outhouse," he whispered as he lifted the dog from her lap. There, under the dog, clenched in her hand was the hammer they used to drive the stakes. Maybe she wasn't as brave . . . or as foolish . . . as Henry had thought.

He climbed quietly back down and set the dog off to take care of his business and went to take care of a little of his own. When he came back out of the trees, Cora was standing next to Gil, who seemed to be ignoring her as if she had really succumbed to Henry's will and disappeared in the night.

"Well, are we entertaining here today, or moving on?" she asked brightly. "I personally think we should move on. Get a nice early start. Maybe head to Lafayette. You know those engineering students at Purdue will be wild for a plane ride."

With a cigarette dangling from the corner of his mouth, Gil kept his eyes on the newspaper. "I am an aviator. I do not 'entertain.' "

Entertainment, excitement, spectacle — call it what you will — was exactly what Gil sold. Henry's short acquaintance with Gil had given him enough insight into the man that he understood Gil viewed selling rides as a means to an end. That end was simple, to keep his plane filled with fuel and his feet off the ground. Regular meals resided as a distant third.

And Purdue? Cora clearly wasn't using good logic. Plenty of towns were closer that would require less fuel to reach and still had more than enough people for a good crowd. And those university kids — Henry didn't feel at all good about going and mixing with them. Farm folk he understood. Of course, he kept all of these thoughts tight inside. His only concern now was making sure he was in the cockpit of that Jenny when it left here.

Gil went on, "You can make whatever arrangements you want with Mr. Sowers for the use of the pasture for your little *entertainment.* We're leaving."

We. He said we.

Gil got up, dropped the newspaper on the ground, and walked toward the plane.

Cora was right on his heels. Mercury was right on hers.

Henry looked down at the newspaper and saw the headline for one of the front-page stories: MANHUNT CONTINUES FOR MURDERER OF DELAWARE CO. GIRL

Somehow physical contact would link him more closely with both the words and the act, so he squatted and read it right where it lay on the ground.

126

The man who brutally murdered eighteen-year-old Emmaline Dahlgren is still on the loose. Her body was discovered in a stream on the family farm earlier this week by one of her six sisters, who witnessed the murderer fleeing the scene.

The Dahlgrens' charity to a German orphan led to this unfortunate tragedy. Henry Schuler, the man sought by authorities for the crime, was taken in by the family five years ago. The troubled young man never adjusted to his new home or community and had shown aggression toward Emmaline on several occasions.

Eighteen-year-old Schuler is over six feet tall with blond hair and blue eyes and was last seen traveling on foot.

Dear God, how he hated that girl.

Had Gil read it? Did he make the connection?

Henry kicked the paper into the low embers of the fire, waiting until the edges began to blacken and curl before he got up and walked away.

5

Henry grew nauseated and clammy when he thought of the considerable number of people who'd been on this field yesterday looking at a tall, blond stranger and then gone home and read that newspaper. He knew he looked older than eighteen. He hoped a lot older. And neither Cora nor Gil had used his name. He'd never thought he'd be happy to have Cora call him Kid.

He double-checked the road just to make sure the sheriff wasn't already barreling his way. When he went to hustle Cora and Gil along to get camp packed up, Cora seemed as anxious to clear out as he was. Maybe she figured if she acted as if they were all leaving together, it would just happen.

Henry vowed to himself to be smarter. He was used to keeping out of the way, but that was entirely different from hiding from the law. This time far more was at stake than banishment to the barn or a withheld dinner — even though when Mrs. Dahlgren had dictated the no-supper punishment, Mr. Dahlgren had always managed to sneak out a little something for Henry to eat after his wife had retired for the night.

But overall, Henry had been too slow in seeing the risks on that farm. And it had led to his current predicament.

Henry's first Christmas Eve on the Dahlgren farm had come exactly twelve days after his arrival. He'd watched with a disjointed kind of sadness as Mr. Dahlgren dragged a giant evergreen into the house. Ma had always made Pa chop a tree, usually a pitiful, scrappy thing that probably wouldn't have survived the winter. And they'd sung carols around it — at least Ma, Peter, and Henry had. He was used to missing his family, but the long, work-filled days kept him occupied in his waking hours and pressed him into an exhausted sleep afterward. But Christmas Day would be different. The only work that would be done was feeding the livestock. He would have an entire empty day stretched out before him.

He thought maybe Mr. Dahlgren's troubles inside the house were getting worse instead of better when it came to Henry. It was hard to tell. Mr. Dahlgren ate supper with Henry most nights. More than once, through the kitchen window, Henry had seen Mrs. Dahlgren arguing with Mr. as he headed out with two plates. It didn't seem to sit well with the older daughters either. One time he'd seen Emmaline thrust herself between her papa and the door, refusing to let him pass. After a bit Emmaline moved and Mr. Dahlgren had come out. As the door closed behind him, Henry had seen Emmaline run from the kitchen. Henry felt bad about it. But he really liked his time with Mr. Dahlgren.

Henry didn't expect Mr. Dahlgren to eat with him that night. Not on Christmas Eve. So he stretched out on his cot and opened the book Mr. Dahlgren had brought out on Henry's second night. Mr. Dahlgren had a big library and said Henry could read any book he wanted. He was still trying to figure out how he was going to choose a book if he wasn't ever allowed in the house.

He was only about three-quarters of the way through *The Adventures of Huckleberry Finn.* That's how he would fill tomorrow. Then he'd ask Mr. Dahlgren to pick something else; he'd done real good picking this one.

Right at regular dinnertime, Mr. Dahlgren appeared with two plates. "*God jul,* young

Henry." He smiled and nodded. "Merry Christmas."

Henry sat up. "Merry Christmas, sir."

"I cannot stay long tonight, there are gifts and songs and too many high voices, but a papa must sometimes be strong." He winked as he handed Henry his dinner. "But I did not want you to eat this important meal alone."

"Thank you, but you don't have to stay." Henry looked down at the plate heaped with more food than he used to eat in a week back home.

Before long, Emmaline called from the house, "Papa! Papa, come now! You promised!"

Mr. Dahlgren shook his head, but he was smiling. "I must go." He reached into his pocket and pulled out a wrapped, flat package. "I did not have much time, so I hope you will not be disappointed."

Henry stared at the package. "Disappointed?"

"In your gift. Next year I will have time to plan a proper boy's gift." He handed the package to Henry and nodded for him to open it.

It was a book. *The Wonderful Wizard of Oz.*

"For me to keep, sir?"

"Of course!"

"Thank you. I've never had a book of my own before."

"You will have many more. I have also ordered a periodical publication I think you will like. It is about machines and science. It will come in the post all year long."

Henry sat there staring at the book in his hand, unable to speak.

Mr. Dahlgren put his hand on the top of Henry's head. "You are a good boy. You deserve better than this barn. I will work on it." He started to leave, then turned around. "Oh, and this book is about an orphan, too. You must see orphans can have the most amazing journeys."

"But Huck Finn wasn't an orphan. He had Pa Finn out there running around."

"He was still left to fend for himself. Huckleberry was as alone as a boy could be." Mr. Dahlgren nodded. "*God jul,* young Henry."

"*God jul,* Mr. Dahlgren."

Two days later Henry found the book splayed open in the mud of the pigpen when he got back from helping Mr. Dahlgren mend a fence. He snatched it up and tried to wipe off the mud, then tucked it in his coat before Mr. Dahlgren could see. How had it gotten out there?

The next day, Emmaline had passed

Henry on her way to the henhouse. She barely slowed when she spoke to him for the first time ever. "This was a very strange Christmas. First one that Papa didn't give me a book."

She'd made it to the chicken-yard gate before Henry shook off his surprise that she'd spoken at all. The first thing that hit him was guilt; he'd received something intended for her. Then his stomach grew cold when her meaning sank in.

He called after her, "All you had to do was ask for it."

She paused, halfway through the gate. "For what?" Then she went about her business of collecting the eggs.

Staying on the move was probably better for evading the law than hiding in a city, where, once Henry got a job, people would grow to recognize him, to know him, including the local beat cop — he'd read about those in the newspaper. It would be best if people didn't think he and Gil had only been knocking around together for a day, a week, or a month. Folks noticed the plane and the war hero. Henry was just a voice building the excitement. He needed to keep it that way.

What if Cora does come with us?

133

She was on Gil's heels as he did his preflight. She could ruin everything just by holding them up now. Mercury seemed in collusion, tripping Gil at every turn.

A woman in our act would make us seem more inviting, more family friendly.

The dog grabbed one of the tie-down ropes and took off with it. Gil chased it ten feet before he realized it was useless. Then he yelled for the dog to come back . . . in a tone no creature in his right mind would respond to.

Henry tried calling, but the dog kept going.

One sweet whistle from Cora and the mutt came trotting back and sat obediently at her feet, rope trailing from his mouth as the sausages had done.

When Gil reached down to retrieve the rope, Mercury backed away with a growl. Henry saw just how much doggie loyalty could be bought with a shared half sandwich.

"We might not want you to have that," Cora said. "Not until we settle on a deal."

People will assume the three of us have been an act for a good while; Henry Jefferson the barnstormer will be one step further removed from Henry Schuler, the man on the run alone.

Gil growled back and made a quick lunge for the rope. He missed. Mercury once again took off at a run, ears flapping and flopping with each bounding lope.

There is no job in Chicago.

"I can always call him back," Cora said.

Wasting time was a peeve to Gil, but could prove disastrous for Henry.

People want new amusements. Radios. Moving-picture houses. Can I promote this act enough to support all three of us? People wanted more thrilling, more outlandish. And Cora is both in so many ways.

He finally pulled Gil aside and pointed out that the motorcycle could match the Jenny's speed, so it wouldn't be all that difficult for Cora to follow them to their next location.

"What's the harm?" Henry asked. "She won't last past the first rainstorm anyway. We're just wasting time when we could be making money to take care of the Jenny."

Gil's face was unreadable.

"As long as she's around, we can use the motorcycle to make runs into town for supplies. Maybe we can even attach a sign advertising that you're selling rides. The motorbike will burn less fuel than the Jenny drawing a crowd. Lots of things could be easier." Then Henry added, "At least until

Cora gets tired of the whole business and goes home."

Gil's shrug of surrender was accompanied by a raised brow. "I doubt anything to do with Cora Haviland will make life easier." Then he turned and walked back toward Cora. "Call the damn dog."

"We have a deal? I'm in?"

Gil crossed his arms over his chest and gave a curt nod.

She whistled for Mercury, retrieved the rope, now covered in nettle burrs, and held it behind her back awaiting verbal confirmation.

Apparently, Gil couldn't quite bring himself to say yes. "Just don't expect special treatment because you're a woman."

She stood there for a long moment, her eyes narrowed with suspicion and her mouth pressed tight. "You're tricking me somehow."

Gil gave her a take-it-or-leave-it look.

Henry waited, fighting his urge to open his mouth and give a nudge.

Finally, she handed over the tie-down rope.

As Gil climbed up on the wing to stow the last of the gear, he asked, "Do you have a map?"

"No." She stepped toward the plane with

136

her hand out.

He climbed into the cockpit. "A shame." Taking a look at his own map, he held it high enough to make a show. Then he signaled Henry to prop the engine. "See you in Crawfordsville, Miss Haviland."

Maybe, Henry thought, I should ride with her. A woman alone . . .

By the time he looked her way, she'd already scooped up Mercury and was trotting toward the motorcycle.

As Gil tied down the plane and the last customer motored back toward Crawfordsville, thunder rumbled in the west. Gil glanced at the sky, then grinned wickedly at Henry.

Henry looked away, knowing Cora was about to wipe that smile right off Gil's face.

She glanced without concern at the clouds tumbling over one another in the sky. "Just so I'm not being favored with special treatment, Gil, you can ride the motorcycle to the hotel. Henry and I will walk. It's the Crawford Hotel, right on Main and Green. Reservations in my stage name, Cora Rose."

Henry had been surprised when she'd told the hotel clerk her name. When he'd sent a questioning look her way, she'd quietly put her heel on top of his foot and pressed.

137

Later when he'd asked why she hadn't used her real name, she'd gotten snippy. "Cora Rose is my real name, just not all of it. Besides, I can be whoever I want now. Don't mess it up."

"So you're hiding?" The instant those words had come out of his mouth, he'd regretted them. He needed to be careful about asking questions that could be turned back on him.

"I'm reinventing, leaving the old behind."

"So you're not worried that your uncle will come looking for you?"

"Seriously, Henry. Uncle Clyde doesn't want me to be miserable; he doesn't even like Mother. She'll be angry for a while. But she'll figure out something, she always does. The only difference is now she can't sacrifice me to get it."

"But if you're of age, how can she make you marry someone even if you stayed?"

Cora had huffed, "My God, you don't know anything! She'd make every day so miserable, eventually I'd either have to get married or leave. I didn't have enough money to take off on my own. If I got a confining job as a teacher or secretary, I might as well be married. I was still working things out. But then, opportunity landed in Uncle Clyde's pasture. I'm Cora Rose because I want to be, not because I have to be."

Henry had left it there. She was right, he had no idea what living in a rich, or once-rich, family was like. And before he'd met Cora, he'd never given a thought that some women might not like their place in life. It was all quite confusing.

Gil's voice was icy when he said, "Reservations?"

"Yes. I made them while we were in town getting gasoline. And after we've cleaned up and had dinner, we're going to the dance at the 4-H grounds." She gave a little shimmy. "I can't wait!"

"We don't stay in hotels," Gil said. "We camp."

"Don't be silly. We've done so well these past two days! You deserve a hot bath and a nice dry bed."

"And what gauge are you using to tell that we've done well?" Gil asked, the "we've" coming out through clenched teeth.

"Henry said."

Henry busied himself with retying his shoes. Every dime of Gil's newly made cash still sat in Henry's pocket. The man hadn't so much as asked how much they'd collected.

From under his eyebrows, Henry saw Gil

shoot him a look that should have been reserved for those committing high treason. "We camp."

"Fine." Cora shrugged. "I can camp." The wind gusted, pushing the smell of rain. A loose strand from Cora's braid blew across her face. "But I'm going to that dance. What better way to spread the word about our act? It'll be a good opportunity for people to meet you, too, so they'll trust you more as a pilot."

"Dancing has no correlation to being a good pilot."

She rolled her eyes. "Don't be deliberately obtuse. You don't need to dance. You need to meet people. Show your face so you're not just some mysterious stranger with a dangerous airplane."

Henry said, "She has a point. And it'll be better than sitting out here in a thunderstorm." Henry needed a bath and didn't know when the next opportunity might arise. She'd already given a name and signed for all of the rooms, so even if the police questioned the clerk, Henry would remain anonymous. He hoped Gil's desire for Cora to suffer the maximum misery didn't outweigh his own for a dry bed. "Cora bargained with the hotel manager — our rooms are practically free. I got a couple of ideas for promotion while I was in town today. It'd be a lot easier to talk them over if we're not drowning every time we open our mouths."

"Come on, Gil. I promise I'll sleep out in the next rainstorm," Cora said.

"Nearly free, huh?" Gil said, and Henry noticed a glint of admiration in Gil's eyes. "Your night in the rain is coming, lady." Gil stomped over to the motorcycle. "See you at the hotel."

Henry walked alongside Cora, hoping the rain held off until they reached the hotel — at least she wasn't wearing a white blouse. Mercury trotted beside them, occasionally heading off into the roadside weeds to investigate some smell or other.

"No thieving from butchers when we get to town, young man," Cora said, shaking her finger at the dog. "We want everybody to like us."

Once a thief, always a thief. Miss Julien's words echoed through time. Henry's third-grade teacher was overfond of character-damning maxims. She'd been trying to ferret out a confession from whoever had been taking food from lunches, pilfering pencils, and lifting pennies from coat pockets, but her eyes — and the eyes of every kid in class

— had landed on Henry. She'd been scrutinizing his every move since war had broken out in Europe. Even though America hadn't been in the fighting yet, Miss Julien had been preaching the villainy of the Huns with the fervor of a tent revivalist. Her grandparents and uncles still lived in France.

Henry hadn't been the thief in that classroom, but as an act of self-preservation he'd been on the lookout for who was. When he'd seen Billy Edwards, a runt of a kid with eyes too big for his face and a body so skinny you could almost see through him, help himself to Annabelle Butler's lunch, Henry had turned away and pretended he hadn't. Billy reminded Henry of a mouse skirting the room trying not to be noticed before skittering back into the safety of his hole. He was *always* sent home with a note on lice-check day. Henry's family was poor, but Billy's was *dirt*-poor; there was a difference.

"Maybe if we keep him fed," Henry said to Cora, "he won't be tempted."

She shrugged. "Sometimes it's a different kind of hunger that drives bad behavior."

"Speaking from experience?"

She flipped her hand in the air. "You already know what I want out of life — and what I'm willing to do to get it."

Cora seemed tough. She seemed ambitious. But Henry wondered how strongly her conviction would hold when hunger bedded down with her at night, when the damp cold from the hard ground filtered into her bones.

"What do you think Gil wants?" she asked.

Henry chuckled. "To be left alone. To be a thousand feet off the ground where nobody can touch him." The only time Henry had seen peace in Gil's face was when he was in the air.

"He has to want more!"

"I'm pretty sure he doesn't."

"Well, that's ridiculous. He's one of a handful of people in this country with an airplane. If he wants to, he can chart the future of aviation! He can set records. Stunt for the moving pictures. He can change the world!"

"I think the world has already changed *him.*"

"I thought you two just met."

"We did."

"He must be a whole lot more forthcoming with you than he is with me, then."

"It's not what he says," Henry said thoughtfully. "It's . . . it's what's behind his eyes." *Particularly when he's been startled out of a doze.* "There's something, I don't know . . . detached in the way he walks through the world." Henry shrugged. "I can't explain it exactly."

"He *is* intriguing, isn't he?" Cora sounded like the silly girls he'd heard talk about Rudolph Valentino. Cora knew no more about Gil than those girls knew about Valentino; they just filled in the void with things they wanted to believe.

Henry stopped and looked down at her. "He's broken, Cora." Her face showed surprise at Henry's sudden intensity. "Broken." The years had blurred the memory of what Henry had seen deep in his pa's eyes, but that memory had refocused the instant he'd glimpsed the same wreckage in Gil's.

Henry walked on. Picking up his pace, he whistled for Mercury to come out of the weeds. "We need to hurry or we're going to be caught in the storm."

Cora trotted to catch up. For a while they walked in silence; he could almost hear the mental tussle in her head. He was pretty sure her girl brain was inventing all sorts of fascinating details, concocting romantic, mysterious reasons for Gil's reticence. But it wasn't intrigue, it was damage. Sometimes life stole a piece of you, chewed it up, and swallowed it down. Henry didn't know if Gil had lost that part of himself to the war or if it had been stolen before that. Henry was pretty sure, though, that a girl like Cora would only tear out more chunks if she tried to shove herself into that dark, empty space.

After a while, Cora asked, "So what drives you, Kid?"

Desperation was on his lips, but he kept his mouth closed long enough to think through his answer. "Up until now, my life has kind of happened *to* me. Not a lot of driving."

"Compelled by your family's choices? I know how that is!"

"I don't have a family. Haven't for a long time."

"Oh." She paused. "No one to dictate your every move, then. You're lucky."

For all her city sophistication, she didn't seem have a good grip on reality. Maybe it was because she'd grown up rich. "Not lucky at all, Cora." He couldn't keep the chill out of his voice. "Not one little bit." He could feel disaster nipping at his heels.

"Hey." She grabbed his arm and stopped walking, pulling him to face her. Then she touched the scratch on his forehead, trailing her fingers to the corner of his blackened eye. "I'm sorry. I shouldn't have . . . I just can't seem to stop knocking you around."

He looked into her eyes for a long moment, his heart turning slow rolls in his chest. Then he turned and started walking again before he said something stupid.

She looped her arm though his and fell into step. "I'm going to be more careful with you. You're a good person, Henry."

Good? Hardly. Not deep down where it counted. He'd been twisted and wrung out by his lifelong companion, disaster. He hadn't risen above it, as he pretended to the world. He'd just buried everything deep inside where it sat with a green-eyed hatred searching for a way out. At times he felt it pulsing, pushing, clamoring to get free.

Henry was just coming to suspect his true self . . . and it scared him.

The storm blew through while Henry sat soaking in a steaming bath on the fourth floor of the Crawford Hotel. He didn't deserve such luxury, but with each volley of thunder he mentally thanked Cora for keeping them from riding out the storm huddled under the wing of the Jenny. He'd never been in a hotel before, never seen anything like the lobby with its fancy lights, huge potted plants tucked between clusters of bloodred velvet chairs and couches. He'd never walked on such a thick carpet runner down such a long hall, never ridden in an elevator — which seemed like a lazy man's way to get to the upper floors. He supposed the ladies might need it, though. He'd ridden it out of curiosity. What he really wanted was to see the electric motor and pulleys, but the elevator operator had looked down his nose and informed him that those areas were strictly off-limits to guests.

Henry considered searching for it on his own in the wee hours when the rest of the hotel was asleep, but he wouldn't want to get Cora and Gil tossed out with him if he was caught.

At the appointed time, Henry went down to the lobby. Gil's hair was slicked back, he'd shaved, and he wore a clean shirt and tie. He looked much less dangerous. Henry wondered if this version of Gil would be more or less intriguing to Cora.

"Nice hat," Gil said, nodding to Henry's newly acquired newsboy cap. He'd seen it in the clothing-shop window on the ground floor of the hotel. He'd parted with the money because his straw-colored hair and his height were his most recognizable features — and he couldn't do anything about his height.

"Nice tie. Going dancing?"

"Absolutely not. But I do plan on a decent meal."

"I want to show you something." Henry walked Gil to the door. The spring storm had left the air cool and damp. The lights from the store display windows reflected off the wet sidewalks. The lobby was busy, but the street outside even busier. Overalls, trucks, and farm wagons from earlier in the day had been replaced by buggies, automobiles, and tidy-looking couples strolling into the movie house and restaurants. Henry suddenly realized it was Saturday night.

He pointed to a banner advertising a June dance marathon: *Foxtrot to Fame; Wabash College Armory and Gymnasium; Beat last year's record of eight days; Orderlies and nurses will be in attendance; Ice packs and smelling salts provided on the premises; Cash prize $100.* Henry hadn't believed it when he'd first read it. Even the Midwest seemed to be falling to bouts of ridiculous frivolity. Selling airplane rides should be easy. At least they were offering an experience of historic substance.

"If we make one or two of those, we can put them up in towns before we get there. Like circus posters, get the enthusiasm up."

And make us appear more well established.
Henry felt a tug of guilt; this was most likely the farthest thing from what Gil wanted. Yet, if it would keep Gil better fed and the Jenny in gas, oil, and parts . . . Henry could maybe make some improvements on the plane with the increased cash flow . . . wouldn't it be beneficial to Gil in the long run?

Gil, not surprisingly, shook his head. "We won't know where we're going to be able to land the Jenny, or even when we'll get there — weather, repairs . . ."

"We don't need to be specific, just advertise the daredevil act. With this kind of advance word, the instant you fly over, word will spread like church gossip and people will come."

"Daredevil act?" Gil glared at Henry.

"Well, now that Cora can do stunts on the ground while you do them in the air, it's more than just airplane rides. And it'll draw more people — isn't that what you want?"

"You make it sound like people get the chance to ride in an airplane every damn day."

Cora's voice came from behind them. "From the look on Flyboy's face, I take it you've told him about Mercury's Daredevils."

Henry winced. The girl's timing was impossible.

"What — ?" Gil's voice cut off when he turned.

Henry spun around and his mouth went dry. She wore a fancy sleeveless dress, a gold cuff on her upper arm, and a string of pearls against her throat. And her hair . . .

"Like it?" She patted the ends of her newly short hair and spun around. The pearls swung out; she was wearing the long strand backward so it hung down her back . . . where her dress dipped so low Henry couldn't swallow. "I've been wanting to get it bobbed *forever,* but couldn't get mother's suspicion up. Had to play the obedient daughter up until the last minute."

"Where'd you come up with that getup?" Gil asked. Henry wondered how the man could find his voice.

"I had the hotel dress shop send several up."

"Very practical investment for a barnstormer," Gil said.

"I know you're just being an ass, but it actually is. Tonight's all about attracting attention . . . for Mercury's Daredevils." Her brows rose over eyes glittering with challenge.

Henry's insides shriveled. Why couldn't

150

she have waited, like they'd agreed?

"Mercury's Daredevils?" Gil said it with the same welcoming tone he'd use for, say, the bubonic plague.

"Catchy, huh?" Cora said.

"You're part of this?" Gil asked Henry.

Henry shrugged.

"No," Gil said. "No banner. No *Mercury's Daredevils.*" He walked out into the puddle-spotted sidewalk.

Cora trotted past Henry. "But it's brilliant! People will remember it . . . especially after they see who Mercury is."

Henry moved to catch up.

Gil and Cora stood face-to-face, interrupting the flow of people on the sidewalk like an island in a river. The only movement between them was where the breeze teased the fringe at the hem of Cora's dress.

"You're just being obstinate," she said.

Gil didn't respond.

"Think of the improvements you can make to the airplane. We could even buy a second one! You can teach Henry and me to fly. We can buy a truck to haul our equipment and personal items as we travel — have the name painted on the side. We can be more famous than Eddie Rickenbacker, bigger than Barnum."

Gil's gaze shifted to Henry. "I don't like

being shanghaied." To Cora he said, "I'm a barnstormer. That's it. Don't like it? Leave."

He walked away, leaving Cora sputtering and Henry panicked.

She turned to Henry with a smile. "He'll come around tomorrow when the crowd shows up."

There was confidence and there was foolishness. Cora had yet to discover the difference.

When they walked into the crowded dance hall, Cora gasped and her face fell.

"What's wrong?"

"This is not the kind of dance I was expecting."

Henry looked at the band: fiddle, banjo, guitar, Jew's harp, same as the barn-dance band back home. The caller stood in front with a washboard.

She took a deep breath. "Could be fun." She grabbed Henry's hand and pulled him, dragging feet and uttered protests ignored, right into the thick of the dancers.

After being dragged around the floor through four songs, stepping on Cora's toes enough to cripple her, Henry pulled her to the side. "Shouldn't we be talking to people? Spreading the word?"

"Ab-so-lute-ly." She fortified herself with

a deep breath. "I was just having such fun."

"At least one of us was." He made himself sound sour, tried to make that feeling go deeper than words. But for the first time in as long as he could remember, he'd felt . . . light — even on his plodding feet. While the music had played and he'd concentrated on following Cora's moves, nothing else was in the room, nothing else in his heart and mind, no past, no future, no worry.

"I'll start on that side of the room." She pointed. "You start over there."

"Okay." He went in that direction, planning on lurking in a corner, staying unnoticed, and keeping an eye on her.

That obscure corner turned out to be already occupied. A sullen-looking man missing an arm sat in the shadows, his shirtsleeve pinned to keep it from flapping. His eyes stared at the crowd, unfocused, unengaged. Henry usually took a wide path around men with outward signs of what they'd lost in the war. He started to gravitate to another corner, then stopped. Peter. What if that was Peter — stripped of his place in the world, of his spirit and vigor?

He went and sat in one of five empty chairs near the man. "Warm in here, isn't it?"

The man blinked and nodded, his eyes

still focused in the distance.

Henry offered his hand. "Name's Jefferson."

The man's eyes shifted to Henry's outstretched hand.

"Oh. Sorry." Henry quickly switched to his left.

The man stayed still for a few terrible, embarrassing seconds, then he shifted sideways and shook with his left. "White, Bob White."

"Nice to meet you, Bob."

The man looked as if he was waiting for something. "What, no bird jokes?"

"Do people really do that?"

Bob smiled; it looked like an involuntary muscle movement, not at all associated with emotion. "Almost always."

Henry shook his head. "Don't see any humor in it. A person can't help their name."

The man nodded and shifted his gaze back into space. "Birds and broken wings."

Jesus.

Henry realized he'd lost sight of Cora in the crowd. He found her, stepping onto the band riser. She stood there until the end of the song, clapping her hands with the music. Then she walked to the caller and leaned close to the old man's hairy ear. He nodded, then said, "Folks! Folks! Give your attention to this lovely young lady for one moment."

Cora's dress shimmered as she stepped forward. The sight of her was enough to stop a train; this crowd was easy pickings.

Henry breathed, "Clever."

"Hello, everyone!" The crowd murmured a hello, like the call and response of a church program. "For those of you who missed the exciting arrival of Mercury's Daredevils today, you haven't missed out. Due to popular demand, we'll be staying on for a second exhibition. My partner" — she waved a hand toward Henry, surprising him that she'd kept track of where he was — "Mr. Jefferson and I want to invite you out to the Sloderback farm tomorrow for a once-in-a-lifetime opportunity to ride in an airplane with our war hero, Captain Gilchrist, and to experience the thrills of a daredevil act without peer. Our exhibition will start at one o'clock . . . after Sunday services. Tell your friends. No one will want to miss this!" She kissed the caller on his cheek. "Now let's dance!"

The applause told Henry just how much power a pretty woman with an enthusiastic smile carried. Even Bob White had watched her with interest. And she'd timed it perfectly, right in the middle of the evening, after people were wound up and before they'd tired and started to drift away.

The music started. Several young men jostled to be the first to ask Cora to dance.

Bob looked Henry's way. "You're with the Daredevils?"

"I am."

"And your flier is a war hero?"

"He flew in the war, yeah." One-on-one conversation wasn't like barking. It required something closer to the truth.

The man nodded. "I tried air service. Didn't make it out of training. Crashed two trainers. They let you get by with one. But the second got me booted."

"Is that how you lost your arm?"

"Nah. Germans got the arm." Bob was quiet for a minute. "Turned out to be for the best. Most of them fighters didn't come home at all."

And some came home broken. "Come on out tomorrow . . . if you're not off the idea of flying. We'll give you a free ride."

Just then, Cora appeared in front of them. "Would the handsome gentleman like to dance?"

Henry shifted his weight to his feet before he realized she was talking to Bob.

"Sorry, miss." He lifted the stubby

shoulder to accentuate his empty sleeve. "Not much of a dancer."

"Well, how are your feet?"

A faint smile came to his lips. "They're good."

"Then come on!" Cora reached down and took his hand, hauling him behind her.

At first his self-conscious eyes skated around the room. But it was hard for a man to ignore Cora, and she soon absorbed his full attention. About halfway through their second dance, that man changed; Henry saw the man he'd been before the war. It was startling to see the two sides of that divide right next to each other. Was Gil's old self just a dance away? Or had it slipped so far into the distant past that there was no retrieving it?

When the band took a break, Cora spent some time mesmerizing a group of twelve-year-old boys loitering near the obviously spiked punch bowl. Then she moved on to a little knot of lady wallflowers and received a less enthusiastic welcome and a more suspicious eye. She left them with a smile and a wave (and got several glowers in response) and went toward a group of couples just outside the door smoking cigarettes.

Henry followed her like a ghost, now

lingering just inside the building's open double doors. Not doing his part in promotion for sure, but it seemed wiser to draw minimal attention to himself in a place where people could ask him questions that might venture beyond the Daredevils' exhibition. Besides, where Cora went, he suspected trouble usually followed.

And it did. Before long a flask-toting dandy slid an arm around her and slipped his hand inside the low back of her dress.

A flash of tingly hot possessiveness shot through Henry.

He wasn't even one furious stride toward them when Cora's elbow flew up and caught the man in the Adam's apple. She did it without even turning, not the slightest movement except that snake strike of an elbow. The man stumbled backward, hand to his throat, a long, thin squeak coming from his gaping mouth. His friends, so engrossed in passing the flask they didn't notice what had happened, turned his way.

Henry had to satisfy himself with beating the man on the back instead of delivering the punch to the face he wanted to. "You all right there, old man?" Each blow of Henry's hand was so hard it was more likely to knock the breath out of the man than to help him regain it.

The man gave a bug-eyed wheeze.

Henry took him roughly by the arm and moved him toward his companions. "Maybe he needs some water." Then Henry turned to Cora. "I've been looking all over for you."

She leaned close and whispered, "I can take care of myself."

"I wouldn't get too cocky about it." She didn't seem to know the world held much more dangerous things than a single sloppy drunk at a crowded dance. Henry didn't waste his breath bringing it to her attention.

The music started again and he pulled her to the center of the dance floor — just in case the guy got his wind back and came looking for retribution. For rich-looking dandies, retribution always seemed necessary to mend their egos.

Henry had never liked dancing. It drew too much attention; and attention always led to trouble. But as he and Cora danced to "Cotton-Eyed Joe," as her energy filled him and her eyes held his, he forgot anyone else was in the room, in this town, on the planet. He'd never before met a city woman, but he doubted many of them were like her. How could they be? The world would be in chaos. Men would stop working, factories would stall, banks would fold, as men succumbed to a web of desire and carnality.

The dance ended and another began. Henry didn't consider leaving the floor — for her protection, and to head off any scene with the dandy that might draw the police.

Thoughts of the police made him wonder about Cora's mother. The woman didn't seem like someone who would accept the defeat of her plans without a fight. But Cora was right, a woman of age couldn't be made to return to her family against her will, those days were gone. Money, security, and guilt over neglected duty were the only weapons that could be brought to bear. And Cora had said none of those things would alter her course.

But it was still early, she had yet to go hungry or sleep out in the rain.

The last song had played and Cora had made one last pass around the room to remind people of the Daredevils' performance tomorrow before they stepped out into the humid night hand in hand, red-faced and still breathless. He felt as if he'd fallen into another person's life. He supposed he had. Maybe Henry Jefferson would always be the man who danced with Cora, maintained flying machines, and rescued stray mutts.

For now he allowed himself the indulgence of belief.

As they got farther from the lights, he took a careful look around, just to make sure Mr. Fast Hands and his friends weren't lurking in the shadows; fellas like that tended to prefer the advantage of a sneak attack — and they rarely came alone.

The flow of people thinned as couples and families drifted different ways, the voices that had surrounded them for hours becoming more blurred and distant. Henry listened for the sound of steps behind them until he was satisfied no one was dogging them.

Cora sighed and leaned her head against his shoulder. "That was more fun than I've had since . . . I don't know when!"

"You must know every dance ever created." The dampness prevented Henry from cooling down much. Heat seemed to radiate from where his palm pressed against Cora's and the place on his shoulder touched by her temple.

"Oh" — she looked up at him, little dots of perspiration lingering on her brow — "I didn't know any of those. It just took a few minutes to figure out the calls; after that, the guy told us every step."

Henry had heard the calls, but he'd been so wrapped up in following Cora that he'd never made sense of them. Truth was, it had been impossible to concentrate on much of anything other than Cora moving with the music in that dress.

"I can't wait to teach you some modern dances, the fox-trot, the Baltimore Buzz. Oh, you'll love ragtime music, Henry. It has so much *life*!"

Henry wasn't sure how much more "life" he could withstand holding Cora in his arms without grabbing her off that dance floor and hauling her off like a caveman.

As they walked back to the hotel, she kept his hand in hers. "We really did great tonight. Gil won't be able to deny it either."

A clammy chill ran over Henry's skin. "Don't be so sure." They'd pushed him. Too far? From here on out, Henry had to keep his own goals in mind and not get railroaded by Cora's. If there was a here on out.

They reached the hotel. Cora kept his hand in hers until they entered the elevator. The elevator operator's eyes stayed on Cora until Henry said, "Third floor, please."

"Oh, um, yes, sir." The man's eyes snapped to the front of the elevator car, his cheeks redder than Cora's after dancing for an hour.

"I'll take Mercury out before I go up to my room," Henry said.

"No need. I had one of the hotel employees take care of him." She stood on tiptoe and kissed his cheek. "Good night, Kid."

Kid. He rode to the fourth floor as deflated as a blown tire.

Once in his room, he looked at that nice dry bed and fluffy feather pillow, then he turned around and went back out the door.

6

Henry walked with his head down, his hands fisted in his pockets holding on to the sensation of Cora's palm against his. The sky had cleared, leaving the night still and moonless. The weight of the darkness draped Henry's shoulders and settled heavily against his chest. The air was full of sounds from unseen creatures, leaving him feeling like the last human on earth. An owl hooted and another answered. The grit of the wet road grated beneath his feet. Something about the sound of his lone footfalls in the night comforted him, a testament to the course of his life. Alone. Separate. Not his choice, but his fate. He had to be content as an outsider, watching others live lives with families and love and belonging. The irony that he now shared his path with a woman who'd fled the very things he longed for did not escape him.

He wondered if Gil was like him, once

part of a loving family that life had stripped from him; or like Cora, fleeing the constraints of family bonds. Or maybe Gil had always been an outsider, even in his own family. The more Henry thought on it, the more he felt the man Gil was now was not the man he'd grown into from child-hood. Although Henry could see the same brokenness he'd seen in his pa, something else was in Gil's eyes, too, a foundation of warmth Henry doubted Pa had ever had. All of the softness in Gil lay deeply buried under harder emotions that Henry couldn't quite pinpoint. Anger? Loss? Because of the war? It had certainly changed Peter — a fact Henry only knew because of the letter his pa had hidden from him.

Pa's pride in Peter's service had made him stand a little taller, even in the accusing glare of the most suspicious of anti-German souls. Pa and Henry read and reread every letter from Peter until they were wrinkled and grayed from handling. Those letters had been filled with the conviction he was fight-ing the good fight, proudly serving his country. His fellow soldiers didn't question his loyalty. To them he was a Hoosier, not a German. For that alone, he'd written, join-ing up was worth it. But as summer faded to fall, and fall turned to winter, so did

Peter's letters, losing all color and life. Until the last one, written just two days before he died:

Dear Pa,

Please don't show this letter to Henry. He's too young. I'm already on the verge of madness, and if I don't tell someone, I fear I will lose my mind completely.

You've never seen a place so stripped of life. Truly hell on earth. There isn't so much as a living blade of grass standing between us and the Germans. Mud. Mud. Mud. Our daily battle isn't against the enemy, but against the rats for the driest places to sleep, for a stale ration of food. Sickness downs more soldiers than weapons, while the incessant shelling shakes the ground and rattles nerves to the point of insanity. Our line has not moved from this trench in weeks. I know I will die here.

Make sure Henry never goes to war. It won't make any difference.

Peter

Not *Your loving son, Peter,* as all other letters. Just *Peter.* Pa *had* hidden it. Henry found it when he'd been getting Pa's funeral clothes from the drawer; the paper and envelope were as worn and muddy as Peter must have been.

I will die here. Had Peter really known? He'd been surrounded by death for months. Even before he'd shipped overseas, the training camps had been overrun with killing influenza. But Peter had never once expressed a fear of death, let alone the conviction of it. Had he sensed death's presence at his own door, just as Henry had known it stood outside the threshold for Pa six months later? Henry had wondered, what guise had death been wearing when Peter had opened that door? That question had been a cancerous partner in Henry's grief.

When the telegram informing them that Peter had been killed at Belleau Wood had arrived, Pa crumpled it in his work-worn hand and held it to his heart so tightly his whole body shook. "We sacrificed him for nothing. Nothing," he sobbed, his German accent even thicker in grief. After that day, he was a silent kaleidoscope of guilt and pain. Even though his body continued to move and breathe for months, Henry knew his pa had died on that bloody battlefield with Peter. Pa had stayed locked in his silent repentance, fading a little more every day, until the memory of his voice became just a distant whisper in Henry's head.

What if Peter had survived? For years, Henry had held on to the shiny images of Peter's life, imagining a joyful reunion that could have been, pretending he'd never laid eyes on the naked, broken spirit of that last letter. But he'd been a foolish child. What new form of his brother would have come home? Who had Gil been before war plucked him from his ordinary life and cast him into a sky that was now his only refuge? If Henry could understand Gil, maybe he would better understand the change that had come over Peter.

Soon Henry passed the hulking, black shadow of a brick farmhouse. He felt it as much as he saw it, heard the change in the reverberation of the sound of his steps. The Jenny was tied down in the next pasture, which was still hidden in the blanket of darkness that swallowed everything more than five feet in front of his face.

He found the gate more by touch than sight. After he let himself through, he walked toward the far side of the field, stumbling and twisting an ankle more than once on rough ground that he could easily have navigated in the daylight.

Gil had mentioned on occasion he'd had folks help themselves to bits and pieces of his unattended plane — which accounted for his tying down far as he could get from the road, in the shadow of a cluster of trees. He'd said he didn't know if people wanted souvenirs or what, but he *did know* it made his life a damn sight more difficult to return to discover a missing magneto switch, altimeter, or control stick. Once he'd come back to find the propeller gone. Times like that, he lost days waiting for a part to come by train.

Henry finally saw the black outline of the wings against the grass — close. Startlingly close. The grass was wet, the ground boggy under his feet. He wondered if it would be too soft for Gil to take off in the morning. Wouldn't Cora be disappointed —

He hit the ground face-first, teeth clacking, breath leaving in one huff. A weight landed on his back and a hand pressed against the back of his head, driving his face, nose to chin, deeper into the soft ground.

He opened his mouth and it filled with mud.

He couldn't breathe.

Fighting the urge to flail, he braced his hands by his chest and drew his knees as far beneath him as he could. He heaved his belly off the ground and threw himself to one side. Not far, but enough to topple whoever was on his back. As the man beside him scrambled to right himself, Henry threw himself on top of him, determined not to let him get away with one of Jenny's vital parts.

The man thrashed. His hands found Henry's face. Thumbs pressed against his eyelids, pushing his eyeballs deep into their sockets. The pressure sharp, building.

Henry grabbed at the hands, pulled the wrists. No use. He balled his fist and took a wild swing, landing a solid punch on the side of the man's head.

"Fuck!" A confusion-laced groan rode out on a ragged, booze-soaked breath.

Well, Christ. "Gil! It's me, Henry." Henry slid off and they sat thigh to thigh. He swiped the mud from his mouth with his shirtsleeve. When he put his teeth together, grit ground between them. He spat a couple of times but it was still there.

Gil sat up slowly. "You're supposed to be at the damned hotel."

"So are you."

For several minutes they sat. Gil's breathing evened out. Henry's limbs eventually stopped trembling.

"I'd think a shout would be enough to scare off someone trying to steal a control stick," Henry said. "Suffocating the poor bastard in the mud seems a might extreme." He'd meant the words as a joke, but the truth of Gil's intent sank in. A chill ran over Henry's skin.

Sounding uncharacteristically rattled, Gil said, "It's not . . . I . . . I didn't . . . I wasn't . . ."

"Here," Henry finished for him. "You weren't here. Like in the hall at Cora's house."

After a few minutes of silence, Gil got to his feet and reached out a hand to help Henry up. "Sorry."

Gil went and sat near the tail of the Jenny.

Henry followed and sat next to him. "The war?" When he blinked, he saw Peter's scratchy writing on that tattered, muddy letter; *Truly hell on earth.* "That's where you were, wasn't it?"

The weight of Gil's sigh told Henry it was.

Tonight had gotten him to thinking. People generally fell into two categories: ones you wanted to be near, and ones you wanted to give a wide berth. Gil's behavior should place him in the second category. He was gruff and distant. He didn't seem to particularly care if anyone liked him. Yet Henry was compelled to stick with him — and not just because he offered a place to hide. It was because of Peter. Gil was nothing like Henry's charismatic brother. Yet when he looked at Gil, he saw war. Peter's war.

"What was it like over there?" Gil was Henry's chance to fill the blank space in his brother's life. Peter had been his parent, his teacher, his best friend — and the keeper of their mother's memory. Ma had died when Henry was just six; too young for many recollections to survive. But Peter had kept her alive, sharing stories of her life, telling him just what Ma would think of this or that if she were still here. He and Peter had been more than brothers. And they did not have secrets. Ever. That's probably why Henry had eagerly accepted the wartime fantasy Peter had spun. If not for the discovery of that final letter, Henry might have lived forever believing Peter's war life had been lived almost completely away from the fighting, filled with nothing but camaraderie and dedication up until a quick, unquestioning patriotic end.

Gil shook his head. "It's over and done."

Henry was half-surprised that Gil didn't get up and stalk off. That he didn't wasn't quite an invitation to cross the threshold, but at least it was an unlatched door. "Is it? Over?"

"More over than I deserve it to be."

"What's that supposed to mean?"

"It means I shouldn't have made it home. I made some bad decisions. And others paid for them."

"I'm pretty sure war comes from bad decisions — and others *always* pay for them."

Gil sat silent.

After a moment, Henry said, "I lost my brother in France. At Belleau Wood." He rubbed his forehead with the heel of his hand, as if he could scrub away the false images Peter had planted; the adventure of seeing a new country, life with a family of soldier-brothers positioned far away from the danger, idle hours filled with jokes and high jinks.

"He was a marine, then?"

"Yes." Henry gave a scoff. "Oh, I know he lied to us — to me. I just want a better picture of what war is really like. I've read some military accounts, seen photos in the newspaper. But what he *lived* . . . I have no idea. And don't just say 'hell.' Everybody says that."

"Why in God's name do you need to know? Your brother didn't want you to."

"Because I was just a kid then! If I'd been older, he would have been honest with me — that's the way it was between us. I owe him the respect of acknowledging what he went through." Henry paused, his throat constricting. "Without him —" His voice broke and he sounded like the scared little kid he didn't want to be anymore. What would his life have been like without Peter; with Ma gone and Pa so . . . so closed off? Henry found himself on the verge of tears. He hadn't cried over Peter for years.

Gil sat quietly for a long while. Henry imagined that door Gil had left ajar was inching closer to latching. And then, his brooding voice slipped softly into the silence. "Belleau Wood. The marines took a hell of a beating those first days. I can't even imagine. . . ." He stopped and swallowed hard. "It was a waste, you know. All of it. The blood. The destruction . . . And for what?" His voice rose. "Promises were *not* kept. Nothing changed."

"My brother said something like that in his last letter — the one he had Pa hide from me. That it didn't make any difference."

"Your brother had it right."

"Maybe. But there's this whole part of his life that I don't know anything about. It makes it worse . . . not knowing."

Silent seconds stretched into a minute, maybe two, before Gil finally said, "I was just a green kid who wanted to fly — had ever since I saw Lincoln Beachey race a Curtiss Pusher plane against a car at a racetrack in Columbus when I was fifteen." Henry heard the awe of the boy Gil must have been in his voice. He fell silent for a bit. As much as Henry wanted to press for more about the war, he didn't interrupt Gil's memory that seemed to hold wonder instead of wounds. Henry got the impression there wasn't much of Gil's past that was like that.

Finally he went on, "I went over there before we were in the war, joined the French *armée de l'air.*" He rubbed his hands together just beneath his chin; Henry heard the sandpaper roughness. "I didn't go for any noble cause. I did it to run away." An edge of self-loathing was in his voice. "And I just wanted to be around planes."

Running from what? Those dangerous words were on Henry's tongue, but he managed to stop them before they left his lips and got turned right back at him.

Gil drew in a deep breath and exhaled loudly. "Air service was different than ground soldiering. I didn't live in the trenches. I wasn't shelled incessantly. I didn't slog a hundred miles in the rain on muddy roads. We fliers didn't even leave our billets when the weather didn't cooperate. I flew my patrols and returned to the airfield, got fairly steady meals, and slept in a mostly dry cot." He shook his head. "I can't help you. It wasn't the same."

Henry knew things had happened to Gil, things that made him tense and vigilant even in his sleep. "But you saw."

Gil closed his eyes. "Oh, yes. I saw." His eyes opened again. "You don't want to hear any of it. Your brother was right about that, too."

"I do. I want to know what his days and nights were like. Nobody who wasn't there can help me. I . . . I know it was bad."

"Bad?" A bitter, breathy laugh reached across the darkness and slapped Henry's face. "Just don't blame me for your nightmares." Gil sounded as if he were getting ready to teach a child a spiteful lesson, one to prove curiosity comes to no good. "I wasn't a fighter pilot — just so you know. I flew reconnaissance patrols — just a taxi for a photographer most of the time. Sometimes I few artillery observation." He turned to face Henry, the whites of his eyes showing an eerie blue-gray in the darkness. "So stop goddamn glorifying me when you're hawking rides."

Henry knew Gil wanted him to argue,

176

wanted to divert the conversation. But Henry was too close to filling in the gap in Peter's life to fall for distractions. For years Henry had spent sleepless nights imagining Peter playing cards on the ship to France; Peter climbing a bell tower of an ancient church to serve as lookout for an enemy miles and miles away; Peter walking a foreign landscape in step with his soldier-brothers; Peter dying in a place called Belleau Wood — a name so beautiful it conjured images of his brother lying down on the soft forest floor, folding his hands over his chest, and falling peacefully into an everlasting sleep. Henry wanted . . . no, he *needed* to replace these foolish, childish memories with the reality of Peter's last months. So he waited.

Finally he prompted, "My nightmares are waiting to be fed."

"I was probably never in the same place as your brother."

"Tell me what *you* saw." Even if it didn't give Henry any true insight into Peter's last days, it would at least offer a more realistic picture than what Peter had painted . . . and it might help Henry figure out what made Gil so taciturn one minute and so dangerously jumpy the next.

Gil scrubbed his hands over his face,

beard stubble rasping as a background to the crickets and tree frogs. He shifted the way he sat, drawing his knees up and linking his arms around them. "I heard one guy describe the artillery noise not as a sound — because after hours and hours without a break your hearing went — but as a pulverizing beating of your chest, it compressed your lungs and changed the rhythm of your heart. I can believe it. When artillery guns fired at our planes, an explosion within twenty yards nearly shook me out of the cockpit. The first time it happened, I thought the wings would blow off." Gil said the last words with a dismissive laugh, but with an undercurrent of strain that made Henry glad it was too dark to see the finer details of the look on Gil's face.

It seemed that if artillery was firing at his airplane, his patrols weren't exactly the safe air-taxi rides he wanted Henry to believe. Maybe downplaying the danger was a habit of everyone who lived through war. Maybe it was the only way they maintained a shred of sanity.

"I suppose," Gil said quietly, "the worst thing on the ground was gas."

Henry wondered if talking about it would release Gil from some of his secret torment. Sometimes the things you kept bottled inside festered; the only cure was to let them out into the air.

"From my nice, safe altitude," he went on, as if he were talking only to himself, "I could see the spots where the canisters landed — the plumes moving with the air currents, widening as they spread across the battlefield. They looked like thick smoke from a dozen brushfires." He stopped.

Henry waited.

"The first time I saw it, I circled until the gas dissipated, then made a low pass so the photographer could take some shots. God knows why we thought our air-to-ground shots could tell command anything that those poor bastards on the ground couldn't." The sound of Gil's swallow was dry and constricted. "I couldn't hear the screams over the noise of the engine, but I didn't need to. There was nothing down there but writhing pain and chaotic movement."

After the war, Henry had seen a picture of a line of survivors of a gas attack, shuffling along, following one another hand to shoulder, their eyes bandaged and their skin blistered. Although each man's face was half-covered by white gauze, Henry had seen Peter behind each and every bandage.

"We were ready to pull up when I saw a

man crawling through the mud right toward the German line. He had to have been blinded. I buzzed low — maybe fifty feet — and yelled down, telling him to turn around. My photographer shouted in French. I don't know if the man didn't hear . . . couldn't hear . . . was out of his mind with pain . . . The Germans started taking shots at us. Then at him — I don't think they would have seen him if I hadn't drawn attention. The soldier kept crawling, crawling, like he was headed to salvation . . . maybe he was. A bullet finally caught him in the head." The last words had a take-that tone, as if Henry should be so repulsed he would never ask anything about the war again. "*That's* what your brother went through. Cold and mud and fear and pain with a bullet at the end of it."

Horrified? Who wouldn't be? But Henry had been prepared for the horror. He hadn't been prepared for the rush of shame he felt for pushing Gil into painful memories; shame and sympathy. Would he want anyone to do that to Peter if he'd survived and put it behind him?

"You had to try," Henry said. "Even if it did make the enemy" — he couldn't bring himself to say *Germans* — "notice him."

After a moment Gil said, "It was a man's

life. My intentions don't mean shit."

Henry didn't know what to say, so he kept quiet.

"Glory went to the flying aces — Rickenbacker, Gillet, Lufbery. And they deserved it; I'm not saying they didn't. But the soldiers living like sewer rats in trenches filled with water, having their skin and eyes seared with gas, *they* were heroes. Your brother was a hero." Gil turned to face Henry. "I was just a fucking flier."

Suddenly Gil stood up, but did not stalk off. Instead he peered in the direction of the road. "Who's there?"

A dog barked. Mercury shot out of the dark and jumped into Henry's lap. He smelled like soap. His fur felt smooth, mat-free.

"Well, well. You fellas having a party and didn't invite me?" When Cora got close enough, Henry saw she was wearing her pants and knee boots again. "Or maybe we're *all* afraid the plane will take off and leave without us in the morning."

Henry cringed. That had been exactly why he'd left that warm, dry hotel room. But the truth was, their presence did nothing to ensure Gil's cooperation. He could jump in that plane and disappear anytime he felt like it. Mercury's Daredevils! Henry should have shut that idea down the minute it came out of Cora's mouth. In reaching too far to cover his own tracks, had he ruined his chances to keep traveling with Gil? And he'd topped it off by dragging the man through the hell of his worst memories.

"I didn't hear the motorcycle," Henry said.

"That's because Gil rode it out here . . . at least it'd better be with Gil."

For a long moment, Gil stayed silent. Henry could hear his own blood throbbing through his ears as his gaze shifted between the two shadowy figures, surprised by the cold dread that gripped his heart when he thought this might be the end. Chicago was less and less appealing. No matter how much he liked the Cubs.

Gil's rough breathing gradually smoothed out. "It's here. Best get some sleep, Henry. Cora's got a crowd coming in the morning." It was said with minimal condescension, and Henry's muscles stopped quivering.

From that moment on, Henry didn't even miss that nice, soft hotel bed.

With Mercury curled at his side, the nightmare images Gil had painted stayed away. A new and unexpected warmth came over Henry as he lay on that boggy ground, listening to Gil's liquor-induced snores and Cora's soft sleep sighs. For the first time in years, he looked forward to tomorrow.

7

The grass lost the emerald green of spring and the corn grew tall. By Independence Day, Henry's fear of the past's walking up and tapping him on the shoulder had quieted to an ever-present, but distant, hum. Getting out of Indiana had probably helped. He'd stopped learning the names of the towns they passed through; they were here and gone so quickly they'd all begun to run together.

Gil had relaxed his rule about nobody's touching the Jenny but him. Now nobody touched the Jenny but him *or Henry.* He'd even gone so far as to teach Henry how to pilot the plane — with the threat of a long and painful death if Cora found out. Although Gil acknowledged Henry's gift with machinery, he always did his own walk-around before each flight session — oiled the rocker arms, checked the oil sump, and primed the carburetor. *You don't hand someone else a half-loaded revolver and have them take a shot at you. And you don't let another man preflight your plane.* Henry took no offense.

Cora had stopped sleeping with the hammer hidden beside her — even after Henry had given her fair warning not to startle Gil out of a sleep — which just showed how naive she truly was. Even though the three of them spent day and night together, she didn't know any more about either his or Gil's past than she had that first night. It surprised him that she hadn't tried to find out; most girls were full of questions. It also made him suspicious. He knew why *he* didn't pry into people's pasts. The crowds generally came, tromping down the purple clover and yellow wood sorrel in field after field. Some days people shoved money into his hand in a near-desperate way, as if they were in danger of being left on the sidelines of a once-in-a-lifetime opportunity. He supposed for most of these folks that's exactly what this was, once in a lifetime. And so the three of them were making enough money to keep the machines running and to feed themselves. Henry considered it acceptable. Gil thought it a cornucopia. Cora insisted they were missing opportunities.

Early on, Gil had told Henry and Cora

that as long as they were all working together, they would both get a 30 percent share of the take after expenses were met, including maintaining the machines and their meals. Henry thought it more than fair, especially since he was only contributing his mechanical skills and not a machine.

As the weeks passed, things were changing step by step. Mercury's Daredevils (despite Gil's refusal to say the words, the name had stuck) was in flaming yellow and red on the sides of the airplane and on the handbills Cora had sweet-talked out of a young printer in Rockville. (The paint on the plane came about less from sweet talk and more from a water-on-stone wearing down of Gil's resistance.) They now had a routine, a schedule of events for their shows.

Henry had modified a pair of goggles for Mercury (Cora had dubbed them doggles). If she put on her leather jacket and his goggles weren't on yet, he ran and got them and commenced a jumping, whining fit until they were on his head. She'd been teaching him some good tricks both on and off the motorcycle. He could now ride on the little seat over the gas tank that Henry had crafted for him. The dog still preferred riding inside Cora's jacket. Henry couldn't blame him — for multiple reasons.

That they were charging *only* for plane rides had been a sticking point with Cora. At their last stop she'd set out a can with a sign asking for what she called "tips." She'd said — with a whole lot of wanna-make-something-out-of-it in her voice — that it was the only way people could show their appreciation for her daredevil act. Amazingly, Gil hadn't risen to the bait. It had been the first glimmer of hope (false as it turned out) that things would settle down between the two of them.

They were somewhere in central Illinois getting ready to perform at an oval, dirt racetrack used for sulkies and motorcycles. The main attraction, other than the selling of rides, was a heavily publicized race between man and woman, airship and motorcycle. A true competition between the sexes. It had been Cora's idea — a reenactment of their first meeting. The stakes, also devised by Cora, would not only establish the equality of the sexes, but the loser would be forced to "challenge the Grim Reaper" by submitting to dangers at the hands of the winner. If Gil lost, he would "ride the bucking and swerving mechanical bull" (the handlebars of Cora's motorcycle) as she cut didoes and thrilled the spectators with "terrifying speed." If

Cora lost, she would put her "delicate feminine physique in mortal peril" as she sat on the wing while Gil performed "death-defying feats in the air." Cora had a way with the ballyhoo.

Gil hadn't been at all happy when he'd discovered the stakes she'd advertised. Henry was pretty sure it wasn't because he was afraid to ride on the handlebars of Cora's motorcycle. Gil's acknowledgment that she was every bit as much a daredevil as he was coming hard and slow. Henry thought perhaps it was compounded because their motivations for taking life in hand were so different.

Henry sat across the fire from Cora, a position he repeatedly chose. He could look at her without drawing attention to the sad fact that he couldn't keep his eyes off her — it was getting worse by the day. Luckily Gil hadn't noticed. And Cora, well, she was all-business, focused solely on building this show into something more than a second-class act held together by spit and determination.

She got to her feet. Gil's eyes came open.

She leaned over him and poked him in the center of his forehead. "If you let me win tomorrow, I swear I will skin you alive. Be a man and accept this challenge with integrity."

"Oh, I have no integrity." Gil stood and looked down at her. "But you won't win. You're just a girl." As he turned and walked away, he threw Henry a rare smile.

Cora's fists settled on her hips. "Keep thinking that, buddy! Right up until your fine dinner of crow," she hurled at his back.

She sat back down right next to Henry.

He thought of his first sight of her, tearing across that field, determined to win that race come hell or high water. "Is this need to win something Gil brings out in you, or were you born this way?"

She grinned. "Oh, I was definitely born this way."

His stomach knotted. "Don't let your pride get you killed."

"Pride? Seriously, Kid, pride's got nothing to do with it."

"What is it then?"

She sat staring into the low-flickering flames for a bit. "I don't know what to call it. It's basic, primal; like hunger or reacting to pain. I think it all started with Jonathan. He loved to show off by doing things I was too little to do. That's why I started doing handstands on the rafters in the stables, because Jonathan could run across them faster, but he was too scared to try a handstand." She smiled. "It was always so tedious when girls visited the Hudson Valley house; it was all about pushing dolls in prams and having boring tea parties. But when they were boys! Of course, they always assumed they could beat me at everything.

"We had a pair of giant Norway spruce trees that were great for climbing competitions. I always got higher. Then I'd set the top of the tree to swaying. I was the pirate queen in the crow's nest, and those boys would have to do whatever I told them to. It was great." She sighed. "Maybe I'm really a boy inside."

Henry looked over at her. "Oh, I seriously doubt there's anything boyish anywhere in you."

She cast him a sideways look. "Well now. I suppose I'll take that as a compliment." She waved toward her pants and boots. "Considering how I dress."

Henry decided to leave it right there. He stood. "You'd better get some sleep."

She reached out for him to give her a hand up. He pulled her to standing, then spent the next few heartbeats staring into her eyes. "Good night, Cora." His mouth was unnaturally dry.

"Night, Kid." She slapped his shoulder.

He slunk to his blanket like a kicked puppy.

Henry set up the race finish line with a rope decorated with checkered flags rigged with a thin thread to break away when tugged, suspended between the top of the grandstand and a tall pole near the inside of the oval. It was just high enough that Gil could nab it with his wheels as he raced above Cora's head. Another finish-line rope was at motorcycle height.

Gil stood with his hands on his hips, looking up into the overflowing grandstand. "By God, you do seem to know how to get a crowd, I'll give you that."

Cora looked up at him with a smile. "Lookey there. And you didn't even have to spit those words out from between clenched teeth."

"I'm starting to think we might be able to do pretty well in a city," Henry offered. "Maybe Chicago."

A glimmer of panic in Cora's eyes was quickly overcome by a bold smile. "Let's not push it, Kid. Remember, Gil made it plain, he's a barnstormer — and he owns the Jenny."

Then she spun on her heel and walked away.

Henry recognized the anxiety in her eyes. Fear of discovery, of exposure. Logic said Cora should be jumping at the chance to hit a city like Chicago. It was a curious reaction, for sure. Of course, he was in no position to ask questions, lest he be asked some himself.

The airship/motorcycle race would be the grand finale of the show. Prior to that, it was business as usual. The motorcycle revved up and Cora signaled Henry to pick up the megaphone and announce her first stunt.

She did some tricks with Mercury on the motorcycle, saving his on-the-ground doggie antics for entertaining folks waiting while Gil was giving rides.

When she took a break, she came straight to Henry. "You know, I've been thinking. You're so good with modifications, I want you to work on a way to lock the throttle on the motorcycle."

"Lock it? To keep it off?"

She looked at him as if he were stupid. "Not off! What good would that do? On. So I can let go of the handlebars. And I'll need something I can engage to help stabilize the front wheel — you know, make it harder for it to turn."

He knew where this was going. "No.

Impossible."

"Kid, you're a horrible liar and a great inventor. You can do it."

"You have no business riding a motorcycle standing up on the seat. That's what you're aiming at, right?"

"Only when we've got a smooth enough surface. I've already been practicing doing a handstand on the handlebars, but it's really tough to keep the throttle just right."

She was crazy. "Too impractical. Every surface will need a different speed, and probably a different gear, to keep you upright and not have the motorbike run away."

"Did you just say *impractical*? Good golly, Kid, everything we do is impractical." She started back to the motorcycle. "Time to light it up."

Gil had landed and was fueling up. It was Cora's turn again.

As Henry prepared the Flaming Arch of Death, he was already figuring in his head how to give Cora what she wanted.

After a fast lap around the track, she stopped in front of the grandstand and unzipped Mercury from her jacket. She sat him on a little platform on the ground that was just above seat height of the cycle.

Henry picked up the megaphone and

played it up to the audience. "The next stunt is so dangerous, Cora Rose, woman daredevil, will not risk the life of her faithful companion, Mercury."

Mercury spun around in place on the platform, stopping every third revolution to paw at Cora, trying to get her to pick him up. She made a show of soothing him and kissing him good-bye. Then she took off with a spray of dirt and went to the fourth turn of the track.

"Easy, boy," Henry said through the megaphone as he walked past Mercury. "If she makes it through, she'll come back and get you." He walked back to the arch. He'd crafted it out of a lightweight, collapsible metal frame (for transport), to which he attached tightly wound kerosene-soaked rags. When it was first finished, he'd wanted to do the first test run. But Cora had argued there was no difference between the combustibility of men and the combustibility of women; and she was the one who had to be able to do it in a show. Of course, she'd won.

"And now, ladies and gentlemen, if you'll keep your eyes on the young lady on the motorcycle as she attempts to speed through the Flaming Arch of Death." Henry lit the narrow arch. Flames licked high. "As you can see, there is only a narrow opening, which is completely filled with flames, above, below, and on both sides. Now, let us pause and offer a quick prayer for Cora Rose's safety." Henry bowed his head. Mercury buried his nose in his paws with his tail still in the air. Men's hats came off and the rumble of the crowd silenced.

Henry raised his hand over his head. Cora revved the engine. The kid Henry was paying fifty cents started a dramatic roll on his drum.

Henry dropped his arm.

The motorcycle roared down the straightaway.

"Oh, no!" Henry shouted through the megaphone. "No! Mercury, stay!"

Mercury was pawing at the air, standing on the very edge of the platform.

As Cora flew by, the dog leaped.

The crowd gasped.

"It's too late!" Henry shouted.

Cora caught Mercury, doubled over him, and barreled right through the arch.

Every straw boater, fedora, and flowered hat in the grandstands turned toward where Cora stopped and put her feet on the ground. She held Mercury in front of her face for a moment as if lecturing him, then lifted him up over her head.

Mercury yipped and waved the way she'd taught him.

The applause was so loud, Henry could feel it in his chest. "Ladies and gentlemen! A true death-defying miracle! Cora Rose and her faithful dog, Mercury! Next time we'll have to tie that little feller up!"

Henry announced the race. Gil took off in the Jenny and did a loop and a spiral before he disappeared into the west.

Cora did a lap on the track. Henry's narration kept the drama high as he explained she was getting warmed up. "We've come into a modern age, for sure. Women have the vote. Now we have to ask, what's next? A woman president?" Men booed. "Ah, now, gentlemen, it's time to put something else to the test. Can a mere woman master a machine well enough to beat a man in an aeroplane? Impossible? Well, ladies and gents, keep your eyes on the sky in the west. History is in the making!" Henry explained the race would be run down the front straightaway, a competition with no turns, just as their initial meeting had been. Although, Henry said, Cora had been at a keen disadvantage then, racing over an uneven pasture.

"If Captain Gilchrist isn't at the start line in time, then it's too bad for him."

Just as Cora rounded the fourth turn, Gil's plane swooped low.

Henry was transported back to that day on the Fessler farm. The sight of those two machines matched against one another still set his heart racing.

It was anyone's race. As it had been that day.

Just short of the finish, he heard Gil throttle back ever so slightly.

Cora's string of flags snapped free and trailed her around the first curve.

"Sorry, gents!" Henry called. "Looks like our time as masters of machines has come to an end. Let's hear it for Cora Rose, woman daredevil, faster than a man in an aeroplane."

Henry thought he heard more daintily gloved hands clapping this time than men's bare palms.

After Gil landed, Cora stomped up to him. "You'll do anything to keep me out of that plane, won't you?"

Gil looked perplexed. "You think I'd *let* you win? In front of all of these people? Concede for all men around the world?"

She smiled falsely and waved to the crowd. "Henry?"

Henry knew she couldn't have heard the

break in throttle. Gil's stern gaze landed on him.

"You won fair and square. Now see what you can do to toss his ass off of that motorcycle. The people are waiting."

According to Cora's rules, the loser's penance had a three-minute time limit. Cora used every second of it. By the end, Gil's palms were raw and his legs black-and-blue. As she stopped to let him off, she said, "Next time I *win* a race, I'm going to think of something much more . . . damaging." Then she gunned the engine and sped off.

The dirt sprayed both Henry and Gil.

The crowd roared.

At the end of that day, Cora asked Henry about the take. "A hundred and ten dollars in rides, plus fifteen extra dollars for kids on someone's lap."

Gil nodded. "A good day."

"And?" Cora had quirked an eyebrow at Henry.

"And the tips are in pennies, nickels, and dimes. You'll have to count them yourself." Henry felt he'd owed Gil a little solidarity.

"If you and Gil each get thirty percent of the tips, you should help count." Even as she said it, she stuck out her hand with a resigned look on her face.

Henry handed the one-pound coffee can over. It was so full a few coins slid off the top and hit the ground.

"Golly" — she hefted the weight in both hands — "people must think Mercury and I are worth something."

"I didn't say you two aren't worth anything," Gil said. "Hell, everybody loves a dog. What I *said* was, it's impossible to charge admission when all people have to do is stand on the other side of the fence and see everything."

"Today we could have charged for the grandstand."

Gil groaned.

She tapped her chin. "Hey, what if we blocked off the road when we're in a farm field? People coming to the show pay. Those traveling on through don't."

"Don't be ridiculous," Gil said.

"Well, we don't have to make it so easy for them," Cora said. "At least we can perform in a pasture farther from a main road. We could charge people to come down the farm lane. Or" — she was almost breathless with her idea — "what about exclusively booking our act with county fairs and racetracks? They already have gates. And we'd be guaranteed a crowd."

Henry cringed at the word *booking.* That

meant something planned. Something permanent. A commitment. All things sure to set Gil off.

"No," Gil said.

"You can't just keep saying no without a reason. You're not the only one in this act."

Gil looked her in the eyes. "I can be."

Henry finally stepped between them. "Let's get the Jenny tied down. Then we need to get fuel out here for tomorrow."

After they'd turned their backs, Cora rattled the coins in her can. Her version of the last word.

Three days later they were in yet another Illinois town that had proven fruitful enough to warrant a second day. Early in the morning Cora came dragging some scavenged boards into the pasture with the idea of Henry's building her a ramp. There wasn't enough lumber to build it right, so he refused. He shouldn't have been surprised when she started to work on it herself. In the end he figured her chances of coming out in one piece were better if he constructed it, so he did.

At least Gil wasn't around to grouse about it. He'd gotten in a dark mood — dark even for Gil — last night when one of the men from the local VFW had tried to get him to come and talk to the veterans at the local post. Cora had tried to coax him out of his glumness, an effort that backfired completely. Soon after that he'd disappeared.

"This is a bad idea," Henry said as he looked over his best effort with the materials he had. "It's way too narrow and too steep."

"It's good enough to at least give a try. Then we can figure out how to improve it."

"I *know* how to improve it. No need to risk your neck."

"I'll take it slow and easy."

"It's a ramp. Slow and easy will just land your front wheel first and you're guaranteed a crash. You have to hit the ground rearwheel first — both level at the very least."

"I know that."

He looked at her. "But did you before I said it?"

"Good Lord, Henry, I've spent every day for over two months on that motorbike. I know how to handle it. Besides, today's my birthday. Even Mother lets me have my way on my birthday."

Henry had almost forgotten about celebrating birthdays. Ever since Peter had left, Henry's had passed unnoticed by him or anyone else. The last one that counted,

Henry's tenth, Peter had made a cake that had fallen apart when he'd taken it out of the pan. He'd poured icing all over the broken-up pile, and he and Henry had eaten the entire thing right off the serving plate in one sitting.

"Well, happy birthday, Cora. I'll take you to a bakery for a cake later. But right now I'll take the first run at that ramp."

"Bushwa!" He didn't know why she thought saying that was any better than saying *bullshit* outright. "It's my stunt. What good does it do me to know *you* can do it?"

He'd been through this argument enough to know it was pointless. The first time had been when he'd tried to switch with her when they traveled from town to town. A woman alone out on the road was just foolish. She'd stuck to her guns, accusing Henry of trying to give Gil a reason to boot her from "the team." When he'd appealed to Gil, he'd gotten, "She's woman enough to live up to her bargain. No special treatment." It had taken two weeks before Henry's gut had grown accustomed to the wait for her safe arrival.

She handed Mercury over. Then she rode the motorcycle to the far end of the pasture.

Henry shouted, "Be sure and hit it square!" She waved, but he doubted she'd heard him.

When she revved the engine, Henry's pulse accelerated, too. The longer they were together, the more stunts she did, the more nervous he got for her. It seemed counter to logic.

She raced across the field. It was too rough for a stunt like this, even with a decent ramp.

Twenty feet. Fifteen. Ten.

Her approach angle was off!

She swerved at the last second, racing past the ramp.

Henry waved her to come back, but she rode to the far end of the pasture again.

As Henry watched with a dust-dry mouth, she came at it again. Better approach.

Twenty feet. Ten. Five.

She hit the ramp square and was airborne. The engine whined high. Henry had a flash of her unmoving body floating facedown in that pond. *I can't lose you now.*

She landed on the front wheel. The handlebars jerked to the side. The bike got sideways and slid out from under her. She hit the ground and rolled like a rag doll.

"Cora!" Henry set the dog down and ran, his heart in his throat.

She was on her side, facing away from

him. The motorcycle engine chugged to a stop.

He slid the last three feet on his knees.

Just as he reached her, she rolled onto her back. "Uuuuugggghhhhh."

She was blinking under raised brows, as if trying to get her vision to clear.

"Hold still!"

Mercury lay down and put his face next to hers and laid his head on his paws. His questioning brown eyes shifted between Henry and Cora.

"I'm . . . I . . . I'm all right." She blew out a breath that puffed her cheeks.

"How do you know? Your eyeballs haven't stopped rattling around in your head yet."

She started to sit up.

He grabbed her shoulders and held her down. "Hold on." He needed a minute to get his heart tapped back down into his chest.

That she lay back without a bunch of sass told him just how shaken up she was. He unbuckled and pulled off her leather helmet, then explored her head for lumps with his fingertips. From there he checked her neck, arms, and legs, running his hands over her limbs, gently checking flexibility and probing for broken bones.

"See? Fine," she said, seeming to get some

of her starch back.

Mercury inched closer and licked her cheek.

"Unzip your jacket."

"Why, Henry, you rascal . . ."

He rolled his eyes. "I want to check your ribs."

"That's the worst line I've ever heard from a fella trying to get in some heavy petting."

"Shut up." But now that she'd said that, when he put his hands on her midsection and ran them over her sides, all he could think of was the way she'd looked in that wet blouse. When he pushed that image away, the sight of her in her fancy dance dress crept right in and took up residence in his head. "This hurt?" He gave her sides a squeeze.

She kicked her legs and swatted his hands away. "Tickles."

At that he pronounced her intact enough to get up.

"How's the motorcycle?" she asked as he helped her slowly to her feet.

She wobbled. He wrapped his arms around her and held her to his chest. "Just stand here for a second." He pressed his cheek against the top of her head and closed his eyes. After all of his years alone, he'd forgotten how good holding another person could feel.

She pulled away slightly and looked up at him. "You're shaking." Touching his cheek, she said, "And white as a ghost."

Mercury jumped up and gave a bark. It brought Henry back to his senses before he lost his mind completely and kissed her. There were a hundred reasons why he couldn't let that happen.

Letting her go, he said, "I get a little shaken up watching bullheaded recklessness resulting in near death."

She blinked and the soft kiss-me look left her eyes. "You're being melodramatic. I wasn't even hurt."

"Keep doing stupid crap like this and your luck will run out."

"The ramp worked! I just needed more speed and to shift my weight a little more."

"No. No. No. No more on this ramp. You'll have to wait until we can build a proper one."

"If we spend money on it, we'll want to knock it down and take it with us. And we can't do that without a truck."

This kind of talk always led to the flint-and-steel sparks between her and Gil. Expand. More exciting stunts. More daring exhibitions. She sang that song morning and night. Some of her ideas were crazy, sure, but a lot of them were good. But Henry was the only man balancing the canoe, so he had to act accordingly. He'd grown accustomed to his role as referee and peacemaker, quietly nudging Gil this way and Cora that. But he had a growing feeling Gil had just about hit his limit. Henry feared the next clash would spell doom for their partnership.

Reason 101 why he couldn't let himself fall for Cora.

Gil returned just before showtime, looking like a man who'd spent his night making love to a bottle of bootleg. Henry wanted to take the man by the shoulders and give him a solid shake, one that would no doubt send Gil's hungover head off his shoulders. If people saw him like this, their show was doomed. Goddammit, didn't he know what was at stake?

It hit Henry just then. Gil didn't *care*. None of this mattered to him.

For some reason that made Henry angrier. He gritted his teeth and breathed deeply before he did something that would just make things worse.

Gil probably wouldn't even have noticed the ramp if Cora hadn't marched right up to him and said, "Don't even waste your breath trying to kill this idea. It's going to be a great draw. I'm thinking of raising the Flaming Arch so I can vault from the ramp right through it."

For crying out loud. They weren't even incorporating the ramp yet, let alone adding fire to it. Did she think getting a preemptive volley in was some sort of achievement in itself?

The truth was, Gil didn't usually actively object if additions were quietly incorporated; approval by abstention. But for some reason Cora felt the need to go after everything head-to-head. For a woman with a fancy education and fine social graces, she sure didn't grasp the concept of finesse. Or maybe she just liked fighting. Henry couldn't tell for sure.

Gil stared at her with bloodshot eyes. Before he gathered his ammunition for a return barrage, Henry stepped between them. "You look like hell. We need to get you cleaned up. You're intimidating enough to the customers without this added air of . . . degenerate drunkard." He nudged Gil toward their camp setup. "I left water by your shaving kit."

After Gil walked away, taking the fumes of residual alcohol with him, Cora asked, "Why do you always step in like that?"

"Why do you always want to fight?"

Cora looked momentarily startled by the biting anger in Henry's voice. She seemed to weigh her options. Then Henry saw belligerence win over good sense. "You *never* want to go against him. Why?"

The show was in less than a half hour. Someone had to put an end to this foolishness.

"He's been nice to me." He sounded like the pathetic orphan he once was.

"Well, isn't that just ducky. I suppose I haven't? Honestly, what has Flyboy done for you, other than keep you from your job in Chicago?"

She referred to that job as if it lived in the same universe as unicorns. Which was pretty darned accurate.

"Come on, Henry. These bush hounds are eating up our little exhibition. We can make this big if you'll back me up once in a while. Who wouldn't want a life like this over working twelve hours a day, six days a week, in a smelly meat-processing plant or shoveling coal in a steel mill? There's no shame in admitting you want something and going after it. You need to stop being afraid Gil's going to up and leave you."

"You aren't?"

"If Gil *really* wanted to be alone, he would

have left you standing in Uncle's pasture that first morning." Her smile turned devilish. "Flyboy wants us here. He just won't admit it."

At that moment, Henry understood the real root of his fear, a fear that had grown stronger day by day. It wasn't his worry over losing a place to hide, to reinvent himself. It wasn't missing out on the rare opportunity to work on an airplane, or losing the connection he felt to Peter when he was with Gil. Mercury's Daredevils had become his home. His family.

That awareness brought with it the kind of deep-seated peace he hadn't felt in years. He hadn't even known it was missing until it slipped back into his soul.

On the heels of that realization was the certainty that disaster would soon come to call.

Gil's recovery was remarkable. Even that first customer wouldn't have guessed the man had been out all night drinking. By one o'clock, black Model T's and a few fancier and more colorful makes — Oaklands, Studebakers, Henry even spotted a Pierce-Arrow and a Stutz Bearcat — were parked cheek to jowl with wagons, buggies, and horses along the side of the road. Shops had been closed, fields abandoned. Boys walked prized bicycles through the gate, parking them within eyesight — not that anyone kept eyes on the ground when Gil took to the air and performed loops, spins, and barrel rolls.

The first time Henry had seen Gil do a loop, his ears had told him the carburetor was gravity fed, which meant that when it was upside down the engine didn't get gas. When he'd asked Gil about it during their first day together, he'd said that it wasn't a problem, as long as you got the plane upright while the prop was still turning fast enough to restart the engine.

"And if you don't get it turned over in time?" Henry had asked.

"If I have enough altitude, I can nose it down and use the wind speed to turn the prop." Gil had sounded quite matter-of-fact.

"If you don't have the altitude?"

"I've done plenty of dead-stick landings."

"Dead stick?"

"Prop is wood. No power and it sits there like a dead stick."

"You glide? Steer using those flapper things on the wings and tail?"

Gil had given Henry one of his few true smiles. "You always steer using those 'flapper things.' If you're going to talk airplanes, you need the lingo or you're going to sound like an idiot."

Henry hadn't argued the point, but it seemed an extremely slight risk; so few planes were around he'd probably never come across someone who could tell the difference.

"The flaps on the wings are ailerons. They control banking. The wood posts between the wings are struts. The tail has a rudder behind the vertical stabilizer; it works same as a rudder on a boat." Gil had used his hands to demonstrate the movements. "The stationary crosspiece is the horizontal stabilizer. The flaps on the horizontal piece are the elevators, move the nose up and down."

It had been Henry's first flight lesson. At that moment, he had begun to love the beauty of the whole, not just the wonder of the engine. As he learned more about piloting, his respect for Gil's extraordinary talent in the cockpit grew. He had put that plane into a spin just to teach Henry how to pull it out. Even after the instruction, Henry was pretty sure if *he* ever lost it to a spin, he was just going to be one dead pilot. With increased knowledge came the ability to tell when Gil was pushing too far — even for his skills.

Such as now, when he turned the Jenny upside down while on a much-too-low pass over the field.

Henry stood on his straw bale, megaphone to his mouth, adding ballyhoo to their exhibition. Words died in his mouth. What in the hell was Gil doing?

People went wild, yelling and waiving their hats in the air.

Turn it over. Turn it over. Turn it over. Gil might be good at dead-stick landings, but inverted dead stick was impossible, no matter how good a pilot he was.

At the engine's silence, a unified gasp came from the crowd.

Turn it over. Henry's eyes stayed on the prop. *Over. Roll over.*

Gil finally turned the ship right side up.

Henry's stuttering heartbeat filled his ears. He leaned forward, as if his physical urging could keep the plane's speed up.

Gil was headed straight for dense woods. With no power.

Then the engine caught, thrumming once again. It had only been seconds, but to Henry it had been an eternity.

Gil pulled up and banked left, barely clearing the trees. Cheers and whistles rose after the breath-held quiet of the pasture.

Cora's voice came over Henry's shoulder.

"Now that, Kid, is the monkey's eyebrows . . . to make every one of those people stop breathing like that." She thumped him on the back. "Just think how much better it'll be with a wing walker."

He was surrounded by lunacy. Pure lunacy.

He turned to tell her to forget it, but she was already throwing her leg over the motorcycle and zipping Mercury into her jacket. At least since the dog was with her, he was assured she'd steer clear of that damned ramp.

Henry took up the megaphone again as she and Mercury took the field, starting off with some crowd-pleasing, dirt-tossing figure eights. Cora's uncommon show of female daring was nearly as unique as the appearance of an airplane. When she stopped and the engine idled, Mercury barked and howled for more. The dog was a natural showman, just like Cora. Henry was surrounded by attention-grabbers. This was to his advantage; to most people watching the show he was no more than a hand to take money and a voice in the background.

Gil made a pass overhead. He waggled his wings and flew off, giving Cora the field. She rode balanced with her knee on the seat, then navigated through the course she'd set up that morning, plucking hankies off various obstacles as she raced past.

Then, her routine completed, she rode pell-mell to the end of the field, stopped, and unzipped Mercury from her jacket.

Henry flashed hot. He dropped the megaphone and took off at a run. "No!" She revved the engine twice and took off with a rooster tail of grass clumps and dirt.

She hit the boards good and square and shot off the end. She shifted her weight, landing on the rear wheel. But the motorcycle hit the ground hard, causing her to jerk the handlebars. The front wheel wasn't perfectly straight when it hit the ground. She wobbled wildly, but somehow saved it. She'd only been airborne for about ten feet, but the crowd reacted as if she had flown halfway across the pasture.

Henry's teeth hurt from his clenched jaw. His tight fists pumped as he ran. *Selfish. Spoiled. Bull-goddamned-headed.*

She swung the bike around as she stopped, raising her fists in what Henry was beginning to think of as her Warrior Maiden pose. Her careless attitude blurred his vision.

Mercury barked as he raced up and launched himself into Henry's arms. The jolt brought him back to his senses. He drew up and forced himself to stand there while he drew deep breaths and got ahold of himself.

By the time he and Mercury reached her, she was surrounded by a dozen adoring boys still in knickers. A newspaper photographer was setting up a camera-topped tripod, asking to take her picture. She rolled the motorcycle back on its new stand and held out her hands for Mercury. Henry bit his tongue and handed the dog over. She posed astride the bike with his furry, doggled face sticking out of her jacket. Henry had never seen anyone look so pleased with herself. Which went through him like a red-hot dagger.

Gil landed the Jenny and people finally stopped oohing and aahing over Cora and began to drift away. Henry jerked her aside. "That was so damned stupid!" The words shot from between his clenched teeth. "You could have broken your fool neck."

"It's my neck."

His fingers dug deeper into her arm.

"Ouch!" She tried to pull away, but he held tight.

"Yes, it is." Henry barely refrained from shaking her. "And I reckon you're welcome to break it when no one is looking. But we need to make sure these stunts are going to work every single time before doing them in front of an audience."

"But that's what they like! Daredevils!"

She was so damned green. "They like *the idea* of a daredevil. It's excitement they want; the *possibility* of disaster. But none of these people wants to see a woman get broken to bits. Not one! That kind of publicity can ruin everything. You have big ideas for this show." He pointed a finger in her face, his own face heating up. "Keep that in mind when you get the itch to do something this stupid again. If the newspapers get convinced we're going to kill someone — especially a woman — if they decide to write about our foolish reckless-ness instead of about our amazing show, we're through." *He* was through. Accidents brought investigations . . . and the law.

Her eyes grew wide. "I never thought of it like that."

"Well, think on it." He leaned over her, his breathing rough. "When public opinion turns against you, nothing you do will change the course."

Henry snatched Mercury from her arms and walked away, his hands shaking hard enough that the dog's ears quivered.

"Henry!" she called after him. "Come on. Don't get in such a lather."

He knew better than to stop. He'd been

lucky Mercury had saved him.

Throughout his life, Henry'd had plenty of practice controlling himself. He'd thought himself a calm person, able to weigh out consequences, put reason before reaction. Only lately had he become aware of the danger that lived behind the bars he kept on his emotions. Something had been growing. Building. Once it broke free, it thrashed like a wild beast, wounded and blind.

Henry sneaked out of camp while Gil and Cora were still talking to the hangers-on. The weather had closed in and put their day to an early end, a reprieve for Henry. He needed some time alone to sort himself out. He walked under a gray shroud of sky that draped itself clear to the ground; a hot summer sky that should, but wouldn't, rain. The air smelled of sluggish rivers and his lungs felt clogged with wet cotton. The dense air bent, muffled, and amplified the sounds of birds, of his footsteps, of a barking dog.

He moved through the stifling haze separate from the world. Looking not outward, but in toward his deepest self.

His temper still simmered, just below a boil. Was that the price for locking it away all of his life — a restless soul on the verge of eruption, edgy and volatile?

Airing out the soul posed a certain danger. Open that door just a crack and the currents stirred the cobwebs, revealing the shrouded shapes beneath, things he'd fooled himself into believing he could leave behind.

It was growing dark as he neared town. The thickening of people and vehicles all seemed to be flowing in a single direction, toward a large white tent in the center of a firefly-studded field. The canvas top glowed with light from within. A melody rose and fell, distant and broken, yet the scraps he could hear were familiar. He strained to listen. He knew that song. "What a Friend We Have in Jesus." He stopped, closed his eyes, and could feel his ma on one side and Peter on the other. They'd been in a tent similar to this one, arm to arm with their neighbors, riding the beauty of the music. He'd been too little to know the words, but he'd liked the way all of the voices came together as one sound. He remembered how his insides had grown quiet and calm. He'd been . . . safe.

He opened his eyes and let himself be drawn into the flow of people, across the field and into the airless tent.

"Welcome, brother," a man said as Henry

filed past, and "Welcome, sister" to the woman behind him.

There were no chairs. People crowded close to the stage, shoulder to shoulder, oblivious of the heat. Paper paddle fans with a picture of Jesus bathed in a heavenly glow fluttered below chins, waved over babies. On the stage stood a woman in a white robe, flowing sleeves moving as she led the crowd in song.

Henry stepped out of the slow, steady tide of bodies and stood near the wide opening of the entrance.

Next onstage was what looked to be a family, outfitted with guitar, a banjo, and a tambourine. They did a couple of songs unfamiliar to Henry that set the crowd to clapping and offering shouts of "Hallelujah."

Then a young girl, maybe ten or eleven, dressed in all white stepped onto the stage, her holy Bible held high over her head. The place got so quiet Henry heard his own breathing.

"Many of you have come tonight for the Lord's healing. And he will heal you. He *will* heal you. But first, come to Him with your troubles and your sins. Let Him carry your soul to glory so your body may follow." Her voice was amazingly strong and loud for such a little thing.

"The devil is sin!" She waved her Bible in the air, her voice even louder.

"Amen." It seemed Henry's was the only silent voice.

"The devil is darkness!"

"Amen!"

"The devil is hate!"

"Amen!"

"You must repent for your *sin*!" She smacked her hand against the Good Book. "Spurn *hate*!" Thump. "Shun the *devil*!" Thump. "Yes, brothers and sisters, do this and embrace the word of the Lord, God Almighty.

"Do not fall for the devil's lies, his denouncement of the Word, his blatant rejection of Adam and Eve and the wonder of God's creation. *'Then the Lord God formed the man of dust from the ground and breathed into his nostrils the breath of life, and the man became a living creature.'* " Her voice had built to a shout. Then it dropped low. "There are those who say God did not make man. Those who try to tell you man came from ape . . ."

Her voice, the people, the tent, all faded.

One word kept echoing in Henry's head: *hate.* Hate was the devil. Disaster must be his child.

When had Henry's hate started? No one was born with it, were they? When he'd beaten the crumbs and scraps of it back and stuffed it away, had it grown in the darkness like a fungus?

All of the petty childhood cruelties, all of the death, all of the loss — when had he turned all of those corners that led from disappointment, to hurt, to anger, and ultimately to hate?

Looking at the whole of his life, he saw the moment when the real hate started.

If he'd understood the dark, manipulative forces of jealousy, his life on the Dahlgren farm might have been different. But even after his jagged, cutting childhood, he'd been slow to learn too many lessons. At first he'd been deluded — or maybe outright deceived — into believing Mrs. Dahlgren was his only adversary on that farm. It turned out the enemy you didn't see coming was the most dangerous.

From the outset, the three littlest Dahlgren sisters had been giggly and curious, spying shyly around corners and from behind bushes — against their mother's admonitions. Over time Henry had coaxed them into the open, using games and kindness the way a person would use a handful of grain to lure a timid but starving fawn.

However, the four older girls, with the exception of Emmaline a few days after that first Christmas, hadn't exhibited much interest in him at all, offering only the occasional sidelong look when they passed at an influenza-avoiding distance in the barnyard. At the time Henry had assumed they were simply more obedient to their mother's rules than the young ones. An idea that turned out to be laughable.

Once the epidemic had passed, the three little ones openly trailed behind him like puppies. He fished lost shoes out of the mud, retied hair ribbons, and answered endless questions about everything from where butterflies came from to where their favorite pig had disappeared to during slaughter season. That last one had been tricky, but he'd managed to tell it in a way that didn't leave them crying over their morning bacon. As they'd grown older, one by one they'd joined the ranks of the distant older sisters. All except the youngest, Johanna, who, up until Henry had been forced to flee, occasionally still spent time with him. She rarely asked questions though. She was self-conscious of her stammer, which hung up most severely on the *J* in her own name. Henry couldn't blame her for staying quiet. Her sisters pelted her with relentless teasing, and her mother was convinced that a sharp rap on the knuckles at each hung-up consonant would break the offensive habit.

Henry worried about Johanna now that he was no longer there to offer her silent solidarity.

One morning, eighteen months after Henry had moved into the Dahlgren barn, he'd been surprised when Emmaline, the second eldest, stopped as they passed one another as he was headed to roll up the carpets and carry them outside to be beaten. She told him that with the epidemic over she would like them to be friends. Then she pulled a gold chain bracelet from her apron pocket. On it was a nickel-size, gold four-leaf clover. "Keep it in your pocket. It's lucky. Orphans need luck."

Henry had barely gotten his stunned "Thank you" out of his mouth before she walked on. He looked down at the shiny charm in his hand. Henry had no idea if it was real gold or not. He looked at Emmaline's retreating back, feeling as if maybe his luck was turning.

He spent the rest of the day feeling the warm presence of friendship in his pocket.

The next morning Mr. Dahlgren was waiting outside at the barn door. "Young Henry! Do you have something to tell me?"

His tone made Henry's mouth go fresh-straw dry. Mrs. Dahlgren might consider Henry a farm animal, but Mr. Dahlgren had always favored him; treated him like a son, even if he did live in the barn.

"I don't think so, sir."

Mr. Dahlgren frowned and stayed quiet, waiting for an admission. Yesterday's chores ran through Henry's mind. All done. No shortcuts taken. No mistakes that he could think of.

"I don't know what you're asking."

"Do you have Emmaline's gold bracelet?"

Henry reached into his pocket. When he opened his palm, the charm lay there like a burning accusation.

Mr. Dahlgren's gaze cut to the kitchen door. For the first time, Henry noticed Mrs. Dahlgren and Emmaline standing there. Emmaline's shoulders shook with hanky-muffled sobs.

"She said it disappeared from the top of her dressing table yesterday — after you had been in the house to carry out the rugs."

Henry shot a jittery look toward Emmaline and her mother. On her most charitable days Mrs. Dahlgren's expression looked as if she suffered from dyspepsia. That day she was red faced with fury. Her fists opened and closed at her sides, looking as if it took all of her restraint not to fly down those back steps and club Henry to death.

Confusion swirled a cold, crackly leafed wind in Henry's soul. Had Emmaline gotten in trouble for giving it away? Had she lied to lessen her mother's anger? Why not just ask Henry to give it back?

He faced Mr. Dahlgren and held the man's gaze with the conviction of the truth. "Emmaline gave it to me yesterday, sir. For luck."

"Ah, Henry." Mr. Dahlgren heaved a sad sigh. "What am I to believe?"

The truth! "I didn't take it."

"If you want something, you should come to me. I will make sure you have what you need."

"I didn't take it! I would never —"

Suddenly Emmaline was beside them. Her blue eyes glittered with tears and she gasped at the sight of the gold bracelet in Henry's hand. "Oh, how could you, Henry? After all Papa has done for you — after he took you for his *son*?" That last word held the poison of bitterness. She snaked her hand around her papa's arm and clung tight. "How could you steal from us?" She sounded as heartbroken as Mr. Dahlgren looked.

"You gave this to me! Right here on this path," Henry shouted. Hot, shameful tears stung his eyes. "Tell him!" The image of the book lying in the mud came into his mind. He'd thought it had been just a reaction to his newness. Jealousy over the gift.

Emmaline shook her head as if he were a pitiable idiot. "Why would I give it to you? Papa gave it to me for my seventh birthday. It's my favorite thing in all the world. Right, Papa?"

The disappointment in Mr. Dahlgren's eyes cut Henry deep.

"I didn't take it! Honest. Why would I?"

"Please give it back to her." Mr. Dahlgren's voice was flat.

Her hand came out, palm up.

Henry dropped the gold clover into it, staring into her eyes, trying to shame her into telling the truth.

She closed her hand around it and turned to walk back to the house. As she did, she gave Henry the tightest, *coldest* smile he'd ever seen.

That day laid the foundation for what was to come. As careful as Henry tried to be, Emmaline somehow always outmaneuvered him, making him appear responsible for taunts and damage to her possessions. Mr. Dahlgren always admonished Henry in a halfhearted way that said he had doubts about his daughter's claims. Mrs. Dahlgren's favorite punishment was the only one in her control, the withholding of food.

Henry grew to hate Emmaline in a way he'd never thought possible.

She'd been his nemesis. And in the end, she'd won.

God damn it, she'd won.

Henry slipped out of the revival tent, no closer to settled than when he'd come in. It seemed anger relived was as powerful as anger in the moment.

A hand touched his arm. His eyes weren't adjusted to the dark, but he knew it was Cora even before she said his name.

"Did you follow me?" His voice was sharp. Lashing out felt good.

"Jeepers, Henry, what's eating you?"

He clamped his teeth together and shrugged his arm away. "I just want to be left alone."

"In a tent crammed with people?"

"Damn it, Cora! Leave. Me. Alone."

"Come on, Kid. Don't be mad. I'm sorry I did the ramp. What more do you want me to say?"

He started walking, hoping she didn't follow.

He heard her trotting along behind. "Well, to be perfectly honest, you surprised me. I didn't think you had it in you."

He stopped and spun around. "What's that supposed to mean?"

"You actually showed some emotion — although I wish it hadn't been anger with me. But still. Bully for you! Where I come from, nobody says what they're thinking and certainly not what they're feeling. And you, Henry Jefferson, you always think before you open your mouth, measure the consequences. You're afraid for anyone to see inside you."

He could feel his pulse throbbing in his temple. "You make me sound like Gil."

"No. Gil's different, a charred and burned shell protecting the soft flesh underneath. But you, you're just deliberately cautious." She touched his arm. "Something made you that way."

"You don't know either one of us, Cora. This business we've got going will work a whole lot better if you leave it that way. Neither of us needs to be unearthed."

"Oh, come on! I just meant it seems like you've been knocked around by life. What deep, dark secrets could a nice fella like you possibly have?"

He looked beyond her. Breathing in. Breathing out. "No secrets here." In. Out. "And leave Gil alone. We've already pushed

229

our luck with him."

She waved his words away. "I promise I won't dig into Gil — I kind of like all of that mysterious brooding."

She was such a silly girl. "Then pretend I'm a mysterious brooder, too." He sighed and rubbed the throbbing in his temple. "I just want this show to work."

"Me, too. So, on that score" — she made an *X* over her heart — "no more stunts in front of customers without first perfecting them. Thank you for believing in our show." She kissed him on the cheek. "Now come back to camp. Gil's opened a fabulous can of beans."

He wanted to send her on her way, to spend the night wandering through the darkness on his own. But it was getting late and camp was a couple of long, dark, lonely miles away. Who knew what kind of trouble might find her?

She held on to his arm as they walked, until Henry pulled it away. Everything grated on him, even her touch. For a while he thought she'd at least give him the peace of silence. Then she said, "Do you believe all of that faith healing and Bible banging? Or are you a follower of Darwin?"

He shrugged, hoping his lack of response would discourage talking.

"And that was just a little girl doing the preaching! Not that I don't think girls can become preachers . . . if that's what they want. It just seemed she's too young to know anything about the real world."

"You'd be surprised what a kid her age could have experienced."

"Well, I think it's all theater — ballyhoo. You just don't come in there blind as a bat and walk out fully sighted because a little girl says so."

"Hard to say. I left before the healing started."

"And I don't think you have to choose between God and Darwin. I mean, what if evolution *is* God's plan? How are we to *know*?"

"Stop talking. My head hurts."

"Look there! You said what you thought again. This could be a real breakthrough."

"I mean it. Shut the hell up."

She sucked in a little breath of surprise.

They walked the rest of the way in silence.

He left her at their field with Gil and walked on into the night. Alone.

8

Even though Gil gave a lot of lip service about giving Cora no special treatment, he was obviously keeping their stops on main routes and relatively short distances apart for her motorcycle rides. It drove Henry crazy that neither Gil nor Cora would acknowledge that. They'd been hopscotching from town to town, skipping back and forth across the state line between Illinois and its neighboring states of Iowa and Missouri, having varied success. When a town proved to be a total bust, logic would say Gil should have blamed being tied to a planned route, should have insisted that he could have eliminated it as a stop by flying over and seeing the lack of interest. A couple of places had even had a barnstormer through in the previous month. But after that first complaint, Gil never again mentioned the loss of spontaneity because of the addition of Cora and the motorcycle.

Logic also said, between the amount of badgering he took from Cora and the fruitless stops, he should have dumped Cora and Henry weeks ago. Even more telling of Gil's deeper feelings was that MERCURY'S DAREDEVILS was emblazoned on the sides of his beloved Jenny. Naturally, it had been Cora's idea. For the first time and only time, she had teamed a little of her charm with her determination to persuade Gil. Plus she'd plied him with some fine moonshine before she'd made her final push. She'd started out with more outlandish suggestions such as pulling a banner behind the plane to advertise (the poor bird's engine was taxed enough carrying Gil and Henry and a small amount of supplies). It had been a compromise in the end, facilitated by Henry — who'd also sketched and painted the lettering and some flames on the tail. After his somewhat inebriated agreement, Gil did as always and just ignored the new paint job — approval by abstention.

All considered, Cora was probably right; Gil did want them around. Not that Henry was eager to test the theory.

After the ramp incident and the tent revival, Cora seemed less cocksure of Henry. As she should have been, considering all she didn't know about him. Still, he felt the loss with a sharpness that surprised him. Oh, she still teased, but something about it was more reserved now, a reluctant wariness showing deep in her eyes. From that first day when he'd pulled her from the water, it had been him and Cora as a team with Gil an essential, yet distant, participant. Now there had been a shift. She showed a new closeness toward Gil. Henry wondered if he'd made a huge mistake in staying away that night, leaving Cora in her wounded mood alone with Gil; for that had clearly been the turning point, the slight shift in her allegiance.

It was done. Like so many other choices Henry had made, it couldn't be changed. He knew Cora's distance was for the best. It prevented him from making another foolish mistake.

He'd been distracting himself by focusing all of his mental energy on the airplane. There was something to be said for the uncomplicated nature of a relationship with an inanimate object. In that one single aspect, he understood Gil completely.

The better he got to know the Jenny, the more apparent it became that the main things holding her together were baling wire and a big heap of faith. The wooden and cloth plane was built on an accelerated wartime schedule and was designed to be used only in the short term as a trainer. The old girl was already on borrowed time. A steady stream of ideas paraded through his mind, not just to keep the plane hanging together, but to improve her. All of them required at least some cash, which was coming in at a rather haphazard flow. His wish list was steadily growing.

Henry sat in the rear cockpit as they flew over southern Illinois coal country, readying for his first solo landing. He'd come a long way since he'd first put his hand on the throttle and edged it forward, sending his heart into double time and taking his breath away — for the first time not from the propeller wash. Gil had informed Henry before they'd taken off that he was as much on his own as if he sat in the plane alone. Sink or swim, the Jenny was in Henry's hands. As the miles disappeared and the landing neared, his heart hammered as if he'd run ten miles. And he completely forgot to breathe.

If he made a successful solo landing — *please, God* — he could call himself an aviator. Only not in front of Cora.

Part of what Gil had been training him to do since their first trip together was to continually scout the ground for a likely landing place. *Emergency landings don't give you time to look around; keep that in mind every mile you fly. Flat as possible. No cliffs. No big trees. Lakes can be good, but keep in mind, hitting water is no softer than hitting land. Shrubbery, tree stumps, and mature corn crops help dissipate energy and slow you down in a field that's too short.* Henry had taken the lesson to heart. Whenever he was at an altitude that wouldn't allow for a long glide, he always knew where he'd put down if the engine quit.

They'd passed over the Marion courthouse and he spotted a likely field for their show. Henry checked the cows below to figure out the wind direction. *Ass end to the wind.* He banked the plane for a low pass to check the field more closely, confirming the wind direction by the movement of the grass. After Tilda, Henry didn't trust cows.

His hands were sweaty on the control stick and his stomach had tied itself into a knot, simultaneously creating both the worst and the best feeling he'd ever had. The field looked good. He couldn't decide if he was glad or disappointed. Now that the moment was upon him, he felt totally unprepared — just as Gil had said he would. At least Gil hadn't trained in a plane that risked someone's livelihood. Besides, the Jenny wasn't just a meal ticket to Gil, she was his whole life. And then there was Gil's actual life.

There wasn't enough fuel to fiddle around and take another pass. This field looked good, so it was a go.

What if he'd missed something, a tree stump or a boulder in the high grass?

Gil signaled from the front cockpit for Henry to set down.

That helped. Still, confidence in the field was only part of it. He needed confidence in his own ability. Hesitation and second-guessing had no place in the cockpit. Assess. Decide. Execute.

Henry circled and made his approach. He pulled back on the stick a bit, pulling the nose up slightly, setting the pitch for landing. Throttle back. They dropped lower, lower. A crosswind caught the plane, pushing them sideways from the landing spot, heading them for the cornfield on the right. *Destroying crops sets up entirely the wrong tone for negotiations with a farmer.* He fought the crosswind by crabbing the plane, using the stick and the rudder, aiming for the landing spot he'd picked on his pass. The ground was rushing up, the corn like a rolling green sea. They crossed the fence.

Nose up, kill more speed.

Dropping. Dropping. He should be feeling the wheels hit by now. Had he overshot?

He had to get the plane on the ground or he'd be out of room. A safe landing that ended in a fence was no better than a crash landing.

The wheels hit hard. The Jenny bounced into flight again. He had to get that tail skid on the ground. He killed the engine and kept the stick in his lap. The wheels hit again. It was so bumpy it rattled his teeth. The tail finally lit and began to drag and slow them.

What he wouldn't give for some brakes.

He leaned to the right, looking ahead around the nose and loosened his grip on the stick. They were going to stop with yards to spare.

He, Henry Schuler, homeless orphan, was an aviator. An aviator! Peter wouldn't believe it. Hell, Henry hardly believed it.

His tense muscles finally relaxed as they rolled toward a stop.

Suddenly the front dropped. The plane nosed down.

The tail's coming over.

Gravity shifted. Henry was on the upswing of a seesaw.

His lap belt cut in as his body jerked

forward. He stopped moving at a downward angle ten feet off the ground.

What the hell happened?

Gil was silent as he pushed himself out of the front cockpit and slid forward off the lower wing to the ground. Henry braced his feet on the rudder bar and unfastened his lap belt, wondering how Gil ever kept his concentration hanging by the thing during inverted flight.

Henry climbed out, disappointment filling his stomach and shame coloring his cheeks.

Words stuck in his throat as he stood staring morosely at the Jenny, her nose in a shallow ditch that had been camouflaged by the grass, her tail in the air.

After a second, Gil slapped him on the back. "Good job, old boy!"

Henry's horrified gaze cut to Gil. He appeared to be sincere — and he had a purpling goose egg on his forehead.

"I nearly killed your plane."

"When I was in training, most fellows not only killed the plane on their first landing, but themselves, too. The plane's still got her tail and wings. You look hale and hearty." Gil smiled at Henry with what looked like pride in his eyes.

No one had looked at Henry like that since Peter had left home. Henry had almost forgotten what it did to a person's insides.

"You corrected for that crosswind. You didn't panic when she hopped. I didn't see that ditch either. It's all part of flying."

Henry's eyes lit on the splintered prop. "Ah, hell." He put his hands on his head and walked in a circle. "Damn. Damn. Damn it to hell."

"We'll need a new propeller." Gil's voice was matter-of-fact.

"How much?"

"Around fifty dollars." Then he looked at Henry. "Do we have it?"

Henry had become the unofficial accountant, handling the intake, paying for supplies. He even divided their shares at the end of the week — not that there was ever much left to divide. "We do. But it should come out of my share. It might take some time for me to get it covered though."

"Did we take the money for Cora's replacement chain out of her cut?"

"No, but —"

"Our shares are after operating expenses. Fixing broken stuff is operating expenses. Besides, we can't let Cora know you were piloting or she'll be all over me to teach her. A woman on a motorcycle is bad enough. A woman aviator . . ." Gil visibly shuddered.

Henry didn't think now was the right time to mention Cora had ideas for getting airborne that had nothing to do with piloting. Gil was going to be resistant enough, and Henry had a feeling Cora was right, they were going to have to step up their act if they were to keep drawing a crowd. The barnstormer who'd beat them in harvesting several towns had a wing walker; when Mercury's Daredevils arrived, they were already second-rate. In the exhibition business your act had to provide the most thrills or you were doomed.

"We'll telegraph for the propeller when we get to town," Gil said. "Might take a week to get here. Maybe a little less, since we're right on a rail line."

"You and Cora shouldn't get nicked because of my —"

Gil's eyes nailed Henry with their fierceness. "Before you started working on the plane, I'd never gone three weeks, let alone six, without something grounding me. I count us money ahead. And Cora had better not say a word about it. She needs to learn the money has to keep what we have glued together, not buy more to maintain or line our pockets."

Henry didn't think a desire for money fueled Cora's wanting a bigger crowd, a more daring performance. If she just wanted money she'd marry a Father Time. No, it was something else entirely. She seemed to need excitement and the adoring eyes of strangers the way most people needed a good square meal; not as an aspect of vanity, but a necessary part of survival.

No sense ruffling Gil's feathers by saying that aloud right now either. "So now what?"

"We're going to need help getting the tail down and pulling her out of this gully."

Just then, Henry noticed a middle-aged man with a thick mustache trotting across the field toward them. He was red faced and huffing when he reached them. "Ever— body — all — right?" He stopped, put his hands on his knees and sucked in a few deep breaths. "I seen that tail go up and knew you was in trouble."

"Fine," Gil said. "Could use some help getting out of the ditch."

"Need more'n me? Got my son back at the barn."

"Him, too."

The man nodded. "Name's Gather. Hugh Gather."

"Gil. This is Henry." Henry nodded at the man and Gil asked, "This ditch run all the way across?"

"Nope. Only 'bout ten feet long. You managed to hit it right square, you did."

Henry groaned.

Gil gave him a that's-how-it-goes look. To Gather, Gil said, "We're here to sell rides. We'd like to use your pasture. We'll give you a percentage of the take." Gil's approach, although short and to the point, had certainly improved. Henry felt a twinge of uselessness. "And we'll *all* make more money if you keep this little incident to yourself."

"I didn't see no plane get tipped in the ditch. No, sir." Gather stuck out his hand. "Let me be the first to welcome you to Bloody Williamson."

"Bloody Williamson?" Gil and Henry asked together.

"Don't you folks read the newspaper? Mine trouble. Strikes. Been nothin' but beatin's and guns and lynchin' round here for quite a spell. Had ourselves a regular massacre of scab foreigners last year. Course, bootleggers is still a problem. But the Ku Klux Klan's gettin' involved in the fracas, cleanin' things up.

"Got me a cousin over to Ohio writes me that every paper in the whole country's callin' this Bloody Williamson, on account of it's Williamson County — and all the killin'."

Henry looked at Gil, wishing like hell that he hadn't just ruined their chances to get out of here. And that Cora weren't riding all alone on that motorcycle.

"Oh, now, don't look like that, boy," Gather said to Henry. "Most of the trouble's been up Herrin way. And unless you're scabs, bootleggers, or gangsters, you'll pro'bly be just fine." Gather winked.

Henry said, "I need to get to town. Cora's alone."

"Oh, now, I'm just joshin' ya," Gather said. "Ain't all that bad right now. And the Klan's all about protectin' womanhood and virtue. That's why they come, to rout out the lawlessness, get rid of them bootleggin' foreigners that habituate to wine. Klan'll make this a place for decent Americans to live again."

Gil said, "We'll get this plane moved later. Do you have a car or truck we could borrow?" To Henry he said, "If she's not in town, we'll start looking on the road."

"Road? Ain't your lady travelin' by train?"

"No. She's riding a motorcycle," Gil said. Obviously he'd never had to tiptoe around public opinion before. Gather didn't seem the kind of man who welcomed the progress of womanhood.

Gather's eyes got wide, then squinty. "Well

now . . ." He looked to be making a decision. "Truck's up to the barn. You're welcome to use it to find your *lady* if you bring it back full of gasoline." He said *lady* differently this time, as if he considered any woman traveling alone on a motorcycle and meeting up with two men to be far less than one. The implication irritated Henry beyond measure. He wanted to punch the man for his disrespect, but held his hands at his side; they needed that truck.

For the first time he understood Cora's complaint about the unfairness of the public attitude toward independent woman, that they were either immoral or suspiciously masculine. How quickly she'd begun to change his perspective. He recalled his shock at Cora's initial appearance and over her asking for Gil's cigarette. That shock seemed prudish to him now, and he felt a little ashamed that Cora still needed to remind him that women were equals now, the old Victorian ways were being left back "in the dark ages where they belong."

Change came slowly, no matter how justified. Some places were slower to come around than others and Henry hoped this wasn't one of them; they needed to replenish their cash before they could move on.

When he laid eyes on Gather's truck, he

feared it didn't have seven miles, the distance to town, left in it. Henry had to crank it so many times, he broke a sweat and nearly his arm, too. When it started, it coughed and ran rough. As it sluggishly chugged out of the barnyard, Henry prayed it wouldn't die on the side of the road before they found Cora.

The motorcycle always took longer to reach their destinations than the Jenny. Most roads weren't good enough for Cora to travel anywhere near top speed, an unhappy discovery for her. Their plan always was, if she didn't see Henry and Gil in a field on her way into town — as she wouldn't today because they'd flown past Marion — the fallback was to meet Henry in the center of downtown. Originally, she was to stay put and Henry was to wander until he found her. But Cora wasn't a woman to stay put when she could be talking up the exhibition. After that first time, Henry stayed put and let her find him. It simply expedited things.

Gil pointed the truck toward Marion. He might not have said he was worried — or anything else for that matter because he'd gone silent — but his jaw muscles flexed and his fingers kept opening and closing on the steering wheel of the old truck.

"I think we need to find another field to operate out of," Henry said.

"We already shook on it. It'll be fine."

"But you heard him. He seems —"

"We can cut back to just rides and keep Cora out of it. We'll just do one day."

"I don't like being stuck here."

"Don't believe everything that old coot said. We'll judge for ourselves."

The late-July sun beat down and the hot wind lashed Henry's face. His tense stomach turned sour. He suddenly missed the cool rush of high-altitude air that he wouldn't feel for at least a week. As self-centered as thinking about how much he'd miss flying was, it was better than thinking of Cora getting caught up in a shoot-out.

Henry didn't know if Gil's wild driving was because of panic or if he was just a terrible driver. They hit every rut and pothole in the road, and Henry steadied himself by holding on to the door. Gil's hands, so smooth on the control stick and the throttle, were erratic on the steering wheel; the side-to-side jerking of the truck was making Henry's neck muscles cramp.

"Up there." Henry pointed to a mining company coming up on the right. "Slow down so we can get a look."

Gil slowed, but not by much. They both

turned their heads, searching the grounds for signs of trouble. No guards armed with tommy guns. No angry union workers storming the area. No white KKK hoods.

"Think Gather was just saying all that stuff to scare us?" Henry asked.

"Why would he bother?"

"He seemed to have a kind of perverse sense of humor."

Gil gave a grunt — whether in agreement or dissent Henry couldn't tell.

As they entered town, Gil swung wide to go around a buggy being pulled by a broken-down old horse and almost hit a touring car head on. He swerved into the grass, barely missing an electric pole. Thank God there wasn't a curb or the tires would have peeled right off the wheels.

"We're not going to do Cora any good if we're lying dead on the damn street!" It was a relief to yell at someone.

Gil finally slowed, mostly because he didn't have a choice. They'd reached town proper with its mix of pedestrians, dogs, bicycles, and street traffic.

He looked over at Henry. "When I'm not around anymore, it's going to be your job to look after Cora. She thinks she's different from other women. But the rest of the world doesn't see it that way. And she's so damned sure she's invincible, she's bound to get into trouble."

Henry frowned. "What are you talking about?"

"Protecting women is the only good use men have. Everything else we fuck up."

"Well, then you two stubborn asses should have let me trade places with her weeks ago and she wouldn't be out there on her own right now!"

Gil's right eye twitched but he didn't argue.

"And you don't need to tell *me* about Cora," Henry said, his tone icicle sharp. "I was asking what you meant by 'not being around.'"

"Cora wants this to be something more . . . bigger. And I'm pretty sure whatever she sets her mind to she'll do. And you've got a future in you, too. But none of that is for me."

"So we're going to wake up one day and you'll just take off without us? Is that your plan? Why in the hell have you kept us around at all? Jesus, you talk about protecting Cora. If you're going to leave us, then you should have done it that first day. Why build up her hopes?" *And mine.* "Now she's a long way from home. She threw everything away for this."

"I should have. This plane won't last." Gil paused. "I won't last."

"I can make the plane last. And you're what, twenty-six, twenty-seven? I wouldn't call that an old man."

"I'll never be an old man." Gil said it so quietly, it took a moment for Henry to pluck the words out of the wind. "I've cheated death more times than a man should be allowed. Time is coming. I feel it."

"You want it, you mean."

Gil shrugged. "Cora'll find another plane, another flier." The way Gil looked at Henry made his heart sink.

"Is that why you taught me to fly?"

Gil gave a half shrug.

"You're wrong."

"About Cora, maybe. About you, possibly. But not about me."

They reached the courthouse square. The brick streets didn't border it, boxing it in. They made T's right into the center of the courthouse on all four sides, leaving wide-open bricked areas between the courthouse and the surrounding businesses. It made it easy for Henry to see most of the downtown with one lap around the square. Everything looked peaceful. No sign of Cora.

"Isn't she supposed to wait on the square for you?" Gil asked, his hands nervous on the steering wheel.

"You don't know Cora at all." Henry felt a little smug saying it. "I park myself. She finds me."

"There're plenty of open spots. Would she have parked off on some side street?"

"Not a chance. Her plan is to attract as much attention as possible."

"I was afraid of that."

"That's our job, promoting, drawing a crowd. The *problem* is letting her ride that motorcycle all over creation by herself. If it breaks down, she's stuck." Henry didn't give voice to his true fear, that it wasn't a breakdown that had kept her from reaching Marion.

Gil stopped at a corner. Henry called out the window to a bent-backed man in a bowler hat walking slowly by. "Excuse me, sir!"

The man stopped and looked their way.

"Have you seen a woman and a dog on a motorcycle anywhere around town?"

"Why, I sure did."

Henry's heart lightened.

"There was a monkey on her shoulder, too. Think an elephant was followin' 'em — a pink un." With a shake of his head, the man swatted a hand in their direction and walked away muttering, "Dang youngsters."

He disappeared into the door of Duncan-Baker Hardware Company.

Gil headed west out of town on one of the first hard roads Henry had ever seen outside of a downtown area. It was narrow enough that the truck had to drive down the middle to keep all four tires on the concrete, but so smooth Gil could push the truck as fast as it could go. Henry thought of Cora tearing into town at sixty miles an hour on this road — as she surely would. He was pretty sure it was something people would remember.

"She doesn't ever get off the main road, does she?" Gil asked.

You'd know if you ever talked to her. Henry quickly swallowed those words down. Cora and Gil were talking more now, and Henry had discovered that he preferred them fighting. He'd never been a jealous person, but then he hadn't felt close to anyone since Peter died . . . until Cora.

"No. That's one plan she sticks to. If she breaks down, she doesn't want to waste promotion time having us looking for her."

They motored on, Henry growing more nervous every minute.

"You think she's finally turned tail and run?" Gil's voice sounded sad. "Barnstorming is pretty rough for a woman."

"You're kidding, right? If anything, she's

more determined than ever."

"Maybe the novelty's worn off."

A bark of laughter came out of Henry. "How could it? She comes up with a new scheme every other day."

An open-topped car raced toward them, not yielding an inch of the width of the road. Gil had to pull completely off the pavement. Henry hung out the window, waving his arms to get the man to stop. Maybe he'd seen Cora. But the car sped on past, the driver either not seeing or not caring.

They were heading into the setting sun, the white glare on the windshield blinding them to most everything. Henry kept his head out the window, his hand on his hat, the bill shading his eyes.

Halfway to Carbondale, Henry finally spotted her walking toward them on the road. "There she is!" he shouted, but Gil was already slowing and pulling off the road. He cut the motor, jumped out of the truck, leaving the driver's door open. The truck kept rolling down the slight grade at the side of the road. "Shit." Henry had to slide over and cram it in gear and set the brake. By the time his feet hit the ground, Cora was already in Gil's arms, hers tightly around his neck.

Henry's stomach turned to lead.

Mercury shot toward him, launching himself toward Henry's mid-section. He caught the dog like a football. That little, hot tongue started licking Henry's chin. At least someone was glad to see him.

Gil held Cora by the shoulders and looked her over. "You're all right?"

That was Henry's first good look at her . . . and she didn't look all right at all. Her clothes were muddy, the knee of her pants torn. It looked like a rasp had been taken to her left cheek. His mouth went cottony and his hands clenched. "Who did this?"

She grinned at Henry and he saw her lip was swollen, too. "Easy, Kid. I did it. Well, it was mostly me."

Gil's hands lingered on her shoulders. Henry wanted to smack them off. What was worse was the way Gil was looking at her. Henry had only seen that I-touched-God look in Gil's eyes while he was flying.

"Had a flat I had to get fixed," Cora said. "Then got into a race with a breezer a couple of miles back that didn't turn out so well. I tried to pass him off the pavement and ended up in a ditch."

" 'Breezer'?" Henry asked.

"You know, a convertible. Golly, you can really fly on this cement road! I can't wait until more are paved . . . I'll probably *beat* you two from town to town."

"No, you won't," Gil said. "You'll be flying with me. From here on out, Henry rides the motorcycle. It's not safe for a woman alone."

"Good God, it's usually Henry bossing me around." She shoved Gil in the chest and stepped back away from him.

"You've proven you don't need special treatment, so let it go. Henry and I agree it's not safe for you alone."

"Oh, you do, do you? If I wanted someone, or two someones" — she pointed to Gil, then Henry — "to tell me what to do, I'd have stayed with Mother and gotten married to a man with money. At least then I wouldn't be sleeping on the ground."

"Come on, Cora!" Gil said. "Be sensible."

Henry stood back and waited for the explosion.

"You really just said that to me?" she shouted. "I'm a daredevil, Gil. A *daredevil*!"

Gil looked to Henry for his usual intervention, but Henry just shrugged and stepped a little farther away. For the first time he actually liked the idea of her being mad at Gil.

"Then save it for the show, when people are paying good money to see it. What in the hell? Racing? Last time it didn't turn out too well either. When are you going to stop?"

"Hey, if I hadn't raced you, we would never have met! And poor Henry would be stuck in some factory in Chicago."

Gil. That's whom she'd regret not meeting. *Poor Henry* ground his teeth together and told himself it was for the best.

"It's almost dark," Gil said.

Dark? The sun rested on the tops of the trees. Hours until full dark.

Gil went on, "What if instead of me and Henry finding you, it'd been some ruffian?"

Cora burst out laughing. "Ruffian?"

"Stop laughing!" Henry's sharp tone sobered her up. He thought of Mr. Gather's stories. "Gil's right."

"I own the plane. You want to stay in the barnstorming business, you fly with me. Henry rides the motorcycle. Now where is it?"

"I *said* a couple miles back." She crossed her arms.

"Since you're on foot, I assume it's too damaged to ride."

She nodded, looking just a little contrite.

"Get in the truck." Gil walked to the driver's door.

"Maybe I'll walk the rest of the way," Cora said.

"Jesus." Henry grabbed her by the arm and moved her toward the truck. "Stop being such a pain in the ass."

She didn't resist. "You used to be on my side."

"Not when you're acting like a three-year-old. Use some sense."

She sat in between Gil and Henry with Mercury on her lap. As she petted the dog, Henry noticed her palms were skinned. The stab of sympathy he felt for her injuries irritated him even more.

In a few minutes she said, "I'll think about it."

"What?" Gil asked.

"Flying with you." She leaned a little more Gil's way.

Henry's stomach bubbled and boiled. The hateful taste of jealousy lingered in the back of his throat. He wasn't sure if it was over Cora's taking his place in the cockpit, or the idea of Gil and Cora being alone together. But in that moment, he did begin to understand Emmaline Dahlgren just a little better.

9

Three days later, Henry, Cora, and Gil had spent enough time scouting Marion and riding the electric train to neighboring towns to discover that, while Gather's stories were indeed true, Williamson County was currently no bloodier than any other. It did seem like a place in desperate need of a lively diversion from its troubles, so that boded well for the show.

Once Gil was good and convinced there was no immediate danger, around halfway through the second day, he stopped going with Cora and Henry on their "little outings," a term that normally would run up battle flags with Cora, but somehow slipped right by on placid waters. That change in temperament nettled Henry like a hair-fine pricker under the skin. He was feeling like the third wheel on a bicycle.

At least Cora was inching back to her old easy ways with Henry.

Finally, they received a telegram saying the new propeller had shipped. It was time to get geared up to get back to work. Henry was glad for it. Even though they were taking the opportunity to give the Jenny's engine an overhaul, Gil's spirit seemed to be fed by altitude, not just proximity to his machine. He got quieter and more distant each day they were grounded. Cora had even started to avoid him — which was a bit of a silver lining to Henry.

Gil had disappeared before dawn to who knew where. Henry and Cora decided to take the motorcycle into Marion to give out more handbills. Mercury was in her jacket. She sat in front of Henry, sideways on Mercury's seat, boxed in by Henry's arms with her legs draped over his right thigh, an intimate contact that was getting harder and harder to keep in perspective.

"All set," she said. Mercury woofed. "He likes to go fast, so goose it, Kid!"

The rumbling machine felt good under him. He took off. Cora shrieked. Mercury howled. For the first time in a week, Henry grinned.

He parked next to a bright green Hupmobile touring car in front of the Goodall Hotel.

"Meet back here at six?" Cora set Mercury

on the ground and pulled the stack of handbills out of her jacket before she took it off. Underneath she wore a sensible dress that hit her leg at midcalf. Henry mentally applauded her rare nonconfrontational choice; no need to irritate those who opposed women dressing like men.

"I think we should stick together," Henry said.

"Don't be ridiculous. We'll cover twice as much ground separately. It's the middle of a Tuesday afternoon." She looked down at Mercury, waiting patiently at her side. "And I have my guard dog. Besides, you said you wanted to go to the service garage. Why should I waste my time there?"

He hesitated and looked around.

"We've been here for four days," she said in a huff. "It's just like anyplace else. Stop being such a mother hen."

Even with the afternoon heat, plenty of townsfolk were on the streets, many of them unescorted ladies. A girl of about ten was sweeping the sidewalk in front of the store next to the hotel. Four boys stood near the bins of fruit in front of the market, no doubt looking for the opportunity to help themselves. A young woman pushed a baby carriage down the sidewalk. People were coming and going from the courthouse. It did look just like anyplace else.

"Okay. But five o'clock. Don't leave the downtown area."

"Yes, Father."

Henry left her thinking, *Good God, mother hen, Father, Kid.* That's how she viewed him. Was it so wrong to want more?

Safe. This was safe. For both of them. *Keep that in mind.*

He went straight to Cagles Garage on Market Street, intent on getting back to her sooner rather than later. He paused at the wide door to the service area and waited for his eyes to adjust. The odor of exhaust, gasoline, and oil had been absorbed by the floor and the open rafters. He breathed deeply. The smell was more welcome to him than that of freshly baked bread. He was a lucky man to be living in a time with the miracle of the internal combustion engine and all of the wonders it had spawned.

The man inside the garage was working on the axle of an old black carriage with a cracked leather bonnet and weathered wood wheels. Oh, how times were changing. There would come a day when horses and mules were completely replaced by machines, Henry just knew it.

What if airplanes became commonplace? What would Gil do? His being grounded these past days showed just how much he needed to be airborne. If he lost that, it'd kill him. Henry's thoughts stopped cold in their tracks. After witnessing Gil's recent behavior, Henry thought maybe that's what he was hoping for; the plane to kill him before progress killed barnstorming.

Henry turned his thoughts away from the day-by-day tightrope walk of their lives. Right now the Jenny needed new spark plugs and a never-ending supply of oil.

He introduced himself to the man and told him what he needed.

"Well now, I heard you fellas was in town." The man wiped his hands on a rag so oily it was a useless gesture. "Been wantin' to get out there and take a look at that airplane. Ain't seen one since I got back from the war. So your pilot fly over there?" He pulled a pad from under the counter and started writing up a ticket for Henry's purchases.

"He did."

"Dangerous business — but then ain't that war in general?"

"Yes, sir. You serve?"

"Army medical transport."

"You saw a lot of bad, then."

"I did. Not many fighter pilots though. Not much left to fix when they got it."

Henry nodded. "Our pilot flew reconnaissance."

The man whistled. "He must be one lucky bastard. Wasn't hardly none of them come back at all. Had to fly low, always behind enemy lines. Easy targets. Get shot down and" — he shrugged — "that was the last we seen of them."

Just a taxidriver for a photographer, huh?

Henry paid for the supplies and the man agreed to deliver everything out to the Gather farm free of charge.

As Henry was tacking a handbill for Mercury's Daredevils on an electric pole, he saw Gil walk into the post office.

Henry walked the half block and followed him up the granite steps. Inside, Gil stood at a tall marble-and-wood table set before one of the large front windows. He was putting paper money into an envelope. Henry waited, feeling like the spy he'd once been accused of being, while Gil licked the envelope and then picked up a pencil to address it.

Shame finally got the better of Henry and he walked over to the table. "I didn't know you were in town."

Gil jumped. His hand covered the envelope and his eyes looked guilty. Henry could only see the last name in the address:

Gilchrist.

"Where's Cora?" Gil asked.

"Delivering handbills."

"By herself!"

Henry's back stiffened. "I thought *you* decided it was safe around here."

"No place is safe when Cora's running loose."

"True enough." Henry wanted to suggest that if Gil felt that way, he should keep an eye on her, but that was the furthest thing from what Henry wanted. "I was arranging for the spark plugs, oil, and gasoline. She didn't want to come. I'm headed to find her now."

"Good idea." Gil slipped the envelope off the table and held it against his leg. "See you back at camp." He walked away and got in line at the window.

Henry left the post office thinking Gil must have family of some sort. Sending money to parents? Not that it could be much; their cuts had been pretty darn lean.

How would you feel if Gil were sneaking around after you?

Henry hurried down the steps and decided to forget about seeing Gil in town at all.

He ducked in and out of businesses looking for Cora. Finally it neared five o'clock and he went to the Goodall Hotel. Five minutes later, Cora and Mercury came down the street. Mercury had a swagger in his trot and a huge bone in his mouth.

"He didn't steal it, did he?"

Cora laughed. "He actually worked for it this time. Did a dozen tricks for the butcher before he got it."

Henry reached down and picked up the dog. The bone made him half again his normal weight. "Didn't they have a smaller one?"

"Mercury was allowed to choose. Being a fella, he had to go overboard." She scratched behind the dog's ears. Then she looked up at Henry with a sparkle in her eye — the kind that usually meant trouble. "Hungry? I know just where we're going for dinner."

"Let me guess, under the stars at Gather's farm . . . perhaps with a high-hat, delicious can of beans?"

"No." She grinned as if she'd just won the blue ribbon at the county fair. "We're dining out."

"Your treat? 'Cause there's not much left in the till."

"As a matter of fact, we're going as guests."

"Whose?"

"A fella from the hardware store."

"A fella from the hardware store?"

"Yes, he was quite nice."

"I'm sure he was . . . to you. Does he know you come as a package deal? And I'm not just meaning the dog."

"Of course! He wants to show off with a war hero."

Henry decided to just let Cora deal with Gil's reaction to that. "Where are we meeting him?" This town had plenty of nice places, and the Daredevils' meals had been plenty lean. Henry's mouth watered.

"Oh, it's not in town." She moved toward the motorcycle. "It's along some creek or river or something. He's picking us up in his car."

"Just what kind of place is this?" Henry hoped his hunch was wrong.

"It's a supper club. You'll like it."

"I think we should stick to some place in town. It's better for business."

"Come on, Henry. People who like fun will be there." She stopped and looked over her shoulder at him. "*Fun,* Henry. As in a good time. We could use one, too."

"As in *illegal.*"

"I have it on good authority that the pro-hees are well taken care of, so it's hands-off."

"Prohees?"

"Prohibition agents."

"Ah. This from the hardware-store owner you just met?"

"Oh, it wasn't the owner. It was a fella *in* the hardware store. He goes out there all of the time."

"This is a really bad idea."

"Come on, Kid. I've been in plenty of blind pigs. None of them were ever raided."

"Then the odds aren't in your favor now, are they?"

She tsked. "*Nobody* enforces that stupid law. There's too much money to be made ignoring it." She walked on. "What's the worst that'll happen? Anyone I've ever known who got pinched in a raid just spent the night in the pokey. Big deal."

"Yeah. Big deal." Henry had actually gone a couple of consecutive weeks without looking over his shoulder; now he wondered if wanted posters made it from Indiana to Illinois.

She plucked her jacket off the handlebars of the motorcycle and slipped it on. "Get a wiggle on! I need to get myself dolled up and ready to go."

He followed, certain Gil would put a stop to this whole supper-club business.

When they got back to camp, Gil's dull, restless eyes lit up at the mention of it.

"It doesn't really seem like your kind of

place," Henry said. The man barely tolerated being inside a restaurant long enough to get a meal down. When the crowd pressed too close at the field, he climbed up on the wing of the Jenny to distance himself.

"They serve alcohol?"

"Yeah. That's the problem. I don't want us to get off on the wrong foot. We should avoid trouble. Not to mention support a restaurant in town, buy some goodwill, make people want to come see us."

"If they serve a drink, it is my kind of place. We'll catch plenty of fish there, too."

Henry furrowed his brow. "Oh?"

"What kind of people buy airplane rides?"

"Curious ones."

"And?"

Henry shook his head.

"Risk. They like risk. So stop fretting."

"I don't think ending up in jail will be good for business."

"But the drink will be worth it." Gil laughed, a sound so rare Henry could count the times he'd heard it on one hand. "They would have eaten you alive in Chicago, old boy."

Henry didn't like the "fella from the hardware store" on sight. He drove too fast, skidding to a stop on the road in front of the field. He honked an overly large, polished brass bulb horn — a farce in itself — mounted on the side of a shiny green Packard. Then he hung his slicked head out the window, waved a straw boater as if he were beckoning cattle, and yelled, "Hey, beautiful! You ready?"

Gil looked toward Cora with his head tilted and his brows raised.

Henry muttered, *"Ugh."*

Cora rolled her eyes. "It's a ride, boys." She waved cheerily and started toward the Packard.

Henry had already decided he wasn't going. Since he'd left Indiana, luck had been on his side. He wasn't going to tempt fate over some illegal hooch. If he was arrested, it was all over. He was waiting until the last minute to back out so Cora wouldn't have time to wheedle him into going. Once she and Gil were gone, he'd send the Gather boy, who was supposed to watch the plane, off with his dime in his pocket for no work at all.

Setting eyes on this reckless fancy man changed Henry's mind. What if Gil drank too much to look out for Cora?

At least she wasn't wearing that too-short, low-backed dress. Still, her lips were scarlet red and her city polish didn't need fine clothes and feathers to draw men's attention. She wore jodhpurs and polished knee boots, a blue blouse with too many buttons undone, and a white scarf around her neck tied in the back, its ends trailing to her waist. No doubt her clothes were intended to mark her as part of Mercury's Daredevils and not just some ordinary girl.

Even dressed in those mannish jodhpurs, she made a man think of things he shouldn't.

"This should be interesting," Gil said as he fell into step behind her across the grassy field.

Henry debated only a moment longer. "Ah, hell." He told the Gather boy, "Take care of the dog. He'll try to follow her." Then Henry headed toward the Packard, dread dancing on the back of his neck like spider's feet.

They climbed into the car, Cora in the front seat. The man shoved his hand over the seat back toward Gil — a soft, pasty kind of hand that didn't know work. "Pierce Whitley. Glad to have you join us, ace." The proprietary way he said "us" made Henry's ears get hot.

Gil shook his hand. "Gil. Not an ace."

Henry reminded himself that he was Henry *Jefferson;* occasionally Schuler still wanted to slide off his tongue. But Pierce Whitley apparently didn't deem him worthy of an introduction. Whitley turned back around and ground the gears so loudly that Henry wanted to smack the back of his brilliantined head for the mistreatment of a fine machine.

"I plan on getting an aeroplane soon." Whitley said it just like that, *aero*-plane, as if he thought he were on the radio. "I'll have it built to my specifications, of course. It needs to be fast." He glanced over his shoulder at Gil. "Is yours designed for speed?"

"Sure," Gil said, keeping his eyes on the passing landscape.

Pierce didn't pause long enough for Gil's sarcastic answer to register. He moved on to his family's mining holdings and the bank they owned. He was particularly proud that the Whitleys had paid for power to be run out to the supper club they were going to. It quickly became obvious the man enjoyed the sound of his own voice. From his family's wealth he moved on to an uncle of his who was apparently neck deep in Chicago politics and had a hand in shipping a trainload of nonunion "foreigners" down from the city when the UMWA went on strike.

As twilight shifted to dark, the headlights flashed on the occasional set of reflective eyes crouched in the weeds at the side of the road, giving Henry what Cora called a case of the screaming meemies. Everything about this night was off, he felt it right down to the center of his bones.

Pierce turned off the main road onto a narrow lane squeezed by woods and growing a strip of weeds between the tire tracks. Henry's teeth clacked together as they bounced along too fast for the rough, curvy trail. He began to think maybe his dread had been spawned by an impending car crash and not a speakeasy raid.

Finally they rounded a curve and saw lights blazing in every window of a large, fancy two-story house with a deep porch that wrapped around two sides. Lit paper lanterns were strung between the porch posts and from the house to some of the trees, swaying in the light breeze. A mix of cars and buggies were haphazardly parked all over the lawn.

Noise poured out of the open windows, a piano, squeals of laughter, and a drone of voices. The top half of the front door was lace-covered glass. Pierce kept a possessive hand on Cora's arm while he knocked three times on the glass, followed by four lighter raps. A man the size of a mountain with a neck that hung over his collar in a giant roll opened the door. It seemed absurd to have this secret knock when all of the windows were wide-open to the porch. But then, what did Henry know about speakeasies?

They stepped into an entry hall, and the mountain closed the door behind them. A wide staircase was on the left side of the hall. On the right, a double door opened into a room packed with people and clouded with cigarette smoke. A three-piece band played on a low riser in the far corner, its sound all but drowned out by the loud voices and laughter. A chalkboard beside the door held the menu. For a supper club, it didn't offer much in the way of supper: ham sandwiches or fried chicken and potato salad. Most folks weren't eating.

As Henry had mentally predicted, Cora's appearance caused a stir. The hot urge to punch each of the ogling men in the nose took Henry by surprise. He was used to people looking at her, it happened every day on the field. But here, in this close-packed place filled with liquor-besotted fools, it felt different.

Pierce led Cora to a round table in the center of the room and pulled out her chair. "This is my *personal* table."

Henry sat across from Cora, Gil on her other side. Pierce pulled out a cigarette, then offered the monogrammed gold case around the table. If Henry hadn't been afraid he'd make a fool of himself choking on it, he'd have taken one just to make the point that he wasn't invisible.

"The slot machines are in the upstairs gallery." Pierce pointed two fingers holding a cigarette toward the staircase. "Poker's in the rear parlor. And, as you can see, liquor is everywhere." He leaned close to Cora. "They have very fine smuggled whiskey. What can I get you, my lovely?"

Gil made a noise in the back of his throat.

"I'll get my own in a moment, thank you," Cora said.

Pierce looked as if she'd just slapped him. "As you wish." He shoved his chair back and walked over to a marble soda counter that was dispensing something other than soft drinks and chocolate sodas. He started talking to a rouged woman wearing a short, sheer dress and a sparkly turban around her head. Her earrings were so long they brushed her shoulders when she moved. She held a long cigarette holder between her gloved fingers and kept her nose pointed toward the ceiling as she talked to Pierce. Henry thought she looked ridiculous.

Unfortunately, Pierce didn't stay away long. Apparently his masculine pride healed quickly.

A middle-aged woman wearing a white-collared, navy dress suitable for church came to their table. She had a fine lace-edged hankie tucked under a bracelet on her left wrist. "Good to see you, Junior." She rested a motherly hand on his shoulder. "Will your father be coming in tonight? I have someone interested in his spot at the poker table."

Pierce drew on his cigarette and blew out the smoke before he answered. "I have no idea what the old man is doing." He gestured with his cigarette-holding fingers again, this time around the table. "We'll have four ham sandwiches."

"Actually, I'd like the fried chicken, please," Cora said, and smiled at Pierce's frown. "It's easy to get a ham sandwich on the road, but fried chicken . . . that's a treat."

Pierce was still frowning. "You heard the lady, Belle." He looked to Gil. "Ace? Ham sandwich good enough for you?"

"It's Gil. And, yes, that'll be fine." Gil looked to Belle. "And a bottle of your best whiskey."

She looked surprised. "A bottle?"

"Make it two," Gil said. "Pierce is treating. His family is in coal, you know."

Belle gave Gil a sly wink and laughed. "You're those daredevils everyone is talking about, aren't you?"

Cora said, "Yes, we are! Captain Gilchrist seems to think my handbills are a waste of time, but you just proved him wrong."

Henry watched with a sinking heart as Gil smiled at her. None of the usual challenge was in it.

The night grew deeper. Gil frowned each time Cora and Pierce left the table to dance, but refused to dance when Cora asked him. Henry was too nervous to dance. Two bottles of whiskey turned into three. Cora sipped all evening on a single glass — a bit of surprise, as well acquainted as she seemed to be with "blind pigs." Henry abstained, not because he didn't want to try a drink, but because he wanted his wits sharp. He'd been eyeing the exits in case they had to make a run for it.

Pierce and Gil seemed to be having an undeclared contest to see who could hold more liquor. Pierce's eyes looked to be floating in his head. Gil grew so still and silent Cora checked to make sure he was still breathing.

At eleven thirty the place was still full —

and it was the middle of the week. Suddenly, Pierce pitched forward, his forehead landing on the tablecloth with a thud.

Gil mumbled, "I win." Then his chin hit his chest.

"Swell," Cora huffed. "I'm going to the powder room." She got up and Belle directed her up the stairs.

Henry sat with his elbow on the table, his cheek propped on his fist, wishing they could just clear out. When Cora got back, he was going to throw Pierce over his shoulder, toss him in the car, and drive them back to camp. Fancy man could sleep it off in the backseat. Gil could probably still stagger to the car on his own.

A flicker of light outside the window caught Henry's eye.

His nerves snapped to attention. Police?

When it flashed again, it was obviously not a headlight. Lightning?

He stood up.

Balls of fire flew through the open windows on his right and the one behind him. Flaming bottles shattered on the hardwood, spreading fire across the floor, nibbling at trailing tablecloths.

Screams broke out. Tables and chairs overturned.

The music screeched to a stop.

Feet thundered toward the door, bodies jammed shoulder to shoulder in the opening.

Another bottle came through another window.

Fire licked up the draperies on two walls. Tablecloths caught.

Gil came sluggishly to his feet.

Bodies were ten deep in the doorway, arms and voices flailing.

"Go out through there!" Henry shoved Gil toward the open window near the band riser. It had the least amount of fire near it. A hand holding a clarinet was clutching the sill, then disappeared. Gil's gait was unsteady, but he moved in that direction.

Pierce's head stayed on the table. Henry grabbed him up and threw him over a shoulder. Gil disappeared across the sill. Henry shoved Pierce through and let him fall to the ground six feet below. He landed with a thud.

Henry heard more glass breaking. The whoosh of fresh flames.

He looked over his shoulder. Why wasn't anyone else using the windows? He yelled and waved his arms, even gave a shrill whistle, but all of the bodies continued to surge against the doorway.

Cora. He stood on a chair and looked

across the room, but didn't see her. He hoped she'd been near the front door and was already outside.

The smoke was getting thicker. How could fire spread so fast? The heat stung his skin.

He went through the window, dropping down right on Pierce's still, soft body. The man's breath left in a whoosh.

Gil sat twenty feet away in the grass . . . right in front of a line of white-robed and hooded men.

"People are dying in there!" Henry shouted, waving to the men. "Come on!"

One by one, they turned around and walked away.

Henry grabbed Pierce by the heels and dragged him to Gil. Then he ran around to the front yard, hoping to hell that Cora had made it out.

He shoved the dazed and the panicked, jumping to see over heads, calling her name.

He heard her call to him.

Spinning, he couldn't see her.

All of the windows on the first floor were nothing but flames. People stumbled over and stepped on those who'd fallen near the front door. Several of the paper lanterns on the porch were balls of fire.

"Henry! Around here! On the side!"

He ran around the corner of the house, to

the side without a porch. Her upper body leaned out a second-floor window, smoke rolling out over her head. Flames were climbing up the outside wall. Henry realized it had been doused with gasoline.

"The stairs are blocked," she yelled.

A man ran around the corner of the house, his coat on fire. Someone knocked him to the ground, beating at the flames with bare hands.

Henry moved as close as he could and smelled his own singed hair.

"Jump to me!" He held out his arms. "Push off. You have to clear the fire."

She folded herself up, feet on the sill, hands on the frame. "Get out of the way! I'll just hurt you."

"Come on! Move!"

A loud pop came from behind her and she leaped off.

Her body hit Henry square in the chest and knocked him backward off his feet. He wrapped his arms around her and held her in front of him to keep her from hitting the ground.

"Holy hell!" she said against his chest.

"Is there anyone else up there?" He rolled to his side and let her go.

"I don't know." She jumped to her feet and they both stepped farther from the heat.

"Everything was so crazy. The bathroom window exploded, then there was all of this fire. What happened?"

Henry ran his hands over her arms, her hands. "You didn't get burned?"

"No. Where's Gil?"

"Around on the side. Safe. Go to Pierce's car and wait there."

For once, she didn't argue.

Henry made a circle of the house to see if he could help anyone else out a window or off the porch roof. He didn't find anyone.

Gil and Pierce lay like two rag dolls on the ground, far enough to be safe from the fire. That's where Henry found Cora, not by the Packard. Gil's head was in her lap. The sight of it stabbed Henry's heart as surely as any knife could have.

Why not me? I went to find you in the confusion of the fire. Me. Not Gil.

Henry sat a few feet away, as if the space might take his heart out of striking distance. But his eyes were drawn to the sight of Cora stroking Gil's head more than they were to the fire consuming Belle's — which at the moment felt less destructive than what was happening inside Henry's chest. They should leave. Before the sheriff or fire department showed up. Before questions could be asked. Most everyone else had

281

fled. But suddenly, Henry didn't care. Cora was with Gil. Nothing else seemed to matter now.

Belle's burned to the ground. Neither the sheriff nor the fire department showed up. By the break of dawn nothing was left but embers and smoking ash . . . and the blackened marble bar, now sitting in the basement.

Belle walked in ceaseless circles around the ruins, her lace-trimmed hankie pressed to her mouth.

The injured had been loaded into cars and taken away. Were there dead? Who knew? Four cars other than the Packard were still in the yard.

Finally, Cora looked at Henry. Her eyes were hollow. He couldn't help but move closer and put his arm around her shoulders. She leaned into him. "It was so fast. How did this happen?"

Henry told Cora about seeing the Klansmen.

Cora looked up at him. "My God, why?"

Gather's words echoed in Henry's mind. *Mine trouble. Strikes. Been nothin' but beatin's and guns and lynchin' round here for quite a spell. Had ourselves a regular massacre of scab foreigners last year. Course, bootleggers is still a problem. But the Ku Klux Klan's get-*

tin' involved in the fracas, cleanin' things up.

"Bloody Williamson," Henry said under his breath. "Bloody Williamson."

10

The newspaper reported the fire at Mrs. Thomas Franklin's private residence as accidental, a tragedy that cost the "quiet widow" all of her worldly goods, a lifetime of memories, her aged cat, and a pet canary. No mention of the hundred people inside. No mention of bootleg liquor. No mention of the Klan — even though he'd overheard someone telling Belle about seeing the hooded men. Henry wondered if there really were no deaths, or if that, too, was a fiction of reporting. He quickly scanned the paper but found no mention of "missing" people.

He tucked the paper under his arm and headed toward the train station. He'd drawn the short straw and had to go into town to check the freight depot for the propeller. He didn't like being separated from Cora. And he sure as hell didn't like leaving her alone out there with Gil. But what choice did he have? He was used to being alone, but Cora stirred a new sort of loneliness, one he'd never before experienced, a peculiar aching of the soul.

"You there! Hold up!" The voice startled him. He was usually more aware of his surroundings, wary of eyes locked on him for a second too long, but his thoughts of Cora had waylaid his caution.

With his heart off to the races, he stopped and adjusted his cap just a little lower over his eyes before he turned around.

A middle-aged man in a dark suit and fedora was getting out of a car parked at the curb. He carried himself like a lawman — the serious kind.

Henry's mind raced to organize his story, all the while he was praying this was about the fire at the supper club.

"What's your name?"

"Jefferson."

"You're not from here."

"Sir?"

"Where do you come from?" The man opened his coat and showed a badge pinned to his vest. Not a sheriff's star.

Henry's heart stopped beating. He was sure of it because it stopped rushing in his ears. He forced air out of his chest. "St. Louis." *Why did I say that? I don't know anything about St. Louis.* It was the only place he could think of that was in the opposite direction from where he'd really come from.

"You're with that airplane pilot. The one advertising the show?"

Henry nodded.

The man stepped closer and Henry's muscles tightened. If he ran, where would he go? He couldn't go back to Cora and Gil.

"How long you been with him?"

"Three years." An oil slick of panic rose in his belly. *What if the man goes straight to Gil and asks the same question?*

"He ever fly to Canada?"

It took a second for Henry to process this unexpected question. "Canada?" He'd gone so dry the word clicked against the roof of his mouth.

"You a parrot? Yeah. Canada."

"No. Never. We just fly to farms and little towns . . . in the United States. Mostly west of here."

"Been to Chicago?"

"What? No."

"French Lick, Indiana? West Baden Springs Hotel?"

"No." Henry did know mineral springs were in French Lick. Supposed to cure anything that ailed you.

"Ever heard of Johnny Torrio or Al Capone?"

"The gangsters?"

"Aren't you just as green as spring grass? Yeah, the gangsters. Ever cross paths?"

"Of course not."

"You and that pilot ever *deliver* anything for them?"

"Never met them. Never been to Chicago. Don't do anything but do shows and sell rides." His gut unclenched. This was about bootleg, not murder. So much for Pierce's assurance to Cora that the prohees were all well-oiled. "Is that all?"

"For now. I might just be here long enough to check out your show."

"We're grounded. Broke the propeller." Henry walked away on legs as wobbly as two wet mop strings.

He felt the man's eyes on his back as he went straight to the depot. He was so distracted that he stepped in a pile of horse manure as he crossed the street.

The propeller wasn't there yet.

When he came back out of the depot, the lawman was standing in front of the hotel, leaning with his back against the corner of the building, his raking gaze peering from under the brim of his hat.

Henry took the long way around to head

back out to the Jenny.

When he reached the Gather farm, he still felt as if he were filled with ants. He had to figure out a way to get Gil on board with his story, just in case the lawman showed up out here. But how to do it without giving himself away?

When he got to the pasture, he slowed and lightened his step. He couldn't see Cora and Gil from the gate. Some perverse need to torture himself arose, the need to sneak up on them and catch them in whatever they were doing.

Cora's laugh tripped across the field. Not a ha-ha laugh, something more . . . intimate.

Henry's stomach soured. He crept even more slowly.

They were on the far side of the Jenny's tail.

Henry moved as if he were tracking a deer. He edged closer. Peered around the tail. He didn't want to see. He had to.

Gil was sitting on the ground with his legs crossed. He looked to be gapping spark plugs. Cora was behind him, one arm draped over his shoulder, leaning forward, tickling his chin with a piece of foxtail grass.

"Stop it." Gil dropped the spark plug and reached up, pulling her around and onto his lap.

That's when she saw Henry and her eyes widened. "Oh!" She scooted off Gil's lap, looking embarrassed. *Cora* looked embarrassed. That fact shot straight through Henry. He wanted to run. But that would let Cora know how much he cared. He stood stock-still with his ears ringing.

Gil looked up. Guilt clouded his eyes the second he saw Henry. "Was it there?"

Henry willed himself to stop trembling like a leaf in the wind. "No. But we might have another problem."

It surprised him that Cora, not Gil, jumped up. "What problem?"

Something overtook Henry. Suddenly he wanted to make her feel as badly as he did. It was wrong. But it was true. The only way he knew how was to draw out the anxiety that had unexpectedly shown on her face. "There was a man in a suit. Asking questions."

"What kind of questions? About me?"

Henry stood there and looked at her for a moment. Why was she so jumpy? He began to think maybe she worried that her ma hadn't just rolled over and accepted that her little girl had decided to be a gypsy. "Why would he ask about you?"

She was quick to shrug. "Well, you were looking at me when you said it."

He stared at her long enough that she looked away. "I think he was a prohibition agent. He thinks we might be flying bootleg for gangsters in Chicago."

"Why on earth would he think that?" Gil asked.

"We have a plane. There was a supper club that just burned to the ground. Maybe somebody was killed in that fire. I don't know. But I was thinking, it might be best if we make people think we've been working together for several years, knocking around west of here . . . far away from Chicago or the Canadian border."

"That's a good idea," Cora said. "A very good idea. It'll make us seem more established to our customers, too." He couldn't figure her enthusiasm, but Henry wasn't about to look a gift horse in the mouth.

Gil shrugged. "Anything that keeps the government out of my business."

"I was thinking maybe three years would be logical — anything longer might flag us up because of Cora's age."

"My age!"

"You could maybe pass for twenty," Henry said. "But more than that is stretching it."

Gil picked up the spark plug he'd dropped. "Help me get these back in the

Jenny. I want to be ready to get out of here as soon as that prop arrives."

The relief Henry felt over getting Gil to agree to saying they'd all been together for three years was weighted down by his surety that Cora was in love with Gil. Gil was a man. To Cora, Henry was still Kid.

There wasn't a damn thing he could do about it.

And he couldn't bring himself to leave them. Not yet.

The propeller arrived the next day. Mercury's Daredevils pulled out of Marion without putting on a show. They gave Mr. Gather three dollars and free plane rides for him and his son for helping them pull the plane out of the ditch and allowing them to camp in their field. Gather was decidedly unhappy about the loss of imagined massive revenue from the show, but took the three dollars and the rides.

Cora and Mercury took off in the plane with Gil. Henry watched them lift off with jealousy coloring his vision. Was his heart hurting just because of Cora? Or was it because, as he watched that plane climb into the sky without him, he realized how much he loved flying?

He supposed that was the way of human

beings, wanting what they couldn't have, not appreciating the things they did until they were gone. Through all of his years of loneliness and isolation, Henry had promised himself he wouldn't be like everyone else. He would never want what belonged to others. He'd appreciate everything, no matter how small, and take nothing for granted. And yet there he was, loving both Cora and the Jenny more as they disappeared into the distance. He truly did not want Cora traveling on the motorcycle alone, but all the same he wished she weren't leaving with Gil.

He pointed the motorcycle west, his destination Cape Girardeau, Missouri. Cora had made a good point when they'd been discussing moving on: "You know this kind of stuff happens everywhere. The Klan's declared war on liquor and gambling all over the country — not to mention trying to rout out Catholics, Jews, Negroes, Germans . . . well, pretty much everybody else. We can't let it stop us from putting on a show." Even so, in the end they'd all agreed to leave as soon as possible, to put a significant distance between themselves and the cold ashes of that supper club.

In the years without Peter, Henry hadn't had anyone to talk to about his troubling thoughts, his painful emotions. Maybe that's why they were suddenly clamoring for release. Although he viewed Cora and Gil as his family, in truth they all kept their deepest selves hidden from one another, dancing on the edges of intimacy but never stepping in. A big part of him wanted to tell them everything. Carrying a secret alone was bad for the soul. It fed the darkness.

As the graveled miles rolled under his tires, Henry's thoughts circled back around to the fire. The anger in his soul that night had matched the heat of the flames. But what had he done? Nothing. He'd watched those hooded men turn and walk away just as if they'd been leaving a church social. He should have done something to stop them. At the very least he should have gone to the sheriff and told what he'd seen. But he'd been too worried about his own skin.

He'd seen Klansmen in Indiana, marching in parades with their white robes, peeking out of the eyeholes in their pointy hoods. It was laughable, those hoods in their small town. A lady standing beside him at one parade had pointed and said, "There's the mayor. That's Judge Chamberlain. John Haskins. Fred Williams." She leaned Henry's way and whispered, "I recognize their shoes."

He hadn't given the Klan much thought before now. They were politically powerful, for sure. What those men had done at Belle's supper club was based on a blanket belief that left no room for individual humanity, the same as the way people treated German Americans during the war. He was pretty sure not one of those men would have attacked Belle's if he'd been alone. Like all bullies, the KKK traveled in packs.

Henry thought on that cowardly kind of broadcast hate, hiding behind masks in the dark, delivering sneak attacks. He supposed maybe generalized hate was easier; you didn't have to look a person in the eye.

Was what those men felt any different from the anger Henry had stored up inside? Suddenly just locking it away wasn't enough. He had to kill it. To stamp it out before it invited his old friend disaster in to sit down at the table once again.

He pushed the motorcycle faster, the wind tearing at his hair — but he only felt angrier.

Henry's first sight of the Mississippi River made him pull off the gravel road and stop. For several minutes he sat there, his eyes moving up and downstream. He knew it was the biggest river in the country, but he hadn't been prepared for the astounding width, the amount of river traffic. The bank was low and muddy on the east side, the last mile or so leading up to it a flat plain. The land was higher on the west side. The current didn't flow like that of the Indiana rivers he was used to, the White and the Mississinewa, rippling steadily in a single direction, so shallow they could only float a canoe or a fishing boat. Here the water seemed to roil, reverse itself, and in some places it looked as if it flowed straight up from the bottom and spread in all directions. It was so muddy it was opaque as brown paint. He supposed that its concealing everything beneath its surface made it even more forbidding.

He wished he could see it from the air, the splits around sandbars, the curves and twists of that wide brown ribbon. A giant barge, assisted by two big boats, was carrying side-by-side strings of railcars, the brown water behind them looking as if it were stirred by a massive underwater tail. He could see two steamboats, belching smoke from their twin stacks. A coal barge chugged north — Williamson County was following him.

After finding a ferry, he crossed to his destination of Cape Girardeau. He spotted trouble the instant he drove his motorcycle alongside the trolley tracks on Main Street. On every other utility pole were posters — not just handbills, but large posters with *color* printing and a depiction of a biplane with a wing walker standing spread-eagle on top.

Henry pulled to the curb and shut off the motorcycle.

HOFFMAN'S FLYING CIRCUS
TOP-NOTCH AND UP-TO-DATE ATTRACTION

4–YES, FOLKS, 4!–SPECTACULAR AIRCRAFT
PERFORMING DAREDEVIL THRILLS

WING WALKER DEFIES GRAVITY AND DEATH

COME SEE PILOT EXTRAORDINAIRE JAKE
HOFFMAN PUT HIS PLANE THROUGH
TAILSPINS, BARREL ROLLS, SPIRALS,
FALLING LEAF, IMMELMAN TURNS AND MORE

DECORATED WAR VETERAN REECE ALTHOFF
MAKES A THRILLING LEAP FROM A PLANE
2,000 FEET IN THE AIR
PERFORMANCE AT 2 PM
JULY 28
BROADWAY PAST FAIRGROUNDS
PASSENGER FLIGHTS ALL DAY BY SAFEST,

SANEST PILOTS IN THE AIR
ADMISSION $2 CHILDREN UNDER 12
FREE RIDES $5

Safe and sane? No one who did those stunts could be. All four corners of the poster were stamped with an insignia bearing the show's name. This air circus had enough cash to print fancy flyers specific to date and location. Chances were none of their airplanes had patches and mismatched paint. How much of Missouri had this circus already covered?

With a sickness growing in his belly, he yanked down the poster, folded it, and stuck it inside his shirt. Then he went to wait at the courthouse for Cora and Gil so they could decide their next move. Options were few; they'd used the last of their cash to put gasoline in the machines to get them here.

Cape Girardeau was laid out differently from any other county seat Henry had seen. He supposed that was because of its being a port on the river. Instead of a courthouse square in the center of town, Main Street ran along the riverfront and the courthouse sat on a high hill a few blocks to the west.

Henry rode the motorcycle up Themis Street, which T'd into the courthouse.

Directly ahead were six long tiers of grand, wide steps that led up the hill to the pillared front of the two-story courthouse. The tiers extended in the grassy lawn on both sides of the steps and were dotted with trees and park benches. It was probably the most beautiful approach to a building Henry had ever seen.

He parked on Lorimier next to a block-ice delivery truck.

Sitting on one of the park benches were Cora and Gil. Mercury sat between them and let out a bark when he saw Henry.

"Henry!" Cora came running down the steps, waving a poster in her hand. Mercury bounced along behind her. "Did you see this? They have a *wing walker*! And *four* planes! What are we going to do?"

Gil stayed slouched on his perch with one arm on the back of the bench. Henry wondered how the man could stay so calm considering their dire straits. Yet it gave Henry some satisfaction to know that in said dire straits, Cora turned to him.

He took her by the arm and turned her around. They walked back up the steps, toward the bench. "We'll figure it out."

"How? I thought we were out of money." Then she turned her attention back to the poster. "See." She tapped the bottom of the poster. "*They* figured out a way to charge admission!"

"Looks like they've figured out a lot of things." Mercury was nipping at Henry's heels. He bent down and scooped the pup up; petting him always soothed Henry's raw nerves. "Bet they don't have a dog."

"Seriously, Henry! If people wanted to see a dog do tricks, they'd go to a regular circus. We need an air spectacle! A wing walker."

Henry shook his head. "There's no way we can compete here and now with this show. We'll have to find another way to skin this cat."

They reached Gil, and Cora said, "For some reason, Flyboy is as cool as a cucumber and thinks this will all just work itself out."

Once he got closer, Henry could see that Gil had already found himself some local bootleg — which probably accounted for his boneless ease and lack of urgency.

Gil looked at Henry, blinking as if he were looking into the sun even though it was after six o'clock and the sun was well behind the courthouse. "We don't have enough gas to get the Jenny to the next county seat. And we sure as hell aren't going to sell any rides with these fellas in town. It's time to call it a day."

Cora's eyes grew wide and her mouth tight. "What are you saying?"

"I'm saying Mercury's Daredevils are over. Maybe you can get on with this air circus. Doesn't say they have a motorcycle . . . or a woman."

"That's it! You're giving up, just like that?"

Gil shrugged. "I can scrape by alone. But I need to be agile to do it. And with you two to feed and the motorcycle —"

"You can't be serious!" Cora shouted. Her jaw flexed as she gritted her teeth. "We've worked so hard! We just need to think bigger to compete."

Henry pushed down his panic as he looked at Gil's resolute and somewhat relieved face.

"Hey!" Gil finally looked her in the eye. "*I* didn't want any of this. It worked when I was on my own. I'm going back to that."

"You'd just leave us stranded?"

"Henry's welcome to stick with me if he wants; he's a much better mechanic than me. It's the motorcycle —"

"This air circus obviously plans ahead!" She shook the now-crumpled poster in her fist. "They don't just fly over a town and do a few stunts to draw a crowd. We just need to take the next step. Expand. Henry and I can learn to fly. We'll get another plane. We can ditch the motorcycle —"

"Stop! Cora, stop." Gil raised his hands as if warding off a physical attack.

"We can pool the money from each of our cuts and buy the gasoline to get out of here, at least. Regroup."

They probably could limp on to someplace else, as long as that someplace wasn't too far away.

"You'll do that, won't you, Henry?" Cora looked at him. "And with mine and Gil's we should have enough money —"

"I'm broke," Gil said.

Henry thought of the money going into the envelope at the post office.

"What do you mean, you're broke? How can you be broke? I haven't seen you buy anything other than the occasional drink."

"Feel free to check my pockets." Gil lifted his arms away from his body in invitation.

"Henry?"

"Ten dollars and seventy-six cents."

"I have —"

"No," Gil said. "This is the end. I don't want a bigger act. Hell, I didn't want this act. It's better to call it quits here where you can join up with another show."

"But you'll take *Henry* with you."

Henry cast a sideways glance at her. Her face was filled with fury, but her eyes shone with unshed tears.

"It's up to him. He can probably get on with Hoffman if he wants, too." Gil's face grew almost cruel. "And by the way, he already knows how to fly."

This was not the same man who'd taken off from Marion this morning. Henry stood there listening to Cora's ragged breathing and studying Gil, trying to figure what had triggered this sudden decision. With the increased travel time in waiting for the ferry and the condition of the roads, Henry figured Gil and Cora had been in Cape Girardeau at least five hours longer than he had. What had happened?

"You are such an ass," Cora finally said.

Gil lifted a nonchalant shoulder. "I admitted it the first day we met."

"You're just . . ." She snapped her mouth closed and looked to be collecting herself. "I'll leave you to burn off that hooch and come to your senses." She spun around and stomped down the steps to Lorimier Street.

"What the hell, Gil?" Henry asked. "You're not serious, are you?"

"Go after her. Make sure she's all right."

Henry pegged Gil with a suspicious eye. "You won't go climb in the Jenny and leave?"

"Can't. Not unless I can figure out a way to get her to run on my own piss." Gil paused. "And, yes, I'm serious. Get her to see reason and join up with Hoffman."

"What makes you think he'll take her?"

"He's not a man to miss an opportunity to grow his show."

Henry looked at Gil more sharply. "You know him?"

"Crossed paths more than once. Served with Althoff."

"Something happened today." Henry didn't pose it as a question.

Gil gazed out over the town and the river, pressing his lips together. His chest rose and fell with a deep breath. "I need her away from me."

Henry glanced over his shoulder. Cora had reached the street and was heading down Themis toward Main. Henry was getting emotional seasickness trying to keep up with the changing tides between Gil and Cora. "Why?"

"Just go." Gil got up off the bench and started across the stretch of lawn.

Henry watched Gil's back for a few seconds, then turned to follow Cora, feeling his life once again shifting under his feet.

11

By the time Henry caught up to Cora, she'd already come back up Themis to Lorimier Street and turned north. She was walking with determined purpose. Mercury hustled along beside her.

"Where are you going?" Henry asked.

"I'm doing what Gil wants." She didn't slow or look at Henry. "Going to find Jake Hoffman." Her feet were hitting the ground so hard it shook her breath and words.

"I don't think he meant for you to do it this minute. It's late. You don't even know how far out they are." He hadn't decided which course he was going to take, push her out or draw her back in — not until he'd found out what had happened today.

She kept moving. "Fairgrounds are about a mile and a half. They can't be too far from there if they advertised that location."

"With a show that big, they're probably staying in a hotel."

"I'll wait. What else do I have to do?"

"Cora, don't be ridiculous." He grabbed her arm and stopped her. "What in the hell happened today? What made Gil start this?"

"Oh, who knows what's going on in that thick head of his?" Her words sounded hard, but her chin quivered and she looked as if she was about to cry.

For the first time since Henry had met her she seemed vulnerable. Even when she'd nearly drowned, her spirit had been unbroken. The pain in her eyes set Henry's heart on fire. Just as he reached for her shoulders, she turned and started walking again.

He called after her, "We do have a motorcycle, you know."

She stopped dead, but didn't turn around. It looked as if she was wiping her eyes. Her shoulders squared and she spun and headed back in his direction with as much determination as she'd been going the other way. "Well, come on, then."

"Ho-ly moly," Cora breathed after Henry shut off the engine.

Henry could find no words.

The sight of four majestic, identically painted airplanes lined up in the golden glow of the setting sun was enough to make

Henry's heart stutter. Three were Jennies, and the other looked similar but was bigger; all had red and white sunburst stripes on the wings and body. Parked beside the planes were a panel truck and a trailer, both with paint schemes similar to the planes'. The tails of the planes and the doors of the truck had circular insignias matching the ones on the poster.

Nearby were several roomy, neat camping tents, also bearing the Hoffman Flying Circus insignia. A long table held a couple of portable stoves, one with a coffeepot on it, the other a soup kettle. Beside those was a loaf of bread ready for slicing. Five tin plates and cups were stacked at one end.

At first Henry thought the place was deserted as a ghost town, then a redheaded man emerged from one of the tents pulling his suspenders up over his shoulders.

"Sorry, kids. No rides until the show opens." He looked beyond them, then back to Henry. "Nice motorcycle you got there."

"Thanks," Cora said. "It's mine."

Mercury leaped from Cora's arms and headed directly to the outdoor kitchen. He danced on his back legs with his nose high in the air, trying to reach the tabletop.

"Beg pardon for my assumption, Miss . . ." The man looked impressed.

She extended her hand, not in a girlie way, but as a prospective business partner. "Rose. Miss Cora Rose. Are you Mr. Hoffman?"

He shook her hand. "Reece Althoff. Jake's in town getting supplies." He offered a hand to Henry.

"Henry Jefferson." The name was finally beginning to slide off his tongue like a well-oiled lie. "You served in the air corps with Charles Gilchrist?"

Reece grinned. "I did."

Cora cast Henry a surprised glance, then went on smoothly as if that hadn't been news to her. "Henry and I have been working with him this summer. We call ourselves Mercury's Daredevils. Stunts in the air and on the ground." She said it like a pitch.

With a marveling shake of the head, Reece said, "That bastard's still alive?"

"Quite," Cora said in a tone that said she might be wishing otherwise.

"I never saw anybody try to get himself killed as hard as that man did. Can't believe he hasn't managed it yet." Reece seemed to catch himself. "Come on over here and have a seat." He pointed to a group of camp stools. "Can I offer you some stew? Plenty to go round."

Cora said, "No, thank you," at the same

time Henry said, "Yes, please."

Reece went to the table and handed Henry a plate. Then he looked at Cora. "You sure?"

"I couldn't choke down a bite right now." She looked at Henry as if he were a traitor. He sure didn't see how starving himself would do her any good.

After Henry filled his plate, Reece handed him a thick slice of bread, then tossed a chunk to Mercury. They sat down on the stools.

As Henry sopped up some of the gravy with his bread, he said, "Were you in reconnaissance, too?"

"Oh, no. I was a mechanic. Stayed nice and safe on the ground the whole time. Worked on Gil's plane quite a bit. Kept coming back with pieces missing . . . never figured how he kept it in the air long enough to get back to base most of the time. Recon had to fly low enough that ground artillery had no trouble hitting them, and German fighters went after the recon planes first; considered them the biggest threat — plus they weren't even armed with more than a pistol, like ducks in an arcade." Admiration colored Reece's features. "Pretty sure that man could fly an orange crate if you stuck wings on it. He got shot down twice — but

I suppose you already know that."

"He's been pretty closemouthed about the war," Henry said. "I'd like to hear it."

Reece rubbed his chin, recollecting. "First time, lemme see. Oh! That was when he showed back up after two days of sneaking from bush to bush, dragging his wounded photographer along with him. Wouldn't leave him." Reece paused as if thinking. "That poor bastard got killed not two months later. Second . . . well, Gil wasn't so lucky."

Up until now Cora had been fidgeting impatiently. "What happened?"

"Never heard all of it. Gil wasn't much of a talker back then — only gave the full account to the brass. Course lots of the pilots were standoffish. At first I figured they thought they were better than us. But once I paid attention, I saw they were that way with each other, too. It was more like they didn't want to get connected to anyone. Stood to reason. Weren't many came back."

"And?" Cora prompted.

"That time the photographer was killed outright, took a bullet in the head before the plane went down. Gil got captured by the Germans and sent to some camp. Took four months, but he escaped. Came back from the dead, as far as we were concerned.

Probably only weighed hundred and twenty pounds by then, skin and bones. If he'd made it back with the recon intelligence from that mission, there might have been a lot of soldiers lived to fight another day. I think that bothered him more than being in a prison camp."

Gil had said, *"I made some bad decisions. And someone else paid for them."*

Henry thought of the soldier who'd been gassed. The dead photographer. The lost intelligence that could have saved lives. Gil carried all of these as personal failures that others had paid for. But it was just war. Fate swinging lives in the wind. Perhaps Gil's salvation lay in getting him to see that. Armed with these facts, Henry would have a better chance of helping him.

Cora gave a little telltale sniffle.

Henry wanted to cry for the lives left twisted in the wreckage of that war.

Cora couldn't help being drawn closer to Gil now. He'd been mysterious before; now he was a tragic hero who'd earned her admiration.

Just as he'd earned Henry's admiration, as Gil needed to be made to recognize himself.

The war had left a lot of men with a lot of stories. Some closed the book and refused to let those stories see the light of day. Others seemed to need to recite and relive them time and again. Henry didn't know which was more poisonous to the soul.

When Phillip Whicker had first come courting on the Dahlgren farm, Henry hadn't been able to tell which of the three eldest sisters he was interested in. And maybe the man himself hadn't known. He'd been away for years, conscripted into the war, which had left him with a scar on his neck and a large number of heroic stories that the Dahlgren girls had eaten like candy. Eleven-year-old Sarah had been so overcome, she'd followed Henry around while he'd done his chores, sharing the exciting tales.

Instead of returning to the Whicker farm (across the river from the Dahlgrens') when a ship had delivered him back to the United States after the war, Phillip had stayed in New York City. He'd spent his time there "working on Wall Street." His stories of elegant parties with tuxedoed men and a million dollars' worth of jewels hanging on the women had "made Mother's eyes turn practically green," according to Sarah.

"When his papa got sick," Sarah had said, admiration coloring her voice, "Phillip said his 'conscience demanded' he return to

Indiana and take over the farm."

Henry had been milking a cow at the time. For coming home to work the farm, Phillip didn't seem to do much farmwork, but Henry kept his thoughts to himself. Especially the one how he suspected Phillip's confident swagger hid a weak character. Why else did he prattle on so about himself?

One night, Henry's curiosity had gotten the better of him. He'd sat outside the open parlor window while Phillip visited with the family. Henry was able to get a glimpse into the room and saw that Phillip was seated next to Violet, the oldest, who looked at him as if he were Christ risen from the grave.

Phillip was telling of his scar, which he'd received from a German knife with a nine-inch blade. "We were all asleep. This giant Hun must have belly-crawled into our camp with his knife in his teeth. He was working from foxhole to foxhole, silently slitting throats. He'd already gotten McPhee in ours. The instant the knife touched my skin, I sprang on him, sending the knife to make a jagged cut that missed the vessels. I wrestled him to the ground. He was a fantastic specimen of German brute strength. It was touch and go there for a while, but I finally overpowered him. Saved all but McPhee. That German never sneaked into another foxhole again." Phillip paused. "I couldn't leave my men behind on the lines while I went off to the hospital. I wrapped my neck and fought on until Armistice. They say if my wound had been tended properly, I might not have such a horrible scar."

"Filthy Germans," Emmaline had said. "No more than animals. Sneaking up with no honor like that."

The next day both Violet and Emmaline had looked at Henry as if he'd been the one to slice Phillip's throat. From then on, Henry had made sure to stay out of Phillip's sight. But the man's tales continued to feed the girls' suspicion and disgust, making the war as fresh as yesterday.

After that, they got busy recruiting anyone who would listen into their little band of loathing.

Henry realized he'd drifted from the conversation. Cora was clearing her throat and saying to Reece, "Thank you for telling us. Gil is silent as a mummy when it comes to his past . . . or anything else, for that matter. Opaque as an oak door."

"Same old fellow, then."

Things fell silent. Henry's thoughts were

weighted as much by his own recollections as these new revelations about Gil. Plus he'd facilitated Cora's quest as far as he was going to, so he kept his mouth filled with food, not conversation.

He hoped by the time they got to the Jenny, Gil would be over whatever had made him want to cut ties with Cora. Even as he hoped it, he knew it was a waste of energy; this didn't feel like any normal rift. Something significant had happened; something unalterable and course changing. Over the years, Henry had come to recognize the smell of it.

"Well," Cora said, "I've come with a proposition. I'm looking to get on with a bigger show, and Gil suggested yours would be a perfect fit."

Reece's ginger eyebrows rose. "That so? What do you do with Mercury's Daredevils?"

"Stunts on the motorcycle." She looked over and gasped. "Mercury!" The dog had jumped up on the table and had his head down in the pot of stew. "Get out of there!" She jumped up, and Mercury's head came out of the pot. He looked at her, licked his gravy-covered chops, leaped off the table, and ducked behind one of the tents. "I am terribly sorry, Mr. Althoff."

"Meh." He waved a hand. "The fellas will never know the difference . . . as long as he left enough to feed them."

She sat back down, her cheeks pink. "As I was saying, Mercury rides with me. He also does some very entertaining tricks on his own —"

"So I see!" Reece jerked his head toward the outdoor kitchen.

Cora managed an embarrassed chuckle. "I have a stunt where I ride through fire, I can do a ramp jump, and I've got ideas for lots more."

Reece looked intrigued. "We could use some ground entertainment, keep the folks happy while they're waiting their turn for a ride."

"Exactly! And being a woman working with a dog, it makes us more unique. It's all about the draw."

"That it is." He studied her for a moment. "You do any wing walking?"

"As a matter of fact, I have . . . although I only started recently."

Henry's spoon stopped halfway to his mouth. A chunk of potato plopped back onto his tin, splattering gravy on his pant leg.

"I quite like it. And have a *million* ideas for air stunts. I honestly don't know how you pilots can just sit there for hours on end flying a straight line. I suppose I'm truly a daredevil at heart."

Henry closed his eyes as his dinner turned in his stomach. It was all becoming clear.

When they got on the motorcycle to leave, Henry asked her, "Do you really want this, or are you just doing it to prove to Gil someone else wants you?"

"It's good business to have options." She'd cheered up considerably.

Henry was quiet for a minute. "He wants you to go, you know. He's not just trying to punish you, or prove a point."

"Punish me? For what?"

"Seriously, Cora? When was your first opportunity to climb out on the wing of a flying plane?"

"That did make him mad . . . really mad. But he's been mad before."

"Not like this."

When she looked at him, Henry could see she knew it, too. "His loss." She tried to make it sound glib, but Henry heard the hurt underneath. "This act is well funded. They have *contracts* for work through most of the winter down South. I'll be able to implement all of the stunts I've been thinking of. And the crowds! Did you hear how many people they average per show?"

"I did." It was a significant operation, no doubt about it. And Gil was right, it was perfect for Cora, no matter what her motivation. But an undercurrent to all of this remained unexplained. Her climbing out of the cockpit might have been the fuse, but there had been plenty of fuses over the past weeks. Where had the gunpowder come from for the explosion?

What Reece had told them cast a new light on Gil's personality; Henry now knew Gil's flirtation with death wasn't in Henry's imagination. And it wasn't new. Did Gil push because he felt invincible, bulletproof? Or was it darker? A true open invitation? Henry suddenly wondered if the escape from the prison camp had been just another way of waving a red flag at death.

Gil was complicated for sure, but everything Henry learned only raised more questions. He owed this new life to Gil, no matter how reluctantly he'd offered it. What they'd heard tonight had doubled both Henry's admiration and his worry. He was going to do his damnedest to keep Mercury's Daredevils together. But if keeping Cora was going to push Gil over the edge he seemed to be teetering on, Henry would have to stop fighting.

When Jake Hoffman had returned from town, he'd been surprisingly receptive to the idea of Cora's joining the air circus. She'd gone right to work on selling Henry, too, "a crack mechanic, inventor, and a pilot to boot." Hoffman wanted to see what Henry could do and asked them to come back tomorrow. The air circus was about to lose a pilot; Hoffman explained it was too hard to fly all over the country year-round when you're attached to a ball and chain. Reece had chimed in saying it was a rare woman who'd tolerate a man in this business; he'd been lucky enough to find one of the few.

"Since you two would *both* be with the circus" — Reece had eyed Henry and Cora — "it shouldn't be a problem."

Cora had said, "Oh! No. We're not . . . together, at least in that way."

Her forcefulness more than her words cut Henry to the core.

At that point, Jake Hoffman had raised a brow. "Not married? Or not . . . romantic?"

"We're strictly professional colleagues," Cora said, and Henry felt an inch shorter.

"Well, this show's got no room for romantic hoo-ha distracting the concentration and the trust. If there's any history between you two, I don't want to know about it. Be clear on this," Hoffman had said. "I got no tolerance for man-woman drama. *None.* As long as we all got that straight, we should do fine. If we agree tomorrow, there'll be a probation period, in case either party changes our minds in a few weeks."

"Well," Cora sounded flustered, "I still need to confirm things with Gil." She brightened. "Perhaps I can convince him to bring his Jenny on board, too. Then you'll have five planes and pilots."

Reece Althoff chimed in, "He's a damn fine pilot, Jake. Most naturally gifted I've ever seen."

Hoffman had nodded slowly. "We might work something out with Gil. Really good pilots are hard to come by. Have him come by tomorrow."

Cora had beamed as if all problems were solved.

Henry had kept his mouth sealed. Gil's coming "on board" was beyond unlikely. It would completely defeat the man's purpose for getting Cora on with the circus. Henry tried to untangle the hurt and the gloom of the situation from the possibilities and hope. Cora had just insinuated her being with Henry romantically was laughable. There was no getting around it. Even so, no matter how she felt about Gil, she would probably go with Hoffman, it was everything she wanted right there for the taking.

How much of a heel would Henry be if Hoffman offered him a job and he accepted? It would be good for hiding; he'd be even more invisible than he had been with Mercury's Daredevils. Even if he flew, with four other pilots and Cora, he could slip by virtually unnoticed. His conscious piped up, *Admit it, you think you might have a chance at Cora with Gil out of the picture.*

He closed the door on that voice; no need to put up with the self-shaming and guilt, because it wasn't going to happen. The very idea of Gil knocking around there all alone, courting death instead of living his life, with no one to pull him back from the brink . . . Henry had a sick feeling that Cora's leaving was not going to set Gil on the road to recovery.

No. Henry couldn't leave Gil. No matter what.

Now, as they left the fairgrounds, Henry put his arms on either side of Cora and started the motorcycle. Oh, yes, everyone was excited — except him. As he pulled away from the fairgrounds, his insides were full of slithering black snakes of dread.

Cora directed Henry out from Spring Street to the field where Gil had landed the Jenny. Henry half suspected Gil had lied about how much fuel he had left and had taken off just as soon as he'd left the courthouse lawn. Henry's heart beat like overworked pistons, only slowing when he saw the Jenny still sitting in the dusky light, looking as if she floated on a low cloud of awakening fireflies rising out of the grass. Gil, however, was nowhere to be seen.

"Let's go into town and find him," Cora said, just as brightly as if she and Gil had parted on the best of terms. "I want to tell him the news."

"I don't think either one of those things is a good idea."

"Fine. You don't have to go. I'll take the motorcycle."

Henry stayed put on the seat, blocking her from getting off with his arms by gripping the handlebar. "Tell me what happened."

"You already know. He didn't like me getting out of the cockpit."

"There's more." Henry wasn't sure he really wanted to know, but all of their

321

futures were at stake.

She shrugged and looked away.

"If you want my help in convincing him to pitch in with Hoffman, you're going to have to tell me."

"Why would I need help? It's a great opportunity!"

"For you. For me, maybe. For Gil . . . you know that's not what he wants."

"Gil doesn't know what he wants! Believe me." Only her stubbornness kept those tears that suddenly sprang to her eyes from falling.

"What happened?" Henry wasn't going to make it easier on her by voicing his suspicions.

"I got bored. Really, Henry, how do you stand just sitting there? I decided to try riding out on the lower wing for a while. I was perfectly safe, holding on to one of the struts. It's not like I climbed up on the top wing or hung from the landing gear. . . . I wasn't actually wing walking. I was just sitting. It wasn't a big deal."

"To you. But to Gil?"

"He needs to get over being so protective. I choose the risks I take. Not him."

"You could have hit an air pocket. You're not used to making adjustments for that kind of movement." Although if the girl could do a handstand on a moving motorcycle, her balance and reflexes had to be extraordinary. Still, encouragement was the last thing she needed. Fearlessness was useful, foolishness deadly. He worried Cora didn't know the difference. "You need to prepare for stunts. Plan. You do know that moving your weight around on the airplane requires corrections by the pilot, don't you? You probably scared the crap out of him." Henry could only imagine how he would have felt sitting in the cockpit, unable to stop her as she unexpectedly climbed out on a wing. Scared didn't come close.

"It scared him all right. Scared him enough to give me a good shake when we got on the ground. Scared him enough to admit his feelings for me."

Tingles shot over Henry's skin. His mouth went dry. He'd suspected. But hearing it made it sickeningly real. "He told you?"

"He kissed me." Her cheeks flamed uncharacteristically red. "Or maybe I kissed him. It all happened so fast. Things got out of hand."

Henry didn't want to know how far "out of hand" things had gotten. He dropped his hands from the handlebars and let his arms fall to his sides. "Get off."

"Why are *you* so mad?"

"Because Gil's already a fucking mess. And you killed our show."

"*I* did?" She jumped off the motorcycle and shoved her hands on her hips. "It's not like the kiss wasn't mutual! Besides, I can help him stop *being* a fucking mess."

"Pack up your stuff."

"Didn't you hear what I said? Gil needs me! I just have to convince him to go with us."

"Us? Hoffman hasn't officially offered me a place. And I won't leave Gil unless he forces me to."

A new worry bloomed in Henry's mind. What if Cora did convince Gil to go with Hoffman and then the air circus decided they didn't need Henry? He'd be left out in the cold.

Gil never showed up that night, or the next morning. Henry scouted around town but didn't find him. He hadn't held much hope that he would. So he and Cora finally went to talk to Hoffman without him. Henry only agreed to interview, as Cora called it, to ensure that she left with them. No matter what the offer, he wasn't taking off and leaving Gil behind. The man's absence had cleared any doubt. There was no way he'd agree to bring the Jenny to the circus. He had to be away from Cora. That was all that mattered now.

When they reached the fairgrounds, the show was over, the camp packed up. While Cora went off with Hoffman, Henry spent some time talking to Reece Althoff about the mechanics of the machines. Occasionally Henry would catch sight of Cora climbing on one of the tied-down planes — doing a handstand on the upper wing, dangling from the half circle of a lower wing skid (no danger at the moment as she was lying on the ground, but Henry's gut twisted when he thought of her doing it several hundred feet in the air). He had second thoughts about declining an offer to join the circus, should it come. He wanted to devise some safety devices for Cora's wing-walking stunts. He was sure he could reduce the risk without tipping off the spectators.

After Reece was convinced of Henry's competence, the two of them walked over to Hoffman and Cora.

Hoffman said to Althoff, "We've got one here near as crazy as you." To Cora he said, "Reece left space on the truck for the motorcycle. We can load it up and be on our way. Need to use all the daylight we can, get some miles under our belts toward the next stop."

Cora looked a little panicked. "We have to find Gil and talk to him. We can't just leave."

She thought her committing to go would force Gil to join up, too. But she was wrong, so very wrong.

"I understand your loyalty," Jake said. "Admire it. But we've got a schedule. We'd be happy to have you and Henry on the team, but would understand if you decide to stay here with Gil."

"What if we come along in a day or so?" she said.

"Monday we order new posters. If you're on board, now's the time. No sense in adding a woman if we can't advertise it."

Henry grabbed her arm and pulled her aside. "This is what you want. Go. I'll get a schedule from Hoffman. If I can convince Gil, we'll catch up to you. If he won't agree to join up, I won't either.

"But, I can't just leave him."

"*He* just left *you.* He doesn't want you around him, Cora!" Her startled expression made Henry soften his words. "Maybe he needs time to come around. Give it to him. If you're gone, he'll get a new perspective." The thought of being away from her nearly brought Henry to his knees. The idea she'd be taking on wing walking without him to help guide her preparation and minimize her risks was enough to turn his stomach. But he couldn't abandon Gil, and Cora was better off with the circus. Henry wondered if caring for a woman this deeply always caused this much pain. "Mercury's Daredevils can't make it against shows like this. You know it as well as I do. Don't tie yourself to a sinking stone. If you want to keep being a daredevil, go with Hoffman. Gil and I can always find you."

"Do you think you can convince him?"

"Yes. It might take a while, but yes." It bothered him a little, how easily the lies were coming.

Reece nodded to the cycle. "So? Do I load it?"

Cora clutched Mercury tighter, uncertainty in her eyes.

"Load it," Henry called. He walked her to the passenger side of the truck, where he shook hands with Hoffman and Althoff. "This is best, Cora. You know it."

"I do. I just . . ." She blinked against tears. Then her face hardened. "To hell with him! You come, Henry. Let him wallow in his self-pity alone."

Gil's problem was a whole lot deeper and more complicated than self-pity. "I know where to find you. And they don't need my name for the posters."

One by one, the planes chugged to life.

"Go," Henry said, raising his voice over the machines and the prop wash. "If nothing else, we'll meet up with you at the last show in November."

"You promise to find me? No later than November?"

"I promise."

She shifted her weight from foot to foot. "It's all happening so fast. . . ."

"You told me there's no shame in admitting you want something and going after it. Is this what you want?"

She bit her lip and nodded.

Henry inclined his head toward the waiting truck. "Then go after it." Those words cost him more than he'd ever imagined four little words could.

She kissed his cheek and climbed into the truck. Once she was inside, she held Mercury in the window and waved his paw good-bye.

Henry stood where he was until the truck was gone and the planes were no longer even specks in the cloud-spattered sky. It was done. She was gone. His heart seemed to grow larger with every beat, trying to burst from his chest, climbing higher in his throat, threatening to suffocate the life out of him. But he wouldn't die. He'd live every painful day with the yawning hole of her absence in it.

His knees gave way and he sat in the matted field, listening to the whir of grasshoppers and drone of clover-seeking bees. Picking up blade after blade of grass, he absently shredded them along their stringy veins. He couldn't go back to Gil without untangling his own emotions first. He had to weigh the risks of talking Gil into following Cora. The risk to Gil's soul. The risk to Henry's own heart.

The break was made. The worst was over.

The sky streaked and shifted with a sad-looking sunset. Henry got up and started walking with heavy steps back to the Jenny. It was fully dark when he reached the plane. Gil was sitting slump-shouldered with his elbows resting on his knees next to a little fire. His unblinking eyes stared into the low, yellow flames. A half-empty bottle of whiskey dangled from his fingertips, glowing amber in the flickering light. Henry saw a corner of paper with its edge curled and blackened at the side of the fire. One of the flyers for Mercury's Daredevils.

Henry sat down on the ground. "She's gone."

Gil's eyes stayed on the fire as he nodded

slowly, then he took a pull on the whiskey
bottle. "So I saw."

12

Four days after Cora left their lives, on August 2, President Harding dropped dead. The country went into mourning. Black crepe draped nearly every door. Out of respect Gil and Henry stayed grounded — and near starving — for a week.

Then days stacked upon days and Henry had yet to say a word to Gil about the offer Hoffman had made. Even Henry's shame over his behavior couldn't nudge him over the hump. He had plenty of justifications; he worried most of them were ultimately selfish. He and Gil were somewhere in central Missouri, Henry having encouraged Gil to head west out of Cape Girardeau. Hoffman's Flying Circus was working its way northeast and then south. Henry had convinced himself that Gil's unquestioning acquiescence to Henry's suggestion was confirmation that he had no second thoughts about sending Cora away.

Were the fellas with the circus keeping her risk-taking in check? The worry was keeping him awake at night, and emptiness rattled around in his heart during the day.

Henry had known he would miss her — and that thieving mutt — but he'd never experienced anything like this, the mix of aching and longing, the sense of missing something that was crucial to his very being. Every evening as he sat in the gathering darkness, every morning when the sun came over the horizon, his misery grew. That he knew he could join her and the circus, with or without Gil, anytime he wanted, made it worse, not better.

Her name had not been uttered by either of them since she'd left. It seemed best to leave it that way.

Henry thought it telling that Gil had been lurking nearby, watching as she got into that truck with Reece Althoff and rode out of their lives. Gil's feelings for her obviously went deeper than a regretted kiss. Henry wondered why, then, had Gil sent her away? To protect her from his darker side? Or had he been sacrificing what he wanted in order to put her in a place where her talents could shine? Or could Gil simply not bear to watch Cora take such continual risks? If things went wrong, it'd be one more death collected on his soul.

With Hoffman's Flying Circus she would finally be able to implement daring in a way that didn't involve piecemeal equipment like ramps of scavenged wood of questionable integrity. But would it be enough for her? Henry suspected an empty place was inside Cora, too — although better concealed than Gil's — an empty place she tried to fill with adoring eyes and applause. Maybe that's what had drawn her and Gil to each other, that deep, aching need for something to fill the cold, empty void.

As Henry sat in the still, late-August heat beneath a giant elm at the edge of a Missouri field, he contemplated a compelling need of his own. One he'd been willing to sacrifice his feelings for Cora in order to satisfy: a family; as simple and as complicated as that. It didn't seem like such an outrageous wish. But fate intended for him to be alone. Why else did it keep putting a family — natural, adopted, and makeshift — within his grasp and snatching it away?

He was feeling sorry for himself. But he thought he'd earned a good day of wallowing. Then he'd have to figure out what he was going to do about pulling Gil back from the brink.

Gil had always vacillated between stony silence and sparse communication. But something about his silences was different now, as if he'd found a way to make an absence of words even more oppressive. Before Cora left, Gil had stood with his toes curled over the ledge that fell away into darkness. Now that precipice had narrowed to a knife edge. Henry feared the waft of a single feather could send him either into the black void or shift him back to, if not the light, at least the shadows.

And then there was Henry's own darkness. Yes, he was going to have to do something about that, too.

After he'd joined with Gil and Cora, he'd taken the wrongs — done to him and by him — of his previous lives and locked them away in the cellar of his soul. For the most part, he'd been successful in keeping them weak and starving down there in the musty dark. He didn't know if Gil's current despair fed the monsters in Henry's cellar, or if his own tormented feelings for Cora had given them second life. Whatever the cause, his nights had become littered with the colliding fragments of pain he'd gathered throughout the years, each one a shard buried deep, cutting away at the foundation of a deceptively sturdy-looking dwelling.

How could he turn Gil away from his demons if his own continued to grow out of control?

It was time to admit the sad, horrible fact that Cora's absence was as destructive as her presence had been.

Henry ached for the loss of possibilities at the same time he rejoiced that at least she wasn't Gil's. What kind of person did that make him? Selfish? Certainly. Thankless? Undoubtedly. A betrayer? Probably. Just as he'd been in the end at the Dahlgren farm.

The sound of the Jenny's turning over jerked Henry out of a drooling doze he hadn't realized he'd fallen into. The heat was suffocating, even in the shade — just one of the reasons he'd been dreaming he was facing the fires of hell. Cows stood in the creek that ran on the other side of the nearby fence, huddled in fly-swatting masses in the spotty shade.

Why was Gil climbing into the plane? It was too hot to draw a crowd, the air too choppy to put on a show or give rides that wouldn't return customers to the ground shaken and sick. Henry got to his feet and walked to the edge of the shade, watching as Gil took to the air.

Instead of heading toward town to attract a crowd, Gil started his aerobatics right out there in open country. It was a ridiculous waste of gasoline, considering how low they were on both money and fuel. The man must really need the sky.

While the crowds were thin, Gil had been taking Henry through some basic stunts, first on the ground to explain how to execute them, then in the air so he could feel them, which was simultaneously terrifying and like arriving at the gates of heaven. Stunts used the basic principles of all flight — power, yaw, roll, drag, and lift — manipulated by the same tools: throttle, rudder, ailerons, and elevators. You had to know the right combinations and when and to what degree to apply them to keep yourself out of trouble — or in the case of a spin, get into trouble and then back out. Gil had said Henry was a natural pilot, but warned him not to rely solely on instincts when stunting, because in a spin your instincts would lead you in the wrong direction. Henry wasn't sure he'd ever be ready to try a spin. But riding through the stunts had made him even more aware of the value of a well-maintained and well-tuned machine. Of course limitations of budget prevented their Jenny from achieving either.

Gil did a climb that inched toward vertical until the Jenny stalled and nosed over to the right and went into an accelerating dive. The plane was too underpowered to complete loops without gaining airspeed in a dive, so Henry anticipated a loop next. Gil plummeted past the point where a prudent flier would have pulled into a loop.

Cold lead fingers gripped Henry's heart. He'd known this was coming. He had. He thought he had more time.

A handful of seconds from doom, Gil pulled up into a loop that started and ended much too close to the ground.

Climbing to a semi-sane altitude, he did a spiral and a lazy eight. Just as Henry was beginning to think he'd overreacted to the dive, Gil put the plane into a steep-angled spin, nose much lower than the tail. Henry watched the descent with dread. Pulling out of a spin took a lot more skill than pulling out of a dive — and it needed more altitude for recovery.

That altitude passed.

Henry ran into the field, squinting against the sun, shouting and waving his arms — a useless gesture. Gil's world was a rotating blur of sound and color, his ears filled with painful pressure.

Gil's instructions shot through Henry's mind, a jumble that would do no good if he needed them. But Gil wasn't Henry. Gil could fly an orange crate if they stuck wings on it. Reece had said.

Pull out. Pull out. Pull out. Now!

Henry squeezed his eyes closed. Every muscle in his body was stone.

The engine roared, passing so close overhead that it rattled Henry's teeth.

His eyes snapped open. The Jenny inverted, righted, then climbed.

Henry's hands fisted at his sides. "Dammit. Dammit. Dammit. God*dammit!*"

Gil swung around in his landing approach.

Then he was on the ground, taxiing to the tie-down stakes.

The second his feet hit the ground, Henry was on him. He shoved Gil in the chest hard enough to knock him off his feet.

"If you're so goddamn set on killing yourself, just get it over with! And don't fucking make me watch!"

Gil stayed on the ground, leaning back on his elbows. The calm look on his face made Henry want to punch him and keep punching.

But he held his hands in check and let his voice deliver the blows. "What is *wrong* with you?" He took a step backward. "Do you *want* to die?" He took a step forward and leaned down toward Gil's face and shouted, "Do you?"

Gil's voice was soft when he said, "I should have died a long time ago."

"But you didn't! Goddammit, you didn't! Get the hell over it." Henry walked in a tight circle. "All of this talk about 'should have died'; 'I won't live to be an old man' . . . it's bullshit! Bullshit you hide behind so you don't have to make the effort to rejoin the human race. The war fucked all of us. All of us!" The last words were closer to an insane roar than a shout. Henry was trembling so hard, he sat down hard right where he was. The sun beat down on him. He was covered in fresh sweat. Nauseated. Weak. Spent. "My brother *did die.* If he had lived, I hope he wouldn't have wasted that gift the way you are."

Gil got up. Peeled off his helmet and goggles and tossed them up into the Jenny. His leather jacket followed.

"She thought she could save you, you know," Henry said, trying to slow his breathing.

Gil stilled, but didn't turn to look down at him.

"I don't think you want to be saved."

Gil started walking toward the road.

"Where are you going?" Henry called.

"To find a drink."

Henry threw himself onto his back and

balled his fists against his forehead. He whispered, "Yeah. You do that. Maybe you'll stumble off a bridge and be put out of your misery." Then he muttered, "I should have gone with Hoffman."

Henry crossed his arms over his eyes and just stayed there in the shadow of the Jenny. It was too hot to think. It was too hot to worry. And it was damn well too hot to hike after a man who didn't want to live.

He awoke a while later to a gust of wind, roiling clouds, and green-hued light.

"Oh my God!" He jumped to his feet. Thunder rolled overhead like a barrel across an empty hayloft.

He grabbed the tie-down rope nearest him and hurried to one rocking wing. The rope was three feet too short. The plane wasn't square in the same spot as when tied down before.

He ran to the other side, glancing around him. The wind buffeted the trees in multiple directions. The Jenny shook on her wheels as if she were racing across a bumpy field as Henry grabbed the other wing rope and lashed it tight. He could swing the tail easily enough. He hoped to hell two tie-downs would hold it until he could reset the other stake. It didn't look as if he had much time.

The tail rope wouldn't reach. Henry got the tail off the ground far enough to give it a jerk inching it closer to the tie-down.

He heard an advancing rumble and looked up. A wall of hail was headed across the field, bouncing off the hard ground. "Oh, no, no, no, no."

The first baseball-size ice chunk went through the turtleback behind the cockpit and clanged against the metal tools inside. The second hit Henry's shoulder, sending a knife of pain clear across his chest. He covered his head with his arms and tucked himself under the horizontal stabilizer. He stretched out on his belly, trying to get the rope through the tail skid. Still too short.

Suddenly it sounded as if Henry were in the middle of a cattle stampede. The ground vibrated. A hailstone struck his ankle. It felt as if it chipped a bone through the leather of his boot. He balled himself under the tail and helplessly listened to the fabric being pummeled and ripped. His gaze was even with the ground. It was thick with hailstones.

Then the hail stopped, but the roar did not. He raised his head and peered out from under the bucking shelter of the plane just in time to see the tornado shatter the Browns' barn. Debris circled the funnel like flies swarming garbage.

He looked around for a low spot.

The creek.

He rolled out from under the Jenny's tail and made a dash for the fence. The cows had all shifted their tails toward the fence, into the wind. Henry put his left hand on top of a fence post and leaped over. It sounded as if he were being chased by a train.

He threw himself into the creek bed where it made a slight curve and the water had hollowed out a shallow divot in its west bank. He pressed himself into it, turning his face to the dirt and covering his head with his arms.

His ears popped. The sound around him intensified. Cows' moos were cut off in screams. Wood popped and snapped. He heard and felt debris hitting the ground.

A great thud shook the earth. Something huge landed at his back, pressing him into the bank.

The noise moved off and left only the muted static of rain.

Henry's torso was pinned tight. He pushed with his knees against the dirt and didn't feel the slightest shift at his back. The tree. He was pinned. No one could see him . . . if anyone ever came.

The cool flow of water stroked his side.
What a fucking unlucky way to die.

13

The creek continued to rise, even after the storm left behind silence punctuated only by tranquil bird-chirping. Henry shivered, unable to believe an hour earlier he'd been suffocated by the heat. He'd tried to dig his knees deeper into the bank, hoping to get better leverage, but had no luck. He could only move his elbows forward about six inches before they jammed into solid dirt. Debris pressed against his forearms, leaving them pinned uselessly over his head.

He tried to wiggle and worm toward his feet, but only wedged his shoulders tighter.

Blind animal panic set in. He yelled for help until his voice started to fail.

He forced himself to stop, to lasso that panic and rein it in. *Use your head. Breathe. In. Out.* Yelling was useless. The nearest farmstead to the Browns' was only a small bump on the horizon.

Someone will come. *Gil will come.*

That brought a slow parade of ways Gil could have died: a cracked skull from a hailstone, impaled by debris, his body lifted and tossed by the tornado, struck by lightning, crushed by a fallen tree. Or was Gil trapped alive somewhere? His return to the field was Henry's only hope. Unless the farmer came out to check on his cattle. Doubtful it would be in the next little while; Henry had seen the house and barn being hit.

Sooner or later someone would come to check on the Brown family. Later was definitely feeling both more likely and too late. Being trapped was terrifying, but the complete loss of the sense of time rattled him nearly as much. The only timekeeper he had was the slow, steady rise of the creek up his side and back.

There wasn't a lot of light, but staring at the exposed roots and rocks less than a foot from his face was starting to set off the crazies again. He closed his eyes, hoping to keep a rope on his bucking panic. The smell of wet earth and water seemed even stronger. Buried alive. His eyes snapped back open.

Not for the first time today, he wished with all of his soul that he'd gone with Cora and left Gil to his self-destructive ways. Being consumed by guilt was preferable to the death he now faced. The water was halfway up his shoulder blade.

Then he heard it. Footfalls.

"Here! I'm here! In the creek! Help!"

The steps came closer. Henry let out a breath of sweet relief. "Under the tree! I'm pinned against the bank. Heeeeere!"

He heard the branches of the fallen tree rustle. *Oh, thank you, God.*

Then it grew quiet again. "Hello? Is anybody there?"

No answer.

"Here! Help me! Hurry. The water's getting deeper."

He listened carefully for a voice over the rush of the water.

The branches rustled again.

"Can you hear me?" Henry shouted.

Footsteps splashed into the creek.

"Here. West bank. Under the tree." His voice squeaked the last bit. "Say something!"

Mueoooooooooo. The tree shook.

Henry screamed, the hoarse sound of it bouncing back in his face. He thrashed, his movements restricted and useless. He screamed again. And again.

Henry walked through the woods near the

Dahlgren farm. The hunting rifle Mr. Dahlgren had given him for his fifteenth birthday rested in the crook of his arm, barrel down, just as Mr. Dahlgren had taught him. Fall leaves called for slow, careful steps. He was hoping to spot the big buck that had been eluding him for two years. That deer hadn't grown into an eight-point by being stupid. Henry had come home from his last four hunting excursions empty-handed. He could never bring himself to shoot a doe.

He walked into the wind. He'd seen plenty of large tracks along this area for weeks. But the best sign was that he'd found a fresh buck rub on a tree not twenty yards back. A big one.

He slowed with even-more-careful steps.

Sweat beaded on his brow — anticipation, not heat.

Step by step. Minute by minute.

Then there the beast was, in belly-high dry weeds on the far side of a thicket of bush honeysuckle that was dotted with berries that looked like beads of blood. The buck rubbed a tree, working to shed the velvet from his antlers, totally unaware of Henry's presence.

He quelled his excitement and moved with deliberate slowness, raising his rifle to his shoulder, sighting the deer carefully. Ever

347

since the day he'd received the rifle, he'd practiced, sharpening his skills. One-shot kill. Anything less was cruel.

He slowed his breathing and pulled the trigger.

The buck dropped instantly.

Henry stood stock-still for a disbelieving moment.

Then he trotted toward his kill, pushing through the scrub.

When he looked down, his body went numb. Emmaline's head grew out of the buck's body, magnificent eight-point antlers sprouting from her blood-soaked blond hair. A blue hair ribbon clung to the weeds nearby.

Her eyes moved and looked up at him. "What have you done, Henry?"

"Henry?" Pause. "Henry?" Pause. "Hennnnry!"

Henry jerked awake, his heart hammering. It was pitch-black.

"Gil." It was a whisper. He tried again. "Gil! Here."

"Henry?" The voice sounded farther away.

The water wasn't yet hitting his ear. He twisted, trying to cast his voice outward. "Gil! Here! Here!"

"Henry!"

"In the creek. Under the tree. Stuck."

Footsteps. The branches rustled.

"Where?"

"West bank. In the curve."

Gil splashed into the water. Henry thought he caught a glimmer of light.

"Here!" he called, hoping the sound of his voice would draw Gil to the right spot.

"Are you hurt?"

"No. Just pinned."

Henry heard more branch rustling and Gil grunting. "Ahhh, Christ."

"That bad?"

"I need tools. And help."

"Are the Browns all right? Maybe they can —"

"I'll be back."

"Wait!" Henry called stupidly; he wasn't getting free until Gil got help, but he felt like a kitten being abandoned in an alley.

Gil was already gone.

Henry kept himself from losing his mind by mentally repairing the damage he imagined the Jenny had received. With the felled elm, he knew it had to be more than hail tears in her skin.

A rooster crowed. It sounded close enough to be sitting in the branches over his head. The light grayed before he heard Gil's voice again. He was talking to another man.

A saw set to wood. It cut through in a few

minutes. Then another. Branches.

"I see your feet!" Gil called. "We couldn't find the felling saw in the barn rubble . . . lucky to find a saw at all. I think we should use the shovel to dig you out. It'll be faster."

"Good. Do it!" The water was still rising, but slowly. It tickled his ear now.

After more sawing of branches, and after what felt like a full day of digging, Henry was pulled out by his feet.

Gil fell to his knees in the water and grabbed Henry to his chest. "You gave me a scare, old boy."

Henry couldn't believe he was laughing. "Me, too."

Gil helped him to his feet. Then Henry looked around. In the calm gold light of sunrise, the devastation was sharp and clear. A dead cow was under the fallen tree on the other side of the creek. Barn boards, shingles, a fringed pillow, and an iron kettle were caught in the wire fence, which miraculously stood intact. He looked beyond to where the Jenny should have been and saw only a hole-riddled lower wing.

"Where is she?" Henry looked full circle.

Gil pointed to the far side of the cattle pasture. "There."

The engine sat nearly upright, exhaust tubes buried in the ground, the propeller facing the sky.

"And there." He pointed upstream from the wing. The tail lay upside down, held off the ground by the vertical stabilizer. The painted flames now billowed downward instead of up. "And who knows where else."

Henry's gaze widened. Gil's description of the war came to Henry's mind. Skeletal trees, some twisted and bent over, tops hanging from raw, ropy fibers, while other trees appeared untouched. Half of the barn roof sat in the middle of a wheat field, the other half either carried too far to see or smashed to pieces. A lightning rod stuck out of a nearby tree trunk like an arrow. The tractor had landed on the henhouse. A good portion of the roof was gone from the Browns' house; the outside wall of one bedroom was missing, leaving it looking like Johanna Dahlgren's dollhouse. The bed inside the room was as neatly made as morning.

Henry looked to Mr. Brown. "Your family?"

"All fine. We rode it out in the storm cellar."

The three of them stood there, knee-deep in water, staring at the randomness of the destruction in the deceptively beautiful light of the early-morning sun.

14

Gil's mourning didn't set in right away. He and Henry were too busy helping the Browns recover what they could of their possessions and burn what wasn't salvageable. Days went by with their bodies exhausted, their minds focused on the Brown family, and their eyes averted from the scattered pieces of the Jenny.

The worst job had been dealing with the cow, whose carcass couldn't be left in the creek to spoil the water. Once they'd cut it free from the tree, Brown's single mule hadn't been strong enough to pull it up the slight bank, and the tractor wouldn't be operable until damaged parts were replaced. They'd had to dismember the poor cow before it could be dragged in pieces to where it was burned. The second that decision was announced, Gil had remembered he'd promised to "help Mrs. Brown clear the henhouse." Even Henry, used to butchering season, had been thankful there had been only one bovine casualty.

Finally, the time had come to say good-bye to the Jenny.

Henry and Gil salvaged what could be sold: the prop, the engine, the mag, the altimeter, a few cables, the rudder, one wheel. Mr. Brown let them use the mule to wrestle the engine onto a skid and drag it closer to the house, where it would wait to be shipped when Gil telegraphed with the future buyer's information.

The Jenny's funeral pyre burned fast and bright as Gil and Henry stood side by side, paying silent homage as they watched the flames dance and the smoke rise. At least this was one death Henry didn't have to mourn alone. He would never admit it out loud, but this loss felt as heavy and sad as any other he'd ever suffered — for a *machine.* It was shameful.

But it wasn't just the machine. He was saying good-bye to yet another life. Would it be good-bye to Gil, too? That airplane had been what bound them together. Without it, without Cora, Gil was sure to fall off the wrong side of that edge he'd been teetering on.

They stood there until the flames died and the embers cooled. It took a surprisingly short time considering the miracle against gravity the machine had wrought and the significance it had in their lives.

The schedule for Hoffman's Flying Circus was still in Henry's left pants' pocket, having suffered only dampness during his entrapment. He wasn't sure Gil could survive if he was cast back into Cora's atmosphere; hell, Henry wasn't sure *he* could survive it.

But she was right, Hoffman would find a new pilot if Henry and Gil waited too long.

Henry finally spoke. "What now?"

That two-word question seemed to hit Gil like a hammer blow. He sank to his haunches and covered his face.

Henry laid a hand on Gil's shoulder and waited.

The day was at its colorful end, the wide sky streaked with what Cora called "baby colors." Henry had thought it a contradictory choice of words for her unsentimental nature.

"We'll figure it out tomorrow," Henry said with a pat on Gil's shoulder.

Gil shook his head as he rose to his feet. Then he turned and walked out of the field, probably in search of a drink. Henry couldn't blame him, not this time.

By the next afternoon there was still no sign of Gil. Henry went into town in search of him. As he walked, he saw the path of the tornado clearly marked by a trail of flattened crops and twisted trees. On either side was a scattered-debris field. He passed a broken bed frame a mile from the nearest dwelling, a soggy rag doll, and a family Bible. Hoping the owners were safe, he picked up the doll and the Bible. He'd leave them at the telegraph office when he sent his message to Hoffman and hope they found their way back home.

He tried to quell the niggling fear that Gil hadn't gone to town for a drink but had kept on walking. Surely he would at least have said good-bye. By the time Henry reached the main drag, he hadn't been successful in quieting his unease.

He was glad to see that the little downtown had been spared the brunt of the storm. Some shingles were missing from a church steeple, a few tree limbs were downed and windows broken along with hail-dented cars, but all roofs still sat on top of their respective buildings and life appeared to putter along normally. As Henry walked among the ordinary and the undamaged, he felt as if he were finally emerging from a nightmare — or a battlefield.

Henry made his stop at the telegraph office, then went to ask around about Gil. He wasn't overly worried about lawmen — whom he avoided in general. This small town rocked by the tragedy of the storm was far from Indiana, and Henry Jefferson had been traveling for months without hounds on his heels. He wasn't safe, he'd never be that. But the heavy hand that had threatened to flatten him seemed much farther away.

On his third query about Gil it was suggested — with an uncomfortable expression — that he check the mercantile.

An attractive war-widow who looked several years older than Gil owned the business. She led Henry back out the front door of the shop and up a narrow staircase that opened between two storefronts. Upstairs was a tidy apartment. Starched doilies rested on the chair backs, and a vase of colorful zinnias sat on a table. An empty liquor bottle and two glasses were on another table. One had lipstick on the rim.

"Forgive the mess. I was running late to open the shop." She swung open a bedroom door. "He was such a wreck, I couldn't bring myself to wake him."

"Sorry for your . . . inconvenience, ma'am." She didn't even ask Henry's name or why he was looking for Gil.

She smiled sadly. "Lots of folks around here have needed some liquid encouragement to get through the aftermath of that storm. No shame in it."

Apparently, there wasn't much shame in a lot of things. Gil was sprawled on his belly, one arm hanging over the edge of the mattress. One bare leg stuck out from the sheet. While Henry's face grew hot — and undoubtedly an unmanly shade of red — the widow didn't seem the least embarrassed by what had obviously gone on last night.

"I'll let you roust him out." She started to leave, then stopped. "He's really worried about letting you down." She slipped out the door, and Henry listened to her soft footsteps going down the stairs. He took a bit of satisfaction from the widow's comment. Cora had been right all along; Gil didn't want to be isolated, not deep down. Henry wondered if he'd ever get the man to admit it enough to let himself fully live again.

Henry shook Gil awake, got him into a cold bath, and then to the café down the street. As they sat staring at cups of black coffee, Gil finally spoke. "Listen, kid. I —"

"Hey, I'm not your keeper. She seems like a nice lady." Henry had something else he wanted to talk about. "Guess you're over that kiss with Cora."

"That shouldn't have happened."

"I won't argue there." Henry made himself ask, "So why did you do it?"

"Things were . . . heated."

"Things have been heated between you two plenty of times before."

"Listen, it doesn't matter. She's gone."

"It might matter."

"Why?"

Henry steeled his heart. "Do you love her?"

After the slightest hesitation Gil replied, "No."

"Then why did you send her away? The truth."

Gil took a long sip of coffee, then kept his eyes on it after he'd set it back down. "I told you before. She's going places. You should have gone, too."

"Well, yeah, now that the Jenny's gone, that's pretty damned evident." Henry stirred cream into his cup. "What happens now? Will you finally go home?"

Gil's eyes snapped up and Henry saw

something he'd never seen in them. Fear. "No."

"Then what?"

Gil shrugged. "Earn some money. Then find a new plane."

"What if I told you I could get you back in a plane? Right now."

"And how would you do that?"

"Hoffman offered you a job. They're losing a pilot."

"You mean he offered that when I had a plane to contribute."

"Yes. But he's still losing a pilot. Reece Althoff won't let him miss the opportunity to get you on board, Jenny or no Jenny."

"What about you?"

"He offered me a job, too."

Gil scrubbed a hand over his mouth. "You know it won't work."

Was he talking about Cora? Or working with a larger crew? In either case Henry's response was the same. "Only if you don't want it to."

"You should go. You can fly the fourth plane for Hoffman. You're ready. I just can't —"

"If you don't love her, it shouldn't matter. Just let that mistake of a kiss go, like you're obviously planning on letting the lady in the mercantile go."

When Gil raised his eyes to meet Henry's, Henry read the naked truth. This was going to be a whole lot more complicated — and more painful — than he'd imagined.

With no other real options, he'd just have to do as he'd advised Gil. Let go of his own unrealistic feelings for Cora and focus on making his life worth something.

The telegram from Hoffman arrived at the Brown farm the next day.

SORRY FOR LOSS OF JENNY-STOP-WELCOME ABOARD-STOP-MEET IN LIMA OHIO
30 AUGUST

If they joined up on the thirtieth, that'd give them three days to practice before the Labor Day show. Plenty of time.

Henry handed the telegram to Gil and waited for his response.

Gil's eyes narrowed as he read it, then he shot Henry a cold, withering look that, back in the beginning, would have scared him shitless. "You accepted for me."

"What's to lose by giving it a shot?" Henry said calmly, holding eye contact. "How much worse off will you be if you decide to leave in a few months — or even weeks? At the very least you'll have more money in

360

your pocket — that much closer to buying another plane."

Gil didn't respond.

"So it *is* Cora." If Henry was willing to toss his heart under her boots to keep flying, why couldn't Gil? Henry was willing to take the risk of traveling through Indiana to get there. Perhaps something inside him was as self-destructive as that inside Gil. Only a fool would return to Indiana, where no matter how many months it had been, they weren't going to forget a murdered girl. Of course, Henry couldn't very well admit that to Gil as incentive to buck up.

"No."

"If that's true, there is no downside in going with Hoffman. You're going to have to tolerate being around people to earn the money to replace your plane. Why not this, doing something you like that pays better than average? Or I suppose you could just give up and become the guy who used to be a damn good pilot, but now just knocks around romancing lonely widows and drinking himself to death."

Gil grabbed the front of Henry's shirt and yanked him until they were nose to nose. Henry didn't flinch. He stood there with his eyes locked on Gil's, waiting for this to go one way or the other. Right now he didn't care which; the monster in the cellar was pounding on the door. Delivering a few punches might feel real good, but he wasn't going to take the first swing and render that door useless.

Gil's voice was tight and his teeth gritted when he said, "I thought I told you I don't like being shanghaied." He let go of Henry's shirt and shoved him back a half step.

"Shanghaied!" Henry shrugged his shirt straight. He concentrated on his breaths and held his temper. "Goddammit, I'm not just trying to get you to do this because *I* want it. I will go without you. But you know in your gut this is your best shot. Why in the hell are you fighting it?"

Gil didn't respond.

Henry started to walk away. "I'm going to buy train tickets. Should I buy one or two?"

He made himself keep walking, counting his steps. Their daredevil money, pooled with what Henry still had in his pockets of his own share, was just enough to buy two day-coach tickets; he'd checked the fare when he'd been in town yesterday. That would wipe them out. If Gil didn't go, Henry would hand over everything that was left.

Finally Gil called, "Buy two."

■ ■ ■ ■

Once the train crossed the Illinois/Indiana state line, Henry felt as squirmy as the devil in church. He pulled his hat low, then thought that might make him look suspicious, so he resettled it higher off his face. Gil was snoring in the seat next to him, and Henry wished he could disappear into sleep. His stomach grew more sour with each eastward mile.

He nudged Gil awake to change trains in Frankfort, then had to make a stop in the lavatory to throw up before they boarded the next train. He was glad Gil was too groggy to question Henry's sprint to the men's room. The Nickel Plate line would take them through the most dangerous and most familiar stretch of their journey — north and northeast right through the section of the state where Henry had lived . . . and Emmaline had died.

Just handing his ticket to board challenged his nerves. It was now possible to run into someone who either knew him or recognized him from the newspapers. He kept Gil partially between himself and the man who checked their tickets as they boarded.

"Let me have the seat by the window," he

said when Gil started to sit down first.

"Sure." Gil seemed to take a real look at him for the first time in hours. "Hey, you're looking a little peaked."

"That's why I want by the window, in case I need air."

"Hope it isn't catching."

"Don't think you need to worry about that," Henry responded automatically, then regretted it. But Gil didn't ask any more questions. A rare moment when Henry was glad of Gil's silent ways.

It felt as if the train stopped at a depot every five minutes and lingered there an hour before chugging on to the next stop. They rolled into Muncie, the closest station to the Dahlgren farm, still some miles away, and yet smack-dab in the lap of the Delaware County sheriff. Henry got clammy again, his saliva ran hot, but he managed not to be sick.

"Folks," the conductor said from the front of the car, "we'll be here for thirty minutes, so if you'd like to get off and stretch your legs, feel free."

Gil stood. "Coming?"

Henry didn't dare open his mouth to answer. He shook his head and waved Gil on.

"Want a newspaper or anything? You can

catch up on Indiana news." Was he taunting Henry? Did he suspect?

Four months. Was Emmaline's murder still making the newspapers?

He shook his head.

Then another thought struck him hard. Several train stations had wanted posters on display. Was there one inside with a sketch of Henry on it? He nearly threw himself around Gil's legs and begged him not to go in.

His coiled muscles stayed put.

What if someone gets on who knows me? The list was short. And he didn't know anyone from Muncie.

Why had he not checked out the exact route before he bought the tickets? This was too close. Far too close.

He turned his head away from the aisle, pulled his hat low, and pretended to be asleep. Through slitted eyes, he took the occasional look outside the window, just in case lawmen were out there.

He was still pretending to sleep when Gil came back, newspaper in hand, and the sound of the engine increased.

"All aboard!"

Finally! Finally, the train began to inch forward.

A man in a suit ran out of the depot, yelling, "Wait! Wait!"

Henry's mouth went dry and his heart sped up. He looked for a badge.

The train rumbled forward.

Henry didn't relax until the speed increased to the point no man could jump on.

It was probably just a late passenger. He didn't see a badge. No gun. No warrant waving in the air.

He thanked God trains do not wait.

When they stepped off the train in Lima, Cora and Mercury were there to meet them. She smiled and waved, bouncing like an excited schoolgirl. Henry had prepared himself for the sight of her, but his heart still did a double beat and his fingers tingled. He was careful not to look at Gil, unsure if it was because he was afraid of what he'd see in the man's eyes, or fear that Gil would see what was in Henry's own. He'd told Cora that while she was gone, maybe Gil would come to understand how much he missed her. But dear God in heaven, it had happened to Henry.

He felt awkward as he walked toward her. The urge to throw his arms around her and hold her close to his chest, to bury his nose in her hair, was strong. Time had made

Henry shamefully lovesick. But if they were to survive this reunion, both he and Gil had to bury their feelings for Cora — and keep them buried.

Mercury howled and launched himself out of Cora's arms. Henry was glad for the diversion of scooping him up.

"Hey there, little fella!" Henry scratched Mercury's ears and accepted enthusiastic doggie kisses.

Henry should have known Cora would take control of their greeting. She threw one arm around Henry's neck, the other around Gil's, and kissed them each on the cheek. "I'm so glad to see you two!"

"How did you know when we were coming?" Henry asked, keeping both of his own arms wrapped around the dog and off Cora.

"Only two trains a day. You had to be on one of them."

Gil backed away, putting more distance between himself and Cora. Henry soaked up her nearness.

Gil said, "I'll go collect the prop."

After he walked away, Henry told Cora, "He wouldn't come empty-handed. If Hoffman wants the OX-5, it's his, too."

"The rest of the Jenny?"

"Ashes."

She looked at Gil's retreating back. "That

must have just about killed him."

"Just be careful not to finish him off." The words were sharp and out of his mouth before he put any thought behind them. He was glad for it.

"What's that supposed to mean?"

"You can't fix him, Cora. If you keep trying, that's going to be either the end of him, or at the very least the end of him with the circus."

He prepared himself for a glib response, but instead she stood silent and serious.

"Was he better after I was gone?" Pain shone in her eyes.

"Yes," Henry lied.

He might burn in hell for things he'd done, but lying to Cora to protect Gil — and probably her, too — wasn't one of them.

15

As the days rolled on, Gil gradually shed some of that thrumming tension. The changes were subtle but undeniable. He slept more peacefully in the tent he and Henry shared. The constant parallel creases in his forehead eased. Those lurking shadows behind his eyes even receded. This was quite contrary to what Henry had prepared himself for. In addition to the stress of having Cora back in their lives, Henry had worried that Gil's being around Reece Althoff would be a constant reminder of the war. But as far as Henry could tell, Gil and Reece kept their conversations rooted in the present. Although Gil still remained quiet most of the time, he no longer disappeared without a word for hours at a stretch.

Maybe this new flying circus would be what that quick-step dance had been for the one-armed veteran, a way for Gil to find his pre-war self. Maybe he felt unburdened; the responsibility for generating enough money to feed Cora and Henry now sat on Jake Hoffman's shoulders. That idea was reinforced by what the widow from the mercantile had said: Gil was worried about letting Henry down. That really bothered him, the idea that he and Cora had worsened Gil's already-stressed emotions.

Henry secretly watched for subtle changes, wind socks to indicate a shift in Gil's disposition that could lead him back to that dangerous precipice he'd been on just a couple of weeks before. Sitting and waiting for his darkness to return set up an expectation that it would, and that seemed disloyal somehow.

Aside from his concern over the possibility of Gil's backward slide, Henry was in pig's paradise. Night after night, his and Reece's conversations stretched into the wee hours as they devised ways to improve the performance of the planes. All of the air circus's planes were outfitted with Hispano-Suiza engines, *Hissos* — nearly twice as powerful as the OX-5, *and* they had a pressurized fuel tank, making inverted flight a little less like flying a gliding coffin. They each had Scintilla magnetos and were overhauled regularly. All things that had just been distant dreams Henry had had for Gil's Jenny.

The bigger plane, a Standard J-1, had been outfitted to carry three passengers, significantly increasing the cash per flight brought in by rides. The flying circus also had a promoter, Marcus Davis, a man with an impressive mustache. Henry only saw him on the days of the air shows. The rest of the time Marcus was on the road, doing advance work. Ballyhoo. Every town they arrived in had been plastered with posters and billboards; the flying fields were marked with a wind sock — no more using cows' asses to decipher the wind direction before landing — and staked with red and white pennants. Newspaper reporters with their cameras never failed to show up as soon as the planes landed. Henry always made himself scarce when the cameras were around.

The fourth pilot, Thomas Reid, was a veteran, too, making Henry the youngest flier. Thomas really had been a fighter pilot, although not an ace. The public loved military men. Marcus always included military ranks, sometimes elevated, for the three veterans when promoting, just as Henry had assigned *captain* to Gil — which, Henry had discovered through Reece, had been a rank too low.

·Even though Henry flew one of the Jennies from location to location and did a little stunt flying, he spent most of his time as a mechanic, which was an even better setup than Mercury's Daredevils had been — for hiding purposes. Mechanics and prop swingers were a lot like the hired help, invisible but for their function. Oddly, no one ever questioned who was flying the fourth plane when they were all airborne. Henry sometimes felt like the pea hidden under the huckster's shell. It suited him just fine.

Reece was the only one who parachuted. The promise of his jump was a huge draw and was featured in all advertising. No one really wanted to see a man fall through the air until his helpless body hit the earth, but human nature made people unable to resist being there. Just in case. Same for stunting and wing walking, Henry supposed. Morbid curiosity kept the crowds coming.

Cora and Gil seemed to have taken a necessary step away from each other. They didn't exactly avoid each other, but neither of them now seemed inclined to nudge certain boundaries — not surprising from Gil, but Henry had expected a reckoning with Cora that never came. After the first ten days, Gil stopped looking as if he were facing a firing squad when she came around. Even their differences of opinion had lost some of their fire. Henry supposed that was because the seat of power had shifted. Jake Hoffman now held the keys to the kingdom, and he and Cora were reaching for the same goals.

As for Henry, he was so happy to have his "family" back that he was able to keep his own puppy-dog longing in check around Cora — it somehow made it easier if he trivialized it with such words: foolishness, inconsequential. He started to wonder if maybe he was just like everyone else; he wanted Cora all the more when Gil had her. Is that why the urgency and intense need had now become manageable? He didn't want to look too closely at it — and fortunately didn't have to.

Time rolled on, show after jam-packed show. Even though the entire team flirted with disaster every day — it was the essence of their jobs after all — Henry had started to feel that he'd finally beaten his old nemesis. The second that thought crossed his mind, he knew it was a foolhardy temptation that disaster could hardly ignore. For days he waited for the trouble he had beckoned to arrive.

Eventually, he forgot about his taunt.

Next stop, Nashville, Tennessee. It was mid-October, later sunrise, earlier sunset, and they were going to need all of the daylight in between to get there. But when Henry came out of his tent, he faced a world shrouded in fog. It was so thick he couldn't see the plane tied down farthest from him. Nashville was a big show. They couldn't miss it. Last night as the haze had begun to collect around the moon, they'd decided that if they had to fly into darkness to get there, they would.

Reece, Cora, and Mercury left in the truck. The four pilots, Jake, Gil, Thomas, and Henry, hunkered down and prayed there would be enough sun to burn off the fog before the entire day was lost. They were all tired from nearly daily performances, yet not one of them considered catching a couple more hours of sleep, as if the fog couldn't be trusted to lift unless they were staring at it.

At ten o'clock it began to thin. A light coin of sun shone through. At noon, it was clear enough to fly. Henry trusted the judgment of the seasoned fliers, keeping his worries to himself. They assured Henry that by the time they reached their destination, Reece would have barrels stoked with fire to light their landing strip.

Henry's worst fear was that his plane would become separated from the others and then he become disoriented in the darkness. If he couldn't find the field, he'd be executing his first nighttime crash instead of his first nighttime landing.

At their fuel stop, Gil slapped him on the back as they walked to their planes. "I'll stay behind you from here on out. Don't worry."

Sunset turned to twilight. Twilight to dusk. Dusk to dark. They slowed their airspeed. Below, he saw the occasional twinkle of light, looking like no more than a firefly in a field. They'd agreed on an airspeed to keep from running up on one another too quickly in the dark, but Henry was sorely tempted to slow further. He couldn't keep his mind from mentally calculating how quickly at fifty miles an hour he could come up on a stationary object. It was foolish. The only objects this high were birds and planes. The birds had gone to roost, and only four pilots were foolish enough to be in the sky.

Darkness gave way to moonrise, letting Henry clearly see the white stripes on the other planes. Those few minutes of darkness had rattled him more than he'd expected.

When they neared the lights of Nashville, they lowered their altitude. Streetlight glow reflected on brick and concrete. They flew over the town, and the lights on the ground below were sparse. Then he saw, just ahead, four bright dots of light, two at one end of the landing strip, two at the other. They circled in their approach. Henry's mouth was dry and his man parts drawn up tight. How was he supposed to pick his touchdown spot if he couldn't see it?

They'd already planned the order of landing: Jake, Thomas, Henry, then Gil. Henry would have the benefit of watching Jake and Thomas, not that he'd be able to see much until they touched down in the halo of firelight. He knew he wasn't to set down until at least ten yards after the first barrels. Jake had used this field before and assured him the approach was free of obstacles higher than a fence for at least a quarter mile on either end of the strip.

Henry circled. Then it was his turn.

He made his approach. The white stripes on the landed planes reflected gray in the moonlight. Cora stood in the bright glow of the first set of barrels, waving and pointing to the strip. Very helpful.

In his mind, he kept repeating Gil's words: "You've landed enough times to trust your instincts. Watch the altimeter. The fires will light some of the ground, but don't try to focus on it. You know where the ground is, the barrels are sitting on it. If you *think* about its being dark, your judgment will go to hell."

How did you *not* think about its being dark?

The closer he got to the ground, the more light the barrels seemed to throw. Easy enough to line up.

Keep those wings level.

As he passed the barrels — at what he hoped was fifteen feet off the ground — he saw Cora jumping up and down out of the corner of his eye.

Wheels ain't down yet, lady.

And then they were.

He let out a *"Whoop!"* His body was full of relief and buoyant energy, the two creating a drunkening cocktail of emotion.

Now that he was on the ground, there seemed to be plenty of light to make everything out. He taxied to park next to the other two planes, his spirit as high as he could ever recall.

When he got out, Reece chucked him on the back of the head. Jake clapped him on the back. And Thomas proudly shook his hand. But Cora's kiss on the cheek and hug around the neck sent him to the moon. He didn't even notice Gil had landed until he taxied right up next to them.

Reece said, "Food's on! And Cora and I got all of the tents up . . . you can thank us by doing the dishes."

As they moved as one toward their camp stools, arms slung around one another in a line, Henry thought, *This must be what it is like to feel the soul of a true family.* And his had just grown to include Reece, Thomas, and Jake. With these people behind him, Henry could do anything.

Immediately after the dishes were cleaned up, everyone but Henry went to bed. It was late and they had already been near exhaustion when they'd arisen that day. Jake promised the winter schedule would be less strenuous, with a nice long break over the holidays. But Henry wasn't sure he wanted less strenuous. He was used to living without holidays. He liked being so busy that all he could think about was the next thing needing to be done. He didn't want time to reflect on his life, to have holidays pick at the holes in it.

He continued to sit by the small, flickering fire as the rustling in the tents settled into sighs and man farts. He wondered what Cora thought of the men's nightly rituals and smiled. He just wanted to hold on to this feeling of belonging, of having a purpose, of accomplishment. Sleep would steal it away and tomorrow would be just another day.

The barrels had nearly burned out, nothing left but a glow down inside and the occasional flurry of orange embers rising skyward.

He was so lost in thought that the hand falling on his shoulder startled him. He looked over his shoulder, and Cora stood there in the warm glow of the dying fire. She was barefoot and wearing a nightgown. Mercury must have been dead to the world already not to have followed her out.

"Shouldn't you be in bed?" he asked, but held himself still, leaning forward with his elbows on his knees, as if he might frighten her away if he moved.

"I was going to ask you the same thing." Her hand slid across his shoulders as she took a seat on the camp stool next to him. For a minute, she just stared at the fire, and Henry wondered what had brought her out here. He wasn't about to ruin the moment by asking.

"Were you scared?"

He looked over at her. "Of flying in the dark?"

She nodded, her bobbed hair sliding over one eye.

"Hell yes."

She laughed softly. "That's what I love about you, Henry. You're the real McCoy. Where I come from, a young fellow's first rule is to be hip to the jive; the second is to always be blasé about absolutely everything; and the third is to never acknowledge any human emotion — other than possibly one-upsmanship."

Real McCoy. Even he knew what that meant. And he was not. But all he said was "Nice crowd."

She sighed. She was so close he could feel it pass over his skin, or maybe that was only his imagination. "I'm so happy to be away from all that money."

Now he straightened up and looked at her. "Most folks find money mighty comforting."

"Oh, Henry, just the opposite. It makes people do things they dislike in order to get it, and sacrifice everything in order to keep it. Parties. Jewelry. Cars. Yachts. I'm not saying I want to starve, but I wouldn't go back to that life for any amount of money. It's all so . . . vapid."

Henry had never been so thankful for Mr. Dahlgren's library. "Oh, yeah, parties and yachts are so hollow and unexciting."

"You say it as a joke, but it's true! There is no *substance.* I exist so I can wear the next dress, or Tiffany headdress, or be seen at the polo field. They don't *do* anything."

"Hanging from the wing of an airborne plane, that's definitely *doing* something."

"It's a start. For someone like me, it's a start. I'm not like you, Henry. I'm not clever at figuring out solutions to problems and inventing things. The only thing I can do is birth children or bounce around trying to discover something I'm good at. And I'm good at entertaining people. I know that's not substantial. I know it's not filling a need. But right now, it's what I *can* do."

When he looked at her, tears were running down her cheeks. He reached out and took her hand. "Hey. That's not what I meant."

"I don't want to pass through this world and not cause the slightest stir in the atmosphere. I don't want to die an old woman who's never taken a chance." She swiped at her eyes with her free hand. "I'm sorry. I don't know what's gotten into me."

She stood, but Henry didn't let go of her hand. Instead he tugged her closer. She looked down at him, her green eyes shiny. "Sometimes we're born where we belong and sometimes we have to search to find our place." He took her other hand.

"Which are you, Henry?"

"Both. I was born right where I belonged. But the world took it away. Now I have to find my place."

She surprised him by sitting down on his knee and wrapping her arms around his neck and leaning her head against his. "I think you've found your place."

He didn't dare think it. Not if he wanted it to last.

Cora emerged from her tent the next morning with dark circles under her eyes. He wondered if she'd lain awake as long as he had after they'd said good night. She was dressed for the show: lace-up boots, jodhpurs, a white blouse with a long, red scarf tied around her hair.

"Go back to sleep," Henry said. "You need to be better rested for the show."

"Everybody else is running on this little sleep."

"None of us has to be able to lift our body weight from underneath a speeding airplane. Go back to sleep. The show's not until eleven."

"I'm fine." She moved to the coffeepot and poured a cup.

Reece called Henry over to Thomas's plane.

"Really, Cora," Henry said as he walked away, "get some rest. We can prep for the show."

She waved him away.

Thomas's plane had an oil leak that took until showtime to get fixed. The next time Henry saw Cora, she was climbing into Jake's plane for her wing-walking stunts. She never flew with Henry or Gil. Henry didn't know if it was just because she was used to flying with Jake, or if there was more to it than that. Henry knew he'd never be able to concentrate on his flying if she was hanging underneath the wing where he couldn't even see her. As for Gil, maybe Reece was behind the decision; he knew better than to put Gil in a situation where he might feel responsible for one more person's death.

She went through her routine with her usual flair and drama; hanging below the wingtip from the skid, standing on top of the upper wing, first on her feet and then her hands. Henry heard Marcus begin his ballyhoo about the danger of her next stunt — standing erect on the top wing while Jake did a full inside loop. Henry didn't need ballyhoo to get his blood up. He kept his

eyes on her with his heart tied in a knot.
People assumed the centrifugal force kept
her on the wing, the way water stays in a
bucket if you windmill your arm fast
enough. But there wasn't enough speed to
keep Cora's feet planted — and nobody
thought about how the bucket had sides to
keep the water from breaking free and spinning off in the air. This stunt required a little
trickery. Henry had rigged a thin but sturdy
cable on each side of her. To the spectators
it appeared she was just standing with her
feet braced apart and her arms to her sides
for balance. In reality she had a taut cable
looped around each wrist, the pressure of
her pulling countering the forces that would
send her sailing. It was still dangerous as
hell.

Henry didn't blink the entire loop. He
never did. It happened naturally the first
time. Now it had become a superstition. *If I
blink, she'll fall.*

When Jake took a low pass over the field,
the crowd cheered as Cora stood on that
top wing and waved. Henry's heart unknot-
ted — until the next time.

He got ready for her next stunt. It required
the most strength of any in the show. Henry
had argued to move it up in the program,
do it early before she began to fatigue. But

Cora knew what a crowd-pleaser it was and insisted it be the "big finish." So far, it hadn't been a problem.

Henry took a two-foot-high crate and a long, yellow silk sash and stood in the middle of the runway. No one was looking at him. Cora was 150 feet overhead, where the spectators could watch her climb down under the lower wing and hang upside down by her knees from the spreader bar between the wheels.

Taking his place on top of the crate, Henry held the silk scarf high over his head, stretched between his hands.

Jake circled around, losing altitude, until he was heading straight for Henry, Cora's head twelve feet off the ground, her arms flung wide. She was grinning.

The plane roared over. Cora reached down and snatched the yellow sash from Henry's hands. She held it in one hand and let its full length flutter out behind her.

As always, this stunt drew the loudest response. In reality, it was the least dangerous. It was the only one where the altitude alone wouldn't kill her in a fall. And Henry had devised a "bootstrap" at the top of her knee boot that, while she was still at altitude, she secured to the bar just in case she passed out from being upside down for so long.

Jake returned to 150 feet, circling as she climbed back up onto the lower wing, where she would stand and wave at the spectators as he landed.

He was on his second pass and she was still struggling to get up. She never took this long.

Cold fingers closed around Henry's windpipe. She wasn't going to make it!

He ran toward Gil's plane, which was idling, ready to take off as soon as Jake and Cora landed. Jumping onto the wing and into the front cockpit, Henry shouted, "Something's wrong! Get up there!"

They throttled down the runway.

Henry kept his eyes on Cora. She made a couple of grabs at the spreader bar and missed. Within seconds, she stopped even trying to pull herself up.

At least both legs were still over the bar. He hoped she was just gathering her strength for another go at it.

Jake couldn't know what was happening, only that Cora hadn't climbed back up. He signaled he was increasing altitude, giving them more room to maneuver.

Henry took off his boots and socks. He'd have better grip with bare feet. Then he stood on his knees and faced Gil, shouting and gesturing in case he couldn't hear. "Get under her." He pointed to the upper wing. "I'll pull her down." He ended with his hands crossed over his chest.

Gil nodded. His face held complete calm and confidence. Henry was sure his showed nothing but terror.

Gil came up behind and just below Jake. Henry saw that Cora was now anchored only by that leather bootstrap. Her arms dangled freely; one leg had slipped off the bar. She looked unconscious.

The two planes could never stay steady long enough for him to unbuckle that strap. Not with all of her weight on it. He hoped his pocketknife was sharp enough to cut through it.

He opened it and put it between his teeth, then he stood on the back of the cockpit and inched his head up over the top wing. The wind sucked away his breath and tried to wrap the skin on his face around the back of his head as he hoisted himself up. He lay flat on his belly for a few seconds, trying to gauge how he was going to get out to the king posts three feet from the end of the wing. A wire stretched between the front and back posts; it would only hit him about midshin, but it was all he would have to stabilize himself.

Jake's plane was just feet ahead. Its prop wash added to the buffeting and shoving against Henry. He readjusted his balance.

On the ribs. Keep weight on the ribs under the skin of the wing.

He crabbed along, rib to rib. How did Cora do this?

Jake's tail inched past Henry's vision. Still high and twenty feet to the side. That twenty feet would make him cringe about the closeness had he been flying. Now it looked like an unbridgeable chasm.

Gil maneuvered forward and higher. Jake maintained speed and altitude. Once they were in place, Gil would have to match it.

Those seventeen feet from the cockpit to the king post were the longest of Henry's life. When he reached it, he crouched, keeping one hand on it and the other to the side for balance as he slowly rose. His feet braced wide, one on either side of the wire between the front and back posts. He kept his eyes on the wheel of Jake's craft. He couldn't look at Cora.

He needed to get closer, three feet forward and five to the side.

Come on, Gil. Get me there.

He inched to his full height, slowly and crouched, his arms wide for balance, gauging as he rose how far he had to lean into the wind to keep from being blown off.

Now he looked at Cora. Her face was a deep purplish red. Her eyes rolled back in her head and her mouth hung open. A tingling rush of panic came over him.

Take your time. She's not going anywhere. Figure this out.

The yellow silk sash was inching out of her pocket, the wind quickly tugging it free.

Could he use it? Secure them together somehow?

Before he could even get close enough to reach it, it whipped free of her pocket and was gone.

He was so close to the end of the wing, if he cut the strap, she'd be in free fall. Once he grabbed her, his balance would follow her momentum over the tip of the wing.

Maybe he needed to inch back toward the center of the wing. If he could release her over the front cockpit . . .

He reached out and missed Cora's purple-red hand by inches.

Henry tried for the spreader bar again. The wheel hit him in the head, knocking him off-balance. He grabbed down at the king post to steady himself. The knife fell from his mouth.

Christ!

Red and white stripes appeared on the other side of Jake's plane. Thomas! Reece was perched on the top wing, about even with Henry.

Thank God.

Relief was brief.

Did Reece have a plan?

Thomas gestured to Jake, then pulled slightly ahead, their wings overlapped. Thomas slowed. Jake's lower wing caught Reece in the chest. He disappeared up onto it. Moments later, he climbed down onto the spreader bar beside Cora.

How much weight could it hold?

Reece motioned for Henry to go back and stand in the cockpit.

He made the return trip much faster.

Dropping down and bracing his feet on either edge of the front cockpit, he leaned his hips against the top wing. Cora dangled in front of him. Gil maneuvered so Henry was directly beneath her, then rose higher, until her arms hung just in front of Henry.

He gestured for Gil to climb higher. He wanted to grab her around the chest, not the arms. That would only leave about six feet between Jake's wheels and Gil's upper wing. But that danger was less than Henry's losing his grip when she fell.

Come on. Come on.

There! He signaled for Gil to hold steady.

Reece locked eyes with Henry. "Ready?" The wind tore the word away; it was the lips Henry understood.

He braced and nodded.

Reece cut the strap.

Cora fell.

Henry's arms hooked around her. He bent forward, landing her on her back on the upper wing.

Ten seconds later, he had her pulled into the cockpit with him, his heart hammering against her body.

He made sure her head was higher than her heart and patted her cheeks — purple as beets — and called her name over and over. Finally, her eyelids fluttered.

When they opened seconds later, her eyes were unfocused and bloodred. He crushed her close to his chest and held her there, waiting for his own blood to begin to flow at a normal rate.

He didn't realize they were landing until he felt the wheels hit the ground.

The plane stopped. Gil cut the engine.

Cora smiled at Henry. "Thanks, Kid. That strap saved me."

Jesus, she had to be made of steel. He laughed. It was either that or strangle her. "That and two other planes and four fliers."

"I do love a spectacle."

The crowd rushed them then. Someone was on the wing, pulling her out of his arms. As her weight was lifted from him, emptiness pooled in his chest.

"There's a doctor here! Let him through!"

"Get her on the ground."

Cora might survive against the odds, but Henry was pretty sure watching her was going to kill him.

When he looked around for Gil, the man was stalking away, his stride jerky and his fists balled at his sides.

By the next day, the only traces of the disaster were the live wires of Henry's nerves and the bloodred of Cora's eyes. The doctor said it could take weeks for them to clear. Henry hoped so; he wanted her reminded every time she saw herself in a mirror of how close she'd come to dying.

When she sat down to breakfast, she started right off. "Now that the ice is broken, I want to add an official plane-to-plane midair transfer to the show."

Gil was quick with "You've crossed the line from daring to stupid. Count your lucky stars you're able to see the sunrise today." He tossed the coffee out of his cup and onto the grass, then walked away, leaving the reek of alcohol behind him.

Jake ignored him. "We proved we have steady enough planes and pilots to make it happen."

Reece offered, "Kinda surprised myself yesterday. Prefer jumping out with a parachute though. Think I'll leave the wing walking to Cora."

Although Henry agreed with Gil, he knew there was no stopping her. He needed to think of safety mechanisms and how to train her adequately on the ground before she attempted it in the air.

As fall deepened, the circus migrated south with the other birds. The week before Thanksgiving saw the end of their season — without a plane-to-plane transfer.

But the conversation about it never stopped. Cora had devised a muscle-building exercise program to silence Gil's continually bringing up the failed recovery on the spreader-bar stunt. "It took three planes and five pilots to get you from one plane to the other last time."

Even Henry was getting tired of hearing it. Yesterday, he'd borrowed a couple of trucks and rigged an arm with a loop she had to catch while standing in the bed of the other truck. She'd mastered it so quickly that it seemed a waste of time on both their parts. Before they broke for the holidays it was time to put theory into practice. If it was successful, they'd integrate the stunt into next year's posters and advertisements. They went over the plan one last time. Jake was to pilot the "launch" plane. Thomas had already left to join his much-neglected wife for the holiday break, and Gil was balking at flying the "target."

"Henry can do it, then," Cora said.

"No, he can't," Henry said. He had new appreciation for the kind of skill it took to maneuver two planes that close together and keep them steady enough that a person standing on a wing had a chance in holy hell of getting onto the other plane. "You need the steadiest pilot. That's Gil."

"That's right," Jake said. "No offense, Henry. This time experience counts."

Henry waved the apology off.

Cora turned to Gil. "You know I can do this." At least she'd stopped throwing in that technically she already *had;* at least she'd admitted consciousness counted. "I've been practicing for weeks."

"On the ground," Gil said.

"And moving! It's not like I haven't been on the wings enough to know what I'm doing. I've been hanging from the wing skid and getting back up in the show for three months. And I'm even stronger now. You know a plane-to-plane transfer will set us apart. Only a few people have done it."

"And a greater number have died trying," Gil said sourly.

Reece stood watching the conversation bounce, looking torn between dread and excitement. Only he and Henry knew the cause for Gil's caution, his exaggerated burden of personal responsibility.

"You can't possibly know the exact body count," Cora said in her usual airy way.

Henry thought that attitude was a bad sign. "Cora, if you're not taking this seriously —"

"I am! But getting me all worked up over the number of people who hadn't prepared enough isn't going to help. I'm ready to do this."

Gil said, "We've been drawing plenty of people without it."

"You know that's not how this business works. We have to push," Jake said. "She's ready. Otherwise I wouldn't risk it. She's too damn valuable."

Cora said, "If I don't think I can make it once we're up there, I won't try it."

Gil looked at her with disbelief. "I've seen evidence to the contrary."

"I've learned a lot since then."

"But have you learned enough?" he asked.

"One way to find out."

Gil didn't look as if he was going to budge.

Jake finally said, "Don't you think she can do it?"

For several seconds, Gil was silent. It looked as if it pained him to say, "I know she can."

Reece finally spoke: "Damn right she can!"

Jake slapped Gil on the back. "Let's go."

The ceiling was high. A shroud of thin, gauzy clouds softened the sun's brightness. That would make it easier to watch from the ground, and for Cora to see as she changed planes. Henry wished there were some way to baby-step the transfer at altitude. But that was like baby-stepping Reece into parachuting from a plane. It just couldn't be done. Henry assured himself they'd prepared as much as possible. Now he hoped Cora's stubbornness didn't push her into bad judgment. She was right, she had learned a lot. He'd seen her back off when she wasn't comfortable with a stunt. Her concentration had improved. She was finally using her head for something other than a ramrod.

Henry stood beside Reece watching the

two planes take off, one after the other. Henry was more nervous than he had been his first solo landing; he hoped Cora had a better result with this stunt.

They planned an altitude of two thousand feet at reduced airspeed; it gave them more maneuverability on this first run. When Gil tried to suggest a lower altitude, Cora had pointed out she wouldn't be any more dead falling from two thousand than if she fell from five hundred. Henry tried not to consider what those additional seconds before impact might be like. Right at that moment, he tried not to consider a whole lot of things.

The planes disappeared from sight. They were going to try to time the transfer as close to the field as possible, since that was how it was going to have to be in a show.

Reece bounced on the balls of his feet. His left hand kept sweeping across the back of his neck, a habit of concentration.

Henry strained his eyes watching for their approach. Finally, two dots appeared. By the time he could tell they were airplanes, Cora was standing on the top wing of Jake's plane. Gil's plane flew beside and above, way above, just as they'd planned. He would be doing the maneuvering because he wasn't fighting the off-balance weight of a person moving around on the wingtip. Jake's job — no less difficult — was to hold steady. Step one was to establish that they could maintain the overlap. Then Gil would slowly close the vertical gap for Cora to reach up and grab the wing skid. And then he'd have to correct for an off-balance plane as Cora swung herself up onto the lower wing. Once Jake was sure she had a good hold, he was to drop lower.

It should all work. It *had* worked, for a few. And failed for others. Henry wished he'd convinced Cora to wait until he could figure out a way to tether her to Gil's plane before she made the transfer. But there was nearly as much danger in hooking a rope attached to a belt onto the skid. If she decided to abort, there was no way to undo it. Hit an updraft and it could yank her off Jake's wing before she had a grip on the skid. Then she'd have to shimmy up the rope before she pulled herself up over the lip of the wing — assuming the jolt didn't knock her unconscious or break her neck.

Untethered was probably safer — that thought nearly drew a hysterical laugh from him. *Safe* was a word that seemed absolutely ludicrous right now.

The planes were close to the field. Gil slowly lowered his Jenny.

Henry imagined the wind buffeting Cora, the muscle strain of just remaining upright. She kept motioning for Gil to drop lower, but from Gil's position, he wouldn't be able to see her hands. He'd better be keeping his eyes on Jake's signals — following the plan.

Cora reached up for the skid — and missed. For a heart-stopping second she leaned off-balance. She seemed to recover, right before she disappeared from Henry's sight as the planes passed directly overhead. Henry compared their tails. Perfectly even.

By the time Henry could see her again, she was hanging from the skid with both hands, and Jake was dropping away, falling in under her, a hopeless tactic to catch her if she fell.

She swung her legs, just as she'd done on the practice setup Henry had built, but that had been at a safe eight feet off the ground. Wing skids had been added to the Jenny's design early on to keep a dipping wing from digging into the ground on landing, which meant Cora hung a good twenty inches below the actual wing.

She's come up from this position in the air before. She should be home free.

She hooked her foot on the wing just before they were too far away for Henry to see details. He kept his eyes on the plane as it grew smaller and smaller, praying not to see anything fall from it.

When Jake peeled away Henry finally breathed again. With that first intake of breath he felt as light as a dirigible, ready to float off the earth himself. He shot a fist in the air and thought of Cora's Warrior Maiden pose. He bet she was doing it right this minute as she stood victorious on that red-and-white wing.

Reece whooped and jumped up and down like a little kid.

They spent a few minutes congratulating each other and rehashing the stunt moment by moment before Henry went to retrieve Mercury. He'd tied the dog to one of the cots in his tent so he wouldn't have to witness Cora's untimely end. It seemed important then, but silly now.

Jake landed first. He was out of the cockpit before the prop stopped turning.

"My God, she did it!"

Henry didn't like how surprised the man sounded.

Cora was out on the wing as soon as Gil set the Jenny down, waving wildly, shouting something no one could hear.

They rushed toward the plane. Gil cut the engine. Henry pulled up short when Cora dove into the rear cockpit, toes trailing just off the wing, and kissed Gil on the mouth.

After a few seconds, he pulled her the rest of the way in onto his lap.

Reece whooped it up, cheering them on.

Jake's excited smile slipped.

Henry's mouth went dry and his heart turned to lead.

The boundary had been breached.

16

Something deep drew Cora and Gil together, deep and destructive and fueled by unrealistic fascination. Moths to flames came to Henry's mind when he thought of them, helpless against the lure, even when it singed. That evening, still euphoric over Cora's success, she and Gil sat next to one another during dinner, a first. Henry had hardly been able to eat for trying to hear every soft word that passed between them. Afterward they walked side by side into the darkness and disappeared. Henry nearly crawled out of his skin imagining what might be going on. He tried instead to work on drawings for modifications he was going to make to the planes over the off-season.

It grew late. Henry sat up long after the other men had gone to bed, chewing his pencil, the drawing forgotten. Finally, he turned off his Coleman lantern and went to his cot. Twenty minutes later he heard whispers outside his tent. He strained to catch the words, even going so far as to hold his breath to reduce his inner noise, but had no luck in even deciphering the mood let alone the content. He heard Cora's whisper grow harsh. A bit after that a sniffle. Gil entered the tent a short while later.

Henry felt foolish and juvenile as he pretended to be asleep, listening as Gil sat on his cot with a regretful-sounding sigh. He rubbed his hands over his face with a rasp, and his cot creaked as he lay back. He didn't take off his shoes.

An hour later, Henry was still awake. Gil, however, was thrashing in a fitful sleep.

The wind sock was shifting.

At some point Henry fell into dreams of his own; dreams woven from the rags of memory.

Henry was small enough he could sit at the table and rest his chin on it. This always made Ma remind him, "Table manners," as she did this time, but with a big smile on her face as she brought the roasted hen to the table. Henry knew some people had turkey for Thanksgiving, but his family didn't have a turkey house, just a henhouse. And they only ate hens on special occasions. When he'd asked his ma why, she'd told him that hens were precious because they gave every day, but roosters were good for only one thing. She didn't explain what that one thing was, but he figured it was pretty insignificant.

Pa sat at the head of the table. Henry was shocked by what he saw. Pa wasn't the faded man Henry was used to seeing. Pa's face was shaven, his hair still thick and his eyes bright blue. He still looked stern, but not broken.

Peter sat on Henry's right, pulling at the collar of the clean shirt Ma had made him wear and button all the way up to the neck. Baby Marie was in her cradle because she was too little to eat roasted hen. But when it was time for the blessing, Ma got her and brought her to the table. "A family should always be together for the blessing. When we cannot, we must hold one another in our hearts."

Henry closed his eyes and bowed his head. After Pa said, "Amen," in a strong, clear voice that had grown colorless and weak many years before he died, Henry opened his eyes and looked around the table. Ma and Pa and Peter and baby Marie were gone. Sitting with him were Gil and Cora and Mercury.

The next morning Gil's wind sock had

changed direction entirely, and not for the better. He watched Cora from the shadows. Henry saw the undisguised longing in Gil's eyes as she went about her business, ignoring him completely. That Henry saw all of this only meant he was watching Cora enough to notice Gil watching her. Henry was forced to admit he was probably a moth, too.

All of these repressed emotions and the strained silence were going to be the end of a good thing. Already Henry saw Jake looking perturbed with the curt answers and crappy moods Gil and Cora were offering. And they were acting like twelve-year-olds not talking directly to one another. How long would Jake tolerate it?

"No romantic hoo-ha." Henry's coming right out and confronting Gil about keeping away from Cora when they'd joined the circus would have been about as well received as a knife in the back. Henry had already driven one wedge between him and Gil the day of the storm. The tornado had dislodged it, but you couldn't always count on a handy tornado to undo the damage to a relationship. And then when Gil had seemed better than he'd been since the day Henry had met him, Henry had been glad he'd avoided the subject.

How naive he'd been.

He was packing up the kitchen, getting ready to load it into the trailer, when he heard Jake's uncharacteristically raised voice across the camp. "Dammit, Gil! Get that burr out from under your saddle."

Henry looked toward the voice, but couldn't see more than two pairs of feet on the far side of the three tied-down planes.

All Gil had to do was keep himself together for one more day. Surely the man could do that. They were heading into a two-month off-season. All of the equipment was headed to Reece's cotton farm in the Mississippi Delta — Thomas had already delivered his plane there. Then Jake would head to Omaha, away from all man-woman drama, except for whatever he stirred up himself. Hopefully, Gil would have rediscovered his equilibrium again by February when they reassembled to practice and settle on a show schedule. The circus wouldn't perform again until the first of March.

Gil startled Henry out of his thoughts by appearing and saying, "I'm heading out."

"I thought we were all flying out together — when the truck and trailer are ready to go," Henry said.

Reece had left an open invitation to all

three of them to stay throughout the off-season. Henry had immediately accepted, having no home to return to. Cora had been talking about going to California. Gil's plans for the break remained a closely guarded mystery. Each time Henry approached him, he got the same terse "I have something I need to do."

Maybe that something was spending several weeks off by himself — a bear in hibernation. The holidays always made Henry extraordinarily lonely, but he suspected Gil preferred loneliness.

Gil shrugged. "I'm ready now. Weather might change."

Henry didn't like the look in Gil's eyes. "You'd better be there when we get there." He leaned close and gave Gil a poke in the chest. "You accepted Reece's wife's invitation to Thanksgiving dinner. Even you couldn't be rude enough to sneak off beforehand."

Henry's head told him it would be better to let Gil do just that. But this was Henry's first holiday in over seven years that he would spend with people around a table. He'd been looking forward to it for weeks. Was it too goddamn much to ask? One holiday?

Gil stared at Henry until the anger showing in his eyes mellowed to sarcasm. "No, even I couldn't be that much of an ass."

Henry gave a satisfied nod. "See you before sunset, then."

When Gil's plane took to the air, Cora stopped pulling up her tent stakes and stood watching it until it was no longer visible. Henry waited until she went back to the task before he went over to help her.

Mercury seemed to sense her mood and stuck closer to her heels than usual, which made folding and rolling the heavy canvas tent even more of a challenge. When they were collecting the wooden tent stakes, the dog took off with one, got fifteen feet away, turned to face them, flopped down, and started chewing it. When Cora went after it, he trotted a few more feet and repeated his actions.

"You're going to be sorry you chewed that when the tent falls in on us next spring." Her tone was harsh; she was never harsh with Mercury.

She tried to approach him again, with no better result. "Come over here right now, you little shit!"

Henry took her arm. "Hey, he's just a dog."

She jerked her arm away and stalked back to pick up the remaining stakes. "Well, he's going to be a homeless dog if he doesn't watch it."

Henry sat on the ground right where he was and waited. In a few seconds, Mercury came trotting over and lay down next to him. With a gentle hand, Henry removed the tent stake from the dog's mouth. Then he pulled Mercury into his lap and scratched him behind the ears for a bit. "Maybe it should just be you and me at Thanksgiving, little fella. Less craziness." He chuckled as he thought of his dream, with Mercury seated right at the table, paws resting on either side of his plate as he waited patiently for the meal to begin.

Henry sat there for a few minutes, watching Cora try to fold the tent. He decided to let her struggle with it for a while, maybe work out some of that hostility.

She huffed and tugged, then finally stood up and shot him a glare. When he didn't jump up, she walked over to him and shoved her hands on her hips. "Have you decided if you're coming with me to California or not?" She used the semidisgusted tone a mother would on a misbehaving child.

"Gosh, with a lovely invitation like that . . ."

Closing her eyes briefly, she blew out a long breath, then sat down hard beside him.

"Sorry, Henry. I'm just . . ." She threw a hand in the air.

Henry held Mercury up so his face was near hers. "What about me?" he said in a gruff little voice that he imagined Mercury would possess could he talk.

She finally broke a smile and grabbed the dog from Henry's hands. Holding his nose to hers, she said, "Sorry to you, too." She planted a kiss right between his ears. "Everything's just so — up in the air."

"We *are* a flying circus."

"You should look into vaudeville with a sense of humor like that. Give eighty-year-old ladies a real good laugh."

"Eighty-year-old ladies are not without their charm." At least none of them would stomp on your heart. The three of them sat there for a bit. Henry used his knife to smooth out ragged edges of the stake Mercury had chewed.

"So," he finally said. "You haven't changed your mind? I mean, if I had a family, I sure wouldn't be spending Christmas alone in California." She had made the break and her life was now her own. It seemed pointless to stay cut off from her family.

"It would just be one big fight — Mother ashamed and disappointed, trying to get me to change my ways; me frustrated with her shallow views. We're both better off if I stay away. I sent her a letter saying I had to work over the holidays."

"Going to Hollywood to gawk at movie stars . . . maybe get a peek at Valentino . . . is work?"

"Henry!" His actual name had been coming out of her mouth more than *Kid* lately. "I wish I'd never told you about that tour. I didn't say I was going to take it! The only reason I'm going is to check into stunting for the moving pictures. We can work in the off-season doing pictures, you and I — Gil, too, if he's still around —"

"Wait! What do you mean 'if he's still around'?"

She shrugged.

"He's been better with this circus than he's ever been — even without his own plane. That is, until you two lost your heads." It came out more hateful than he'd intended.

The breath she took was so deep he heard it. "Well. That won't be happening again. No need to blame me if he leaves the circus."

"You think he's going to leave?"

"Who knows? You said it yourself, he's broken."

"And you've finally given up on fixing him?"

"*I* do not give up on things. And I don't want to talk about it anymore. I want to talk about going to California and getting into the moving pictures; they always need stunt fliers."

"Because they keep dying off. Besides, you don't fly."

"Of course I do. Jake taught me. I just prefer wing walking — which they also need in movie stunts."

"Knowing how to fly and stunting are two different things. Out of the three of us, Gil's the only one with enough skill to sell to the movies."

"I've learned everything else. If I decide to stunt, I'll stunt."

Henry laughed. "I don't doubt it."

"So? Are you coming?"

"You know I told Reece I'd stay on his farm and work on the planes."

"That doesn't mean you can't take a couple of weeks off. It'll give Reece time to be with his family without extra people around."

Henry hadn't thought about it that way, as if he was an intruder in the few weeks Reece had with his family. "What about Gil?"

"I'm not going to ask him. You can if you want."

Henry'd have to think long and hard before he did that — for Gil's sake. On the other hand, maybe being alone with Cora for two weeks would be Henry's own undoing. "What's going on with you two?" There it was, out there. Finally.

She turned her head to look square at him. "Absolutely nothing."

Henry's frustration outweighed his reluctance to face the truth. "So you two just kiss and run."

"Never again."

"How can you say that? It hasn't looked like there's been planning in the previous instances. Unless there's more —"

"No! Oh, God, no!"

He was a little taken aback by her vehemence.

"Gil is not . . . available."

He wished she'd stop talking in disjointed statements. "I did warn you, he's a dried-out corn husk, emotionally. He's been through things he can't —"

"That's not what I meant by *unavailable*. He's married." She shoved Mercury back into Henry's hands, got up, and walked off, leaving him to sit there with his head spinning.

■ ■ ■ ■

Jake took off for Reece's farm. Henry watched him gain altitude as Henry propped his own plane. He hoped the hours alone in the air would help clear his head . . . and his heart. This life was suddenly feeling as if it were being held together by as many wires as a Jenny, and one by one they were snapping free.

He hoped the wings wouldn't fall off completely.

He aimed the plane into the wind at the end of the field. Just as he was throttling up, movement off to his right caught his eye.

A car was fast approaching, going much too fast for the rough field. The driver stuck his arm and head out of the window. His bowler blew off. He waved frantically for Henry to stop.

The prohibition agent came to mind. A lawman.

Henry throttled up and took off down the field.

He didn't look back.

The entire way to Mississippi, he assured himself that no one knew where the circus kept its equipment over the winter. His alarm was probably foolish. That man could just have been someone wanting a ride. Or a reporter wanting an interview. Or a dozen other things. Why had Henry assumed he was a lawman?

Because he looked like one. From up north.

17

Gil was true to his word. When they gathered around the table for Thanksgiving dinner, he was sitting right next to Reece's pa — and directly across the nice juicy turkey from Cora. Considering the circumstances, they were both behaving pretty well. Anyone who didn't know them the way Henry did probably wouldn't even get a whiff that anything was amiss.

The Althoffs' house had most likely been grand at one time. It had big rooms with fireplaces, a fancy stairway in an entry hall, and a large porch across the entire front, but much of the white paint had baked to a ghost of itself in the Southern sun, and the old wood floors had lost their finish on the regular paths traced by those who lived there. Two of the most magnificently twisted trees stood in the front yard — live oaks, Reece had called them — a hundred years old. Surrounding the lawn on three sides and across the road as far as Henry could see were broad, flat, harvested cotton fields. He'd never seen cotton growing. Reece had shown Henry pictures and had given him a cotton boll, which looked and felt nothing like he'd expected.

When Reece's pa offered the blessing, Henry said his own silent prayer of thanks for this new life. He prayed for the strength and guidance to help Gil find his way back, and for a boost in his own immunity against his attraction to Cora. If they were going to survive in the circus, they had to keep things friendly. *Just* friendly.

Then he asked for the strength to do what was right, to atone for his weakness. It was a lot to ask of even the most generous God.

After Mr. Althoff had said his amen, Henry looked around the table and offered one more prayer of thanks for these people. Peter had said Ma believed prayers should always end with thankfulness, not requests.

The dining room table had fancy, spindly legs that looked too frail to hold the bounty that was spread upon it. With just the six of them around it, they had to extend their reach to pass the serving dishes. This wasn't exactly the family meal Henry had spent hours imagining, but he realized he'd probably set his expectations unnaturally high.

He'd pictured a crowded table with bumping elbows, happy chatter, and boisterous laughs. This was a bit more serious, with fancy china and monogrammed silverware. Even so, sitting with these people felt like a salve to a burn. All families had rough waters at times. And he committed himself to helping Cora and Gil get through theirs. For years, he'd longed for people to call his own; he wasn't going to give them up without a fight.

Gil worked to be a good guest, talking even when not asked a direct question.

"Wonderful meal, Mrs. Althoff. Best cooking I've ever had," he said as he buttered a biscuit.

"Please, call me Nell. And it's probably just because you're a hungry bachelor. Just wait until you get a wife. Food cooked with love always tastes better."

Out of the corner of his eye, Henry saw Cora sit up straighter. Her fork paused halfway to her mouth.

Henry watched Gil, waiting for his response.

He kept his eyes on his food and mumbled, "Yes, ma'am."

Although Henry had lived alongside Gil day in and day out for months, he didn't know him at all. Married. The man was *mar-*

ried. And still sitting there pretending he wasn't — even though Cora already knew.

That must be what he was going to go do in the off-season, see a wife. The money he'd mailed had likely gone to her. But why keep it such a secret?

Gil was quiet, sure. And initially Henry had had to dig to get anything out of him about his past. But these months with the circus had opened him up some. He still didn't discuss his years in the war, but he did talk about growing up poor in southeastern Ohio, where coal mines and potteries were to him what farming had been to Henry — the only possibility the future held. He talked about how he'd bought the Jenny from the army and his first days barnstorming. In addition to this glaring opportunity to fess up, there had been plenty of campfire talk about homes and wives and children. Gil had been involved in most of them. But never a breath about a wife.

After dinner, Henry followed Gil out onto the front porch. It was chilly, but after all of that food and deception, the air felt good.

"So," Henry said, "your train leaves tomorrow morning?"

Gil nodded as he lit a cigarette.

"Home to Ohio? Or are you going to look

for a plane?" The double question camouflaged Henry's intent. Jennies weren't as cheap as they used to be; lots of them had been rebuilt by Wright Aeronautical with new Hisso engines. But Gil might have a lead on one he could afford — if he hadn't secretly been sending most of his money to a wife. Of course, as far as Gil was concerned, Henry didn't know about that.

Gil's sharp gaze cut from the fields to Henry. "I'm not looking at a plane."

"Ah. I'm sure your family will be glad to see you. It has to have been a long time."

"Uh-huh."

"Are you going to be gone the entire break? Or are you coming back here to help me overhaul the engines?"

"Not sure." Then Gil looked at Henry in the dusky light. "Will you need me?"

"I'll have plenty of time to handle it. Even with the trip to California with Cora." Henry kept his eyes fixed on Gil, watching for the slightest reaction.

But Gil's reaction wasn't slight at all. He stopped leaning on the porch post and jerked to his full height. "California?"

"She wants to look into moving-picture stunting. Something to do in the off-season."

"You're joking."

Henry pressed his lips together and shook his head. "You know how she is when she gets something in her head."

"She doesn't have the skill to be a stunt pilot. She's never done the simplest of maneuvers. She doesn't even *like* piloting."

Henry crossed his arms over his chest and leaned against his own post. "Apparently all irrelevant." Then he asked, "You knew Jake taught her to fly?"

"Yes."

Well then, Henry had missed more than one thing that had been right under his nose. It irritated him enough to motivate him to say, "After that little scene on the field the other day, I'd have thought you two would be going to California together. And yet, you're going off somewhere else and I'm headed West."

"That 'little scene' —" Gil sighed. "It's not like that."

"It looked *exactly* like that. What's going on? You're likely to ruin everything."

"Jake gave me the 'romantic hoo-ha' lecture the other day, so save your breath."

"You told me you didn't love her."

"That doesn't matter one way or the other —"

"Oh, I think it might. Because even if you *say* there's nothing going on, even if you

421

only break down and kiss her twice a season, the undercurrent you two are putting out there is exactly what Jake doesn't want."

Gil took several puffs from his cigarette; he kept his eyes on the oak trees when he said, "If I have to leave the circus before I can buy my own plane, I will. But I'd rather stay."

Henry looked directly into Gil's eyes. "Why would you make that choice? I mean, if you love each other, do something about it. Keep the drama out of it. Marry her, for God's sake. Jake didn't forbid nice, quiet married people." *Tell me. You're not wiggling off this hook again.*

Gil rubbed his forehead as if he was getting a headache. "That's not . . . it's just . . ."

I trusted you. Suddenly Henry went cold. What in the hell was he doing? Trust went both ways. And he wasn't about to stand here and tell Gil that he was wanted for murder back in Indiana. "Forget it. I was way out of line." Henry started back inside the house. "It's none of my business."

"I'm already married." Gil sounded resigned, worn, and sad.

Henry stopped and closed his eyes.

He turned back around. "I see."

"Hardly. It's complicated."

"Men tempted to stray always say that.

422

But usually to get the sympathy of a half-willing woman."

"Can you see if Reece has anything to drink around here? . . . I don't mean after-dinner coffee."

Henry went inside and came back out a few minutes later with a dubious-looking mason jar of moonshine and two very fine cut-glass tumblers. Gil was sitting in a frayed wicker chair. He'd pulled another one close and indicated Henry should sit.

After Henry poured them both a drink, Gil took a sip and stared into the now pitch-darkness that surrounded the house. Henry held his drink in his hand, unsure if he was going to risk drinking it.

When Gil finally started to talk, it wasn't about young love or a wife. "My whole childhood it was just me and my mother. She worked in a pottery." He shook his head, and when he spoke again, he sounded distant, lost in the past. "The dust of that place clung to her no matter how much she washed her dried-out skin. When she hugged me, it came off her clothes. I remember that fine grit in my teeth." His voice grew more focused. "I don't know who my father was. Mother did the best she could after her father turned her out — I only knew him by sight, after some kid at

423

school told me he was my grandpa. The whole town knew more about me than I knew about me." Gil paused and seemed to grow more distant again. "She was so thin. What I remember most about her was that she always seemed . . . faded. Translucent. More gone than attached to this world."

Henry thought of his pa, more gone than here; life seemed to do that to a lot of people.

Gil ran his fingers across the cut glass, as if memorizing the pattern with his fingertips. "She left me with a neighbor lady when she worked. But that lady had eight kids of her own. I don't think she noticed if I was there or not. I just remember it being chaotic. I didn't like all of that motion, all of that noise. So I generally just stayed away."

He paused and took a long sip from his glass.

"When I started school, I met John Andrews and Mary Keating." Gil's voice was still a little hoarse from the burning alcohol. "Being poor didn't make you stand out in our town, but being a bastard and being Irish Catholic did. The three of us were bound by our exclusion."

When he stopped for a moment, Henry said, "Bound by exclusion. Maybe people like us are always drawn together like that."

Gil looked over at Henry and smiled thinly. "Of that I have no doubt." Gil raised his glass. "To misfits one and all." He drank. "I'm not sure why I told you all of that . . . unless it's to make you understand why I did what I did.

"When we got to high school, John and I pledged neither of us would ruin it by changing things with Mary. She was like our sister. There was a time when I nearly broke that promise. No one knew me like she did. But it meant more to me to keep us all together.

"I quit school at sixteen. By then, Mother's health had gone from bad to worse. She was confined to bed. I earned enough at the mine to feed us and keep a couple of rented rooms. Working long hours on a night shift kept me away from John and Mary most of the time. That's when things changed between them. They hid it from me for months. And then I found them together. John and I fought — I beat the bloody hell out of him, all the while Mary screaming for me to stop. That night he drank too much and fell off the railroad trestle where he and I used to sit at night, smoking and drinking and planning how we were going to get the hell out of that town.

I found his body after Mary came to tell me John's mother said he hadn't come home the night before. It was the first place I looked. Mother died the next week. I decided to go to France, determined to make it through flight training. I figured if a German got me, at least I'd be out in the daylight, not buried in a collapsed mine tunnel.

"The week before I left, Mary told me she was pregnant. I was the reason John was gone. All because I was too selfish and too jealous to grow up and act like a man. So I married her; at least I could keep John's child from being branded a bastard. She cried through the whole ceremony. And then I left to make her a war widow. But that just refused to happen. It only took one day after I got back to see that she could not look at me without wanting John — without blaming me. One look at that baby and it was obvious John was the father, cow-licked red hair and all. People had been willing to ignore that fact while I was gone, but my presence started tongues to wagging. She and the baby had a life, a decent life that didn't include me. Divorce was out of the question. It wasn't fair to her for me to stay; I didn't want to, not and face that every day. I haven't seen her since."

"Well. Hell." If there was one thing Henry understood, it was the lengths a lonely soul would go to in order to hold on to family. In his own desire to do that, he'd probably just ensured that Gil would go away and never come back.

And if he did come back?

Henry had demanded trust. Families and friendships were based on it. Gil's own story proved it.

"Did you tell Cora all of this?"

"Only that I'm married. That's all she needs to know."

Henry nodded. Gil was a more honorable man than he. Preventing Cora from learning the hopeless truth about Gil's marriage kept her from throwing convention out the window and justifying a relationship that was guaranteed to go nowhere.

Henry finally took a drink of the moonshine, welcoming the pain of the burn. He punished himself by holding his breath, not allowing himself to cough, to gasp. *Hold it in. Suffer.*

Gil had told Henry his secret, laid his pain naked for Henry to judge. He'd proven his worth as a friend. And Henry could never, *never,* do the same.

He sat there in the dark long after Gil got up and went into the house. Long after the lights went out.

After quite a while, it struck him. He never even asked Gil about the child. Son or daughter?

When had he become such a selfish hypocrite?

18

The sun sat high, hot on the top of Henry's head, even though it was December 12. This, he supposed, made Southern California a perfect place for Northern-born people who didn't want to be reminded it was the holiday season. He stood with his pants legs rolled up, the cold water of the Pacific breaking against his shins, Point Dume's craggy rise behind him. He'd been prepared for the size of the water, but not its constant motion, its power, or the blindingly white sand that fought against the greedy waves. The water surged and receded, each pass trying to knock him off his feet while simultaneously burying them deeper in the sand. He wondered how long he'd have to stand here before his entire body would be buried. A year? A decade? A lifetime? The wind blew steady against his face. He tasted the salt of the ocean on his lips. He was standing in the *Pacific Ocean.*

Impossible.

His life was offering wonders he'd never dared to dream of. All because of the death of a girl. As he watched the hypnotic rolling of the water, he thought on that for a while. It was an ugly truth, but one he couldn't ignore. Time had passed. He'd traveled far. But the reality was, he was a wanted man. He was managing to stay inconspicuous with the circus. If movie stunt flying was in his future, anonymity would be easy to maintain. No one ever saw the stunt pilot's face on-screen, or in the newspapers — until he killed himself during a stunt. In that case, it wouldn't matter anymore.

How would Cora and Gil feel if Henry's death exposed his deception?

He had betrayed the trust of the people he cared about most on this earth — Cora, Gil, and Mr. Dahlgren. But another issue was taking chunks out of his insides with razor teeth. He needed to go back. To face the consequences. But it would be worse now. Now that he'd run. Now that so many months had passed. If he returned, his story would be even less credible than the day it happened. The jail door would slam. The sentence would be read. And he'd be dead.

"Henry!"

He turned. Cora was headed back his way,

her hands clasped at her waist. The wind blew her short hair across her face, even though she had a scarf tied as a headband. The long ends of silk whipped like banners behind her.

When she got close, she held out her cupped hands. Several shells, swirls and ridges of tans and pinks and grays, were in them. "Almost all of them are broken."

When Henry looked into her eyes, he suddenly felt as tumbled and broken as those sea-tossed shells. He'd been a fool to convince himself he could come out here with her and not be drawn deeper in love. Neither of them had spoken of Gil, not since they'd left Mississippi — not of her anger over his disappearance, or why he'd left, or if he'd come back. Without the shadow of his presence, Henry and Cora had grown closer — but he had no idea how deep her affection might run. They never spoke of feelings or futures. They just *lived*. He had fallen harder and more deeply than he'd imagined a man could. Watching her talk to the movie people inside studios so new they still smelled of fresh paint, Henry's heart had actually ached — he'd always thought that was just a silly phrase, but it *happened*.

Yesterday they'd been at Warner Brothers

Studios on Sunset Boulevard, one of the grandest buildings Henry had ever set eyes on, gleaming white with a soldier's rank of tall columns across the second story. The man they met with wasn't overly interested in adding stunt pilots to his roster. Instead, he'd taken them to watch a picture being filmed on one of their massive sets in an attempt to convince Cora to try her hand at acting. Henry's heart had nearly stopped when the man made his proposal. Everything about Hollywood was shiny and new and exciting — and on such a massive scale. And Cora was a woman who admitted she was searching for her place. She needed excitement. How could she resist?

"I'm not an actress." She'd laughed lightly. "Wouldn't have the patience for the tedium. I'm a stuntwoman. Let me know when you need one and we can talk."

After they'd left, Henry had made himself ask, "Are you sure you don't want to take a stab at acting?" She could easily be more famous than Lillian Gish or Mary Pickford, two women this town seemed wild over. Cora needed to think about it and not be blinded by her single-minded stubbornness.

She'd shaken her head. "Really, Henry. Why would I contract my life over to a movie studio so they could tell me what to do? Might as well have gone ahead and gotten married."

The tone in her voice set off a flash of memory. "Those trunks, the ones you kicked on your uncle's back porch, were yours. Packed to leave. You were *that* close to getting married?"

"It wasn't like the wedding was supposed to be the next week, or that I broke anyone's heart. I'm sure he just moved on to the next lady in line to marry his money. Besides, what does it matter now?"

"I suppose it doesn't." But it had given him pause. She'd given her word to the man she was going to marry. Didn't that mean anything to her?

She'd looked him in the eyes. "Henry. I see what you're thinking. Let me ask you — if you were about to be locked up for the rest of your life just because of the misfortune of your birth, wouldn't you stop it any way you could? And for the record, I wasn't involved in any of the negotiations, so *I* didn't break any promises."

Her choice of words had given him a little shiver, and not just because of the mention of being locked up, jail. He'd had the bad luck of being born with the wrong name at the wrong time. Seems they'd both run from their misfortune of circumstance. At

433

least Cora admitted it.

Right then and there he'd decided he wasn't ever going to ask her about the marriage or her mother again. He had no right whatsoever.

Now, under the shining sun of this windswept beach, looking at her smile as she stared down at the shells she'd spent the better part of an hour gathering, Henry's heart got the better of him and he reached out to touch her face.

When she looked up at him with surprise, his panic nearly choked him. "Sand on your cheek." He made a show of brushing his hand on his pant leg. "All gone." Then he looked at the shells. "Do you know what any of them are?"

"No. I've always just liked them for their artistry. If I think of them as houses for now-dead sea creatures, it kind of takes away the pleasure."

"Reality has a way of doing that."

Her eyes met his again. "What's wrong, Henry? You've been moody all day."

The flood of emotions nearly fell out of his mouth. Had they, they would have been incomprehensible, broken as the fragments of shells in her hand. The only one perfect in its wholeness would have been *I'm in love with you.*

He had no right to love her. He was just as unavailable as Gil. At least the reason Gil couldn't marry her wasn't because he was an impostor hiding a brand of *murderer* under his shirt.

He shrugged. "Guess it's Christmas coming. Always makes me a little sad."

She gave a soft smile that squeezed his heart so tightly he had to look away. Then she said, "Maybe the picture show will cheer you up."

Cheer? They were going to the Egyptian Theatre to see *The Hunchback of Notre Dame.* Cheer hardly came to mind. But it would be Henry's first moving-picture show, so that was something. He forced a smile. "I'm sure it will."

She tossed all of the shells back into the waves, brushed her hands against each other, then slipped her arm through his.

Every step Henry took back toward the stop for the bus that would take them through the Cahuenga Pass and back to the Hollywood Hotel was filled with the certainty that he was going to have to stop running — and not just from the law.

It was quite easy to get around. The Pacific Red Cars, electric trains like the interurbans back home, got them most places.

Buses did the rest. Henry and Cora had been working through her list of things "we ab-so-lute-ly *must* see." They'd taken a bus up to see the fancy houses being built in Hollywoodland. Cora said most of them were influenced by European or Mediterranean architecture. Whatever kind they were, they were unlike any Henry had ever seen, with exposed timbers, irregular bricks and stone, stucco, and steep roofs with sharp peaks. They were built on steep hillsides where the winding road had been cut in and shored up with twenty-foot-high stone walls. A string of giant letters up on the top of the far hills spelled the Hollywoodland name. Advertising that could be seen for miles and miles. The promoter in Henry applauded the ingenuity.

One town pretty much led right into the next. Cora said the area around most big cities were like that nowadays. Hollywood and its surrounds gave Henry the impression that it had only recently sprung up out of the orange groves. Everything was gleaming white. Steam shovels rumbled everywhere, taking chunks out of dry, rocky hills, carving new roads and leveling areas for new buildings. Red-tile roofs, towers, and arched windows and doorways were everywhere — Cora told him that was the

Spanish influence. Even the trees looked as if they'd come from faraway lands — tall, naked trunks topped with huge, fanlike leaves. Palm trees. Now they walked into the courtyard of Grauman's Hollywood Egyptian Theatre. It was like entering another country — which he supposed was the whole point. Wide columns lined the sides, etched with lines of pictures and symbols, which Cora explained were Egyptian hieroglyphs, an ancient form of writing. On the walls around them were primitive-looking paintings of brown men with funny headdresses and white cloths wrapped around their waists. Giant pots filled with strange-looking plants sat around the concrete courtyard. There was a statue with a man's body and a dog's head twice as tall as Henry. They entered the wide doors to the lobby. The open air overhead became a ceiling. He was suddenly part of a herd funneled into the slaughterhouse. So many perfumes and hair oils. So little air. The Egyptian decorations inside this confined space felt oppressive.

Then the usherette led them into the auditorium. Henry stopped dead. A man bumped into him from behind.

"Sorry," Henry and the man both said at once.

Cora took Henry's hand and led him down the aisle and into a row of seats. When she stopped in the center, she said, "Now you can look. Magnificent, isn't it?"

She said *magnificent,* not *monkey's eyebrows* or *cat's pajamas* or *bee's knees. Magnificent.* Even Cora was impressed.

She said, "It's like being inside a pharaoh's tomb."

If this is what a pharaoh's tomb looked like, no wonder Cora had wanted to discover one. Four giant, decorated columns flanked the draped stage, supporting a pair of overhead beams with layered step backs, each crowded with hieroglyphs. More people were on the side walls, looking like statues just emerging from the stone.

But the ceiling amazed most. In the center of the first header over the stage was a large gold beetle sprouting wide, eaglelike wings with a circle between its antennae. Above the beetle on the ceiling was a shiny gold half circle that bloomed line after incredible line of carved intricacy, each detail outlined in gold, the inner details painted in yellows, oranges, and bright blues until the arc reached a point where it looked to explode in spikes and shafts of gleaming gold.

Henry leaned close and whispered, "So beautiful. Why ruin it with a giant bug?"

She giggled and leaned close to whisper back, her breath sending tickling shivers across his body. "It's a scarab. Has something to do with Egyptian gods pushing the sun across the sky, or something like that. See" — she looked up and pointed — "it holds the sun in its antennae." Then her hand swept across the graduating arc. "Sunrise."

"Sunrise," he repeated, but he was looking at her. He realized she was still holding his hand.

People had taken seats on both sides of them. When Henry looked around, he and Cora were the only two still standing in the middle of the theater. He sat and tugged her down beside him.

He thought of her comment that the movie would take his mind off his melancholy. Now she sat with happy eagerness on her face. It struck him that she didn't know the story. It had been one of the more tedious books Henry had borrowed from Mr. Dahlgren's library, and parts of it were lost on him entirely as he had no clear frame of understanding, but Henry had pushed through until the horribly depressing end. He looked at her, sitting there with innocent anticipation on her face. All of her fancy education, and he'd read a book that she had not.

He leaned close and whispered, "You do know this doesn't end well?"

She turned to him, eyes wide and mouth a questioning *O*. "You said you've never seen a moving picture. It was just released this year."

"I read the book."

She raised a brow. "Really?"

"I *can* read."

She reached across and put a hand on his forearm. "I didn't mean I didn't think you can read —"

At that moment the lights went out, the curtain opened, and the Fox newsreel came on the screen. Henry sat, unblinking for fear of missing something, as the words *Here's the great ball-game giant himself in action!* gave way to Babe Ruth running the bases. Babe Ruth! And that crowd! Yankee Stadium was rows and rows of people packed like pickles in a barrel. The next pictures showed "the Bambino" visiting the children's ward of a New York hospital. It was incredible to see the man, moving in real life.

The credits for *The Hunchback of Notre Dame* passed and the cathedral and its square came on-screen. The people moved about the Festival of Fools just as if he were watching them in life, although drained of color and sound. For over an hour and a half the orchestra accompanied the photoplay. The words between the moving pictures were brief and used much simpler language than the book. Henry watched, enthralled most by the miracle of mechanics, science, and light that moved on the screen.

Then the end was upon them. The moment when Esmeralda would hang. Only she didn't.

When the lights came up, he shook his head. "That wasn't the story I read."

"Well, things have to be adapted for the moving pictures, I'm sure."

"If they could make a man look like Quasimodo and a cathedral look like Notre Dame, they could darn well tell the story right."

As they walked out into the cool evening air, he explained the changes that had been made: the lustful priest Claude Frollo turned from villain into kind protector, his youthful drunkard of a brother into the villain; Esmeralda's hanging turned into a happy ending with Captain Phoebus.

"Did Quasimodo die in the book?"

"Yes, but he starved to death, grieving at the side of Esmeralda's body."

"Good golly. No wonder they changed the ending."

He looked over his shoulder. "Now you can say you've been to Egypt."

She laughed. "Egypt was not the point. Adventure was the point."

He stopped. She took another step and stopped, too, and turned to look at him. "What's the matter?"

"Have you fulfilled that desire? Adventure?"

She reached back and took his hand, pulling him back to walk at her side. "I have a good start."

"Where do you go from here, then?"

"Who knows? Isn't that part of the adventure, the surprising turns —" She stopped and pointed to a poster in a storefront window. "Look! Maybe that's what's next."

They stepped closer to the window. An aerobatic competition and air race at Clover Field in Santa Monica on Saturday was advertised.

"That must be it!" she said. "More speed. Why else would fate have put that there, right now, when we're talking about it?"

"Fate didn't put it there. Fate doesn't use cloth adhesive tape."

She swatted his arm. "Stop being so literal."

He shrugged and shoved his hands in his pockets. He didn't like where this was heading.

"How many women fly racers?" she asked.

"You don't even like piloting."

"Well, racing would make it interesting! We have to go."

"We can go. But don't get your heart set on it. To be competitive you have to have the best machine. And that means money. Probably lots of it."

"We'll see, Henry. We'll see."

This city had plenty of movie houses to choose from. Why had they come here?

Maybe Fate did use adhesive tape.

19

"I miss Mercury," Cora said as she and Henry sat on the broad porch that wrapped two sides of the original section of the Hollywood Hotel. Henry was getting increasingly restless himself, and not just because he missed the dog, or the airplanes. He was worried about Gil, how things were going in Ohio. Henry didn't think the man could take one more blow. Every day Henry prayed that Gil's wife received him kindly, that the child gave him reason to live.

There was a more pressing problem. This hotel was expensive. Although the circus paid him more than he'd ever imagined, his pockets weren't bottomless. With or without Cora, he was going to have to clear out after the aerobatic competition and race on Saturday.

He did have to admit she'd been right; if they were going to investigate Hollywood, this was the place to stay. Rudolph Valentino himself had lived here. Henry thought it peculiar that anyone would *live* in a hotel. Something about it was just so disconnected and temporary, lacking commitment. Henry's life was rootless by necessity. He longed to wake up each day and make plans for the future around a single place on the map.

Even though most of them didn't live there, film people — studio owners, producers, writers, all identified by Cora — were tucked practically in every corner of the hotel, huddled together with cigars and intense conversations. Cora had already pointed out four different moving-picture stars on the porch or in the lobby, faces that passed just like any others to Henry. But she was no gawking goose around the wealthy and the famous. She conversed with them and remembered their names, and they remembered hers. She introduced herself to those she'd discovered to be heads of studios, producers, and directors. She charmed and beguiled and was accepted as one of them. Henry had to remind himself that she *was* one of them — or had at least been before her father lost his fortune. This world of fine clothes, expensive cars, tennis courts, and elegant dining rooms was hers, the one she'd walked away from to sleep on the ground beneath the wings of a patched-up airplane.

When he'd said something to that effect to her, she'd laughed. "Oh, Henry, this is nothing like the money I came from. This is new money. Happy, progressive money. Open air and starlight, not heavy draperies and cluttered rooms filled with Victorian ideas and archaic social rules."

It made no sense to Henry. Money was money. Rich was rich.

He did have to admit, these people practically vibrated with urgency, as if they were trying to catch something before it traveled on and left them standing on the sidelines. Maybe that was the difference Cora was talking about. He certainly couldn't imagine her stiff and sour mother in this laughing atmosphere.

Even though he felt the momentum rushing headlong into the future, a vague itch deep beneath Henry's skin had started a day or so ago, uncomfortable and nagging. Of everything he'd seen in California, only the ocean and the scattered orange groves and poinsettia fields were real and true. All else worked overly hard at pretending to be places and things they were not — the overdone themes of restaurants and moving-picture theaters, diners and cafés shaped as coffee cups, airplanes, dogs, ice-cream cones, a jail. The industry fueling a good deal of what was going on here sold pretend images of pretend lives lived by pretend people.

That itch had come to the surface and demanded to be scratched. He was done with the land of pretend. He wanted grease on his hands and farm chores to tire his muscles.

"I miss the mutt, too. Ready to go home?" he asked.

"Home?" She turned to him with a raised brow.

Henry chuckled. "I guess home for us is wherever the dog and the planes are, huh?"

"I thought home was where the heart is." The way she was looking at him, with a kind of probing invitation, made his insides turn over.

He was tempted to ask her where her heart resided, but his good sense caught the words before they left his mouth. Cora's heart needed to be guarded from him, just as it did from Gil.

"We should get ready for the big night," he said as he got to his feet. She'd been waiting for this night since they'd checked in three days ago. They were splurging on dining at the hotel and going to the weekly dance in the ballroom. Cora had heard it was *the* place to be seen. He wasn't particularly interested in being seen, quite the contrary.

Yet, for the first time since he'd fled Indiana, Emmaline's dead body seemed too far away to touch him with her cold finger of accusation.

Cora smiled and rose to her feet. "Can't wait to see you in your dinner jacket."

It worried him just a bit, how he was willing to do almost anything she asked. He'd wear that dinner jacket tonight and most likely pack it away for the rest of his life. At least he'd found it at a resale shop.

They headed toward their rooms on the second floor. When he stopped and waited until she unlocked her door, she looked up at him. "Just wait until you see my dress." She winked. "See you at seven."

He'd gone to his room with a mix of anticipation and dread. God give him strength to stand up to whatever she was going to wear tonight.

At seven on the nose, he knocked on her door. The starched new shirt, collar, and cuffs were the most uncomfortable things he'd ever worn. Already his neck felt as chafed as if he'd been following mules with a plow strap around it for a week.

When Cora opened the door, he forgot all about his own clothes. His stomach felt as it had the first time he'd lifted off the ground in Gil's Jenny, jolted out of his body and left somewhere far behind. Her hair was done in close waves with a single curl hugging her forehead. And that dress! No way could she be wearing anything underneath. Something about it was almost otherworldly, a mix of soft fabric, lace, and beads in earthy colors, golds and greens and coral, that split into triangular panels from the hip to below the knee, opening to flowing layers of sheer blue-gray that reached the floor. When she stepped into the hall, it looked as if she were wading in the ocean — a dress perfect for a town based on make-believe.

She spun around. "Like it?" A small, cinched bag covered in glass beads swung out from her arm.

"Hollywood had better brace itself."

"Flatterer."

If only it were flattery. Then he might stand a chance of surviving this evening.

When they entered the ballroom, it was already full of noise and cigarette smoke. The dance floor was surrounded by round tables with short candles sitting in glass bowls on holiday greenery. A few of the chair backs had furs or feathers draped over them. Almost all of the men wore nearly identical black suits with long tails, white vests, and white bow ties. Upstairs, Henry had felt ridiculously overdressed. Now he felt like a poor relative visiting from the farm — which was pretty much what he was.

The band, made up of a piano, drums, horns, saxophones, and clarinets, was on an alcove stage framed by a line of round, white lights. The host led them from the door to a small table for two tucked in a shadowy back corner. Heads bobbed with flashing gemstones and wobbling ostrich feathers in front of the stage, where an energetic dance was in progress. The exposed skin, the movements, the abandonment of feminine morals, would make Midwestern farm wives swoon.

"Don't you have something nearer the dance floor?" Cora asked.

"This is fine," Henry said before the man could answer.

Cora looked at him over her shoulder. "But —"

Henry leaned close and whispered, "We can see everything from here. No neck craning." *And no one watching us that we can't see.* It was foolish. They were in California; he couldn't get any farther from Indiana. Yet months of such considerations had made them habit.

She smiled at the host. "Yes, this is perfect. Thank you."

The man pulled out her chair and she slid into it. "Someone will be by momentarily to take your drink order. Seltzer. Coca-Cola. Tea. And in addition to our regular coffee, we have some fine imported coffee that is quite popular." He bowed slightly and left them.

"Imported coffee," Cora scoffed.

"We are in the land of make-believe."

She reached over and took his hand, her eyes wide. "That's it! That's what's been nagging at me. I just haven't been able to put my finger on it. Everything here is all very . . . artificial . . . isn't it?"

"I thought you might like it."

"Good golly, no. I just hadn't been able to pin down what was rubbing me the wrong way. But that's it. It's different than the false front East Coast society likes to call civility, but it's false just the same." Then she looked more sharply at him. "Do you? Like it?"

"Hell, no."

The smile that came to her face was brighter than the California sun and heated him in places long left cold. They sat there grinning at each other, her hand squeezing his, until a voice came from behind Henry. "Miss Rose? May I have the pleasure of a dance?"

Henry looked over his shoulder. The man from Warner Brothers.

Her smile stayed in place and Henry prepared to let her go. He probably wouldn't see her again until the night was over — judging by the number of eyes that had followed her across the room when they came in.

She said, "Thank you, but I'm promised for this entire evening."

When the man left with disappointment on his face, Henry said, "Why didn't you go?"

"I don't want to spend the night fending off strange hands and offers of careers I don't have any desire to take. I want to spend it dancing with you." She stood and pulled him out of his seat. "I didn't teach you how to dance for nothing. I want to cash in on my effort."

"I'm not sure I'll remember." Suddenly, that night in Crawfordsville seemed a lifetime ago. He supposed it was, of this life anyway.

"Your feet will," she assured him.

"Your toes had better hope so."

She led him by the hand to the dance floor. When she stopped and turned to face him, his breath caught, as if this were the first time he'd ever looked into those eyes. Her hand rested on his shoulder and she snuggled herself close — much too close for propriety. Dangerously close. Henry's whole body was electrified when his hand slid around her waist. He should stop now, pull away, and go back to his dark corner.

She looked up at him, nodding her head in time with the music, and he was lost.

"Ragtime!" She beamed. "Baltimore Buzz." She nodded encouragement. "Two steps right, tap left toe twice. Two steps left, tap right toe twice. That'll get us started."

Henry wasn't sure he could count to two with her so close.

She led him. "Right-right. Tap-tap. Left-left. Tap-tap."

Turned out he didn't need to count, the beat of that ragtime music infused his blood — or maybe it was just Cora infusing his blood. He surprised himself as the dance flowed. Their shoulders and elbows swayed with the fast pace, and they were soon adding turns.

As they moved from song to song, as Cora's body swayed under his hand and moved against his, his blood raced and he understood why some folks thought dancing was a sin. Everything about it made him think indecent thoughts.

The music stopped. The band announced a break. Henry imagined what would be going on in the darkest corners when the stirred-up couples cleared the dance floor.

"Let's go outside and cool off," she said as she turned.

He stood fixed in place, afraid to move, afraid to look Cora in the eye for fear she'd be able to read his mind.

Three steps later she noticed he wasn't following. Looking over her shoulder, she smiled. "Coming?"

He followed her, vowing to keep his distance.

As soon as they were outside the hotel, Henry took off his jacket and hooked it over his shoulder with a finger. If only this tie and collar could come off. But he knew he'd never be able to make himself put them back on if they did. She led him away from the lights of the building, following a path through the garden, looking like a dream moving in the moonlight.

He slowed his pace to let more space gather between them.

"Henry?"

"Hmm?" Guilt rippled over him as he realized how far into impropriety his imagination had strayed.

"I want . . ." She stopped. "I . . ."

Henry stopped walking. Cora was never at a loss for words. "What?" His mind took off with a dozen unwanted possibilities.

She turned to face him. "I want you to know that Gil and I . . . that we never did more than kiss."

Gil? She wanted to talk about Gil? He'd been watching her move in the moonlight, thinking of all of the reasons he shouldn't kiss her, and she'd been thinking about Gil.

Henry stood looking at her, not knowing what she wanted him to say. He had no right to be jealous. None at all.

She seemed to read his expression, her eyes widening. "I just didn't want you to think that I'm some sort of . . . floozy."

Henry barked out a laugh. "Floozy?"

"What you think matters to me, Henry. Don't make fun."

"I'm not." He took a chance and touched her shoulder. "I was just taken by surprise at your word choice."

She patted his hand before she started walking again. "Well, there never would have even been a kiss had I known he was married."

Henry should have been thankful for this turn in the evening. It would keep him out of trouble. "You're sounding downright conventional, Miss Rose."

She shot him an exasperated look. "I don't understand why he didn't just say it right out."

"I thought we already agreed, he's broken."

She looked up at him. "Did you know — about his wife? I mean before."

Henry shook his head.

"I really thought I could make a difference for him. That he needed me."

He did. It was just too late for him. At that second it became clear Cora might have healed Gil if the damage had just been done by the war. And maybe even after all that had happened before, if he'd been a different kind of man. Gil's sense of honor and responsibility was bound to kill him. And that just seemed wrong.

"Was that all?" Henry made himself ask. "Was that all there was to it? He was in need?"

She rubbed her arms and he draped his jacket over her shoulders.

"Thank you." She pulled it closed around her. "I honestly don't know. He set off something inside me. But to be perfectly honest, I have spent so many years fighting *against* things, figuring my way *around* things, that I'm not sure how to let myself just *feel*." She stopped and faced him. "Does that make any sense at all?"

"It does to me." Then he asked the question he knew he must, ignoring the one his heart wanted answered. "Are you going to be able to work with him?"

"Of course. Why would you even ask such a thing?"

"No romantic hoo-ha, remember? If the tension between you two gets under Jake's skin, someone will have to go."

"There was nothing *romantic* about me and Gil. It was all . . . fire."

"I'm pretty sure that's worse."

"Well, stop worrying. I'm not an idiot. And wedding vows have a way of dousing that kind of fire."

He was fairly certain if the fire between Cora and Gil had been left to burn without the suffocation of Gil's wedding vows, it would have blazed bright and hot, leaving at least one of them in ashes. Flames were damned dangerous. When he blinked, he saw Emmaline's blue hair ribbon snagged on a low limb, fluttering in the breeze, its innocence a horrible contrast to the violence that followed.

He shook the image out of his head.

"I just wish I knew why he didn't tell me right away," she said. "Why he let me . . . why he let this thing between us continue."

Because he couldn't bring himself to kill the one thing that made him feel alive. "There is a lot going on inside him that has nothing to do with you." Henry realized too late the sharpness of his tone.

Her eyes jerked to meet his, and a little of that fire flashed in them. He couldn't blame Gil for wanting to be consumed by it.

"I didn't mean that the way it came out." He decided to put a final bucket of water on those embers just in case she had second thoughts about fanning new life into them. "They have a child."

Her eyes flashed again. "That doesn't make him any more or less married."

"No. I suppose not. I don't know why —"

"Henry! I only brought it up because I wanted you to know that it didn't amount to more than a few moments of craziness. It's over and done. I don't want it to mess up everything. When the season starts again, we'll all go back to the way things were."

"All right. I'll stop worrying." And he should. But a blanket of disappointment settled upon him. *The way things were.*

"Good. Now, let's go dance before the

band packs up for the night."

By the time they reentered the ballroom, the band had shifted to more subdued music. Cora led Henry by the hand to the center of the crowd. She turned to him and put her hand on his shoulder. "I can't imagine what I'd do without you, Henry. Thank you for being here with me."

They started to dance.

Be happy your family will, for now, remain intact. As long as Gil comes back.

It was a fear he'd refused to give voice to. But it was a possibility. If Gil didn't come back, would it change things between Henry and Cora? He felt traitorous just thinking the question.

He concentrated on the feel of her hand in his and focused on tonight, on Cora and the Hollywood-induced idea of a make-believe starlit future.

As the sway of the music continued and the night grew deep, she worked her way closer until her head rested on his shoulder and her body pressed against his. They shuffled in the same square foot of floor for an eternity, his cheek against her forehead, the rich and the famous fading away entirely.

20

Saturday morning Henry and Cora took the electric trolley and went to a bakery that looked like a Dutch windmill for doughnuts and coffee. Cora was so eager to get to Santa Monica that she could barely eat.

"Hey," he said. "Us getting there isn't going to make the air meet start any earlier. Relax." He finally gave up on his last doughnut because her bouncing leg was shaking the table, slopping his coffee over the rim of his cup.

They hopped on a Red Car that was packed to the gills and arrived at Clover Field just before the gates opened, bought their tickets, and went in. The first thing that struck Henry was the size of the crowd, bigger than any he'd seen for the flying circus. And the field itself was something. An actual *air*field, with smooth runways and three large hangars. It gave aviation a sense of permanence.

Three forty-foot-tall, black-and-white-checkered pylons laid out the triangular race course. The center pylon was set closer to one end than the other, making one end turn just short of a complete reversal of direction and the other end a little wider. The turn at the center pylon was wide and looked fairly easy. An orange wind sock sat atop each of them. Henry realized just how low the pilots would be racing. Better for spectators. More dangerous for fliers.

Cora used her charm and their ties to aviation to get them past the ropes and onto the flight line, where they could talk with the pilots and Henry could check out the planes. The poster had said the racers hit nearly two hundred miles an hour. He wanted a good close look at machines capable of such speeds. What kind of props were they using? What engines? How were they maximizing the horsepower?

Inside one of the hangars, he struck up a conversation with a man named Cliff Henderson, a Nash automobile dealer in Santa Monica. An avid pilot, he offered a free plane ride with every car purchase. Even before Henry learned another thing about the man, he knew Henderson was an expert at promotion. It turned out he was even better than Henry imagined. Henderson had

461

organized a group of stunt fliers, the Black Falcons, that performed at Clover Field almost every weekend and always drew a crowd. Imagine that. A fixed-base operation that drew a steady crowd. It gave Henry hope for roots someday. The downside was that it would have to be some place with a large population, not exactly what he thought of when he dreamed of a home.

"You know we're launching an around-the-world flight from here this coming year. It's going to help put Santa Monica on the map as an aviation center," Henderson said. "Army crews. Going to be flying modified DT-2s, Donald" — he motioned to the large Douglas Aircraft building at the west end of the field — "is calling them Douglas World Cruisers. History *right here,* young man." Someone across the hangar whistled and motioned that he needed Henderson. He nodded to Henry before he walked away and called over his shoulder, "History!"

History. Henry wasn't used to its treating him kindly. Henderson had said that carrying passengers was the next big thing — for real travel, not just for the experience. Seeing Douglas Aircraft's large building and this crowd made him realize aviation had a real future beyond barnstorming. Maybe Henry was on the right side of history for once. He just had to make sure he looked ahead and adapted to that future before it ran over him.

What if he was free and clear to choose? Would he continue to live a gypsy life? Or would he pick a place to settle, to design and build his own planes? Sooner or later all of the old army-surplus planes would be gone, and then the market would open up. Maybe he could set up an operation like Clover Field somewhere in the Midwest. Give flying lessons.

Foolish thoughts. He would never be free and clear to choose. Not unless he did something about it.

Cora had been unwilling to stand still while Henry talked to Henderson and had ventured off on her own. She came back so excited she could barely string a sentence together. "You won't believe it! I just got a man from Fox News to agree to come to Mississippi and film the midair plane transfer. This is going to be so good for the circus! He said with war veterans and a woman in the show, he was sure he could get the newsreel into the theaters — at least in the Midwest and South." She flung her arms wide. "Look around! This crowd just proves how wild people are for aviation!"

"They're filming here?" Henry looked around.

"Of course! Airplanes are big news."

He made a mental note to keep a wary eye out for a cameraman cranking away.

The aerobatic competition was the first event of the day. Henry watched pilots fly much better planes than Gil's Jenny, performing maneuvers he'd seen Gil do every bit as well, if not better. Henry wondered if he'd be able to talk Gil into entering one of these — maybe Jake would let him use one of the circus planes. There was a cash prize. Gil could use it to help replace his Jenny. And Jake could use the win to promote the prowess of the circus pilots.

During the break between the aerobatics and the races, Henry and Cora stopped at a vendor and bought sandwiches and bottles of Moxie — "guaranteed to produce vim and vigor." Henry worried it might just send Cora flying without a plane. They sat in the shade of a wing to eat. "If you don't slow down, you're going to choke to death," he said to her.

"No time to sit here and lollygag. I need to find out as much as I can from these racers before they start."

"I doubt they're going to be overly

interested in talking until after the race. You know how you are before we do a show. All concentration and snippy answers."

"But what if they leave before I get a chance?"

"Cora. Easy. We haven't even seen a race yet. It might not be anything you'll want to pursue after you do."

"Speed. Danger. *Competition*. Trophies. Cash winnings. What's not to like?"

"My guess is cost might fall into that category."

The announcer called the first racers to their planes.

Cora tossed her lunch in the trash. "Come on! We want to be right on the flight line."

Henry drained his soda and followed her.

They found a spot not far from one of the checkered pylons at the end of the field, where the planes would jockey for position as they circled as tightly as possible.

Two Jennies taxied to the end of the runway. They cut power back to idle at a white line. One wheel was chocked on each plane, on a rope that would pull them free simultaneously. The man with a hand on the rope watched a man just in front of the planes holding a flag. Henry assumed the eyes of the pilots were on the flag, too.

The flag went up. The chocks were pulled.

The flag dropped. The planes throttled forward.

The roar of the engines got Henry's blood moving faster.

Cora bounced on the balls of her feet, her hands fisted in front of her waist.

The planes got airborne, one slightly before the other. The announcer said the race would consist of three laps around the course. The checkered flag would be dropped at the halfway point in the straightaway after the third complete lap.

As Henry watched the planes make the first turn, the danger of pylon racing was starkly clear. It wasn't just the speed and the low altitude. Both planes needed to hug the turn as tightly as possible, which set one slightly lower than the other; or banking just to the outside. The pilot with the higher or closer line was completely blind to the location of the other craft. It was nerve-racking just to watch. He felt confident that if Cora had any feel for flying at all, she'd see how short her skills fell.

By the third lap, the planes were spaced, reducing the chances of a mishap.

He looked at Cora, hoping to see resignation, or at least trepidation. Instead, euphoria bloomed on her face.

"That is insanity," he said, jabbing a finger

toward the pylon. "Pure and simple."

"I want to do it!"

"Your flying skills aren't nearly good enough."

"But they will be. As soon as we get back to Mississippi, I'll start to train. I have some of the best pilots in the country to teach me, after all."

"And what are you going to race?"

"I'll figure it out. And you'll be my mechanic, won't you? I just know you can make any plane competitive."

"You overestimate my skills. And yours."

"Bushwa! We'll start with local races, little ones. Then we'll work our way up to the Pulitzer Trophy."

"Those are some big aspirations, lady."

"What's the point of little ones?"

The next two racers were taking off. Cora and Henry turned their attention to the field.

This race was closer than the first, planes and pilots evenly matched, lifting off wingtip to wingtip. On the second lap, Henry saw disaster coming right before it happened. As the planes came out of the sharpest pylon turn, the lower plane lifted into the higher. Both planes tumbled out of control. Henry shoved Cora to the ground, throwing himself on top of her. Bits and pieces rained down. Sharp blows landed on his head, his calf, his shoulder. The ground shook as one ship met the earth. Henry looked from under his arm. One plane was a disintegrating comet of fire tumbling down the flight line. A large chunk of the other had landed directly opposite him, about twenty yards away.

The pilot was slumped forward in what was left of the fuselage and engine, not moving. Licks of fire were starting; they wouldn't stay licks for long — nothing was more flammable than the dope on the skin of a plane.

Henry jumped up and sprinted to the wreckage. The heat was already building when he vaulted onto the stub of lower wing. He grabbed the pilot's shoulder and jerked him back to release the lap belt.

Henry was too low to get any leverage to pull out the man's dead weight. Not enough was left of the turtleback to climb on. He grabbed the edge of the cockpit and jumped in. Pain stabbed his left arm. He looked down and saw a wood splinter the size of a carrot sticking out of his shoulder. The fire was getting hotter.

He straddled the man's legs, grabbing him under the arms and heaving him up. It felt as if someone were ripping the muscle from the bone in his left arm.

Two other men reached the plane. They grabbed the pilot and pulled him the rest of the way out. The backs of Henry's calves felt as if he'd backed into a woodstove. He vaulted over the side and hit the ground running, putting distance between himself and the possible explosion.

The pilot was safely away, on the ground, surrounded by people. Cora wasn't one of them.

Henry looked around. Cora was facedown right where he'd left her. A few other people were down, clutching wounds, screaming, bleeding.

"No. Nonononononono." He regained his senses just before he yanked her up into his arms. He looked for wounds, blood.

None.

Moans and yelling and chaotic motion surrounded them.

He turned her over, slow and easy, checking for injury.

"Cora!" He patted her cheeks. "Cora!"

He scooped her up, ignoring the firebrand in his shoulder, and carried her toward the ambulance that had raced up and was loading the pilot. Henry hadn't taken two steps when a whoosh of noise and heat came from behind him.

He kept moving.

The rear doors on the ambulance were closing as he got there. "Wait! Wait, god-dammit!"

A white-clad man started toward the driver's door and kept moving. "We gotta get this one to the hospital. They've called for another ambulance." Then he finally looked at Henry. "You look worse off than her. Better sit down."

Henry kept walking.

"You're quite a celebrity," the silver-haired nurse in a starched, white dress and pointy-winged cap said as she finished securing Henry's shoulder bandage. During the fishing of splinters out of his muscle and cleaning the wound, he'd passed out. He squinted at the clock. Apparently for a good fifteen minutes. "There are five reporters out there waiting to talk to you."

"Can you get rid of them?" He started to sit up, but she put a hand on his good shoulder and pushed him back down.

"Too late for modesty. You're already a hero — even if a reluctant one. Every nurse in the hospital has been flittering around here to get a glimpse of the man who climbed into a burning plane and carried an unconscious woman a half mile with a wooden stake stuck in his shoulder."

"The plane was barely on fire when I climbed in." And he doubted he could have carried Cora another step when a man near one of the hangars had guided Henry to his car and driven them to the hospital.

The nurse gave him a sidelong look. "Well, your singed trousers and the blisters on your calves say different." She shrugged. "We'll all get to judge for ourselves soon enough. The fella from the newsreel is out there, too. He got it all on film. Said he couldn't have better footage if he'd been shooting a moving-picture scene. You pulling that pilot out, then walking away with the lady in your arms while the fire billowed behind you. I, myself, can't wait to see it!" She nodded to the white enameled basin filled with bloody cloths and the shard of wood. "Want to keep that for a souvenir?"

"No, ma'am."

Cora appeared in the doorway, a nurse right behind her saying, "Miss, please. The doctor said for you to rest."

"I'm fine." Cora held an ice pack to the darkening bruise on her chin and jaw.

The nurse looked torn between picking her up and carrying her back to bed, and hoping she collapsed right where she was and knocked herself out again.

The silver-haired nurse went to the door and put a hand on the other nurse's shoulder. "We'll leave you two alone for a bit." She looked at Henry. "You've lost a lot of blood. Don't even try to get up yet. The stitches will need to come out of that shoulder and your head in about a week."

His fingers went to the back of his head and felt a shaved spot. He hadn't even noticed the cut, but the back of his shirt, on the table near the basin with the splinter in it, was soaked in blood. "Thank you, ma'am."

Cora came close. "Next time you feel the need to save me, don't." She wiggled her jaw. "I feel like I've been coldcocked."

"You have." By the time Henry, with Cora in his arms, had climbed in the car near the hangar, her eyes had begun to flutter. By the time they stopped in front of the hospital, she was insisting she could walk on her own. He'd carried her in and was greeted by a flurry of nurses. He refused to let them take her from him, sticking with her throughout the doctor's examination and pronouncement that she was fine except for Henry's having knocked her out when he shoved her to the ground. Only then did he leave her and have his own wounds looked at.

"Well, I promise not to tell anyone you're responsible. I'm the most envied woman in the city right now. Don't want to ruin the fairy tale by telling them Prince Charming punched my lights out."

"Do me a favor and don't tell anyone anything. Especially those reporters out there."

"Henry Jefferson! You're supposed to be the promoter. How could we pass up an opportunity like this to bring attention to the circus? You're as good as a war hero right now. They're going to take our photograph as soon as you're able to stand up."

"I'm serious, Cora! I don't want photographs — or news stories." He only hoped that with all of the movement and chaos, the newsreel footage was fuzzy enough that no one would be able to recognize him.

She gave him a sharp look. "Why?"

"I just don't." He took her hand. "Please."

"Well, it's not just me. You saved the pilot, too."

"How is he?"

"Broken in lots of places. Going to be here awhile. But he'll survive."

"Good. The other one?"

She shook her head. "I heard they haven't even found his body yet. Too much fire. I also heard if you hadn't pulled this pilot out, he'd have burned, too."

Henry shook his head. "It wasn't that close. Somebody would have gotten to him in time." Then he looked at her. "How did *you* hear all of this already?"

Her gaze shifted away from him. "From the newsreel fella."

"Who you already talked to . . ."

"How was I supposed to know you didn't want me to?"

"Cora. You need to go back out there and tell him he can't use that film he shot."

"Henry! I know you're modest, but this is ridiculous! Once this gets out there, Marcus is going to be swamped with people trying to book us. He'll be able to negotiate more money —"

"I'll tell him myself." Henry sat up and nearly fell off the table. He also realized that under the sheet draped across his lower half, he was naked.

"I don't think you will." She forced him to lie back. "Besides, he's gone. No one but the newspaper reporters are out there now."

"Everyone knows our names?" Not that his name was a huge concern. It was that damned film footage.

"Of course."

Henry closed his eyes, his stomach rolling

from dizziness. He forced himself to breathe slowly, get his wits about him. One thing he knew for certain: he was going to have to go back to Indiana. If he waited until they came after him, he wouldn't have a chance.

21

By the time their train arrived in Greenwood, Mississippi, Henry's fever was so high that, even with Cora tucked under his good arm, his knees buckled and he crumpled like a rag doll in the aisle of the passenger car. "I told you, you weren't ready to travel."

He tried to pull himself up, his left arm useless in its sling, and was embarrassed to admit defeat. His weakness surprised him. How could he deteriorate so rapidly? He'd been able to change trains to the Illinois Central in St. Louis, unsteady but under his own power. He'd only needed marginal help from Cora in Memphis when they changed to the Yazoo and Mississippi Valley line. Now he was helpless.

His shoulder was a hot, throbbing thing that felt too foreign to be a part of his own body. He'd left the hospital under the protest of the doctor — and the silver-haired nurse — the day of the crash. It had taken two days to convince Cora to book a train to Mississippi. That they were both running low on cash — they'd vacated the Hollywood Hotel for something much less expensive first thing Sunday morning — had probably been what had made her relent, not his determination. With the approaching holiday, they couldn't book two passengers until the nineteenth. By then he'd felt he was on a backslide in his recovery, but kept quiet for fear Cora would cancel their tickets.

He had to get Cora back to Reece's farm. He hadn't decided if he was going to tell them the truth before he left for Indiana or just disappear. The coward in him was leaning toward the latter.

The past day and night had passed in foggy flashes and muddled thoughts. Cora urging him to drink. Chattering teeth. Sharp awakening when the train jolted his shoulder against the window. The changing landscape every time he opened his throbbing eyes. A cool cloth on his forehead. Cora hovering close, whispering words of comfort.

"I'll get the porter," she said. The train car was almost empty; only an old man with a cane and a woman with two small children remained. No new passengers had yet boarded. "And then I'm taking you to the hospital."

She was gone before Henry could argue.

Luckily, the porter was of substantial proportions. He practically carried Henry off the train and laid him on a bench in the new-looking depot. Then he retrieved their bags. When Cora tried to tip him, he politely declined. "I don't take advantage of the sick, miss. Happy to help. Merry Christmas, now." Henry lost the struggle to keep his burning eyes open. He heard Cora thank the man, and then the sound of his footsteps as he walked away.

What day is it? The twenty-second? Twenty-third?

He couldn't seem to do the math.

He felt the eyes of others in the depot on him. He should sit up. Stop making a spectacle. But his body refused to move.

"I'll leave a note with the ticket clerk for Reece. Then we're going to the hospital."

He managed to grab her hand as she turned away. "No. Reece doesn't need to waste his time on two trips to haul us back to his place. It's Christmas. I'll be fine. I just need a good night's sleep."

"This is ridiculous, Henry. You need a doctor."

"We can call one when we get to Reece's."

He licked his dry lips. "Can you get me some water?"

She nodded and walked away.

He closed his eyes, just for a moment.

When he woke up, his head was in Cora's lap and Reece was standing over him with a concerned look on his face. "You need a doctor," he said.

"I just need some sleep. And maybe some of Nell's cooking."

"No doubt about the cooking." Reece frowned. "But I'm not sure that's going to fix you."

"Come on," Henry managed to sit up under his own power. "I'm just exhausted. A train from California is better than a Conestoga wagon, but not much."

"If I'd known he was in this bad of shape, I'd have booked a Pullman," Cora said.

"Our tickets were day coach," Henry said.

"I'd have figured a way."

When he looked at the stubborn set of her face, he knew it was true.

"You're sure?" Reece said. "About the doctor?"

"I'm sure." Henry counted on the man not to overreact.

"Then let me take these bags out and I'll come back and help you to the truck."

"I can get there under my own steam."

Henry stood, determined to get to that truck or die trying. Death seemed preferable at the moment.

Reece had parked near the door, thank God. Henry made it into the seat beside Cora but was so light-headed and shaky he couldn't have gone another yard. His vision was graying on the edges when Reece closed the door. They crossed the Yazoo River before he welcomed the darkness entirely.

Brightness pinked his closed eyelids. Warmth was on his face. Henry slowly opened his eyes and didn't know where he was. A fancy glass light fixture hung from the ceiling. A lightninglike crack in the plaster radiated from its base. The bed was pushed against a wall with yellow, rose-patterned wallpaper. On the opposite wall, lace curtains were open to a rising winter sun. His mouth and throat were as dry as if he'd been eating sawdust in his sleep. The bedsheets were wringing wet.

He shifted. The pain in his shoulder brought everything back. The crash. The train. He looked out the window again. The sun was just peeking over the roof of Reece's barn on the east side of the house.

He heard a snort. Close. The straight-backed chair next to his bed was empty. The room was too small to conceal anyone.

Another snort.

He rolled onto his right side and looked on the floor. There, wrapped in a quilt with her head on a pillow, Cora slept with her mouth hanging open and those god-awful snorts coming about every third breath. Mercury was beside her, laying on his back with his jewels exposed for all the world to see.

"Pssst." He didn't want to wake her, just rouse her enough to stop snorting. Why on earth was she sleeping there? What would Reece and Nell think, her in his room overnight?

She shifted. Her mouth closed. Her breathing quieted.

Mercury rolled over, looked at Henry, then jumped on the bed and offered a faceful of morning doggie breath.

"Whew, buddy, what did you eat for dinner?" Henry whispered, his sandpaper tongue scraping around inside his mouth. "I'm sure mine's no better."

He spent a moment getting his mind in order. Sunrise meant he'd been here a day. So that must make today . . . Christmas Eve?

He slowly sat up, his head swimming. After a few steadying breaths, he swung his legs over the side of the bed, careful not to step on Cora. He eased onto his feet, having to keep a hand on the mattress for balance.

He lifted one foot to step over Cora and tumbled forward. As he put out his arms to catch his weight, fire exploded in his left shoulder.

"Son of a bitch!" With a pitching stomach, he sucked in and blew out breaths between his teeth until the shock of the pain eased. He was on his hands and knees over Cora's now-flailing body.

"What are you doing!" She scrambled to sit.

He blew out two more breaths. "Getting up."

She put a hand on his shoulder. "You're soaking wet."

"I didn't pee the bed. I promise."

"Your fever finally broke!" She put a hand on his forehead and smiled. "Oh, look, you've started your shoulder bleeding again." She helped him up.

Once he was upright, he swayed like a man with no feet.

"Get back into bed."

He sat on the mattress and looked at the bandage on his shoulder. It bloomed bright, fresh blood. "Must have pulled a stitch."

"I don't think so. The doctor had to take them out to flush it and let the wound drain."

"Doctor? I must have really been out of it. I don't remember anything after the train station."

Cora put her hand under his chin and lifted his eyes to meet hers. "We left the train station three days ago. Reece went and got Dr. Shelby the next day. He said you'd be lucky to make it, as festered as that wound was. Gave me a real earful for letting you travel and not watching the wound more closely. I'm so sorry, Henry."

"Three days?" How could three days have gone by without his even noticing?

She made him lie back. "I need to change that dressing. Then I'll get you some broth. Nell has it ready to heat up. Everyone's been so worried."

As much as Henry wanted to stand up and walk to the bathroom, clean up like a man, he found he could do no more than nod. He must have drifted to sleep, because he awoke with her gently removing the bandage. "Dr. Shelby told us that back in the olden days they used to set maggots to work on a wound like this." She visibly shivered. "Can you imagine?"

"Thank God for modern medicine . . .

Do I want to know what he did do?"

She shook her head and gently pulled the bandage away. "At least the fresh bleeding helps keep this from pulling. Now that you're awake, it might hurt."

He turned to look, but she put a hand on his cheek and turned his face to the ceiling, then went back to work.

"Have you been doing this every day?"

"Yep, twice a day. Call me Florence Nightingale."

"Who?"

"Never mind."

There was a light knock on the door before it swung open. Nell came in with a tray. "So happy to see you finally on the mend. I'd love to feed you something heartier, but the doctor said to start you out with broth and tea." Nell had the softest, most beautiful Southern voice. It made him feel safe and childish at the same time. "Reece always tells me my chicken broth can cure anything, so you should be up and about by tomorrow." She grinned and left the room.

When Cora was finished with the bandage, she propped pillows behind him, set the tray on his lap, and handed him the spoon. After he twice dribbled the broth all over his chest on the way to his mouth, she silently took over. "You're just weak. Anybody would be after so long without nourishment."

As he ate, he thought about how many days had passed. If the newsreel made it into the theaters, it would be soon; maybe it already had.

"Is Gil back?" Henry was going to have to explain to him before he went back to Indiana.

"No. Did you think he would be?"

Shrugging with his good shoulder, Henry wondered how Gil's own reckoning was going. Would he come back healed or tattered?

"Henry? Do you know what he's doing? Whatever it is, his moodiness said he wasn't looking forward to it. Which means it's either not about his wife, or he doesn't like her very much."

"He loves her, or he did. Theirs is a complicated relationship." As soon as the words were out of his mouth, he realized his error. He braced for a barrage of questions.

But Cora only said, "What relationship with him wouldn't be?" There was no jealousy, or fire, or longing. She said it in a way that gave Henry hope her fascination with the man was truly gone. The way she was looking at him bolstered that hope.

"You really stayed in here the whole time?"

"Of course."

"Why?"

She looked at him for a long moment. "Because it's what people do for those they care about."

Mr. Dahlgren had cared about him, in his way. But no one had cared *for* him like this through the long, cold years between the disintegration of his family and now.

Then he thought of Johanna Dahlgren. Tiny Johanna with her big eyes and silent ways. The second year he'd been on the farm, he'd had a bad cold. He'd avoided seeing anyone from the house; Mrs. Dahlgren already thought him a disease-ridden varmint. He'd been chopping wood, stopping after every other swing with a coughing fit. Suddenly in the middle of one of those fits, there she'd been, a tin cup in her hand. "I-i-i-i . . ." She'd stopped and he'd seen the concentration on her face. "It h-helps. G-g-inger tea." She'd handed him the cup.

The back-door screen squeaked open. Johanna's eyes had grown wider and her body stiff. A startled rabbit, convinced holding still would make her invisible. All Johanna had ever wanted was to be invisible.

Henry had looked up. Emmaline had stood on the top step, her hand on her hip.

"Get away from him!" Then she'd yelled over her shoulder, "Mama! Mama! Johanna's out there with that dirty orphan!"

By the time Mrs. Dahlgren had made it to the back door, Johanna had fled. Henry had known where she'd gone. She always climbed into the hayloft and hid behind the bales.

"Johanna!" Mrs. Dahlgren had yelled. "You come here this instant!"

Henry had drained the cup and gone back to chopping. Johanna's secret would always be safe with him.

"You've got a funny look on your face," Cora said. "Are you feeling sick? The doctor said the first food might not agree . . ."

He closed his eyes and shook his head. "I was just remembering another kindness someone did for me."

"Was it that rare of a thing, then? Kindness in your life?" Her eyes looked wounded and she took his hand.

This time when the need to confess washed over him, he didn't resist. He owed her the truth. What he'd do after that, he just wasn't sure.

Before he could start, Cora got up and walked over to the small chest next to the window and pulled open a drawer. When she turned back around, she had a package tied with a red ribbon.

"You missed Christmas."

His stomach sank. "But . . ."

"I didn't get this because I wanted a gift in exchange. I bought it because I thought you needed it." She held out the smallish box.

His hand was shaking when he took it. At least it wasn't heavy. Didn't that mean the gift inside was less expensive?

He looked at it in his lap for a long while, reluctant to pull on that ribbon. "I've never —" He clamped his mouth closed.

"Oh my God! Henry? You've never received a Christmas gift?"

"I have, but . . ." How could he explain the sparseness of his life, when she came from a world of plenty? His only real gifts had come from Mr. Dahlgren, no doubt at an expense that went beyond monetary. Back when Ma had been alive, he and Peter had hung small stockings she'd knit special at the foot of their bed on Christmas Eve. In the morning they'd find a stick candy or taffy. The first year they'd hung them after her death, they'd still been empty Christmas morning.

Suddenly he felt more poor and ashamed than he had since his arrival at the Dahlgren farm.

His life collapsed in on him in that instant. He started shaking all over. It stunned him when he realized it was from anger.

Cora was doing him another kindness. Or was it an act of pity?

No. She knew nothing of his past. When she did, it *would be* pity. Or would she hate him for his heritage, his actions, or his lies?

"Henry?" She took the gift off his lap. "Lie back." She offered him a sip of water, then put her hand over his clenched fist. "You need to rest." Her other hand stroked his brow. "Shhh. Just close your eyes."

He did, because he didn't want to look at her, torn as he was between shoving her away and burying his head in her shoulder and sobbing like a child.

22

Cora honored Henry's request to be alone. He'd hurt her feelings. He needed to apologize. He would. After he'd slept awhile. After he'd locked that monster back in its cellar. Why had her kind gesture, the simple offering of a Christmas gift, set off such a flood of resentment?

He fell asleep with his eyes on that ribbon-tied box sitting on the chest of drawers, feeling as if it were just another boy chasing him with a stick, trying to kill Heinrich the Hun.

When the door opened a few hours later, it was Nell, not Cora. "Now that you can eat, we need to keep you filled up, build up your strength. I thought it'd be easier for you this way. I don't know why I didn't think of it the first time." She nodded to the tray, carrying a stoneware coffee mug. It made Henry think of Gil's young mother covered in dust from the pottery. Life had treated him as harshly as it had treated Henry, maybe more so. Henry wondered what was happening in Ohio. Was Gil finally coming to terms with his guilt? Was he finding a way to have a life with the family he supported but did not take part in?

With his right arm, Henry got himself and his pillows arranged so he could sit against the headboard. He liked it that Nell stood and waited patiently, not fussing and fluttering to move his pillows for him. He picked up the mug with a "Thank you." The broth was nice and salty and not so hot that it scalded.

"Cora had to go into town. She'll be back in time to bring you your supper. Do you want me to sit for a bit?" She brushed her hands on her apron. Bits of her hair were escaping from where it was put up at the back of her neck. A flour smudge was on her cheek. Henry smelled bread baking.

"No. Thank you, though." He was enough of a burden to her already. "I'm going back to sleep when I finish this."

She smiled. "Good. That's exactly what the doctor said you should do for the next few days." She started toward the door. "Well, then. Call out if you need anything."

"Thank you, Nell. Reece is a lucky man."

"He knows. Mostly because I remind him

on a regular basis." She closed the door softly behind her.

Henry knew he wasn't going to be able to sleep. Not until he figured out how he was going to explain to Cora — and how he was going to handle going back to Indiana and present his story. Go to Mr. Dahlgren first? Walk directly into the sheriff's office? He had visions of an angry mob ready to lynch him, much like the one he'd read about in *Huckleberry Finn.* But this time they would not be run off and shamed by mere words. This time the rope would win.

He finished his broth and set the mug on the bedside table. Then he laid his head back on his stacked pillows to think.

The next thing he knew, darkness had fallen.

A shadow was sitting in the straight-backed chair. "Cora?"

She got up and turned on the light.

"What time is it?" As he moved, he noticed he was less shaky. And the pain in his shoulder was easing up.

"Nearly seven."

"Listen, I'm sorry about earlier. I shouldn't have reacted like that."

She didn't seem interested in his apology. She swatted it away with a half sheet of paper in her hand. "Forget it."

"I want to talk to you —" He stopped. Now that he'd got a good, clear look at her, he saw her eyes looked feverish. "Something's happened?" The paper in her hand was a telegram. "Is it Gil?" He sat up, his heart accelerating.

"No. No, I didn't even think . . . I didn't mean to scare you." She sat on the edge of the bed. "It's good news. I've been asked to fly in a race in Miami in late January."

"What? By who? You don't race." No one in his right mind would offer a plane to someone as unseasoned as her.

"A man I met at Clover Field. He wants to gain some attention for his new aircraft design. He thinks having a woman pilot in a race against men will be a huge selling point — even if the plane doesn't win."

" 'Such a great plane, even a woman can fly it'?" Henry hoped his sarcasm knocked some sense into her.

"Henry!"

"Just back up." He rubbed his forehead. "Do you know anything about this man's design skills, or his plane? I mean, I have a hard time believing that an unknown woman pilot was his first thought when he decided to promote his plane. There *are* a few women pilots out there who have already made a name for themselves — why not ask one of them?"

"Thank you for the vote of confidence. I happen to be very good at marketing my skills."

"Can't argue that. So who is he?" It was going to take some finesse to wipe that blinding stardust out of her eyes. "Anyone we've heard of?"

"Frank Evans. Lives in Texas. This is his first plane, he calls it the EV-1; one of a kind. So far. It's been flying for a few months. He can't fly it himself because he's in a wheelchair — he was a flight instructor for the army. Student crashed with him in the plane."

"Maybe Gil knows him." Henry had never heard of Evans. "The plane's been tested?"

"I just said it's been flying for a few months. It just hasn't been raced yet."

"Flying it and testing it are two different things. What kind of flying has it done? What stresses has it undergone? How many hours are on it? How is Evans assessing its handling if he can't fly it himself? And you can't just hop in an unfamiliar plane and race it. You need to get to know it. Hours of flight time."

"Well, he's having it flown here this week. You and Reece can check it out all you want and help me get to know it. Then I'm to fly it to Florida for the race — more hours of flight time. His pilot will pick it up here afterward."

"Cora, you can't navigate. How in the hell are you going to fly it to Florida? And why doesn't he just have *his* pilot race it, at least for this first run?"

"You're my mechanic, so you'll be with me. Besides, Miami's right on the coast. All I have to do is fly east, then follow the shoreline south. And I already told you, he wants a woman pilot."

"His idea, or yours?" Henry frowned. "Let me see that telegram."

"I've already agreed." She handed it over. "That's where I was this afternoon, sending an acceptance telegram."

"Four or five weeks isn't enough time for you to prepare. You do remember what happened in Santa Monica."

"I won't know until I try. Henry, you know I'm careful, that's why I'm still alive."

"You're still alive because you've been lucky." His tone was harsh. "Plenty of careful, talented people end up in pieces on the ground. Plenty. If you want to race, you have to do it right. A rushed effort is going to get you, and maybe someone else, killed."

"I won't fly it if I'm not ready."

"By whose assessment?"

She huffed. "Yours. As long as you're reasonable and not overprotective."

"You need to tell Frank Evans that's the condition for you to fly. He needs to know beforehand, so he has a backup plan." *Or nixes the idea of you flying in this race altogether.*

"It's not going to be a problem because I'm going to be ready. Did I mention he's paying me, win or lose?"

"Money to buy your own coffin?"

"Come on, Henry! I'm not as stupid as you seem to think. And I'm not interested in hurrying into an early grave. I know my capabilities."

"But do you know your limits?"

She stared at him for a moment. "There are no guarantees in this business, you know that. It's all about calculated risk."

"My point exactly."

"What more do you want? I hardly think Evans wants to have his plane crash in front of his financial backer — especially when he's wanting to recruit more so they can start production. Which is why he's paying me either way, so I don't take unnecessary risks to win."

If the man had gotten someone to finance his design, it must have some merit. "I want to talk to the pilot when he gets here. Learn more about the plane. And if I check out this ship and find it to be lacking, you have to promise me you'll pull out. Otherwise, no deal. I won't be your mechanic and you can fly all over the South trying to find your way to Miami on your own."

"Fine. But I'm sure it'll pass muster. It flew from Texas to Clover Field and back. We just didn't get to stay long enough to see it fly."

At that moment reality kicked back in. He'd been caught up in a pointless argument. He could stick around long enough to check out the plane. But beyond that . . . "I wish you'd talked to me before you sent that telegram. I can't go to Miami. I have to go back to Indiana."

"What are you talking about? Why?"

"You'd better sit down. It's . . . a long story. I should have told you and Gil months ago, but one thing led to another and . . . now here we are."

She sat on the edge of the bed. "I don't like the way you sound right now. What's going on?"

He supposed it was a coward's way, telling the least offensive truth first. He justified it by convincing himself he had to start at the beginning in order to paint a clear picture of why the later events unfolded as they had.

"My name isn't Henry Jefferson. It's Henry Schuler."

"I assume you have a reason for changing it?" She appeared curious, not yet repulsed. He looked into her face, memorizing it before the way she looked at him shifted forever.

He told her of his childhood, his German parents and how the war had changed everything. He told her about Peter. She took his hand in hers as they shared slow, silent tears over brothers lost. The condemnation of his heritage did not come. He knew drawing this out was only a tactic to delay the end of this life, the one that had treated him the most kindly, where he'd found a place, and the start of yet another.

He told her about Anders Dahlgren, his promises and the quick undoing of them. About Mrs. Dahlgren and the seven daughters. About his life in the barn. About the poisonous relationship he had with Emmaline and how he should have done things differently.

Then he stopped. He didn't have to tell her more. Let her think the reason he'd changed his name was to avoid dealing with prejudice against Germans — that when he'd realized Gil was probably a veteran that had sealed the deal. He could go back to Indiana on some pretense and just never come back — or simply complete his cowardly cycle and sneak away in the night. He would never have to face the change in the way she looked at him.

Then she touched his cheek and looked into his eyes. "There's more."

He recalled all of the times when he'd looked into her eyes and had the urge to confess. Now he turned from her questioning gaze.

"Henry." Her hand turned his face toward her again. "Tell me."

Being a coward had made him a liar, the thing he detested most in all human nature. He could not lie to her anymore. She deserved the truth. And he was tired. So tired.

"Henry?"

His eyes stung with the effort to hold back tears as he absorbed the last of her compassion. Then he forced the first words from his lips.

He started with the day before he'd fled Indiana.

The May Day picnic was at the Chautauqua grounds. Normally Henry wouldn't have gone, but Johanna Dahlgren had asked him specially. She was going to perform the maypole dance. She'd never been picked before. "I-I-I know y-yy-you can't g-go with us. Mm-mama said. B-b-but will you come? She c-c-can't keep you from a puh-puh-blic picnic."

He would have walked through fire if Johanna had asked. This was such a simple thing. He'd gotten Mr. Dahlgren's permission, since it was a regular workday for Henry. Mr. Dahlgren had seemed quite happy that Henry was coming. Johanna might be Mrs. Dahlgren's embarrassment, but she was Mr. Dahlgren's obvious favorite.

The maypole was to be performed at two o'clock, so Henry timed his arrival for about thirty minutes before. He didn't want Johanna to think he wasn't coming; he also didn't want to hang around feeling out of place any longer than necessary. He'd put on his best shirt, cleaned his nails, and brushed his shoes. They were plenty dusty by the time he reached the grounds. He was still glad he'd bothered.

The Chautauqua grounds were just outside town. The road was deserted. Everyone would have arrived early for the day-long event. It always drew a big crowd — only the sick, hermits, and outcasts like

Henry missed it — coming as it did after the sunrise-to-sunset work of the long planting season. He was still about a quarter of a mile away when he heard something crashing through the woods on the right side of the road.

He stopped, expecting to surprise a deer. Instead, he got the surprise. Emmaline burst from the brambles, her eyes red and swollen, tears on her face. Her lips were bruised and the front of her blouse was unbuttoned. She didn't look scared. She looked furious — a look Henry was plenty familiar with.

She skidded to a stop and seemed to just now notice she was out in the open.

Her cold eyes narrowed. "If you say a word about seeing me, I'll tell Papa that you attacked me." She started to button her blouse. A faint bite mark was on her breast.

Henry almost asked if she was all right. But she obviously wasn't.

"I mean it. Get away from me or I'll start screaming rape right now!"

He hesitated. If something had happened to her, he owed it to Mr. Dahlgren to help her.

She grabbed the front of her blouse as if she were going to rip it back open. "No! No, Henry!" Then loud enough someone might actually hear: "No! Stop! Henryyyy, no!"

He took off running. Back toward the farm.

Halfway back to the Dahlgrens', he almost turned around and went back to find Mr. Dahlgren and tell him that he'd seen Emmaline and something was wrong. But the more he thought about it, the more convinced he was that she'd been up to something she shouldn't. She didn't seem traumatized. The threat was only to ensure Henry's silence. But with the way she'd been acting lately, the things she'd been telling Mr. Dahlgren Henry had done, it wasn't going to take much for her to truly convince everyone he'd attacked her. And that was the most troublesome of all. All she had to do was scream once and he'd be finished.

He sat on his bed the rest of the afternoon, anticipating the arrival of the sheriff. Waiting for Mr. Dahlgren to burst into his room with a shotgun.

But neither happened. The family came home at dusk and went into the house, chattering and happy. Henry watched them from the barn door. No one even looked his way, except Johanna. She stood there for a long while, looking brokenhearted. Henry felt horrible for disappointing her, but now wasn't the time to show his face. Not until he got a better gauge on what Emmaline was up to, and how careful he needed to be.

"That's when I realized how far Emmaline was willing to go to ruin me," Henry said, looking into Cora's eyes. "She might not have gone through with it that day. But, I knew, one day soon, she would."

Cora said, "Why do you figure she didn't go through with it right then?"

"I honestly don't know. Maybe she worried that she'd be asked questions she didn't want to answer about why she was out there in the first place. But the way she looked at me" — Henry's blood ran cold with the recollection — "with more hate than I thought any single person could hold. I mean, I admit, I hated her like I'd never hated anyone. But there was something, I don't know . . . evil in her eyes. She'd been filling her papa's head with ideas about me having wicked intentions toward her. It's like she was setting me up. Just waiting for the right opportunity."

"From what you've said, I'm sure telling her father any of this would have backfired on you."

He shook his head, the sickness in his

stomach like a raging fire. "It couldn't have turned out any worse than it did. She was killed the next day." He was shaking. He closed his eyes, trying to get the gruesome image out of his mind. "I'm wanted for her murder. That's why I changed my name. That's why I ran." There. It was out. No taking it back.

Her hand fell from his face. She sat there staring at him with her lips parted and her eyes wide.

He stopped breathing. But his heart kept beating. Each *thub-dub* absurdly loud in his ears. If only it would stop. Before she denounced him.

Finally she stood, an abrupt, jerky movement. Henry felt as if their lives had been momentarily frozen and they were now back in sickening motion.

"That's ridiculous!" She held her forehead. "You couldn't have done it!"

"How can you know that?" His own doubt had grown as he'd told the story. He wanted Cora to see it all now; he didn't want it creeping up on her later when she had time to think, to remember and analyze. Get this over once and for all. "After everything I just told you about her and how much I hated her? After I lied to you from the very first day? After I *ran*? I was there. I had her blood on my hands."

Suddenly his heart slowed. The shaking stopped. A peculiar calm washed over him. If she hated him, if she condemned him, it was better than being suffocated by the knowledge that he was betraying her trust every single day. He felt a small loosening of the tangles in the tight ball of tension that had gotten worse with each deceitful day. "I'm not the person you think I am." And that was the most horrible truth. She had not seen the monster in the cellar.

"I *do* know you!"

"Everyone in Delaware County thinks they know me, too. And they're certain that I did do it."

She looked at him steadily when she asked, "All right, if you insist, I'll ask the question directly. Did you?"

"I can't say for certain."

Her face clouded. "That makes no sense."

"It's the truth. I don't think I did. It doesn't *feel* like I did."

"Stop talking in riddles and tell me exactly what happened." She sat back down, but not on the bed next to him, on the straight-backed chair. Her eyes were intent on his. Was she looking for a sign, truth or lie? "Leave nothing out."

Henry asked for a glass of water and

organized his thoughts while she went to get it. After he drained the glass, he did what he'd done a million times in his head over the past months. He relived that day.

That morning had begun with a screaming argument between Emmaline and one of her sisters, Henry couldn't tell which one, streaming out of the upstairs windows. Emmaline had been meaner than usual since her sister Violet's wedding. But that was to be expected; jealousy ran thick in Emmaline's blood. Any attention directed toward others was an insult to her. Henry had been extra careful to steer clear of her, which she seemed to take exception to, twisting the truth when she complained to her father, "Henry's been following me." He supposed she could hardly have complained that he'd been *avoiding* her. Emmaline's dearest pleasure was enforcing her will upon him. The incident near the Chautauqua grounds the previous day had been the most damning evidence of that.

Several days before, Mr. Dahlgren had confronted Henry about his bothering Emmaline, watching her, following her. Henry felt he'd been convincing in his denial. Of course he hadn't said he'd been avoiding her the way he would a brown recluse spider. Pa had always counseled it was better to hold one's tongue than to turn slights and slanders back on their issuers; it made a man sound weak and petty. Henry should have told Mr. Dahlgren right then about how Emmaline had been disappearing into the woods more and more often, sometimes for hours — a sign of something for certain as Emmaline hated being outdoors. But he hadn't. Mostly because it could lend credence to Emmaline's claim; how would he have noticed her comings and goings if he hadn't been watching her? — which he had, but for quite the opposite reason.

Henry was hilling the rows in the potato patch down in the bottoms when he heard Emmaline yelling, "Stop following me, *J-J-J-Jo*-hanna! I'll have you sent off to the f-f-f-freak show where you belong!"

"I'm j-j-just looking for my k-k-kitten."

"I killed it. Now go back to the house."

Henry's knuckles went white on the hoe handle. Why did she have to be so cruel to poor Johanna? He took five or six wild swings with his hoe, driving it deep into the ground, hard enough to hurt his shoulder and leave his breath heaving. Once he was back under control, it took several minutes before he could go back to work. Even then, his insides still quivered with anger.

Sometime later he heard a quick, sharp shout. Emmaline. Farther away.

He stopped to listen for Johanna, but didn't hear anything more. She didn't usually challenge her sister. Most likely she'd gone back to the house. He'd help her look for her kitten when he got back to the barn.

Then moments later, a shrill scream was cut off abruptly.

Henry broke into a run, his body flashing hot, fury pumping his legs.

There was no path. Branches gouged his face, brambles tore at his hands.

He reached the river, looked frantically around. No one. "Johanna!"

Then he caught sight of a blue hair ribbon snagged on a branch, fluttering in the breeze a few yards upstream.

Fear and anger were lightning in his blood. He hurried toward the ribbon, nearer the water. He reached out —

The next thing he knew, he was lying facedown in the mud, pushing himself up on trembling arms, his head throbbing, his vision blurry.

Then he saw her. Head and shoulders in the river. Emmaline's blond hair stained red, floating around her head like sunburst petals on the water.

■ ■ ■ ■

"I lifted her from the water and turned her over," Henry said, the vision in his head as vivid now as it had been those months ago. Why couldn't he remember those moments in between? "Her eyes were open, lifeless as two blue marbles. That's the image that makes my blood run cold, her eyes. I couldn't help thinking they weren't all that different from when there'd been life behind them." He looked at Cora. "Doesn't that seem strange, that I would have thought that?"

She just took his hand and held it tight.

"Those eyes." He shook his head. "They're what I see when I close my own. Not the bloody gash in the back of her head." He took a deep breath. "That comes back as a feeling, not a sight." He held his hand up and looked at it, his fingers remembering the sensation of gravel where solid rock should have been. "When I cradled her head in my hand, there was a sickening shift of crumbled bone."

Cora's gasp drew his eyes away from his hand and back to her. "Oh, Henry. How horrible. And you've had to carry this around alone."

"Sometimes I feel like I've kept myself on such a short chain that it's done something to me deep inside. Bottled up all of my anger until it rages like a torrent of water through a broken dam. Maybe that's what happened."

"Of course that's not what happened."

"I appreciate your faith in me, Cora. But I have to be realistic. I *could* have done it. I was so angry over her treatment of Johanna. And if I did, I need to know it. I'll pay the consequences."

"What about Johanna? Where was she?"

"I didn't see her. She usually didn't go against Emmaline, so she probably had turned back. It had been ten or so minutes between when I heard them arguing and the scream.

"The fact that I can't say with absolute certainty that I *didn't* do it . . . that's what really scares me." He took a breath and pressed on to the end. "I heard someone coming and stood. Violet took one look at me, scratched and clawed with blood on my hands, standing in the water over her dead sister, and took off screaming, *'He killed her! Oh my God! Henry killed her! Papa! Papa!'* And I ran."

"Blood on your hands? From when you picked her up?"

"I don't know. It could have been there when I came to."

"Surely Mr. Dahlgren didn't just take Violet's hysterics as proof. Maybe they aren't even hunting for you." The hope in her voice warmed Henry's chilled heart. "Maybe they discovered the real killer."

"I *ran,* Cora! My history with that girl. A witness seeing me with blood on my hands. And I fucking ran. What more proof did they need? They didn't *look* for anyone."

"But you don't *know* they're looking for you. Maybe someone saw something that led them to the real killer."

He looked her in the eye. "What if I am the real killer, Cora?" He wanted her to really think about it. Right now.

"I'll believe you are when you remember crushing that woman's skull. That's when I'll believe it."

"The manhunt is for me. It was in the Noblesville newspaper. Name, description, and all. And now that newsreel is out there. It's only a matter of time before they find me. I have to go back by my own choice. If I wait for them to come and get me, there's no hope anyone will believe anything but I killed her. I need questions asked if I'm going to figure out what happened."

"But it's been months. They could already

have found the real murderer by now."

"They had no reason to look for anyone else. If for some reason they found him" — Henry shrugged — "I'll find out when I get there."

"Him?"

He looked up. "What?"

"You said 'if they've found *him.*' You're sure it isn't a woman?"

"I have no idea who it is! Otherwise I'd have been doing something about it."

"So it could be a woman."

"No! I guess." He flung a hand in the air. "It could have been a man, a woman, a band of gypsies, an avenging angel from God for all I know. I. Didn't. See. Anyone. So it most likely was *me.*"

"Did you see any footprints in the mud near her body?" Cora asked, not at all ruffled by his outburst. "That could tell us gender."

"I don't know!" He took a deep breath and answered more calmly, "I can't recall."

"Henry, you told me you live this in your head every day. Close your eyes and move through your memories slowly, not in the rush of reality. There are probably a lot of things you saw that are buried in there. Maybe the reason you said *him* was because you saw something that made you think that. Your answer was instant. You were adamant when you said it couldn't be a woman. *Then* you questioned it. First impulses are usually right."

Henry doubted that. His first impulse had been to run. That obviously hadn't been right. He buried his face in his hands and willed away the urge to throw up.

"Start with Emmaline and Johanna's voices," Cora suggested. "Concentrate on all of your senses, not just sight. Were there any other sounds — maybe so quiet you didn't consider them important? And when you get to where you see her, think of the bigger picture, not just the hair in the water. She was wearing blue."

"She was?" He realized he didn't even remember the color of her dress. His memory was so sparse, how was he going to argue his innocence?

"She was. Or at least it had a lot of blue in it. You said her hair ribbon was blue."

He focused on the image in his mind: the blood, the hair, shoulders in the water. "She was wearing blue! Sky blue." With dark spatters of blood down the back.

"There! It's working already. Sometimes thinking about what you heard will help, too, or what you smelled. Those things trigger memory."

"How do you know?"

"It happens all the time. You smell oranges and think of Christmas. Or you hear a church bell and think of the end of the war. Whenever I smell the exhaust from the motorcycle, I think of Jonathan. I see his cocky grin, his green eyes. Every time. Even now."

Henry nodded. Hope's sails filled with the recollection of the dress. Then he closed his eyes and went through his memories again. Starting with how hot the sun was on the back of his neck. The sound of the hoe hitting and then shifting the dirt. But once started, the memories came in a flood, one falling over the other. He didn't even recall the color of the dress; that only came when conscious thought kicked in. "Nothing more."

"You're probably trying too hard. Try it again as you're falling asleep. Maybe that'll help. For now, we're going to assume it was a man because that was your inclination."

"Probably because I can't imagine a woman committing a bloody murder."

"Then you clearly don't know women very well, Henry."

He couldn't argue that.

"But until you remember . . ." She got up and began to pace the room.

Henry watched her with a sickness growing in his belly. A small voice called out from deep inside him, *You think you're going to convince the sheriff to look for someone else? Convince the Dahlgrens? You can't even answer Cora's questions.*

Then panic launched its own questions: *What if they never come to get me? Would I be throwing away my life for nothing?*

But it was more than the film. He couldn't live the rest of his life hiding, lying . . . wondering. That little voice spoke again: *At least you'd still have a life.* If he couldn't convince the sheriff to consider the possibility of another killer, to do a thorough investigation, that life was over — this time not to be replaced by a new one.

"You can't go back," she finally finished. "It's foolish." She stopped pacing. "You can't."

"I have to. That newsreel proved that somehow, someday, they'll find me."

"You can't be sure."

"No. But I can't live the rest of my life wondering every day if this will be the day they show up — hell, worse, wondering if I did it. Did we get into a fight? Did she surprise me and I reacted? I need to know the truth. And if there is a killer out there, I want him caught. As long as I'm running, they won't even look for anyone else." He dug deep, examining the reasons the need to go back was growing so much stronger and finally understood the one holding the whole stack of others. "And I need to apologize to Mr. Dahlgren for the disrespect of running like a coward."

"Then write him a letter." Cora sounded angry. "We can mail it from Miami. Don't throw your life away."

"I've already come to terms with this, Cora. I can't live with this hanging over me. I should never have run. I'm going back."

She was quiet for a moment, staring out the window. Henry was familiar with the look on her face, one that said her brain was buzzing, looking for a way around an obstacle.

Finally she said, "Not without a good lawyer, you're not. A *very* good lawyer. We need someone who will push them to investigate. Maybe we should hire a detective. Both of those will take money."

"I have a few dollars tucked back." He couldn't believe he hadn't thought of a lawyer yet. He didn't even know one.

"Not that kind of money, Henry. Real money."

"Don't they have to give me a lawyer — if I go to trial?" The word was bitter on his tongue. It started to come brutally clear how ignorant he was about arrests and trials and lawyers. And investigations.

She scoffed, "Sure they do. One that doesn't care about anything but getting you checked off of his list so he can go home and have dinner with the family. And if the sentiment around there is what you say, I doubt he'll even believe you're innocent. How hard is he going to work to free a man he believes is guilty of murdering a young woman?" Cora paused for a moment. "So, if we assume this murderer is a man, do you have any idea at all who it might be? Even the vaguest notion would be a place to start. She was sneaking around meeting someone. Maybe she jilted him and he went crazy. Maybe someone knows who that boy is. Maybe there was someone else she'd been cruel to?"

"Emmaline was manipulative, vindictive, and mean. She finally pushed the wrong person too far." When Cora's startled eyes met his, he realized how vicious he sounded, that his hands were balled into fists. "I'm not saying she deserved to be murdered."

"Of course not." Cora's face softened a bit. "Of course not." She paused. "First things first. We'll leave the memory jogging for later. Now, we need a plan. And money.

Evans is paying me well for flying his plane. We can take that —"

"This isn't your problem to solve."

She started pacing again. "My cut of the purse for winning the race should be enough to get a really good lawyer. I need to make sure I'm good enough to win —"

"Cora!" Henry snagged her hand and pulled her down onto the bed.

She stared at him. "If you think for one minute I'm going to let you go back to Indiana alone, you've lost your mind." Her hands came up to cup his face. "Henry Schuler, everyone in your life might have abandoned you, but I will not." Tears shone in her eyes. "I. Will. Not." She leaned in and kissed his lips. Then she hovered close and whispered, "Promise me you'll wait. At least until after the race. Then we'll have a fighting chance. Promise me."

He looked at her for a long moment. "I promise." The words were a choked whisper. He was weak. So shamefully weak.

"All right then." She nodded. Then she went to the chest of drawers and brought the ribbon-tied box. "I think you should open this now."

He took it from her and pulled the ribbon. Inside was a shiny brass box, just a little bigger and thicker than a pocket watch. On the lid was the inscription MERCURY'S DAREDEVILS.

Cora picked it up. She released the top and it sprang open. It was a compass, its needle quivering from the movement and then settling on magnetic north. She shifted it so the inside of the lid was facing Henry. Inscribed there: SO NO MATTER HOW FAR YOU GO, YOU CAN ALWAYS FIND YOUR WAY BACK TO THE BEGINNING.

"I may not be able to navigate," she said, "but I'll always count on you to."

Henry wrapped his hand around hers and snapped the compass closed. He held it and their hands over his heart when he kissed her. "Thank you. For this. For believing in me."

She smiled and lay down beside him on the narrow bed. He put his good arm around her and pulled her close. A few minutes later, she was asleep with her head on his shoulder and their hands still over his heart.

23

Two days later, the EV-1 showed up. Watching it land, Henry was surprised to see a low-winged monoplane, not a biplane.

Even before its wheels touched the ground, Cora said, "Well, what do you think?"

"Nice paint job. Can't tell more than that from here." Her faith in a completely unfamiliar craft was far too high for Henry's liking. You couldn't take a machine's performance for granted. Nor could you simply take a man's word that it was as airworthy as he claimed.

Henry's initial inspection of the EV-1 revealed no obvious fault in the plane's design or quality. He couldn't wait to get his hands on its powerful Wright J-3 radial, air-cooled engine. He grilled the pilot, who seemed quite experienced, and received a glowing report of the craft. Of course, the man was on Evans's payroll. Henry's full approval would be reserved until he inspected it in more detail and flew it himself. And right then he was too weak to get it done. He'd only been out of bed since yesterday afternoon.

He was shocked by Cora's uncharacteristic patience as she acquiesced to wait for her chance in the cockpit until after he was sure of the craft. Maybe good sense was finally beginning to counterbalance desire.

Reece took the plane up on its first trial while Henry talked to Evans's pilot. When Reece landed and deemed it "respectable," Reece's father drove the pilot to the train station to return to Texas. Before he left, though, he had Cora pose with the plane for several photographs. Mr. Evans was going to use them for publicity.

Henry flew the plane the next morning, after he'd examined the mechanics in detail. Reece was in the front cockpit, just in case Henry's shoulder gave him trouble. The thing that struck him the instant the wheels left the ground was the lack of noise. It had none of the hum and whine of the wind singing through wires and struts he was used to on the Jenny. Without the drag of the second wing, the responses to controls were so much sharper. Overall it felt smoother. And the power! It was fast. Really fast. A hare to the Jenny's tortoise — even those JN-4s with the upgraded Hisso engines. He could have flown this beauty all day long.

When he landed, he gave the EV-1 his official approval. Cora clasped her hands over her heart, giddy as a little kid.

"Calm down. And take a few minutes to just sit there and feel it, figure out where everything is," he cautioned as she climbed into the cockpit. He stood on the wing and went over the additional instrumentation that the Jenny didn't possess.

"Get a feel for that throttle on the ground, taxi it around a bit before you take it up. Test the response of the rudder, too. Remember it has a swivel wheel on the tail instead of a skid, so take that into consideration."

She looked up and nodded, excitement gleaming in her eyes.

"And, Cora, this plane is fast. The controls sharp. She reacts much more quickly. Don't forget that. And she doesn't scrub off speed like you're used to when the nose goes up. That means you can get into trouble a whole lot faster. Take it easy until you get accustomed to it."

Again she nodded.

Then he climbed in the other cockpit.

"What are you doing?"

"I'm going up with you until you get more familiar with it."

She surprised him again by shrugging. "Suit yourself." Then she signaled for Reece to prop it.

She actually did as Henry had instructed before she taxied to the downwind end of the field and took off.

The plane lifted into the air, wheels going silent, bumping ground giving way to silky smoothness. Cora's takeoff was perfect. Henry wanted to look back, watch her face as she flew, but didn't want to distract her. She took it around the pattern; not a single herky-jerky movement from the sensitive controls. The air was cold, the sun behind a haze, making the air glidingly perfect.

He felt the plane's speed even more as a passenger; he wasn't sure he liked feeling this out of control.

Cora kept the plane too low, cutting sharp turns that set the wings nearly perpendicular to the ground. She didn't know this plane; she needed to give herself some room if something went wrong. Henry signaled for her to take it higher. He was actually a little surprised when she did.

It ate up miles so fast, they were quickly

over unfamiliar terrain. Henry wondered if she'd be able to find her way back. Was she paying attention to all of the things she needed to, not just the handling of the craft, but the 101 other things a good pilot had to observe?

She must have paid enough attention. In fifteen minutes, they were back in the pattern to land on Reece's farm. The plane dropped right into place, landing like a feather touching the earth. When she cut the engine, she whooped. "Now that's flying!"

They climbed out. "You did great," he said.

Cora reached up and linked her hands behind his neck. "Now I have to get perfect. I *have* to win this, Henry."

Pressure could lead to mistakes. "No, you don't. You only have to keep Evans's plane in one piece. That's enough for your first race. I might not need a lawyer. I won't take your winnings to pay for him, in any case."

He could see the wheels turning in her head. "You know I don't do things halfway. I *want* to win this. I can make a name for myself. This plane is incredible! This is my shot, Henry. Winning has nothing at all to do with you."

"Bushwa." He used her own term on her.

She put her fingers on his lips. "I want this, Henry. All the way down to the marrow of my bones. And I'm going to do it."

He took her hand in his and kissed the palm. "Of that, I have no doubt. But that doesn't alter the objective. You crash this plane or cause someone else trouble on the course, you're done. There are no second chances for women in aviation." He didn't know that for a fact, but imagined it'd be damned hard for a woman to recover her credibility when most men were already looking for the slightest reason to banish them from most everything outside of keeping house and having babies. "That would be it. Dream out the window. Remember that."

"I have no intention of doing anything stupid."

If it wouldn't add additional weight, he'd insist she fly the race with Mercury in the plane with her. She'd never risk that mutt's life.

The next day, they laid out a three-mile course with turns at a windmill — the closest approximation to a pylon they could come up with — a neighbor's barn, and the place where Reece's lane intersected the road. She practiced first at a much higher altitude than she would race at, getting the feel for the turn and the angle at which she needed to come out of it to set up for the next "pylon." Henry climbed onto the roof of Reece's barn to see the whole course over the trees. She ran the course lower and lower, ultimately making the turns around the windmill and the neighbor's barn at even altitude. That's when he got skin-crawling nervous. That speed at that low altitude, as sharply as that plane reacted, if she lost her concentration long enough to swat a fly, she could be in trouble.

He'd told her to cut those first low-altitude turns plenty wide. There'd be time to shave seconds off once she had some practice. The first low-altitude lap she cut too close around the barn. Henry sucked in his breath and cringed, but she cleared it. He muttered curses and signaled for her to take the next one wider. The windmill turn, the tightest on the course, required the plane to bank to almost ninety degrees. She took that one too close, too. At least the turn at the intersection didn't have anything she could possibly hit.

She ran it two more times, each just a gnat's ass from clipping the "pylons." By the time she landed, Henry was on the ground, hopping mad.

As soon as she climbed out, he had her by the shoulders. "You were supposed to work your way up to those close turns."

"I did. I flew above the pylons seven laps before I got down to altitude. I think I can cut them even closer. There was plenty of wiggle room. You just can't tell from so far away."

Reece didn't help when he came driving up in the truck. "Jake said she was a natural, and by God she just proved it! Well done, lady!"

She tossed a look at Henry. "See. I bet if Gil had cut those pylons that close, you'd be slapping him on the back."

"Probably. But Gil didn't just start flying three months ago." He shut up then. She did have a point.

The next morning, Henry took up one of the Jennies and had her keep her speed low enough that he could fly with her as another racer would. He wanted her to learn to keep track of another plane in proximity. At least this time she did cut the first few laps wider around the pylons. Henry had to force himself to fly close enough that it would do her some good, his inclination being to keep a distance that ensured her safety. He varied his position — inside, outside, above, below, slightly ahead, slightly behind. Finally, she gave it full throttle and ran the course with him tagging behind, way behind.

After they landed and got out of the planes, she threw her arms around Henry's neck. "It's even better with another plane up there!"

He smiled as he wrapped her in his arms, his shoulder giving only minimal complaint. All of this movement had kept it from getting stiff. "You amaze me."

She grinned back. "Why, Henry, no reprimands? You're actually complimenting my flying skills?"

"I'm complimenting your nerve. . . . Remember, overconfidence —"

She cut him off with a quick kiss. "I know. I know. Trust me." She looked into his eyes. "The way I trust you."

Although he and Cora hadn't talked about Emmaline's murder again, the undercurrent meaning was in her eyes. Henry had spent every night trying to float on the boiling river of his memories, but nothing new surfaced. He did however lose plenty of sleep to nightmares.

The kiss that sealed her vow was anything but quick. Henry tumbled, falling as if he'd jumped out of an airplane without a parachute. His arms went around her, and he lifted her off her feet. Only with reluctance and necessity from his painful shoulder did he set her back down. When he lifted his head, he saw Gil standing at the edge of the field, a rucksack on his shoulder, looking like a man who'd lost his best friend.

Henry quickly set Cora away from him and nodded in Gil's direction.

Cora turned. Her intake of breath was audible.

Gil took a pull on his cigarette, then put a forced-looking smile on his face and walked over to them. His appearance was worse the closer he got. He looked as if he'd spent the past weeks taking a daily beating. His eyes were shadowed and sunken; that broken look was back. He'd lost enough weight that his pants bagged.

Reece called out, "If you'd let us know, we would have come and picked you up at the train."

"I needed the walk."

The train station was at least fifteen miles from here.

"Where did you come up with this beauty?" He gestured toward the plane but kept his eyes on Cora.

She seemed to have recovered from her fluster, while Henry's heart was still racing with guilt. She told him about meeting

Evans and how she was going to race in Miami.

Gil's smile was mechanical and no joy was in his eyes when he looked at her. "I knew you were destined for big things."

Something sharpened in Cora's gaze. Henry got the feeling that suddenly he and Reece were on a different planet from Cora and Gil. "How was your family?"

If she'd meant to hurt him, she'd clearly hit her mark. Gil's shoulders slumped slightly; a man defeated. "Well. Quite well, in fact."

Henry stood there feeling like a Peeping Tom as Gil and Cora continued to stare at each other. Thank God Reece opened his mouth. "If you walked all of the way from Greenwood, you're probably starving. Let's get you up to the house so Nell can feed you."

Gil's gaze lingered on Cora for so long Henry thought Reece's comment hadn't been heard. Finally, Gil turned away and said, "Lead the way."

Henry kept his eyes on Cora. Instead of watching Gil walk away, she looked to the ground, her cheeks slightly flushed. Her reaction, compounded by Henry's own creeping guilt, told him that while Gil might have been the glue that initially bound Henry and Cora together, he would also always be the barrier that kept them apart.

Two nights later Henry awoke to the slow, steady back-and-forth creak of the porch swing's chains against the hooks that held it. He smelled cigarette smoke drifting up to his open window. He hadn't had a chance to talk with Gil alone in the two days he'd been back. Cora, Reece, Henry, and Gil had spent every waking moment together, working on improving Cora's skills and going over the EV-1's engine making sure it was operating at optimum capacity. Gil was able to instruct Cora and push her in ways Henry could not, so it was a good thing he'd come back when he did. Yet, deep inside, Henry selfishly wished Gil had waited just a little longer, given Henry and Cora more time to solidify what was between them. If he'd had that time, maybe he could have erased that blush Gil brought to her cheeks.

Although they'd all reverted to their old ways, an undercurrent was between Cora and Gil and Henry that hadn't been there before. Or maybe Henry's guilt was manufacturing it. Even though Gil was married and Henry *shouldn't* feel guilty over his feelings for Cora — or she for him. But there they were.

He got out of bed and pulled on his pants, unsure if he was going down to talk to Gil about Cora, or if he was going to tell him about Emmaline. He knew he needed to do both, but they didn't belong in the same conversation. He left his shoes off, opting for quiet footsteps that would be less likely to wake anyone else in the house. As he crept down the stairs, he decided that talking about murder charges against him would be easier than talking about Cora. And more necessary.

The front door was open to the screen, letting in the cooler night air. As Henry got near it, he heard Cora's voice rising in question. Outside. With Gil.

He stopped dead, then moved closer to the door and listened.

They were quiet for a long while and Henry's imagination conjured images he wished it hadn't.

Gil's deep sigh was sad, not sexual. "I did love her, when I was a boy and capable of love. Now . . . there's nothing left in me. I tried to convince her to divorce me, especially after I saw how obvious it was she loved, and is loved by, the man who owns the house she and Charlie live in — which explains the cheap rent. She is as against divorce now as she had been four years ago — more so, now that Charlie's almost seven and old enough to know. My God, that boy looks like John." The last words carried all of the sadness Henry imagined was stored up in Gil's soul.

Looks like John, Henry thought, *but she named him after you.*

Cora said, "She'd rather her son live believing his father doesn't love him or his mother, and that he basically abandoned them? If she won't divorce you, then she should let you be a part of their lives."

That statement gave Henry a lift of hope. Cora wasn't trying to talk Gil *into* divorce.

"The way she looks at me hasn't changed. She doesn't want me near her child. Guilt penance, that's what she calls my offers to help raise Charlie, the money I send."

"How can she be so unforgiving? John's death was an accident."

"An accident that never would have happened if not for me."

"But Charlie —"

"Looks at me like I might go berserk any minute. Mary told him I came home from the war so scarred that I can't live a normal life, no matter how much I love them. It's best to just let it be. I owe her that. Divorce is a sin she'll never commit. She's become quite pious. I suppose it's a comfort to her."

Gil sighed. "I just can't believe God wants people to be this unhappy."

"Would you be happy? If you were free?" Henry thought he heard just a hint of hope in her voice. And it cut him deep.

Gil was silent for a few seconds. "I haven't been happy since the instant I beat my best friend into a bloody mess. So, no. Married or free, I'm the same. It's Mary that needs freeing."

The grandfather clock chimed, startling Henry and setting his shamed heart to racing.

He retreated silently upstairs and lay awake in his bed, listening to the slow, sad creak of the swing.

24

Henry and Cora arrived at Miami's Chapman Field in the EV-1 — now dubbed by Cora as the Evie — four days before the event. They wanted plenty of time for Cora to get used to taking off and landing while buffeted by Atlantic winds and shifting air currents caused by the water-land mix. They had been unsure if it would be the same as the air turbulence caused by crossing from a sunbaked bare-earth field to a lush green one, or something entirely different.

Henry had expected Miami to be like Southern California, both being the southernmost reaches of the country. But about the only things they had in common were palm trees and warm winter weather. The people he met were mostly East Coast birds gone south, Jamaicans gone north; only a handful were true Floridians. It was low and flat here, water seeping up everywhere as it tried to overtake dry land;

nothing at all like the sparse vegetation on the dry, rocky hills and mountains around Hollywood and Santa Monica. The air was different, too, heavy and moist, as opposed to California's ethereal lightness. When he crawled into his cot at night, inside a tent that was more mosquito netting than canvas, the sheets were damp. The towel from his shower never completely dried.

They allowed themselves the first afternoon to see downtown Miami and search for a reasonable hotel. In the end, the thirteen-mile distance was more than Henry wanted to deal with, considering they had to rely on buses and the charity of others for transportation, so they decided to rent a couple of tents at the airfield, where Henry could keep a close eye on the plane.

Between there and the city, they'd passed huge hotels under construction and signs for new developments that promised to change scrub and swamp into homesites, golf courses, and tennis courts. Henry couldn't see how. The locals at the diner where they stopped for lunch — once they'd discovered Cora and Henry were here for the air race and not among the offenders — had complained about the "land rush"; Northerners who would never set foot in Florida buying up big chunks of land they'd never set eyes on, looking to turn an obscene profit. Cora told Henry her father would have been one of the first — and probably the most crooked.

Henry studied her across the table after that statement. She didn't seemed shamed by it, hadn't made excuses out of love and respect. It simply was. In the same way Henry's pa had been a landless farmer, a poor immigrant. A German. Henry decided he'd rather be poor than have a man he couldn't respect for a father.

And what would Pa think of you *now? Runner. Coward. Choosing self-preservation over honor and principle. Letting the one man who'd shown you kindness believe you betrayed him, without even fighting for the truth. Hiding from your own name.*

These thoughts put another turn in the continually tightening spring inside him. He worried that before long he wouldn't even resemble the man his father had intended for Henry to become.

Just a few more days, Pa. A few more days.

Excuses. Feeble, pathetic excuses. He seemed full of them. Temporary splints on the weakness of his character. Would he find another reason to delay turning himself in once the race was done? The solid moral ground on which his father had placed him was now shifting sand and sinkholes. An ever-evolving parade of justifications. Every day he spent with Cora made him weaker, less inclined to sacrifice his life with her — whatever it shaped into — and more willing to let that sand suck him down. It would be so easy, now that she knew the truth and had not condemned him for it, just to continue on with Henry Jefferson's life and hope against hope that no one ever came after him.

Henry pushed away his half-eaten lunch.

"Are you all right?" Cora looked concerned.

"Fine. Just anxious to get back to the plane. When is Evans supposed to arrive?" Henry asked the question as a diversion, rather than out of any real interest. In fact, he didn't look forward to the man's looking over his shoulder as he did the final fine-tuning of the plane.

"Tomorrow, or the next day. He wasn't certain in his last telegram." She took a sip of coffee. "I'm ready when you are. I want to get in a few takeoffs and landings before the day gets any hotter."

The tension eased up a bit once he was back at the field, attending to the plane, talking to other pilots, discussing the racecourse. It made him feel he was there for a purpose other than avoiding going back to Indiana. After the race, Cora wanted to walk on Miami Beach and see Smith's Casino — which seemed to be all anyone wanted to talk about when they weren't discussing planes and horsepower. If he might be put away for the rest of his life, or worse, it seemed he should put his feet in the Atlantic Ocean beforehand. One more day wasn't going to change anything.

Most of the pilots talked freely about their planes and their experiences — at least to Henry. They didn't seem to know what to make of Cora, so they generally avoided her. It had started getting under his skin the way many of them deliberately excluded her from their conversations when she was standing right there, the sidelong looks of disdain, the turning of backs, the insinuation that she couldn't be taken seriously. Whenever he'd started to comment about it, Cora had stopped him and whispered in his ear, "It's better if they've already discounted me as a competitor. They won't push as hard when racing me. It's an advantage."

Discounting her as a competitor was one thing. Disrespecting her as a person was something else. A couple of the men were teetering on the brink of crossing that line, and Henry had just about had enough.

The next day, practice times were assigned by a random lottery. Cora ran the course as well as any of the men, better than some. When the pairings were drawn and times posted for the following day's practice with two planes on the course — the way they would race — Henry couldn't believe their bad luck. He looked over at the one pilot who hadn't been satisfied with just freezing Cora out; he'd been making completely unfounded comments about her flying skills and had actively tried to get her disqualified.

A squat man with a slow plane and a bad attitude, he was standing two feet from Henry when the pairings were posted. "Hell, no! I won't fly with her. Change it or forget it."

The official informed him that no changes could be made.

Henry said, "She's passed all of her qualifications. You're her draw. You can't just refuse to run with her."

"I don't have to practice at all. So, yeah, I think I can. I'm not going to risk having my plane taken out before the race by an inexperienced *woman*."

"She deserves the same practice as everyone else."

"Maybe you can find someone who'll take an asinine risk like that. Not me." As the man turned to walk away, he mumbled, "Who'd she fuck to get a ride in that plane anyhow?"

Henry grabbed the man's shoulder and jerked him back around. He got a handful of shirt and leaned down so he was nose to nose. "Say that to my face, you spineless little shit!"

Instead of being cowed, the man shouted so everyone within fifty yards could hear, "I said, who'd she have to fuck to get that plane?"

The monster knocked the cellar door off its hinges. Henry wasn't sure how he got there, but he was suddenly straddling the man on the ground, one fist still wadded in the shirt, the other beating the fat face. The punch Henry took in the throat barely registered.

"Henry!" He heard Cora's voice, but it seemed to come from far away. Hands grabbed his shoulders, but he kept pummeling, his vision gone red.

"Enough! Henry! Stop!"

It took two men to pull him off. They kept a tight hold on his arms until he finally said, "Okay." He shrugged them off, panting. "Okay." He pointed a bruised-knuckled finger at the man on the ground. "If you ever utter another word about her, I'm coming after you."

The men who'd pulled Henry off were now helping the bastard off the ground. "You broke my nose!" the man slurred through already-swelling lips, but made no move at retaliation.

Cora stepped directly in front of Henry and looked him in the face. "Don't give them a reason to throw us out of here." Her voice was calm, but her eyes revealed just how shaken up she was, how shocked by his brutality.

He stood huffing. Blood still pounded in his ears. The electric shock of his fury still sparked though him.

She gently took his arm. "Let's go to the tent and get you cleaned up." She tugged more forcefully. "Now, Henry."

After leading him to her tent, she sat him on her cot and went to fetch some water, threatening him with bodily harm if he so much as stuck his nose outside. It was sweltering inside the tent, even though it was in the shade. He looked down at his shirt. It was splattered with blood. For a moment he stared at his bloody right hand as if it belonged to someone else. The skin was broken open on a couple of his knuckles. As his senses returned, he felt the throbbing in his shoulder.

He wished he could say he felt better, that the rage had been sated. Something was different inside, that much was certain. He now knew the monster couldn't be tamed. Is that what had happened with Emmaline?

Nausea gripped him, but he clamped his jaw tight and willed it away.

Cora returned, took one look at him, and said, "Lie down. You look like you're about to pass out."

He stretched out in defeat. He would never be the man Pa expected him to be. Never.

She carefully cleaned his hands with cool water. "You know that wasn't necessary . . . defending my honor like that. Gallant, for sure, but unnecessary."

She was trying to make light of what had just happened.

"It's no joke, Cora. This is me. This is the person I am deep inside. I lost control. Completely. If I hadn't been stopped . . ." He shifted his gaze to the outside.

"Don't be ridiculous, Henry." Her words did not match what he saw in her eyes. Fear now resided there; Henry had carried its bags in with his sudden burst of violence.

Only it wasn't sudden, was it? He'd known

it was there, hiding in the cellar.

He pulled his hands from her and swung his legs over the side of the cot. "Now you see what I'm capable of."

"Henry. The man is an ass. I didn't hear anyone speak in his defense, did you? And they let you get in some good licks before they pulled you off."

"You're missing the point. No one should have had to pull me off. I lost my mind, Cora."

She stopped trying to recapture his hands and looked at him. "Has this happened before?"

"Like with Emmaline, you mean? Did she say the wrong thing and set off my insanity?"

"Well, from what you said about her, I imagine that is likely exactly what happened . . . just not with you." She paused, picked up his right hand, and kissed his wounded knuckle. "Just now you were angry *for my benefit,* not for yourself. You were protecting me. You went to where Emmaline was because you were worried about Johanna. Have there been other incidents where your need to defend overtook you? Something that people might misconstrue? Something that will hurt us when we get back to Indiana?"

He closed his eyes, and all he could see was that man's bloody face, all he could taste was his own shame. "No."

"Good." She said it as if there was no more to say on the subject and went back to tending his hands. "As for that ass, I don't need to practice the course with another plane. You did a great job of preparing me. I'm ready."

He stood. "I'm going to talk to the officials about getting you another pilot to practice against."

She put her hands on his upper arms. "There's no need to make enemies. And what if they force him to fly or face disqualification? I'd rather not fly with an angry pilot nipping at my heels. He'll be more likely to make a mistake and take both of us out. And of course, as the *woman,* it would be my fault. I'll prove myself in the race."

What she said made sense. To his rational mind. But his real concern was her overconfidence if she didn't have a taste of a stranger racing her on the course before the green flag flew.

Then he had another thought. "What if they try to disqualify you because of this fight?"

"I got these first-aid supplies from the office. Didn't hear a word about anything like that. And the ass was in there getting the nurse they've hired for the event to check out his nose. Whining like a little girl."

"It could still come."

"I don't think so. This is a rough-and-tumble man's sport, men get into fights all the time. Besides, they can't afford the bad publicity if they disqualify me, and I can guarantee bad publicity. Evans will toss in his weight, too. And remember, *I* wasn't even in the fight. How can they disqualify me?"

For the next few hours, Henry held himself wary and waiting for the officials to show up and tell them to get packing. By the next morning when they hadn't heard a word, he began to relax again.

He was replacing the spark plugs in the Evie when Cora called to him, "Henry, look who's here!" He turned with a pleased-to-meet-you look on his face, expecting to see Mr. Evans in his wheelchair. But Gil walked beside Cora.

Henry's smile became forced. "I didn't know you were coming."

"You knew I asked him," Cora said.

Henry wiped his hands on a cloth, wincing at the pain in his right. "I guess I got the impression he wasn't inclined." He tried to squash the flare of resentment. The three of them were a team. And God knew, Gil was more of a lost soul now than he'd ever been. He'd continued his downhill slide after coming back from Ohio. Henry should have been doing everything in his power to keep an eye on him. Still, Henry had wanted this air race to be like California, something just he and Cora shared. "Did you fly one of Jake's planes in?"

"Took the train." Gil lit a smoke and blew out the match without taking the cigarette from his mouth. "Didn't mean to *intrude.*"

So Henry wasn't masking his feelings quite as well as he'd thought.

Gil went on, "I didn't want to be sitting around Reece's farm waiting for a telegram to know the outcome." He took a long drag on his cigarette. "Besides, I was curious about Chapman Field."

"Why?" Cora asked.

Good question. There really wasn't much to it, not now that the army had deemed it surplus and sold part of the land to some plant-study program. The airstrip was only used for Reserves' training now.

Gil said, "Victor Chapman was the first American pilot killed in the war. The first of many."

Gil's voice had a hint of envy that Henry didn't like one bit. He felt even worse for his ill-concealed reaction to Gil's arrival. The man needed looking after. He had a strange glasslike fragility about him now, worse even than upon his return to Mississippi.

A black car motored up and stopped nearby. A man wearing a bowler called through the open driver's window, "Miss Haviland?"

"Yes?" She was smiling her publicity-photo smile.

Haviland. The man had called her Miss Haviland, not Miss Rose. That car, that bowler . . . Henry felt sick.

The man got out of the car. When he got close, he tipped the brim of his hat. "I need you to come with me, Miss Haviland."

Henry edged closer to her. *We're about to get the boot.*

As he opened his mouth to explain the fault was all his, Cora's moneyed voice, the one she used to either intimidate or poke fun, surfaced. "Oh, you do, do you? Are you with the race organizers, then?"

"If you'll just get in the car, please."

"Not until Miss *Haviland*" — Henry hoped she got his message — "knows what this is about." He took her arm, as if ready to get into a tug-of-war with the man over her.

"In the car," the man said, then added an insincere "Please."

"I will not." Her chin came up. "Not until you tell me who you are and what you want."

Gil, too, inched close to her.

The man pulled a leather wallet out of the inside pocket of his jacket. He flipped it open to an identification card. "I'm Edward Burrow with the Pinkerton Detective Agency."

"If this is about yesterday —" Henry cut himself off. Didn't make sense. Detectives investigated things, found people. Miss Haviland. Cora. He'd come for her.

So many thoughts took to flight, if they'd been crows, they'd have blocked the sun. None of them made sense.

"And what do you want with me?" Her voice remained authoritative, but Henry felt her muscles tense.

"I'm here to take you home, miss."

"Sorry you made the trip." She made a walking gesture with two fingers. "You can just turn yourself around and head back to wherever you came from."

"I'm from the Chicago office."

"Fine. Go to Chicago, then."

Gil finally spoke up. "What's this all about? Who are you working for?"

"The young lady's fiancé, on behest of her mother."

"Fiancé?" Gil sounded stunned. But Henry thought they'd both been fools thinking no one would come in search of a woman from a rich family, even if the money was gone. He wanted to speak up, but knew this was Cora's mess to straighten out. Him talking would only make it worse — and draw attention to himself.

"You can't be serious!" she said.

"I am. Quite. Now step away from these men."

"Well, I'm not going. Both Mother and Theodore will have to adjust. I'm a grown woman and have made my decision." Then she looked at the Pinkerton more sharply. "How did you find me?"

The pictures, Henry thought. Those publicity pictures for the Evie.

"It's what we do, miss. Now, if you'll come with me, you can get everything sorted out with your mother and your fiancé when we get to Chicago." The detective moved closer, a hand extended.

"I turned eighteen months ago!" She drew away from his hand.

Henry had assumed her birthday was her

nineteenth. He knew assumptions were as dangerous as lies.

She took a step farther from the detective. "You can't make me do anything I don't want to. And I have no intention of marrying Theodore, ever. So shove off." The haughty voice had been banished by the real Cora.

The Pinkerton grabbed her and yanked her away from Gil and Henry.

Henry lunged toward the detective but was shoved from behind and hit the ground before he'd taken a step. Gil was on the ground beside him with a man's knee in the middle of his shoulder blades.

Henry was too stunned to struggle. Too short of breath to argue.

"Stop!" Cora screamed. "What are you doing?"

"You're safe now," the Pinkerton said. "These men are headed to the Dade County jail."

"They haven't done anything!"

"Your mother said you were kidnapped by two men with an airplane. With that other murdered girl just two counties away, she feared the worst. You can imagine how relieved she was when we located you."

"Jesus H. Christ!" Cora shouted. "I left home by myself, of my own free will, on my motorcycle —" She stopped abruptly.

Henry's insides turned to water as his hands were handcuffed behind his back. His shoulder burned with the stretch. No one knew about the motorcycle. She'd been so forceful when she'd explained that her mother couldn't do anything about her leaving, he'd made more than one disastrous assumption. The second being she'd actually informed her mother that she *was* leaving.

Why hadn't he gone back to Indiana the very day he'd made the decision? Now it was too late.

"I left on my own! I caught up with them in Noblesville. They didn't even want me with them. You can't arrest them!"

"The sheriff is going to hold them until we get this all straightened out. We can't take any chances. Especially with an unsolved murder. And the reward money is only to be paid if the kidnappers are taken into custody."

"I was *not* kidnapped!" She looked at Henry with panicked eyes as he was hoisted off the ground. "I'll go home." She took the Pinkerton's arm. "Right now. I'll go. As long as you tell the sheriff to let them go."

"Out of my hands now, miss." He nodded for the sheriff and his deputy to take Gil and Henry away.

Gil said, "It's all right, Cora. We'll go. It'll get straightened out. Don't you dare go with him. He can't force you. You have a race to fly in two days."

Henry closed his eyes and had to struggle to keep from throwing up on his shoes. *So stupid!* He hadn't told Gil about Indiana yet. He was already such a mess. And with the preparation for the race, Henry hadn't found the right time, figuring he'd do it when they returned to Mississippi, right before he headed north.

If he argued against being taken in, against the logic of the truth setting them free, if he resisted, it would just make him look that much guiltier when the discovery was made.

Gil said again, "He can't make you go, Cora!"

Her gaze sharpened. "If this man forces me to leave, he'll be kidnapping!" she said to one of the deputies. "Tell him!"

The deputy looked uncomfortable. "If you're eighteen, no, he can't."

She shook her finger at the Pinkerton. "If you touch me again, I'm pressing charges."

The Pinkerton held his palms in the air, but his face didn't show surrender. "Let these men do their work. Then we can talk."

The deputy's grip on Henry's arm

tightened and nudged him into motion.

He locked eyes with Cora. A single tear ran down her cheek. Her lips were quivering when she mouthed, "I'm so sorry."

This was it. His last seconds before he was locked up, probably forever. He wanted to jerk free and kiss her one last time. But he just nodded and said, "Good-bye, Cora. Good luck in the race."

The last thing he saw as he was put in the back of the police car was Cora arguing with the Pinkerton, her finger stabbing him in the chest. Henry kept his eyes on her until they turned behind the hangar.

Gil sat next to him. "Damn. Did you know she wasn't eighteen?"

Henry shook his head, unable to speak around the wad of fear and disappointment in his throat.

"Well, don't worry," Gil said. "Plenty of people in Noblesville saw her show up on her own. She traveled alone on the motorcycle for weeks. People remember her. It'll get straightened out."

How long? How long would it take? He hoped like hell Gil was out in time to finish prepping the plane for the race. The spark plugs weren't even in it. Henry had been setting the gaps when the shit started to fly. Cora deserved her shot.

And then he'd have to figure out a way to convince her to give up on him, to move on with Gil, the circus . . . her amazing life that lay ahead.

25

The police separated Henry and Gil as soon as they arrived at the Dade County jail, but had yet to officially arrest them. Gil's ignorance of Henry's true identity wouldn't have to be faked, so Henry supposed that was one good thing that came from not yet telling the truth. He hadn't met Gil until two days after Emmaline's death, so they couldn't link him to that in any way.

As they were led to different rooms, Gil dredged up a semiconfident grin and said, "Don't worry, kid." His assurance made Henry feel even guiltier, but he'd responded with a nod, wondering if he'd ever see Gil again. Maybe it would be best if he didn't. Then Henry wouldn't have to see the disappointment in Gil's eyes.

Or maybe he wouldn't be disappointed at all. Maybe he'd welcome Henry's removal from their trio. Gil's face when he'd said he didn't want to intrude had told Henry he'd just undone the last piece of twine holding Gil together. With Henry gone, maybe Cora would be able to retie it. He hoped so. Maybe that would make up for the betrayal and misuse of Gil's friendship.

The small room had no clock. Henry sat on a metal bench attached to the wall, his hands cuffed behind his back, waiting. And waiting. A peculiar calm overtook him. After months of balancing on the knife edge of dread, tasting uncertainty, smelling of fear, he couldn't believe that all he felt was quiet relief; colorless, tasteless, and odorless. This life was over. The decision had been yanked from his hands. He was finally done running.

He sat there long enough that he sweated through his shirt and his ass got numb. The strangest thoughts passed through his head.

Will I be buried next to my family? Will someone make a fifth crooked cross out of fence pickets for me? Do they have a special place they bury executed murderers?

I can't remember my mother's face.

Did Gil know the right spark gap setting for the Evie?

I don't know Cora's favorite color.

Finally, the door opened.

A man in a loosened tie and limp shirt with the sleeves rolled up pulled a chair in from the hall and sat down across the room from Henry, well out of kicking range, he noticed.

"Sorry to keep you waiting. It took some time to get the young lady calmed down."

So Cora was here. A flash of longing came and went like lightning.

Then he wondered, who was meeting Evans? Who was making sure no one walked off with the loose parts of the Evie? "She needs to leave."

"She's not your concern any longer."

"We didn't kidnap her."

"I see. Maybe we should back up and start with the basics. He took a pencil and small pad from his pocket. Your name?"

Point of no return. "Henry Schuler."

To lie would just confirm both his stupidity and his guilt. But he wasn't going to answer any questions about Emmaline's murder. They'd have to ship him back to Indiana for that, so he could at least be where there was a possibility of convincing them to investigate.

The man's eyes snapped to Henry's face.

"Henry Schuler," Henry repeated. "From Delaware County, Indiana."

The man got up and left the room.

Henry was left waiting again.

■ ■ ■ ■

Just before sunrise, Henry was led from the jail in handcuffs. The deputy flashed a piece of paper so quickly Henry could only read the largest print across the top: WARRANT. Henry only asked one question: What had happened to Gil?

"Released." That one word made it so Henry could put one foot in front of the other. Gil was free. He could look after Cora.

When they took him through a back door and loaded him into a waiting car, he supposed he was headed to Delaware County. The city was deserted but for a truck leaving off bundles of newspapers and a milk delivery wagon. Peaceful. He watched the palm trees lining the streets pass by with detachment, as if he'd already left this place of water and unnatural weather.

They pulled up to the train station just as the sun was inching over the horizon, a spectacular display of pink and orange that he soaked in as if it were the last he'd ever see. As he and a grumpy deputy boarded a northbound train, Henry wondered if Cora was asleep in her tent or if she'd been too restless and was watching the sunrise. He wondered if Gil was busy putting the engine back together. And he wondered about Frank Evans. How did he take the news that Henry had been hauled off to jail?

The deputy unlocked Henry's handcuffs and relocked them in front of him so he could sit in the train seat more easily. A man across the aisle frowned, got up, and moved to a different seat, offering the same look of loathing people had given Henry throughout the war. It no longer held the same power.

When he'd imagined this day, he'd thought the train ride would be interminable, with panic clawing his gut and his mind racing. But as soon as the train pulled out of the station, Henry fell asleep with relief coursing through his veins. The deputy awakened him to change trains. Henry refused the food the man purchased at the station. The deputy smiled for the first time as he took Henry's sandwich and added it to his own dinner. Henry was back asleep before the man had finished half of it.

Union Station in Indianapolis was filled with people when they arrived. Neither the deputy hanging on to Henry's arm nor the handcuffs seemed to draw attention. When they walked out of the building, the biting wind slapped Henry in the face. The sky was a sharp blue that hung over Indiana only in the deepest of winter. He welcomed the cold, even though coatless. The deputy shivered in his uniform jacket and grumbled about having drawn the short straw and being forced to travel north in January.

Out on Illinois Street, people did notice the handcuffs, and the deputy's tight hold around Henry's upper arm. They sidestepped to give wide clearance, as if Henry were an unpredictable wild animal that might spring. Maybe they were right.

The deputy hustled Henry along north, straight into the wind. His eyes watered with the cold, yet he still tried to slow down. He'd never seen Indianapolis before. But the shivering deputy kept them moving. Henry wished there were ice, a thick coating that made it so a man couldn't keep his footing no matter how he shuffled.

Unsure where they were headed, he didn't ask. The end destination would be the same, no matter the path to get there.

When they crossed Market Street, Henry looked to the right and saw the famous Circle with the tall Soldiers and Sailors Monument in its center. When he turned left he was looking at the front of the Indiana statehouse a block away. He dragged his feet to get a longer look at both, but the deputy jerked him along. Ice would indeed have been welcome.

They'd only gone about three blocks when they entered the Traction Terminal. Apparently the electric interurban car would take them the last leg to Muncie. The waiting platform was bright and warm. When they passed the large newsstand, Henry wondered if the headlines last May had contained his name. There would have been no photograph because he'd never had one taken . . . until that Hollywood newsreel. Oddly, that footage had not been the vehicle of his demise. Instead it had been the search for Cora, probably led to them by the publicity for Evans's new aircraft. Disaster had a nasty habit of sneaking up on your blind side. He'd known it all along.

The Delaware County sheriff met them in the traction shed as they descended from the car at the Muncie terminal and promptly arrested Henry for the murder of Emmaline Dahlgren. He'd been expecting it. He didn't know why the words echoed in his ears and his equilibrium left him. If not for the sheriff's having a grip on his arm, he might have listed to one side like a sinking ship.

This sheriff wasted no time in asking all of the questions that the Dade County sheriff had not. Henry answered each one the same: "I'll be happy to answer all of your questions after I speak to Anders Dahlgren. And I would like a lawyer." After three separate and equally fruitless attempts at questioning, the sheriff gave up and put him in a jail cell. As the lock was turned, the sheriff said, "He may not be willing to see you. Then what?"

"He will," Henry said with false confidence.

"I'll call him. Too late for him to come today."

Henry nodded and then stretched out on the thin mattress. Dinner was served by the sheriff's wife. He ate with a surprising appetite.

The next morning passed with no Mr. Dahlgren. The farm was only an hour away; Henry was starting to worry. He met with his appointed lawyer at eleven in a small room with a table and a chair tucked on each side. The handcuffs stayed on. The man introduced himself as Xavier Thornburg in a voice so soft Henry had to strain to hear it. Thornburg was probably forty, short, and slight of build, barely coming up to the middle of Henry's chest. Even though it was cold out, the lawyer had a sweaty handshake.

He shuffled some papers. "I see you're

charged with . . . oh!"

"Murder." This was not an auspicious start. Henry thought about Cora's claim that any lawyer provided for him would be uninvolved and careless. Right now, he'd be happy to have one who'd read the charges before he came in the room.

Thornburg cleared his throat. "Yes, I see. How do you want to plead?"

"Aren't you supposed to be telling me?"

The lawyer looked surprised. "Well, anything you tell me is confidential. So I suppose we should start with your version of what happened."

"My version?"

"Yes. The county prosecutor already has their version lined out."

"Which is?" Henry was curious to discover what they assumed had happened and how they supported their theory. It might help him dredge up more memories.

"Defense counsel isn't privy to their case at this point in the process. In due time, they'll have to turn over a list of witnesses they plan to call, evidence filed, and the like. Our plea at this point is simply for the arraignment."

"Arraignment?"

"Where we go before the judge and the charges are read. And then you plead guilty or not guilty. I don't advise guilty. If you're going that route, we can declare it later and use the leverage for sentencing. Not guilty gets us on the trial docket. And we go from there."

"I already told the sheriff that I don't want to discuss anything until I speak to Anders Dahlgren in person."

"Oh, yes. The sheriff told me to tell you that Mr. Dahlgren has refused to come. So, shall we begin with your version of the events?"

For the first time in two days, real emotion gripped Henry. Mr. Dahlgren was so convinced Henry had killed his daughter that he wouldn't even speak to him. It pained him more than he could say, but he couldn't blame the man. If Henry had been in Mr. Dahlgren's shoes, he would probably feel the same way, brokenhearted, disgusted, disappointed, furious. He'd never seen that man angered. He couldn't imagine what it would look like.

At that moment, he understood how much hope he'd been pinning on Mr. Dahlgren's belief in him. How much he'd counted on Emmaline's father to demand further investigation — once he'd heard Henry's explanation.

Now what chance did Henry have of

convincing anyone to ferret out the truth of what had happened? Without a clear memory, what did he have to offer as incentive? For one panicked second he thought about telling Thornburg that he was going to enter a guilty plea if the death penalty was removed as a possibility.

But it didn't *feel* as if he could have killed anyone. Shouldn't that change a person in some fundamental way — whether you remembered it or not? Or was that just his own form of denial, of self-preservation?

Henry recounted to Thornburg what had happened on the day of the murder. For the first time, the tremors that always started deep in his bones did not come.

"That's it?" The lawyer sounded disappointed. "Amnesia is a tough sell to a jury."

Good God, the man missed the point entirely. "I'm not trying to *sell* anything. I told you what I know."

"I'm not sure what you want me to say."

"I want you to help find out the truth, isn't that your job? I want someone to at least look into other possibilities than me killing her. Something was going on with her before that day. Didn't anyone else notice? Is it possible that she just fell? Maybe I did, too. Maybe I didn't see her and tripped over her. There has to be a reason for my own head injury."

"My job is to present the best defense for your case. Investigation is left to the police."

"Then get the sheriff in here."

The sheriff listened to Henry's story. When he reached the point where his memory went blank, the sheriff's interested look shifted to impatience.

"Hear me out," Henry said. "I want the truth, too. I've done everything I can to remember details that might help fill in the blanks of what happened on that riverbank. I must have hit my head, been hit . . . I just don't know how it happened." If he shared the possibility that his own rage had blinded him, that would be the end of it here and now. Answers would never come. "It's true Emmaline and I didn't get along. But it had been that way from the first. I'd lived with it for over four years. Why I would have done something about it last May? Nothing was any different between us than it ever had been." He explained the head injury he'd sustained, probably the reason for the blank spot in his memory; Violet's appearance had spurred his panicked decision to flee. "I'm not an idiot. I know what it looks like. And I don't expect you to believe that I was planning on turning myself in. I don't know what your investigation has uncovered so far, but since I'm sitting here under arrest, I'd say not much other than Violet's statement. All I'm asking is that you take what I've said and look at the case again."

The sheriff crossed his arms and leaned back in his chair, his face a blank mask. "I've known Anders for a long time. He's a good man. He deserves justice. That girl deserves justice."

"I couldn't agree more. I just want justice to be just and not because I was in the wrong place at the wrong time. I'll face up to what I did when I know for a fact that I did it."

"This is an unusual tactic for defense, son."

"It isn't a tactic. It's the truth. And if someone else did this to Emmaline? Then he needs to be held accountable. Remember I told you she'd been in the woods near the Chautauqua grounds the day before. And she was angry."

"So you say."

"Well, isn't that what it's all about? What I say? What someone else might have to say if you ask them the right questions?" Henry stopped short of suggesting the sheriff question Johanna. If the girl had seen anything, he felt sure she would have told her father.

The sheriff rose from his seat. "Let's get you back to your cell."

The sound of the cell door's locking seemed louder this time. Henry had no idea what the sheriff intended to do, if he did anything at all.

26

After his meeting with the sheriff, the calm left Henry on a hurricane wind. Maybe it had just been numbness, a stunned emotional pause, like those brief seconds after you hit your finger with a hammer before the knee-buckling pain sets in. The relief was ebbing, too, being replaced inch by inch with the stark fear that he might never see the outside world again, never see the world from a bird's-eye view with the wind tearing at his hair.

He made laps around the rectangle of his small cell. Only one other occupied cell was near him. Its inhabitant punctuated the silence with the slow rhythmic thud of his head against the bars. It had started the minute the man was locked in there. Henry's pace fell into the cadence of that steady beat.

As he circled, the regrets started. If he'd come when he'd made the decision to, he could have gone to Mr. Dahlgren himself, first thing. Standing face-to-face, even if the man didn't believe or forgive him, he would at least have heard Henry out, he was sure of it. And he could have done some digging himself before he turned himself in, had more to offer the sheriff. If Henry had gone back to the river, it might have shaken something from the mortar of his memory.

He heard the courthouse clock strike one. Today was race day. Or was it yesterday? Time had gotten scrambled.

That he wouldn't know the outcome of the race hit him like a physical blow. No one would share news of Gil or Cora or the flying circus. He was cut off in a way he'd never been. It was true, he'd been alone a good part of his life; but after having had people who'd accepted him, who'd willingly shared their lives with him, this new aloneness was more bitter than any he'd ever had to face.

And Gil? What must he think of me? By now, Gil had to know Henry had been charged with murder, had used Gil to get away and lied to him. If not from the Dade County sheriff, then from Cora. Henry had stupidly thought he had more time. Now he just seemed that much more cowardly. Would he ever have a chance to apologize?

The door to the hall in front of the cells clattered open. "He's at the end. I'll be right here. Don't get close to the cells."

Henry stepped close to the bars and listened as soft footsteps approached. The head-thumping in the other cell stopped. Then it started again.

And she was there. He blinked to make certain his mind wasn't playing tricks on him.

"Hello, Henry." Cora stepped close and put her hands through the bars. Henry grabbed them like a lifeline. She smelled different, but somehow familiar.

"You shouldn't be here. Where's Gil? Did they let him out?" Questions tumbled on statements, fueled by the fear she'd be swept away from him again. "Did the Pinkerton force you back here?"

"Miss! Step back or you'll have to leave."

Defiance showed in her eyes. Henry let go of her hands, took a step back, and nodded for her to do the same.

She took a small step backward. A half smile graced her lips when she said, "The Pinkerton finally gave up when I yelled for someone to call the police, that I was being kidnapped. And the police let Gil go after I went in and explained everything to their satisfaction."

Henry relaxed a bit. "The race?"

"The race was yesterday afternoon."

"How'd you get here so fast?"

"I've been here since early this morning."

"Oh, Cora! You didn't race?"

She shook her head. "I couldn't stay down there and run it with you up here . . . like this."

"But this was your chance! Evans, the Evie —" He'd ruined it for her.

"Gil raced it. You know his chances of winning were far better than mine. We wanted the money to hire you a good lawyer. And as far as Evans is concerned, a war hero is next-best thing to a woman daredevil for publicity."

Henry stood there for a few seconds absorbing the enormity of what she'd given up. "You shouldn't have come. There isn't anything you can do. You gave that race up for *nothing.*"

"I disagree." She stepped closer again and the deputy issued a sharp warning. She stopped just short of putting her hands on the bars. She lowered her voice. "I went straight to the Dahlgren farm."

Henry felt as if he'd been gut-punched. "You what?"

"I wanted to tell Mr. Dahlgren what you couldn't, what you'd been planning to."

Henry didn't even want to ask how it had gone. He knew. He just hated it that Cora had to experience the loathing that should have been his. "He wouldn't see me."

"I know. But I think that had more to do with placating his wife than with you."

Henry shook his head, unable to force words from his lips. She was just trying to make him feel better.

"He doesn't want to believe you hurt his daughter. I can see it. He's just so beaten down by everyone telling him it has to be true."

Henry remembered how Mr. Dahlgren had been about the bracelet Emmaline said Henry had stolen, how he'd not been able to call his daughter a liar, yet hadn't punished Henry in a way that said he believed the lie.

"We don't have time to fool around here, Henry. We need answers. So I asked him what evidence they had that you attacked Emmaline — after his wife left the room with a case of the vapors, of course. You were right!" Cora's voice rose with restrained excitement. She glanced to make sure the deputy wasn't inching closer and listening. "After Violet came back screaming that she'd seen you, that you'd killed her sister, no one looked any further."

This statement aroused no excitement in Henry. Quite the opposite. "That isn't good news."

"Yes, it is! It means there might be something out there I can find that will at least raise enough doubt to get the authorities to take a serious look at the case again."

"It's been months. What could be left to find?"

"Maybe nothing at the river; it's been too long. I'm still going to take a look. But don't you think if some questions were asked of the right people, we might discover at least another possibility for who attacked her? I'd like to talk to Violet, too, away from her mother."

Something clicked in his head, he could almost hear it.

"What is it? You look funny."

"Are you wearing perfume?"

"What? No. When have you known me to wear perfume?"

He had to smile. She was so clever. "Remember when you said smells trigger memory? You smell like Violet."

A sly smile crossed her face. She reached inside the collar of her blouse and pulled out a handkerchief. She waved it in the air in front of him. "This what you smell?"

He nodded.

She unfolded it to show a monogram, *V.M.D.,* in swirly letters. "I might have gotten a little worked up when I was at the farm. Mr. Dahlgren handed me this to dab my eyes."

"That's Violet's. Her fiancé gave her that expensive bottle of perfume. She practically bathed in it, walked around in a vapor that stuck on anybody who got too close. Emmaline kept hiding it from her. Poor Phillip smelled like a girl most of the time. He was probably sorry he bought it."

"Well" — Cora curled up her nose — "I wouldn't like it if you smelled like that. I like you smelling like a man, like motor oil and exhaust."

"I miss those smells already."

"Me, too." She smiled and it nearly broke his heart. "But I'm going to get you back out there tearing engines apart. Soon."

That sobered him up again. "Cora, don't get your hopes too high. The odds aren't in my favor."

Her chin tilted into a stubborn angle, the one he'd grown to love. "I happen to believe the odds are always in favor of the truth. And I'm going to find it. I'm going to poke everything I come across to see if it stinks — something the lazy-thinking police haven't bothered to do." She waved the hankie. "And now I have a reason to go back to the Dahlgren farm, walk the path to the river. Mr. Dahlgren seemed kind, I don't think he'll keep me from it. He asked about you and what you've been doing these months. That's not the kind of thing a man would ask if he thought beyond a doubt that you hurt his daughter. Maybe I can convince him to see you."

Henry nodded. If Mr. Dahlgren could believe in him, if he could forgive Henry's running, that would be some consolation. He thanked God for Cora and her headstrong ways. Then he said, "Did you see Johanna while you were there? She's just eight, the youngest, she probably wouldn't have talked. She's too self-conscious of her stammer. I've been worried about her."

"Oh, Henry, you have such a good heart! See why I don't need proof that you *didn't* do this?"

"Johanna?"

"None of the girls were allowed in the room. But there was a girl, a tiny thing, I saw peering around a tree at me as I came and went."

"That's Johanna. Did she look okay?"

"I don't know that I got a good enough look to say. She was bundled up in a coat, hat, and mittens. Her face wasn't bruised up, if that's what you mean. She seemed . . . curious, and yet skittish."

"Johanna's bruises are on the inside. If you see her when you go back, show her some kindness. Tell her I think of her. Tell her not to be afraid. She's strong."

Cora gasped and put her hand over her mouth. She blinked several times before she said, "I will. I promise."

"Miss? Time to go."

Cora cast an impatient look toward the deputy. "I'm going to do some digging. I'll be back tomorrow." She reached out a hand, but pulled it back with a glance toward the deputy. Instead she held him with her eyes. "Don't give up, Henry."

She started away.

"Wait! The race? Gil?"

"I have to go to the telegraph office. He was supposed to wire last night. I'm staying at the Delaware Hotel." She said it as if Henry might stop by and see her.

"Let me know how he did in the race as soon as you can."

"I will." She wiggled her fingers in a wave and stepped from sight. The door slammed and the lock clattered home.

Henry sat down on his bunk. And tried not to hope too much.

■ ■ ■ ■

They didn't turn on the lights in the jail-cell hall. One large, barred window at the end where the door was gave the only light, so Henry and the head thumper ate their dinners in dusky dimness. At least the man stopped his thudding to eat. By five thirty, it was dark. The head thumping started again. Henry lay down on his cot and closed his eyes, letting the rhythm rock him.

He imagined himself in the air, the vibration of the engine against his spine, the dips and rises of the plane, the wind singing in the wires. He decided this was the way he would fall asleep every night for the rest of his life. That way he'd never forget the sensation.

Then he was running through the tangled woods . . . the blue ribbon fluttering . . . he reached for it . . . and smelled Violet's perfume.

Sitting bolt upright in bed, he tried to hold the memory, follow its lead. But it was gone.

Violet had moved to Phillip's family's farm upon their marriage, but she still spent many afternoons at the home place. She was there that day, for certain. But it could have been Emmaline that was wearing the perfume, triggering that memory. He struggled to remember; the girls' petty arguments were so frequent that the content drifted away on their breath. Had Emmaline hidden that perfume from Violet when she moved out?

Did it mean anything at all? He thought of Cora, how that small scrap of fabric had carried the smell, so it was unlikely.

He lay back and closed his eyes again, willing the memory to return. It was like trying to capture smoke.

Time had been moving quickly from the moment Henry had been knocked down at the airfield. But after Cora's visit it slowed to a painful crawl. How was he going to spend the rest of his life with seconds dragging by, nothing to do but stare at three walls and a set of bars?

Be glad. Once you're convicted, your slow-moving seconds might run out in the electric chair.

Each hour he listened for the clock chime. They were getting further apart, they had to be. After it finally hit three o'clock, the door to the hallway rattled. The deputy issued the same warning as yesterday to stay away from the bars.

Henry stood quickly.

Cora's footsteps were quick, determined, as she approached his cell. The seconds would fly by now.

"Henry!" She looked surprised by the volume of her voice. Henry had to tuck his hands under his arms to keep from reaching through the bars and touching her face. When she went on, she was quieter, but still filled with excitement. "I went back to the farm. Mrs. Dahlgren, thankfully, had taken to her bed with a headache. I pled with Mr. Dahlgren to come and see you. He didn't commit, but I think he'll come around."

"Thank you."

"That's not the good part. When I came out of the house, Johanna was hiding behind the same tree as yesterday. I told her that I had a message for her from you and she came out. I talked her into showing me the path that leads to the river. I didn't want her to go all of the way with me — not to where her sister died. By the time we got to the edge of the bare woods, she was talking a little. My God, Henry, she worships you like a big brother.

"We sat down for a bit. The cold was biting through me, but she didn't seem to mind, so I just let her keep talking. It was like she hadn't spoken a word in weeks — she probably hadn't — and there was so much she wanted to say, so many emotions that needed to see the light. I'm glad you warned me of her stammer. I waited while she found her way. It seemed like that was all she'd ever wanted anyone to do, give her time to speak. I know that's why she loves you. You did that for her."

Henry's heart squeezed for the child. Trapped in silence, when all it took was patience to let her find her way with the words. Why couldn't her family just give her that?

Cora stepped closer and whispered, "When I tried to get her to talk about Emmaline, she looked panicked, her eyes darting everywhere but my face. I thought about her silence and how she'd probably held her grief alone, too. So I kept asking her questions about her sister, giving her the opportunity to work through her grief — I tried to do like you would have, had you been able to be there for her. But it wasn't just grief. She was afraid. I tried to tell her that what happened to Emmaline was tragic, but rare, she didn't need to be afraid that something would happen to her, too. That's when she started crying. Sobbing. Oh, it was so pitiful.

"Finally she told me that she'd seen something. And she'd been too afraid to tell anyone —"

"Christ, Cora, just tell me!"

"Perfume wasn't all Emmaline was taking from her sister. Johanna saw Emmaline and Phillip in the hayloft, taking off each other's clothes."

He thought of Johanna's hiding place up there. "When?"

"Sometime before the wedding. She couldn't say for sure. I'm going to tell the sheriff now, but I had to tell you first! This is enough! They have to investigate now that they have another valid suspect in Phillip. I called one of my father's friends with the federal attorney general's office. He's already calling the state attorney general to get him to put pressure on the local sheriff to examine this case carefully. We're going to do it!" She was already moving away, toward the door. "I love you, Henry."

"Wait! Cora." But the door opened and closed. The lock slid home.

Henry collapsed on the floor right where he was. She loved him.

27

For the next hours, Henry thought about Phillip and Emmaline. He might have doubted a sister could betray another so cruelly if it had been anyone other than Emmaline. If he had to put money on whether it had been Emmaline or Phillip who initiated the relationship, he'd bet on Emmaline, jealous as she was over anyone's receiving more attention than her. This revelation also explained much of Emmaline's behavior after the wedding. Had Emmaline threatened to tell Violet as a way to exert control over Phillip? Had he killed her to keep her quiet? Or had he just lost control? Emmaline could be infuriating.

There was no guarantee the sheriff would consider this enough to make Phillip a suspect.

Henry thought of the scent of perfume right before he'd lost consciousness. It was true, Phillip often smelled of it. Henry supposed it didn't matter whom it came from. Emmaline. Phillip. Perfume wasn't proof of anything. And Henry's memory still had a hole in it.

Phillip's losing control was certainly more palatable to Henry than he himself losing control and harming Emmaline. Still, the pain for the Dahlgrens was too horrible to contemplate. And poor Johanna would have to act as a witness.

He flopped onto his mattress and covered his face with his hands.

All he could do was wait.

And he did. Dinner came and went uneaten. Darkness fell. The clock chimed seven. The head thumper went incessantly on.

He filled his hours with positive thoughts of what he would do when — not if — he got out. He'd see Mr. Dahlgren, apologize for running. He'd spend long hours with Gil, asking forgiveness for his own deceit and try to get Gil to forgive himself for the past. Henry wanted to help Gil find his way back to life; Henry's having his own jeopardized had certainly offered new insight to its value.

Hope held on through the night. Past his uneaten breakfast. But when the clock chimed noon, it vacated Henry's soul so quickly he thought he heard it whoosh past his ears. Nothing had changed or Cora would have forced her way back in here to tell him. The sheriff didn't think the word of an eight-year-old was enough to make Phillip a suspect. Cora was too disheartened to tell Henry. No doubt she was out there trying to come up with another suspect, another scenario that held enough logic to get the sheriff's attention.

He turned on his side, covered his head with his arms, and willed himself not to cry. He shouldn't have gotten his hopes up.

He must have drifted off to sleep because he was startled awake by the hallway door's being unlocked and opened. Was it time for his arraignment?

Sitting up, he slapped his cheeks to rid himself of the dregs of sleep. He stood and straightened his shirt and tucked it into his pants. He needed a shave. He needed more than a splash bath in the sink. It shamed him to go before the judge like this. He probably *looked like* a murderer.

The sheriff himself came to unlock the cell. He swung the door wide. Henry held out his wrists for the handcuffs.

"You're free to go, young man. The charges against you have been dropped."

For a long moment Henry stood frozen, thinking he'd misheard. "Dropped?"

"Yes. You can pick your wallet up at the desk on the way out."

"What happened?" He should be sprinting toward the door, not standing here questioning his good fortune.

"We have a confession. That's all I can say now. You'll be a witness from here on."

Henry's entire body felt as if electricity were humming through it. She'd done it. Somehow Cora had done it.

The sheriff motioned with a nod of his head. "Are you leaving? Or inclined to stay?"

Henry quick-stepped out of the cell and down the hallway. The other cells were empty. He'd gotten so used to the head thumper he hadn't noticed when the noise had stopped and not restarted.

Stopping in the door to the street, he looked at the gray clouds scuttling across the afternoon sky, sucked in a burning lungful of winter air. The cold bit into his skin and he welcomed it.

He didn't see Cora. Instead, Anders Dahlgren stood on the sidewalk, slump shouldered and looking much older than the last time Henry had seen him. Henry waited. Did Mr. Dahlgren know of the confession? Or was he here on Cora's behest

587

of the other day?

Henry walked slowly down the steps.

Mr. Dahlgren took off his coat and put it around Henry's shoulders. "You will freeze." How Henry had missed the Swedish cadence of that deep voice.

"Now you will."

"I will never be warm again. Coat or no coat." Mr. Dahlgren put his hands on Henry's shoulders and looked into his eyes. "I did not believe it was you."

"I shouldn't have run. I'm sorry. Sorry for the hurt and the shame I caused you."

"Young Henry. We are the ones who have hurt you. And you now have my apology."

"What are you talking about?"

His shoulders stooped a little more. "My girls." He sighed and shook his head. "Their jealousy went too far. I am ashamed to be their father. Now Violet will pay. But I fear it is their mother who will pay the highest price."

"Violet?" Then it made sense. "Because Phillip confessed."

"It is all very confused now. Violet had to be sedated. But Emmaline and Phillip . . . there was a fight. She swears Emmaline fell but —" He sighed. "Phillip told Violet to change her dress, not to let anyone see. When she came back, you were there.

Phillip wasn't. She found a way to save them — by sacrificing you. I am sorry and ashamed."

"So Phillip hit me when I came upon him and Emmaline's body." Henry wondered if Phillip had left Henry for dead, too. "If Emmaline's death was an accident, the law should take that into consideration."

Mr. Dahlgren's faded blue eyes locked on Henry's. "And what consideration is given to you, whose life was stolen by their cowardice?"

In that moment the whole of Henry's life broke open, spilling out at his feet in a jumble of fractured pieces. He saw if just one single piece of that life had been different, if it had held together or offered a shred of belonging or comfort, he would not have found this life he now lived, a life in which he truly fit. He would not have found Cora, or Gil, or even that mutt Mercury.

He grabbed Anders Dahlgren and hugged him tight against his chest. The coat fell from Henry's shoulders onto the sidewalk, but he felt no cold. Into the man's ear he whispered, "My life was not stolen. You gave it to me that snowy day you picked me up at the cemetery, a boy with no family, no hope. You can't be blamed for what happened in May. I owe everything to you."

Henry squeezed tighter. "Everything."

The man had gone against his wife. Doubted his daughter. Nurtured Henry's mind with books and conversation, fueled his love of machines. Anders Dahlgren had been as much a father to him as his own pa had been. More in some ways.

When he pulled away, Mr. Dahlgren had tears in his eyes. "Young Henry. I know you will not stay, but you will always be welcome *in my home.* I will put the wife in the barn next time."

Henry smiled. "Thank you."

Mr. Dahlgren's gaze shifted to the jail. "I must go see the sheriff now. See what is to be done."

Henry picked up the man's coat and handed it back to him. They nodded their good-byes and Mr. Dahlgren headed up the steps.

Henry watched him. Then he called, "Mr. Dahlgren."

He turned slowly and looked over his shoulder. "Yes, young Henry?"

"I never once minded the barn. It was home."

Mr. Dahlgren's smile this time was slow and sad. "I minded." Then he turned and went into the jail.

For a moment, Henry stood on the

sidewalk with his eyes closed, wishing he could do or say something that would ease the man's pain. But Henry knew better than most, when disaster comes to call, all you could do is hold on and pray for salvation. He hoped Mr. Dahlgren's salvation turned out as well as Henry's always had — even though he'd been too hurt and scared at the time to see it.

When he opened his eyes, Cora was standing at the curb. And he felt he was home.

She ran to him and threw herself into his arms so hard he stumbled backward a couple of steps. Her fingertips dug into his shoulders and she sobbed.

"Hey. Hey. It's all right. They got a confession from Violet. I'll probably have to testify, but it's over." She cried harder. "Shhhh-hhh." He kissed the top of her head as he rocked her slightly. "Shhhhh." This kind of breakdown was so unlike her.

He peeled her off him and held her by the shoulders. "It's all right."

She took a couple of gasps, then started crying again. "It's not . . . oh, Henry, it's not . . . Gil crashed. He's dead."

Henry's ears started ringing. His body went numb. He wasn't sure how long he stood there frozen before he forced himself to move. *Don't think now. Just do.* He got them a taxi to the Delaware Hotel. The driver looked at them suspiciously as Henry helped a trembling and crying Cora into the backseat. He recalled he *looked like* the murderer he'd been accused of being, out in the January weather with no coat. He could have eased the man's suspicions with a simple "Death in the family," but he was afraid to open his mouth. So he just glowered and nodded for the man to drive.

He got Cora's hotel key from her purse. She had to tell him the room number twice before he understood it. Her mouth or his ringing ears at fault, he didn't know.

When they got inside her room, he took off her coat, sat her down on the bed, and poured her a glass of water. When he handed it to her, he saw his hand was shaking as much as hers. He waited with growing impatience as she drank. The urgency he felt was ridiculous. Gil was dead. Nothing was going to save him.

Henry thought of Gil's steady deterioration since the day they'd met, of his disastrous trip to Ohio. The look in his eyes when he'd seen Henry and Cora kissing. *"It's Mary that needs freeing."*

Oh my God, Gil, did you . . . ?

Henry went cold to his bones. He suddenly understood Mr. Dahlgren's saying he would never be warm again.

Cora took a deep, shuddering breath, then said in a small, quivery voice that sounded like another person's — a weaker person's, "By this afternoon I still hadn't received a telegram. I could understand the first day's delay . . . if he'd lost the race, he'd have been so upset, he'd been determined to get that prize money for . . . for . . ." She swallowed. "I figured he'd drowned his disappointment in a bottle and would send word when he sobered up. At first I was so m-m-mad —" She dissolved into fresh tears.

Henry held her while she got herself together.

Her cheeks puffed out with a breath. "I sent a telegram to Reece, asking if Gil had made it back with Evie yet, and left word how to get in touch with me. Just before I came to get you, Reece called me. . . . I knew it was bad because he had to drive into town to get to a phone . . . to pay long-distance charges.

"Frank Evans sent him word about . . . about . . . th-the crash. Reece's farm was the only contact information he had." She paused. "He won, Henry. He won the race."

"He did? What in the hell happened, then?"

"They aren't sure. Mechanical failure of some kind. After the win, he did some stunts. He went into a dive and couldn't pull out."

Couldn't? Or didn't? Henry's stomach went hollow and sick. Gil pulled out of dives practically every time he was in a cockpit. It could have been mechanical, so Henry kept his thoughts to himself. He owed Gil that much.

Henry moved them so they were lying on the bed. The knot in his throat got tighter and tighter. His heart felt as if it had been torn from his chest and stomped on. When he blinked, he saw Gil's Jenny racing across that field against Cora on her motorcycle. It was only months ago, but a lifetime, too.

Cora cried on his shoulder until his shirt was wet. Finally he heard her breathing slow and realized she'd cried herself to sleep. He lay staring at the ceiling as the light faded. It finally grew dark enough that the streetlights coming through the windows cast two gray rectangles on the ceiling. Henry stared at them until they blurred, then finally closed his own eyes. When he did, he realized the pillow under his head was soaked with his own tears.

The world was coming undone. The

discovery of the truth that gave Henry his freedom was tainted by the tragedies that had come on the same wind. Would there ever be a phase of his life that wouldn't bear the dirty fingerprint of disaster?

He could have done more, for both Gil and Mr. Dahlgren. If he'd told Mr. Dahlgren of his suspicions that Emmaline was meeting someone she shouldn't, the man wouldn't have buried one child and be worrying another would go to prison. And Gil? Henry laid out all of the reasons the crash was mechanical failure. The Evie was a new design. Gil wouldn't have sacrificed another man's plane.

Then he remembered the haunted look in Gil's eyes when he'd returned to Mississippi to find Henry and Cora kissing.

It's Mary that needs freeing.

Henry shook those thoughts out of his head.

Nothing was a surety; life had taught him that. The road not taken did not guarantee a different destination.

Cora was crying in her sleep. He stroked her hair to quiet her. His own chest hurt; his head felt ready to explode from the inner pressure. He didn't want this night to end, to face the morning and the realities that lay outside their hotel door. He and

Cora could just lie here, clinging to one another until they turned to dust. Right now, that idea suited him fine.

He drifted into sleep, but reality followed him there. He stood helpless with his feet in the sand as he watched the Evie plummet out of the sky, heading toward palm trees, water, and death. He saw Gil's determined face, one hand forcing the stick forward and the other on the throttle. The impact jerked Henry awake, sweating and gasping for breath.

The orange glow of the rising sun set the room ablaze.

Please let there not have been fire. Racers didn't overload with fuel, so he'd hold that as truth.

Could Gil have run out of fuel?

No matter how many ways Henry looked at it, no scenario made it less tragic; nothing changed that the man who'd saved Henry's life was dead.

Cora shifted. When he looked at her, she was staring at him. Something had changed behind those eyes.

Without a word, she rolled away, turning her back to him.

28

As February arrived, sadness clung to everything, even the damp, gray Mississippi weather. That moist Southern cold penetrated Henry's bones more deeply than any Indiana winter. He spent all of his waking hours readying the planes. The job didn't require nearly as much time as he was devoting to it, but with his hands busy, his mind didn't dwell on the changes that had come with Gil's death, with apologies left unsaid, with love that had come so close and had now retreated. Flying and Gil were so closely linked in Henry's heart, he wasn't sure how he was going to feel about taking to the air again.

Henry and Cora had spent little time together since their return from Indiana. Gil's permanent absence proved to be more of a wall between them than his presence had ever been. Most days, Cora was out riding her motorcycle with Mercury. She was always in bed when he returned to the house — although many nights he heard her sniffling behind her closed door. She was always still in her room when he left to work on the planes before dawn. But he knew from Reece that Cora was wearing her grief like a coat that she refused to take off, even in the warmest of rooms. Even Nell was worried about her.

Henry wondered if Cora suspected Gil's accident might have been forced. And whether, as Henry did, she felt some culpability for Gil's loss of hope. She'd told Henry she loved him at the jail — before they knew of Gil's death — but had not since. Henry didn't know if they would ever find their way back to that moment. He supposed the loss of what he'd had with Cora was a death of sorts, too. But he wasn't ready to give up to the point of grieving. Not quite yet.

Jake and Thomas returned to Mississippi. Circus life was about to begin again. Cora had lived this life without Gil. She knew what to expect. But Henry had not. He wasn't sure he wanted to. Yet, what else would he do?

On February 7, they held their memorial service for Gil on the grass airfield at Reece's farm, continuing to keep Gil's airborne life separate from his life in Ohio. The weather finally smiled; sunshine and blue skies beckoned those who had aviation in their blood. The red-and-white planes were shined and parked in a semicircle. Cora had bought hothouse flowers and tied them on each propeller. Mercury had a circlet of flowers around his neck. In the center of the semicircle the circus family gathered, including Nell and Reece's father.

The saying of words had fallen to Henry. He'd written and torn up page after page in preparation. In the end, he decided to offer Gil a simple statement from his heart. He hoped the others wouldn't be disappointed.

He held Cora's gaze before he began to speak. Her sad smile broke his heart, and he wasn't sure he'd be able to find his voice.

He cleared his throat. "Charles Gilchrist lived for the air because life on the ground had become too burdensome to bear. Sometimes those who sacrifice the most for others suffer the most, too. He was a good man and I'll owe him a debt of gratitude for the rest of my life. May his spirit fly on."

It was silent for a moment and he feared he'd let them all down. Then there was a chorus of *Amen*s and even a quick *rrrruff* from Mercury. For several moments, they stood quietly, heads bowed in a final good-bye.

One by one, they walked away, until only Cora and Henry and Mercury were left. Cora wordlessly slipped her hand into Henry's. Instead of going back to the house with the others, they walked slowly down the lane. He stayed quiet. The feel of her hand is his was enough for now.

They'd nearly reached the road when Cora spoke. "Do you think Mary and Charlie have received the race winnings yet?"

On the train ride back to Mississippi, Henry had shared the story of Gil's marriage with Cora. He'd known she might turn away from him, knowing Gil's marriage hadn't been a love match, that his love for Cora had been real. But he owed it to her, to Gil's memory. He was tired of hiding the truth.

"I'm sure they have. Evans was taking care of it."

"Gil would be happy to know they were taken care of."

"He would." They walked for a bit, then Henry said, "I wrote her a letter."

Cora stopped and looked at him. "You did?"

"I've discovered the damage of things left unsaid. I wanted her to appreciate Gil.

Forgive him and let go of the pain. That's all he ever wanted from her. He wanted her to be happy."

Cora nodded and started walking again.

"There's something I've left unsaid to you, too." He tightened his grip on her hand and his heart felt as if it were about to burst. The lives they led were all about calculated risk. He was about to take one — but he didn't know the odds. "I love you, Cora. I'm sure that isn't news to you, but I've never said it."

She stepped in front of him and took his other hand. Holding them both, she said, "I love you, too, Henry. Right now it seems so mixed up. That love is so tangled up with Gil and what happened. . . . I don't know if that will ever change. It seems wrong to make promises. I just want to go back to work. I want to have normal, uncomplicated days."

He'd been prepared for the disappointment, but that wasn't to say he hadn't hoped. As much as it hurt, he *still* hoped. He would not give up so easily.

"Normal?" He chuckled. "You're the only person I know who would call wing walking a normal day."

She smiled a smile that was almost her old self.

■ ■ ■ ■

The next week, they began practicing the act. Without Gil they were still short a pilot. But there was no talk of replacing him. Cora could fly the fourth plane from town to town. Jake was still the lead pilot, Thomas the second, and Henry the most inexperienced. Yet, when it was time to practice the plane-to-plane transfer, Cora wanted Henry to fly the launch plane. Jake would fly the target.

"Thomas should fly the launch," Henry said. "He's got more experience than me." No one breathed Reece's name; his piloting skills were probably weaker than Henry's. The man preferred to jump *out of* planes.

Cora had looked at Henry, really looked at him for the first time since the day of Gil's service. "I want you. I'll be most comfortable with you. Besides, Thomas needs to fly the camera fella when he gets here to film it."

"I can fly the camera," Henry said. "Thomas is a better pilot for the stunt."

"I want you, Henry. I don't know how much more clear I can be."

"Maybe we should try it with a rope ladder first."

"What's the point of that? It's not our trick. Lots of people do it with a rope ladder. We do it without. Wing to wing."

Jake had been standing by with his arms crossed over his chest. "It's Cora's stunt. If she wants Henry to fly launch, Henry will fly launch. Unless Henry's skittish over some sort of romantic hoo-ha." Jake frowned.

"I want dry runs until I say I'm good with the transfer." Henry didn't think Jake would give him the boot, but he didn't want to test the theory. The season was young and a lot of experienced pilots out there would be happy to get a shot at flying with this circus.

"Fair enough," Cora said.

They did several passes with Cora in the cockpit. Henry wasn't as nervous flying with his wings overlapped with Jake's as he'd feared. Of course, Jake was a hell of a pilot. When Cora went out on the wing, it was a different story. His fear wasn't that he couldn't keep his off-balance plane steady, but that she would decide to go ahead and do the transfer when Jake got in range.

But she didn't. They landed and discussed the plan for the actual transfer.

"You two are steady enough that Jake can get close enough that I can grab directly onto the wing strut. Not just grab the skid."

Jake nodded. "We were close enough, for sure." He looked at Henry. "It'll be safer for Cora than having to hoist herself up from the skid."

"Safer?" Henry said. "We're more likely to knock her off if we hit an air pocket if we're that close."

"It will be safer, Henry," Cora said. "I can always signal to change if I don't think it's going to work."

As they took off, Henry understood why Jake was so adamant against romantic entanglements. Fear bred hesitation. Hesitation bred mistakes. Henry focused on what Gil had taught him. Assess. Decide. Execute.

He was prepared. Cora was prepared. They were professionals.

And he flew like one. He kept his focus on his job, his eyes on Jake's plane.

The instant she grabbed that strut and her feet left Henry's wing, it sent his heart soaring. He dropped lower and slowed. Jake's plane pulled ahead. Cora was standing on the bottom wing, waving and throwing Henry kisses. He knew it was the excitement of the moment, but it fueled that little flame of hope that she could love him again, without reserve, as she had that day in the jail.

■ ■ ■ ■

Between publicity from the newsreel footage that played Henry as a hero in Santa Monica, and the newsreel shot in Mississippi of the midair plane transfer, Hoffman's Flying Circus was soon booked solid right up until Christmas. Cora was officially an adventuress of renown.

Henry was finishing cleaning the spark plugs for their show on the Chicago lakefront when Cora came stomping up with a letter clutched in her fist. She read Henry the scathing message that had come through Marcus Davis — the only immobile contact who knew where the circus would be on any given day. Her mother had denounced and disowned her, chided her for bringing shame to the family name.

"Shame to the family name! How can she be serious after the things Father did! I don't cheat people or break the law. I'm doing something positive, groundbreaking for women." Cora gave a little growl through her clenched teeth. "And Mother never *owned* me — although she did try to sell me! So how can she *dis*own me? The nerve . . ."

Henry didn't bother to say that Cora's

mother was the last person who saw breaking ground for women in a man's world as
positive. He also didn't say that Cora
shouldn't be surprised by her mother's
condemnation, not when Cora knew the
world her mother was clinging to with all of
her might — a world that was fast evaporat-
ing around her and all of her generation.
Henry actually felt a little sorry for the
woman. He hoped that if his father were
still here, he'd find a way to see past the
sternness and reserve, past his stiff-spined
pride, and make a real connection with
Henry.

"I hope there'll be a day when you two
reconcile," Henry said, knowing he'd probably just set a match to the fuse of Cora's
temper. She'd never quite gotten over her
father's betrayal, not the public betrayal that
had led to his downfall, but his secret
betrayal of the dreams he'd nurtured in her
as a little girl. It was easier to blame her
mother for all of the ills that came after. "A
person shouldn't cut herself off from family
— not when she's lucky enough to have
one."

Cora's temper did not flare. She looked
deeper into what Henry was saying. "Oh,
Henry, don't you see? You *do* have family.
This is your family. Mercury and Jake and

Reece and Thomas and me. *This* is my family, too."

He studied her for a moment. Would Cora ever again see him as more than "family"? He'd sworn to himself he wouldn't push her. Love wasn't something that could be demanded. For now, he was happy to share her life in whatever way she was willing. On the day he'd been released from jail, the day they'd learned of Gil's death, he'd vowed that he was going to spend every moment that disaster did not come to call thankful for what he *did* have.

Today he had the family of the flying circus — and a daredevil still holding his heart.

EPILOGUE

July 1970

Henry took off from Schuler Field in a plane of his own design, one that he had built with his own hands. The airstrip had no control tower, so he kept his eyes on the sky around him for other aircraft. The very idea of "air traffic" had been laughable back in the day. As had the term *experimental aircraft.* Time was when *all* aircraft were an experiment of one sort or another. Now it was law: EXPERIMENTAL had to be clearly printed on the side of a home-built plane. It irked him. Lots of things irked him these days. Maybe his sons were right, he'd lived too long.

He thought of the purpose of his flight today. He'd definitely lived too long.

The Experimental Aircraft Association youngsters flocked to hear his stories of the growth of aviation, which had gone from birth to landing on the moon in less than

Henry's lifetime. But it wasn't the same anymore. Too many rules.

Federal regulations had crept up on them three years after Gil's death. Accidents had drawn the eyes of the bureaucrats. They'd taken their lessons from disaster and hit fast and hard. By 1928, they'd hammered the last nail in the flying circus's coffin. It was a blessing that Gil hadn't lived to see his beloved free-flying aircraft bound by so many restrictions.

"All right," Henry said under his breath. "Let's break some rules." He looked over to the passenger seat at the biggest rule breaker he'd ever known. The box containing Cora's ashes sat where she'd spent so many hours, always doing something while they were cruising along, a crossword, reading — usually tales of groundbreakers and true adventure. She said flying had gotten so boring that she didn't know why anyone bothered anymore. At forty she'd taken up mountain climbing. Henry had followed along.

He dipped well below minimum regulated altitude and opened the window. Cows still inhabited Cora's uncle's field, and he briefly wondered how long Tilda had remained one of them.

Yesterday, he'd knocked on the door of

the old farmhouse and had made his unusual request. The young farmer had looked puzzled until Henry explained his wife's family had owned the land. The farmer had given his permission with a murmur of sympathy.

He held the box in his lap as he made two passes over the field. He cried, even though he'd promised Cora he wouldn't.

"Good-bye, my love. Until we meet on this field again."

The ashes fell in a gray trail, disappearing far too quickly.

Henry made one more pass and then regained legal altitude. He'd planned on flying for a while, just to let the memories play over him in solitude. But his heart was too empty, his soul too tired. He returned to the airstrip.

As the wheels touched the smooth, paved runway, Henry saw his and Cora's sons, Gil and Anders, waiting by the hangar. He said a prayer of thanks that he was still a part of a flying family, even though its makeup was vastly altered since the day he'd seen a motorcycle and a biplane in a reckless race that changed his life forever.

ACKNOWLEDGMENTS

I owe a debt of gratitude to many for their assistance in the creation of this novel. It might not take a village to create a book, but it does take a team. First and foremost, thanks to my patient husband, Bill, for accepting my mental absences on the days I did not "come home" from 1923; and to my family for their endless support.

I have been extraordinarily lucky to have had my fabulous editor, Karen Kosztolnyik, as a partner on yet another book. This is our eleventh collaboration and I hope we will have at least eleven more. Your critical eye and sharp insight, as well as your friendship, make my writing life so much richer.

Working with the team at Gallery Books is a writer's dream. Thanks to all whose hands have touched this project, especially Jen Bergstrom and Louise Burke, who both believed in this book even before it was a fully formed idea in my head.

Thanks to my critique partners, Wendy Wax and Karen White, for keeping me on the rails. I'm so incredibly fortunate to have such talented writers to share in my creative process. It was great fun going through the frenzy of three simultaneous deadlines. Hope we get to do it again . . . it really kept me in the zone.

My father, Vic Zinn, was a private pilot who preferred flying low and slow with the wind in his face. I had the wonderful experience of flying with him in several different aircraft. Although my knowledge was rudimentary, as a teen I learned about tail draggers and tricycle gear, ailerons, elevators and rudder, trim tab and air speed. Of particular help in creating this book were our flights in a tandem-cockpit Piper J-3 Cub with the door open — closest I've come to flying in an open cockpit. To this day I'm sorry I disappointed him by being his only child who never learned to fly. (Congratulations to Tom and Sally for fulfilling his dream.) I also was lucky enough to have gone to the amazing Oshkosh Fly-In with him multiple times, where I was able to get up close and personal with old warbirds and the pilots who love them. Dad's been gone for many years, but I'll never forget his love of flying and machinery —

and his ability to create the functional from scavenged pieces and parts. These experiences gave me invaluable insight into Henry's character.

Because my knowledge of flying and aircraft is so pitifully limited, I reached out to several pilots, who were kind enough to fill in the many blanks. Thanks to my nephew Bryan Zinn for your speedy and detailed replies and not ever laughing at my questions. Larry Jacobi was kind enough to let me crawl all over his vintage Stearman biplane and answer an evening full of questions. And a special thanks to Brian Karli, who lovingly restored a "Jenny" (Curtiss JN-4) and shared all of the finer details of the craft so that my depiction may be as accurate as possible. I am indebted to you all. Any aeronautical errors in this book are mine alone.

My depiction of life in 1923 was fueled by hours of enlightening research and complimented by conversations with my mother, Marge Beaver Zinn, who shared what she recalled from her parents', aunts', and uncles' stories. I am so lucky to have you in my life.

A few historical disclaimers need to be mentioned: The January air race in Miami and the December aerobatic competition and air race at Clover Field are fictional. Such air meets were quite popular in the twenties. Some were short sprints, as I've described; some were long distance. In those early days, they were frequently deadly. Clover Field and Douglas Aircraft were in Santa Monica in 1923. Cliff Henderson did have a Nash dealership in Santa Monica and, according to my research, did offer an airplane ride with the purchase of a new car. I have no idea how many takers he had. He did also organize a stunt team called the Black Falcons, who performed regularly at Clover Field.

While the silent film *The Hunchback of Notre Dame* was released in 1923, it did not play at Grauman's Egyptian Theatre that year.

I made a concerted effort to keep my story framed by historical fact. Belle's supper club was inspired by an establishment of family lore and was definitely not located in Williamson County, Illinois.

This is a work of fiction, filled with fictional characters. Please forgive any literary license employed in the telling of this tale.

ABOUT THE AUTHOR

Susan Crandall is a critically acclaimed author of women's fiction, romance, and suspense. She has written several award-winning novels including her first book, *Back Roads,* which won the RITA award for best first book, as well as *Whistling Past the Graveyard,* which won the SIBA 2014 Book Award for Fiction.